RICKARDS & JONES

The Long Road

The Godless, Book One

First published by Rickards and Jones 2023

Copyright © 2023 by Rickards & Jones

First edition

ISBN: 978-1-7394357-1-4

Cover art by Rena Violet

This book was professionally typeset on Reedsy. Find out more at reedsy.com

To Evan,
who heard the book first
(through no choice of his own).

The long road is winding.

Contents

Disclaimer   iii

THE LONG ROAD   v

I   Part One

1   PROLOGUE   3
2   AUDEYRN   14
3   MARBLE   30
4   AUDEYRN   43
5   NATOLY   60
6   MARBLE   76
7   GREGYN   85
8   THE GHOST   100
9   AUDEYRN   108
10   MARBLE   124
11   NATOLY   133
12   AUDEYRN   150
13   MARBLE   164
14   GREGYN   171
15   NATOLY   190
16   AUDEYRN   208
17   MARBLE   223
18   GREGYN   235
19   NATOLY   256

20 GREGYN   278

II Part Two

21 THE TOWNSMAN   303
22 MARBLE   325
23 NATOLY   335
24 MARBLE   357
25 AUDEYRN   366
26 GREGYN   386
27 MARBLE   405
28 AUDEYRN   414
29 GREGYN   433
30 MARBLE   454
31 AUDEYRN   464
32 MARBLE   485
33 GREGYN   493
34 AUDEYRN   509
35 GREGYN   540
36 THE MONSTER   564
37 THE HERO   577
38 EPILOGUE   598

Acknowledgments   613
About the Author   615

Disclaimer

This book includes explicit language, sexual situations and graphic violence.

THE LONG ROAD

THE GODLESS, BOOK ONE

RHYS JONES
MORGAN RICKARDS

The gods have vanished.
Foul things prowl the wilds.
A war setting the world ablaze.

The great kingdoms of Castan and Sora enter the fifth year
of bloody strife, and pull the lands between them into
uneasy alliances.

The monarchs, sick of war, have tasked the emissaries to
travel the long road and bring peace to the land. But their
quest is fraught with danger, and dark forces are on the
move. Not all wars are fought on the battlefield, and the
emissaries will learn that monsters take many forms.

The long road is winding.

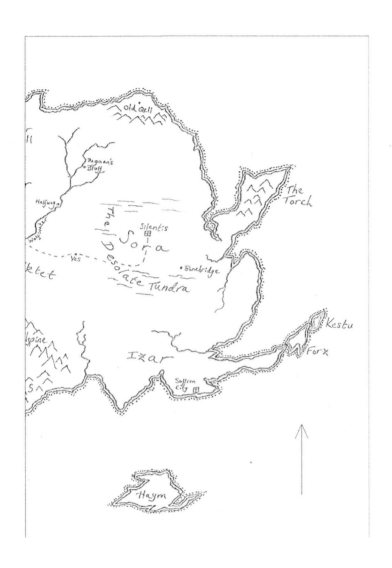

I

Part One

1

PROLOGUE

"Aprize worth dying for…" Maarys spat in scorn. The words billowed out in a fine mist.

She swiped away the rogue strands of dirty blond hair with the back of one hand, sweating despite the cold of the cistern.

It *was* a cistern, and more. Those above kept their goodwater stored in the bowels of the fastness, along with caches for winter and prolonged siege. In the mountain, the natural caverns extended for miles. Every step from her muffled boots sent recondite whispers barreling down the halls of stone. *They weren't supposed to do that...*

The job was easy, or so Lyr had averred at the Warren. *Easy, and simple.* The damn fool had sent her through half-blind. He could not have known where the rift would lead, only that the egress was someplace beneath the castle proper. She made an obscene gesture into the lightless corridor, and carried on.

Finding her way into the stores had been a doss. After all, she had walked right in. The next part had demanded some measure of patience, traversing the vast rooms of dry foodstuffs and raw materials and fodder, all lined neatly on terraces that descended further down into the blackness. On each terrace, locked rooms with heavy doors promised even more stockpiles. All had appeared unmarked to her at first, but lighting the crystcandle, she noticed the markings chalked on the thresholds. She reasoned it must have been a cataloguing system applied by the manciples.

Maarys shelved her curiosity for the nonce, turning the yellow-white light of the crystal along the long shelves of jars full of preserved things. It hummed softly in the rig. Her free hand fingered the nasty piece of hooked steel that the guild liked to call wyrmears. The vats and high-framed crates fell off into an avenue of shadows. Where the light burned away the gloom, the entrance to the passageway appeared stark, a hole gaping wide between two vaulting shelves holding rolls of parchment. The candescence was not strong enough to light the entirety of the way, so the entrance gave in to darkness.

It was there her quarry awaited. The treasure vault within the Sunken Sepulchre. Pulling to mind the face she would make to Guildmaster Lyr and that swine Govier, she threw herself down the python's gullet.

Something was off. She was not a careless hunter- triple-checking her equipment once more before starting out from the Warren. Her habits, if anything, were thorough. She had her grapple and thinweave ropes at her hip, her pouches secured and sealed across her chest and waist. The wyrmear strapped tightly to her thigh. The candlerig had been mended and tinkered so many times that the leather grip was worn to a smooth light brown, and the metal of the fastening arms attached to the crystal amplifier polished to a brilliant gleam.

No. Not the equipment. This place...

Superstition held no place in her heart. The hunter lay more trust at the door of handicraft and cold alchemy than the ramblings of quacks and mountebanks. Even as a child in Sandygate, she had not feared the monsters that supposedly dwelt beneath her bed, instead choosing to stay awake with a knife under her pillow, ready to strike at any spectre that chose to show itself. No ghouls or bogeymen ever appeared, and as she grew out of those childish fancies, she had come to question why she should fear things that she knew did not exist. She often wondered if the guild would have noticed her if it were otherwise.

The passage snaked side to side as she padded on, the crystcandle throwing light on the lurching walls, revealing long unending striations as though the tunnel was not built or excavated, but clawed into being by some great subterranean beast. A cold finger of sweat trailed down her spine. "Snap out of it, gods be damned." Her words echoed ahead, becoming more twisted until it sounded like they were jeering her.

Shadow of doubts and a wandering mind, that's all...

It had been the hushing hour when she had stepped from the Warren's cosy anteroom lit by soft torchlight into the drear cellar beneath the mountain. As always, the first thing she smelled was ozone. The feeling within the cellar was sickening, not helped by the fact that it was a larder full of aurochs meat. On a usual *adventure*, she would have been supplied with a map or a sketch of the place, to at least gather her bearings. But there... the guild had never dared enter before. They could not favour a servant with gold in exchange for information, or find an architect's diagram of the damnable underbelly. The planning stage of the assignment had been beset by trouble. No maps, no plans, and tractable stewards or disgruntled officers didn't seem to exist. Nothing. That meant no doors carelessly left unlocked nor any convenient openings along the rampart walls to rappel safely out of dodge. The doors here would be locked as tight as the bonds of hell, and the guards dutifully patrolling the battlements. Maarys would have loved nothing more than to find suitable servant's garb and mingle among the castle folk. She had been warned against such subterfuge. The manciples were known well, huntmaster Demagul had said. The only women permitted freedom of the castle were the Daughters. *I have more chance of impersonating a roc than a Daughter,* she thought. If the dour Demagul were right, she would need to do more than find the right clothes to blend in with *them.* Had it not been for the soothsman, they would have looked elsewhere for their next job. *He* had promised that the relic was a fruit ripe for the picking, unguarded even. The how's and why's had eluded even him, but it had been enough to sway Lyr.

Day and night no longer existed. Down there, one could lose all sense of time. The tunnels looked much the same, and getting turned about was always a possibility. Luckily, Maarys was not so easily dismayed. She snorted, imagining how the others would fare in such a decrepit place. *Get lost on the first step, no doubt.*

Tunnels led to vaults, leading down corkscrews and switchbacks and what seemed like bottomless barrel staircases. The air got heavier. The cold persisted. For a time,

Maarys plodded onward without the strange sensation she experienced above. She allowed herself a laugh, her lusty tones warped by the pit, like the mouth of the legendary yrt. It was there that she made her descent.

Grappling was nothing to her, the thinweave flowing like silk between her gloved fingers. Her boots skitted off the bare roughhewn rock, the crystcandle on her chest strap a lonely island of light in the vast miasma of night eternal.

The pit that moments before had promised only an endless pitfall... ended. Sand crunched under foot. The crystcandle in hand again, she scooped up a handful. It was warm and as dry as Sora. The crystcandle burned the grains of finely crushed obsidian a gleaming black. *An ebon beach beneath a mountain.* The glassmakers could make handsome glass of it. She let loose a snort and pocketed a goodly amount.

The curved walls were made of cunningly interlocking bricks, each one a different metal or stone. *So this is the Sunken Sepulchre.* Sweeping the light around the multicoloured bricks, the crystcandle revealed a blackened doorway on the opposite side, the midnight sands within coruscating darkly. *Deeper night o'er this way comes.* Someone had told her that. The face eddied in her memory like a pane of cheap glass.

Her breaths came steadily, each footfall noiseless and purposeful. Eventually, the tunnel began to widen, stretching until it was large enough for an oxcart complete with a full team of oxen. Then the walls fell away entirely. The ceiling, too, lifted, becoming aphotic and vanishing completely, and no trying from Maarys could make the crystcandle reveal the roof of the cave.

The air felt stagnant. She could not help but catch a foul taste on her tongue. Huffing, she retraced her steps and marked the nearest wall. She hated children's tales, but she had heard enough to know that when in the lair of the evil witch, one must remember to drop their breadcrumbs.

There was nothing else for it. She resolved then and there that this place was horrid, a veritable hellscape, and the sooner she was back to the Warren and lounging in a steam bath, the better. She might even share a drink with Govier.

"Gods damn this place!" Only after she had lost count of the turns she made in the sidewinding tunnels did the vault find her.

The doors were bronze, thirty feet tall from floor to ceiling. They were old, old enough to have turned an odious green. Embossed on both were images of cherubic children holding fruit and drinking from ornate horns. At intervals were oversized rings. When Maarys pulled at the pair posed at eye-height, the doors yawned outward, scraping at the fine sand at their feet. *Open, just as the soothsman said.* They moved smoothly despite the wear of the great hinges, enough to make Maarys wonder at such a sight. It was too easy.

Then it was over. A gap barely a foot wide was a sidelong metal mouth, ajar and alluring. Maarys eyed the dark recess between. With a sharp intake of breath, she collected her thoughts. *Grab it and be done.*

Within, she stifled to find a breath. A rank stench suffused the air, making her gag. She doused her kerchief with sweet nectar and tied the sodden fabric around her lower face. Her eyes watered as she struggled to breathe, not realising the mass that had taken form in the centre of the vault.

Between tears, she made out a colossal glass container stretching high into the rafters. The liquid within was the colour of meat long gone to rot and shifted with oily motion. The crystcandle left nothing to the murk. A pair of fish eyes watched her, staring white-blind. A bulbous, overlarge head buoying indolently atop an aquatic and atrophied body. It's skin was pale, and the fingers long and webbed, here and there so thin appearing near translucent. It looked aged and decrepit but could not have been taller than a child of six. From neck and wrist, ankle and groin, wires erupted like a bundle of ironskin worms, rising until they were lost to sight. Maarys thought the thing dead, until the body twitched spasmodically. The eyes were unblinking and still, yet she could not shake the feeling that it knew she was there.

She stuck her tongue out at the shrunken thing. Then she made to scour the room for her prize.

At the compass points, worktables had been set up, each erratically decorated with a slew of queer instruments, here some curious devices of steel and copper, there a few porcelain and shaped glass. Everywhere, pages of yellowed paper depicted a man without skin, displaying the torso and the rudiments within. She looked through the stations, finding only reams of old paper covered in spider-like scribblings. A voice inside dared to speak out, whispering, *If the artefact is still here, why were the doors open?*

Then the dread settled in her stomach. Maarys wanted to brush it away, to blame it on the putrid odour, instead of finding the solution to this problem. She would not go back empty-handed. Her eyes went to the glass tube.

9

"We don't get visitors very often." Said the voice behind her.

She spun, deftly pulling the wyrmear free and aiming the crystcandle in the direction of the voice. It worked, and the man stood there blinded by pure white light, shielding his eyes with upraised arms. "Wait. Stop! Don't you know who–" She moved too fast, and in an instant, she had kicked the man to the floor, letting a fine shower of black sand fall around them. With a soft *dhhrick*, she turned out the light.

Instinct took over. All her fretting ebbed away. She was Maarys no longer, but a shadow. A shadow with a nasty piece of steel in hand. The crystcandle had left her night-blind, but it did not matter. She did not need eyes to know where she kept her snuff. From a pouch, she produced a pinch of lustre. Pulling her kerchief off her face, she inhaled deeply. A deep throbbing hid behind her eyes, and she saw.

Light permeated from nothing. Her vision filled, a soft heliotropic gleam painting the brick walls of the Sepulchre, the grains of obsidian beneath her feet glistening as though covered in hoarfrost. The thing in the tube burned a deep violet.

The man crawled towards the glass on all fours, letting Maarys get a good look at him. He was dressed not unlike a godman, wearing plush robes that brushed his knees and bordered his neck with a fluted collar. But his was grey instead of white, his cuffs and breast slashed to reveal crimson silk beneath. "Please... help... *me*."

Maarys made a face of disgust in the dark. His was clean-shaven, with full cheeks and a pointed nose, crowned by thinning hair that hung from his scalp in long dark strands. His hand reached up to touch the glass. "Please... I—" Silent as the grave, Maarys swept up behind him, filled her fist with a handful of that hair, and slammed it hard against the glass. She pinned the wyrmear to his bobbing apple.

"Where is it?" She hissed, letting the steel bite.

A shriek came, and a dark bead of blood fell onto the dark sand. "What?! Where is *what?*"

"The relic, damn you! The treasure!" Her patience was fraying, and she spat out the words through clenched teeth, "Tell me, and you might live to see baldness."

A ragged laugh pierced the gloom. It vexed her, so she twisted the wyrmear. "No! Listen! You don't understand, do you? No... you came here thinking you'd make off with gold or jewels or some such, and then whisk away with your plunder while the evil guards shook their fists at you... No. You are a fool to believe such fancy. You are a fool to have come here. Treasure? *Relic?* Ah. Yes... I see—"

Blinding light filled her world, and Maarys suddenly felt as though a thousand needles had plunged into her eyes. Her scream was something primal. The agony made her drop her knife, and in an instant, through the pain, she felt hard hands pull her off the man.

None of the Daughters were alike, yet they were all the same. Castanni and Soran, Warretumi and Druke, Izarfolk and Paydar, their homelands were plain. But it ended there. The little Maarys could see was pale and tanned and dark skin, scar ridges and brands puckering in the torchlight. Their hair was braided, and their faces painted into masks of skulls and demons. And they were strong, stronger than Maarys had dared imagine. Wordlessly, they had descended on her with torches, her eyes searing at the glare. They proceeded to kick her writhing body, over and over, until

11

the voice called them to stop. The man. His voice was now stern and commanding.

She had thought quickly about using the lustre and knew the risks involved. The sudden change in light, she also knew full well, would leave lasting damage to her vision. Then she reminded herself who had caught her, and she failed to contain her weeping. She went unresisting as they chained her to a wall. The bite of the metal on her wrists was a kiss compared to that in her eyes

"Yes. Yes. My lord, I accept the punishment that awaits me, I do. But the intruder must be dealt with. I have apprehended her, that must be taken into consideration." Opening her eyes only caused more pain, yet she persisted. "I… yes. Yes. You must believe me, lord. I pledged myself to you. My life is yours to command…"

The answer was a wet whisper in her ear from the darkness itself *"Do not lecture me, Wedderburn."* It was faint, hardly more than a croak. *"The justiciars will deal with her accordingly. The contention you present... have fatted yourself on my benevolence... "* Maarys did not like the way it spoke. She forced herself to open her eyes through a bloody shroud. She saw the man called Wedderburn. He was talking to the tube. *"This error will not go unpunished, Didact. Failure is a luxury for the weak."*

"Thank you, magnificence. I accept whatever punishment you deign appropriate. I swear, I will never make this mistake aga–"

"Your empty oaths are worthless to me, boy. I recollect that this is not your first... misstep." Wedderburn looked bloated suddenly, red in the face, but the damage to her eyes tinged the whole world pink. Maarys could not be certain. He

only spluttered.

"M-My lord. Please… I have served loyally for–"

*"Loyalty is a prerequisite of service, not an accolade of service itself. You allowed this…*girl *to infiltrate my sanctum. Your failing to apprehend her tells me all I need to know of your aptitude…* loyal *Didact."* Maarys opened her eyes long enough to look at the thing in the tube. Its mouth did not move when it spoke.

"You are relieved of your duties." Wedderburn seemed to relax at that, and he put a hand through his hair. But his face had turned plum, his lank hair sticking wetly to his forehead. "Thank you, my lord. I will not fail you again."

"No, you won't." The rasped words were unfeeling.

The noise that came from Wedderburn was not human. It was a deep squelching and bubbling that made Maarys narrow her eyes, trying as she might to make out what was happening. A sickening *POP* exploded in the vault, and then everything was covered in a fine coating of red. A headless body collapsed a few feet away.

Maarys blinked away red tears, unsure what blood was hers.

2

AUDEYRN

T he dead men swung lazily in the tree.

"Leave them," he said.

His companions exchanged wary glances under their rain-soaked cowls. Two dozen wet swollen bodies stared out at them from empty black sockets and drooping mouths, dudgeon and accusing.

They always go for the eyes and tongues first, thought Audeyrn, spitting at the foot of the wide oak that held the bodies aloft like some macabre puppeteer.

"Let the beasts of the wood have their feast." *Birds, most likely. But other things too. Things that do not like men...* The sign nailed to the bole marked those hanging from hempen ropes as deserters. None wore uniforms now, nor anything else.

The smell made him wrinkle his nose. A cloying, overripe smell suffused the air. A fetid stench of fruit gone to rot. The young tracker in the group muttered something under his breath. *A prayer?* The emissary did not wish to linger longer at this place than necessary. Even there, so close to home, the first signs of war had bloomed in all grisly opulence.

The going had been good, leaving the high walls of Castan behind them, and they were keen to begin their long journey. The green wall was the first guardian that blocked their way. The forest had wasted no time in closing in around them, with tall, wizened oaks and languid yews and gnarled blackthorn that wound their roots onto the road like burrowing worms and leaving them no choice but to ride at a snail's pace. This was their demesne, and they moved at the leisure of the lords with the leaves in their verdant crowns.

Audeyrn knew some in the city who lived their entire lives in the stone narrows and wynds, always in sight of the walls, never witnessing a sunset. The world seemed an untamed, brutal place to them, a far cry from the protection the castellations afforded them. He could only pity that. The world beyond the high granite walls was dangerous, yes, but one could truly feel free once outside the cramped, soiled thoroughfares littered with muck and faeces and worse, and the throngs of ill-mannered, foul-smelling louts and drunkards, a surfeit of vulgars and cutpurses who would knife you for a copper, dandies who would duel for simply looking at them the wrong way, debt-collectors and vendetta men. All trying to claw themselves a handful of bread, a bowl of porridge. No. Audeyrn was happy to be away. He yearned for the lands he had not yet seen. The road that wound off to the mythic Land of Izar, the Cave-Castle of Phyrafil, the High Secret Mountains of the Windscape Peninsula, the sunken lands of Set, beyond the Tempest Sea. They called to him.

Ten days creeping ride from the castle, and Audeyrn rued coming this way... *Had the trees been so close to the road when I came here last?* The thought discomforted him. Too few people passed this way now, and the forest had been allowed to encroach on the highway until it had been reduced to little more than a broken trail that threatened to break their horses' legs. He readjusted himself in the high saddle, and found little relief.

Leaving had been easy. Owing to discretion, they left before first light, the watchmen prowling the walls being the only faces to see them off. That morning, a sky the colour of wine burned above them. Nat and Deri sang one marching song after another. But the weather turned, and the songs didn't seem so jolly anymore. And then the singing stopped altogether.

The deluge had refused to let up for nine days, and the sun had yet to shine her great golden eye upon them. The forest, for all its closeness, seemed to delight in letting the rain fall on them wherever they rode. At night, they would set up their sorry camp to eat the dry foodstuffs and try to bring some levity to their situation. Audeyrn refused his companions every time they asked to make a fire. Even among the trees, it was too exposed. With the message he carried, it was paramount that they remained hidden. *The mission is always first.* He doubted they could burn anything in that sodden wood anyway.

They saw but few fellow travellers. They passed a goatherd and a greyhame pilgrim, a wandering godman returning to Lar'gara in the north, and once a naked moon-howler ranting that they were not welcome in the forest. No one of importance. No one who posed a threat. He hoped it would stay that way. He reached back to touch the chest perched on his horse's hindquarters. *Safe.* The metal was cold to the touch.

Day followed night followed day. The rain kept falling, and the road stretched through the forest like some dead stone serpent. *The Long Road.* It wound its way from the Great Gates of Castan in the west, through the great expanse of the blackwood, and leading off to Sora to the east. *Best not think about that yet. Only the here and now matters.* In the depths of the arboreal land, the road twisted and turned, swaying back and forth until a rider felt overwhelmed by the distance. Eventually, the blackwood would end, Audeyrn knew. Eventually. *Streams change course and trees fall, but the land ultimately remains the same.* Wet and tired, they would plod on, determined through all. Audeyrn looked back at his friends and saw their mettle.

The bodies in their tree had left a bad feeling in his gut. As the piddling light of day failed them, he resolved that they would rest again in the wood, in that damp hall of uncut wooden pillars that stretched disorderly into the gloom beyond. They led the horses from the road, eyeing a spot to throw up their canvas. The horses came first, of course. They were groomed and fed, and only after hobbled and settled did Audeyrn allow his men to see to their own meals.

Beneath a wide canvas sheet, they all sat, a sea of pine needles underfoot. Deramun, or Hearty Deri as he was called by friends and rivals alike, was the first as ever to find his food, plopping his ample arse on a stump and attacking the tough bread and pork like a starving man. He hummed a marching song as he worked, tuning his lute and cursing each time he heard a loud *clang*. "Damn. I asked old Hadarahk to *fix* it. Gods, and I paid him well this time. I can only use four strings. I'll struggle to even strum *Alder Days* with only four strings. I'll drown that charlatan in a barrel of wine when we get back to Castan, I swear it. He cheated me."

"*Har!*" Jeered the whimsical Nat with his flame-hair, sitting with his back to a tree, his fox face flushed by the humid air. "Like as not, Hadarahk heard you play the damn thing. What was it he said to me?" He ruffled his locks as he stood, rubbing a hand across his jaw in feigned forgetness," Oh, yes! Hearty, the poor fellow, thinks he is the player Lirran the Lyrist reborn. He ruins every lute I place in his hand, and has the gall to blame *me* for the damage. The glutton is made more for playing the flute or Fay-pipe or phal-'"

"That smart mouth is like to put you in all sorts of trouble, gutterling."

The fox smirked at the insult. Audeyrn could only watch. He knew what came next. The knife shot between the large man's legs to a dull thud. Hearty Deri froze, his cheeks suddenly drained of all colour. Gregyn, the tracker, stared wide-eyed from his long callow face. His hand shook as he pointed to Deri. "Ya- He… The-The-The knife! It went straight to his- I can't believe it. Why would ya do that? I can't believe it. I-"

"Don't be a clod, Greg." Laughed Nat. "The good strongman Deramun is not unmanned… well, not in the way you are thinking anyway. See." As though directed, the large man turned about and pulled the bloodless knife from the stump. He tossed the knife back with elaborate indignation. "That was not a merry thing to do, Nat. You have some skill with that thing, I'll grant, but that was too close for comfort."

"I beg to differ, Hearty. That was a fine jape, and even had I been off the mark, say, a hair's breadth, I wouldn't have hit anything important." Hearty Deri huffed at that, and Audeyrn saw that there was a cut in the man's billowing breeches.

Nat swung a long arm around the skittish tracker, who was still gawping at the knife with mouth agape, as though the sly youth had magicked the blood away before his eyes. Pointing the knife at Deri, Nat said. "He's *fine*, don't you see? The knife went right between his legs. No harm, no foul."

"You're neither funny nor clever, fox. I once saw a talking monkey with better humour," snorted the older man, replacing himself upon the stump with a thump that set his jowls to jiggling. "And you still haven't shown me your skill at arms, peck. That is, if you do possess such *skill*, for our good emissary here to praise you. I'm inclined to believe him, but they say that belief is in the seeing. And skill not with that toothpick, I might add, but with a weapon of the field. A weapon like *this*." He tapped the broadsword that hung at his hip.

"Ha! Gladly. I need a distraction from the endless days of rain and nights of snoring fat men. Some action will do nicely. I accept your offer, Deramun."

"No." Audeyrn stretched his long legs. He walked over to them, finding himself reading them all as though they were nothing but words on parchment. The lanky tracker overtopped him by a good two inches. A one-time poacher,

Gregyn had only kept his hands after Audeyrn had paid his ransom, making him a sort of bondsman to the emissary. That debt was long since repaid, and they had become firm friends. Though not as broad or heavy as the fat man, Audeyrn was lean and quick, being a head taller and bearing longer arms. Years on the road had burned away any excess fat from his frame, making the cords of sinewy muscle stuck out on his arms and neck. *The mark of the wild*, his father had called it. *Duty's kiss*.

Deramun was once the champion of the Royal Caldland Contents, a proud warrior prone to boasts, drink, and songs, he was once Coram's protector, and had proven his worth countless times. A formidable fighter still, if not ageing quickly. He was forced to look up at the emissary, and the look on his bearded face was thick with affection.

Audeyrn turned his gaze to Nat, and the emissary's cold grey eyes bore into the carefree face of the warrior. A gutter rat from the lowliest hovel in Castan, the skinny boy had been found thieving from the barracks, and, impressed by his daring, the captain of the guard had given him a place beside his hearth, and a brotherhood with the men he had once tried to rob. When he was old enough, he had been assigned to the Emissary's seat on Langholm, to grow up alongside Audeyrn. His oldest friend. The smile broke, as he knew it would. Audeyrn had a causting glare, and many had remarked at just how uncomfortable it had made them feel.

"We all have a responsibility on this mission. Me, most of all. I understand that I have been distant of late. Very distant... and preoccupied. Hell, I've been a boor." He turned to one of them in particular. "But we must not allow ourselves to bring unwanted attention to our mission. The ears and eyes of the enemy may be probing the land as we speak. The box is important, but I value your lives above all else. You probably all hate me for refusing you a fire. But you know as well as I that it's preferable to have tough dry meat in the belly than the bite of some cold steel." He looked at each of them in turn. Hearty bore his heart on his sleeve as usual, and nodded earnestly in understanding. Nat looked him straight in the eye with a sly-fox smile, as though even this grave situation was some sort of game. The nervous Gregyn was abashed and dared only to look briefly at Audeyrn. But even he made a slight nod and saluted him all too formally.

Audeyrn smiled despite himself. The rain still hammered the canvas and fell from the edges in wet curtains. But somehow his heart was lifted a mite. He was away from that stinking city of narrow streets and cramped taverns, and back in the wild. With his friends. He wanted nothing more than to find the nearest inn and eat a greasy meal and drink too much, and maybe even find a pretty girl along the way. But it was a dream, snuffed out before it was borne. Too much relied on him getting to Sora. It was imperative. Too important. *The mission comes first.*

The chest caught his eye. He thought it mocking him, squatting there in all cold metal and wood, a silent reminder of the life chosen for him. *It is important*, he reminded himself. The king would not have given it to him had it been fit for an oaf to carry. "Deliver *this* to Silentis in far Sora." The aged man stroked the box like a cat. "You shall be given the fleetest steeds, provisions to last for the outward and return, and I shall grant you a boon of me... when you come back."

When you come back. Audeyrn had disliked those last words. The old man had said them as though he was choosing his words carefully. He knew what the king had thought. *If you come back...* not when, but *if.* Fear gnawed at his belly like a bad meal, but he had not let that show to his king, to his master. Then he had chastised for himself feeling it. But now... he wasn't so certain. The danger was real enough. War was here, after all. *And when had there ever been a bloodless war?* The king had laid a kind hand upon his shoulder. His loyal Royal Emissary. His loyal Audeyrn. *A boon. What fool would have believed that?* Then he remembered that he had.

A voice pulled him back to the forest. "Audeyrn? Did you hear that?" Hearty Deri stood with a hand to his ear, the other atop his ample paunch. Nat made a ruse noise. "It was probably your stomach, oaf."

Audeyrn held up his hands for silence. "Quiet!" He hissed through clenched teeth. The wry smile faded, and his head turned to the woods beyond. His hand went to his knife. Through the rain, the emissary could just make out a rumbling. Low and deep, Audeyrn thought it sounded similar to the bellows the glassmakers used in their grand furnaces, as they blew and tinkered and wrought great construction with clear and coloured glass. *The glassmakers don't work outdoors...*

"It is coming from the road ahead. It wound off to the left from where we left it. If it is human, most of it will pass by the road. If it's *something else...*" More by instinct than actual thought, his gloved hand snaked down to the hilt of his sword, quietly loosening the blade in the scabbard. He shot a glance to Gregyn, who was already tightening his overcoat and slung his bow across a shoulder. He knew what was needed of him. Audeyrn gestured to their left, and motioned for the tracker to make a hook around the source of the noise ahead of their camp. He nodded, all signs of boyish fear fleeing him as he pulled his hood up and darted out into the night.

For a time, the only sound was the terrible chorus of rain and the beating of his own heart. The far-off rumbling only got louder. Louder. Louder. The horses heard it too, kicking the earth and snorting nervously. The great grey beast that carried Deri whinnied noisily. Audeyrn moved lightly across the ground to put a calming hand on her neck. He whispered soothing sounds to her, and she quieted.

"I always said that damned mare would get me killed." Said Hearty Deri, his smile usually full of mirth now rueful and grim. He ripped his monstrous sword free of the scabbard and held it ready. Nat had a slender blade in hand, long and curved where Deramun's was huge and unwieldy. "I always thought the poor beast would kill you by collapsing under your weight."

Audeyrn said nothing. He tried to quiet his thoughts as they ran wild, the shapes of childhood nightmares ripping themselves from the nocturne to pounce on their shabby camp. His head pounded with the rumbling aways ahead. *Think! What could it be? Not a Soran scouting party. They make little noise and leave no trace of their goings. Even if the enemy had advanced this far from no-man's land, we would have known about it back at Castan.* With all the rationalising, he still could not shake the feeling deep in his stomach, and the fear chewed away at his courage.

He looked to the men, who had arrayed themselves on either side of him. *Good men.* Hearty Deri stood with his feet planted in the duff of the forest floor. He moved with a quiet strength, and Audeyrn had to remind himself that the older man had not always been so grossly fat. Nat stood to his left, stretching and limbering with all the impatience of youth, cutting the air with his elegant scythe-like blade. Audeyrn finally looked at his own blade. Three-and-a-half feet of good steel, forged by the master armourer Neiron himself, it shone even then in the blackwood. *A sword needs to fit the man.* His father had told him that once. *Or was it the other round?*

They stood that way for a long time. Hours must have passed, for the last light left the world until the dark surrounded them on all sides. Time eluded them, the moon was shrouded by the pall of night and the canopy of the blackwood, so any telling was impossible. After a time, the rumbling ebbed, receding until it required Audeyrn to strain his hearing. A few pitiful whimpers, and then the sound seemed to quiet completely. Even the rain finally decided to die off, easing to a light drizzle. The silence that supplanted the rain was deafening to Audeyrn and his friends.

The emissary had all but decided to investigate himself, when Gregyn came out of the woods like some soaked spirit. He looked all his sixteen years again and frightened. "What did you see?" Audeyrn asked him, polishing his sword, and feeling useless in the effort.

"Yar'll have t'see for yarself. Pardons, emissary... but I don't think ya'd believe me if I told ya."

So they all plodded off further into the trees. From the

east came the first wan rose of day. *A night wasted. Tomorrow will be even harder going.* The trees seemed to thin as they were led by the tracker. The great oaks surrendered to bone-white birch, each weedier than the last. Finally, they fell away completely, bringing the four men to a wide circular swath of grass. The land rose in that opening in the trees, steadily rising higher and higher until Audeyrn saw it was a hillock, an island of grass within the dark confines of the blackwood. Around the base of the hill, stones as tall as a man to as large as a bullock were placed equidistant from one another.

"A faycircle." Whispered Greg, inhaling sharply.

Deri snorted in derision. "A magic circle? Doesn't look all that much. You'd think they'd be more impressive. Ever seen this before, Aud?" The emissary could not recall a faycircle being so close to the road before. The realisation did little to calm his nagging doubts. But he put on his most reassuring face for the men. "After you've seen one, the others look much the same. I may have. I have ridden through the western reach of the blackwood countless times, and most of those I had made good time, without the poxy tree roots hampering my way." He turned to Gregyn. "Faycircles aren't that unbelievable, Greg."

The youth shook his head, scratching at the blonde fluff that sprouted from his chin. "Not the circle. No. On top. Come. I don't know what to say." This time Audeyrn took the lead, happy to stretch his legs and not have his head pommelled by the rain. He chanced making a torch, but he brushed the thought aside. Their night-eyes were on them then, and even if they managed to light a doused cloth, they would risk night blindness and ambush. *Dark becomes our armour.*

It was a light pull. The hillock was gradual, and never climbed steeply. *A month ago trees would have covered this place,* he knew. *A month ago, it would have been as flat as the Ikteti hinterlands. We could have walked right through and thought nothing of it.* No one knew why the circles raised themselves, like sudden tumours built in soil. Some, of the foolish or poetic sort, tried to give reason to it, the rough consensus being that the fay made their clan-homes beneath the hills, raising vast subterranean halls warded by old magics, impossible to access, and invisible if excavated. Audeyrn himself once liked to think that the fay resided in these unassuming rises, but the cold, dispassionate voice of reason and time hammered home a different thought- nothing lived within.

"See. Can't explain it. At least, I think it's an it. I mean, I don't know what *it* is, whatever it, I mean *this*, I mean..."

"Greg, if you don't know what *it* is, how the fuck are *we* to know, eh?" Nat eyed the body uneasily, yet flicked his knife in the air as though nothing was amiss.

The emissary didn't like this, not one bit. He found himself saying, "It's a wyrm."

Deri looked at him incredulously. "Bit bloody big to be wyrm, and bit too bloody big to be anything, if truth be told. I'm just happy it's dead, thank the gods." The creature lay strewn across the crest of the fayhill. *It does look like a wyrm... sort of.* The small draconids were usually no larger than a lapdog, with rich green-scaled skin that betrayed their jungle-dwelling origins. *This* thing was thirty foot long, at least. Audeyrn couldn't be sure. The neck was contorted at an unnatural angle, mangled and broken, and the long meandering tail looped about itself several times. And it was white. A sickly maggot white. In the dark, he thought the colour *burned* somehow, as though it were some sort of moonstone. The wing membranes were tinged an oily yellow, and even they were crumpled and sad looking. The underbelly of the great monster had been disembowelled, he saw, and where the entrails lay in a rude pile, the scales were painted a dark red. "Greg, what could have made such an injury?"

Gregyn scratched his stubble and gingerly went to the gored stomach. He moved a few ravaged organs and flaps of skin, his head momentarily disappearing in the beast's second, bloody maw. "Can't be sure, be it night and all, but I can still smell well enough. The insides are *charred*, Aud. Charred, but not cooked. There is no sign of ripping or tearing, either. Can't make out obvious slashes or cuts. This is no huntsman butcherin' a fawn. It looks as though… the belly ruptured from the inside."

Nat prodded a limp, pale leg with his sword. "Don't wyrms spit fire? Could it have swallowed its own flame-breath and blew itself open? Mayhaps this one was not only monstrous large, but monstrous stupid too."

"The rumbling did seem to come from something of this size." Deri added helpfully.

"I don't think so," Greg wiped the viscera from his hands. "I'll have to look down it's gullet t'see if that's scorched too." He looked to Audeyrn. The emissary nodded, and the tracker walked to the neck and produced his skinning knife. Taking in the sight of this strange thing atop the hill, Audeyrn frowned, glad his friends couldn't see the discomfort plastered across his face. Too many questions ran through his mind. He knew that he should send word back to Castan about the beast. It was his duty. *Hector the Court Alchemist, would be giddy to experiment on it, and the gods only know what my fickle king would say. Probably accuse the Sorans of some fell magics.* He looked to Deri to Nat to Greg and found that he couldn't choose any of them to send back.

To do so would be seen as a slight, he knew. Not that he feared losing them as friends, only that they would believe he thought them disposable.

The mission comes first. He was the emissary, and he needed to make the decision. He found himself thinking of his father, and what he would say if he were there on the island in the blackwood. But the more he thought on it, the less sure he became. He was angry that they had been soaked to the bones every day for a week, for wasting time negotiating the road, for wasting precious riding time gawking at this grotesque- The words took form in his mind.

"Sir, I mean, Aud, I mean... Please, come look at this." Greg looked stricken.

Audeyrn walked around the oversized white foreleg and stood by the tracker.

"Oh..." Was all the emissary managed.

All the angry words he had prepared vanished at the sight of the red sigil. The wyrm's head was three times larger than that of a horse. A brace of horns erupted from a bony crest, becoming longer and curved as they retreated back. Above a triple row of dark needle-like fangs, a single onyx eye stared blindly up at him, the other gouged out and bloody. The third was blood as well, but this was in the flat between the beast's brow ridge, and it was painted. In the dark, he could still make out the shininess of the wet blood that traced a large slit-pupil on the head. Lidless, searching, wanting.

Audeyrn took a step back without thinking. Those around him were shouting, but their voices were drowned out by the blood that thrummed in his ears. He thought he heard them ask something, but he was far away. Fear gripped him. He made his decision.

Dawn saw the rainclouds push west. Clear skies marked the sunrise, and upon the sylvan horizon they saw the sun rise for the first time in days. Rosy light brought colour back into the world. He thought it looked darker somehow, bloodier.

Audeyrn and his friends saddled up, following the long road east, to their goal, to Sora. No one talked for the longest time. He brooded over the great wyrm atop the fayhill, the injuries that had killed it, and the sigil that marked it. *At least it's not raining,* he thought, not daring to say it aloud.

Soon they glimpsed the sun peering between the over-bearing limbs of the wood like some shy lover. They even heard the morning song of some unseen bird. Then Greg surprised them all by blurting into a road song. He sang with a confidence that he lacked in speech. Nat and Deri, appearing too shocked to laugh, joined the boy.

After some coaxing, even Audeyrn joined for a verse or three.

Their mounts trudged on, and for a while, the emissary forgot his worries.

3

MARBLE

Only a little time remained for preparations before Marble was to depart. The time even shorter, it seemed, because the swift departure was unexpected.

Hurrying through the courtyard towards her room, Marble followed the intricate and colourful tiled pathways as they wound their way through the garden in the middle of the structure, protected from the frequent dust and sandstorms by the tall, sturdy walls of the three-story keep. The paths meandered around the lush spaces where citrus trees, colourful succulents and aspidistra grew throughout the square.

A strikingly ornate fountain, an exquisite masterpiece of the purest white stone, dominated the centre of the haven. Sculpted to form the shape of a mysterious woman, skin as smooth as the mirrors in the Palace of Peace, and luscious flowing hair that obscured most of her face and revealed only her eyes, closed in agony from the pain of the spear piercing her chest. The woman, clad in the barest scraps of fabric, most of her clothing torn from her body in the brutal battle that preceded the scene and lay pooled around her, where she struggled to stay upright on her knees as she attempted to remove the spear in vain. The supposed likeness of Quirsus, the God of Rain and Seas.

Smaller, similar structures were sporadically situated around the perimeter of the space, standing guard near the shaded walkway that edged its confines and led to the rooms. The open, shady corridors that heralded the rooms of the upper floors whilst also providing shade to the lower ones were held aloft, supported by elaborately carved stone pillars. The inner sanctum of the garrison paid homage, from the mosaic footpaths to the numerous fountains to the supporting pillars, to the story of Quirsus.

Eleven Gods once walked among men. No one knows from where they came or where they went but for whispers of a distant domain. They laboured together to ensure prosperity, unity, and peace amongst their creations and people.

Tihdite, the god of the living realm and his sister Satia, goddess of the realm of the afterlife. Phozotl, god of souls, husband to Tihdite. The god of life and death, Amarus, brother to Phozotle, husband to both Ezdona, the goddess of night and darkness and Ugnir, god of earth and soil. Neien, goddess of air and wind, sister to Ugnir and wife to Ahdes, the god of rivers and lakes, brother to Ezdona and twin to Quirsus, the goddess of rains and seas. Oxruer, god of fire and flames, husband to Quirsus, brother to Ymtia, goddess of light and day, wife to Satia. Marble remembered the droning voice of the grizzled old godman as he drilled the knowledge into young Soran minds.

Much to do but little time. She must be hasty but thorough,

31

for the journey that awaited her would be long and arduous.

Marble's hurried steps echoed, reverberating around her head as if racing to match her heart's frantic beating and increasingly shallow breaths. Her sandals slapped against the polished floors of her namesake as she climbed the stairs in the corner of the riad. Her bell-shaped breeches flapped in the still, muggy air, and her long knee-length tunic trailed behind her. Her abrupt pace propelled her onwards.

The shade of the landing, a welcome reprieve from the intense heat beating relentlessly from the sun in the cloudless, breezeless sky. Without skipping a beat, Marble ducked and dodged around the people she encountered on her way to her rooms, doing her best to keep her head down and avoid catching the eye of certain people who would be sure to delay her. Thankfully Marble didn't encounter any interruptions on her journey and was soon safely ensconced in her rooms, where she could take a deep breath as she sagged against the heavy wooden door. Tilting her head back, Marble did her best to clear her mind and calm her breaths as she tried to understand why she had been chosen to undertake this task.

She gave herself a second to wonder and despair before she pulled herself together and locked away any doubts in the back of her mind. She had a task to carry out and would complete it no matter what. *Calm in the face of adversity, kind in the face of struggle.* Marble scoffed as her mother's voice whispered unwelcomely in her mind.

Compiling a list of all she might need, Marble rummaged around her room to assemble the items she already possessed. Some, she would not be able to use and have to acquire new; *I can carry nothing identifying on my person.* She had to be a shadow and bear nothing that betrayed who she was, where she came from, her station in life and what her task may be.

As Marble tried to map out her desired route rationally, more items of necessity joined the ever-growing list of supplies she would need to carry with her. She stopped to think again and ruthlessly culled down that list to the barest of essentials. It would not merely be a journey of stealth and speed and importance, she knew, but one of survival. Marble wished for a way to know the path set out for her, and she had a feeling that she would not emerge on the other side as the same person. "Let's not think of that." She said, studying the supplies on her bed.

"Shit. I really have only one pair of plain breeches?" She wondered aloud, looking at the rest of her gathered clothing and her pack. All bore the regalia of the emissaries of the Kingdom of Sora. She had not been provided a purse with which she could acquire new provisions, for none but the Queen and the General were privy to the details of Marble's mission. Therefore, it did not exist, and any purse provided would have alerted those who need not know. Marble would have to exercise her thieving skills and hope they had not grown too rusty in their hiatus.

Marble walked the city in her head, trying to determine the best places to gather supplies unnoticed.

Encircled from the north, west, and south by the roving deserts of the Desolate Tundra, Sora had hot summers and cold, dry winters. Selentis, the city in the sands, had its founding lost to the whispering wastes beyond its battlements. Narrow winding streets with high adobe and

33

brick walls, roofed at various intervals, minimised desert expansion and the effects of dust storms while maximising daytime shade and insulating from the severe winter temperatures. The many manses enclosed and hidden and secreted from the outside world. The architecture designed in a way to provide maximum protection during times of tension and danger while furnishing a microcosm of tranquillity that protected its inner paradise garden.

Neighbourhoods formed around shrines of the old Gods, with no shortage of houses of mourning, bathhouses, teahouses, bureaus and academies throughout the city. Every neighbourhood also had its own ab anbar and bazaar-chec. The Grand Bazaar in the city's heart. The Palace and Garrison, past the outskirts of Selentis, between the city itself and the Tundra proper. Marble's mind ran through all these details as she looked at the pitiful display of acceptable provisions lying haphazardly on her bed that she had long since claimed as her own.

Nothing. She had practically nothing that would be useful to her for the journey ahead. She doubted she could slip out of the Garrison unnoticed. She would have to find her way into someone else's room.

Cursing aloud and attempting deep, calming, focusing breaths, Marble did her best to dismiss the frantic, almost overwhelming doubts that were piling up in her mind. They were irrelevant. She had been tasked with this mission. *Me. Only me.* And she refused to allow worries and insecurities prevent her from accomplishing what seemed impossible. She would prevail. She would not, could not, fail.

Once again resolute, her list of preparatory tasks became more distinguishable in her mind. Marble stood vigil at her door. Ear pressed close to the seam, she waited, listening for any movement beyond its frame. She hoped that the garrison's uppermost level also remained its most quiet.

Despite her careful listening, there was no way to know how full or empty the upper floor was, so with a fortifying breath, Marble opened the door as casually as possible and let herself out. With one last look back into her room, Marble absorbed every detail. There was no time to clear the space of traces of her presence. No time to prove she was not a traitor. That was what they had told her to be. She had to play the part and play it well. With gritted teeth, she crept across to the opposite end of the ancient building, thankful that she had not encountered a soul.

Marble knew which room she would target first. Pausing outside her destination and sinking into the minimal shadows, Marble waited. She was confident that Cliada was currently stalking a particular group of elite soldiers with her minions, but it never hurt to be cautious. Marble couldn't afford to not be either.

The coast seemingly clear, Marble had to toe the line between caution and haste. She twisted the door handle, hoping that Cliada was foolish and vain enough to believe nobody would dare enter her rooms. She *was* that foolish. *Thank you, Cliada.* Marble smirked and hurried inside. With no time to waste, Marble tore about the room and took an inordinate amount of joy in the destruction she caused while searching for anything she could use. She would take it all. She would take what she needed and not feel guilt for Cliada and her family were not wanting for coin. It would be nothing for them to replace the items that Marble would commandeer, unlike some of the people that

Marble may have to relieve of their belongings in the city.

Marble packed three sets of clothing in varying styles, unadorned and bearing no identifying markers, into an equally ambiguous pack. She also helped herself to a decent-sized purse with a generous amount of coin inside and hid it beneath her clothing.

She did not dally any longer than necessary. If her luck held, she could avoid the city almost entirely, needing to acquire a mount from there. *Hopefully*. With that in mind, Marble took her leave. There was one other room she would visit before venturing onto the kitchens.

A loud blaring shattered the relative quiet. The city's raid warning. Selentis was under attack. "Shit." Marble cursed under her breath. *This is not good. Not good at all.* She fought against her instincts and training, to race towards the danger, to help protect and fortify. To arm herself and report to her commanding officer.

Her time was up. Marble had to leave.

Unable to collect a mount or vittles, Marble was thankful she had found a waterskin in Cliada's room. Hurrying to the fountain of Quirsus in the middle of the courtyard, she filled it. The stopper plugged the skin as the frantic approach of expected footfalls reached her ears. Scurrying into some of the more dense foliage, Marble hid. Cursing silently, she calmed her thundering heart.

Tying the water skin to her side, Marble hoped the water was clean and safe to drink, but she did not have the luxury of filling the skin elsewhere. She also hoped drinking from the Quirsus fountain wasn't as sacrilegious as it appeared. She mouthed a wordless prayer to the blind god, from habit more than anything else. It was impossible to know whether the sunlight and bright light of day were to Marble's advantage. On the one hand, it was harder to hide in shadows without looking suspicious, but on the other hand, people appeared less suspicious during the day than at night. However, with attention focused on the raid on the city, Marble was pretty confident that nobody noticed when she slipped out of the back entrance to the garrison.

Marble's initial route would have to change due to the attack. *No mount, no food, and a little, possibly deadly, water. I will have to journey to the Bonebridge.* She could not make it far enough with her limited resources to reach a different outpost or an oasis. Bonebridge was notorious for its lawless culture. Almost a realm unto itself. A haven, if you would, for thieves and criminals and outcasts, from any form of retribution from a crown, kingdom or empire. A savage place where one was always half a wrong look away from meeting their ultimate demise.

If the tales are even half true, you never leave the place. Being robbed would be the least of my worries. Funny... it's no more than a day and night through the sands.

The sand burned Marble's feet as the sandal-clad appendages slipped through the sliding grains in her hurried departure. The slippery grit, ever moving, aided Marble by covering up the tracks she left in her wake, filling in her footsteps as quickly as she made another dent in the ground. One less thing for the emissary had to worry about, and she was thankful for it. This journey was not starting as she'd hoped, and Marble prayed that it wasn't a sign of even worse things. It would be bad enough, she knew, the trek to the lone outpost in a somewhat viable distance considering her lack of provisions.

The sun sat at its zenith and watched her. Marble knew that the heat and the sun and the dryness of the air would get much, much worse before it cooled off to a more reasonable temperature. There was a reason that people did not travel at the height of the day in these parts. It was easy for people to die in these conditions. *Heat stroke, dehydration, and general dangers of the desolate tundra. Creatures that made the place their home after coming through rifts. Sand storms were frequent and deadly, sprouting from nowhere, with no warning and in no time at all.* She ticked off the reasons in her head. The list, drilled into her since she had moved to Selentis with her mother as a young girl.

One blink, and the land would change from calm stillness, if not pleasant, at least not so instantly lethal, to raging storms with grains of sand flying so quickly and so sharply that a person's skin would be ripped to shreds within a couple of breaths. Not that anybody would be able to breathe in that situation, for the air would be so thick with the tiny shards of glass that nostrils would be filled and bleeding and any attempt even to open one's mouth would result in an even more horribly painful death. They would be torn apart from the insides as well as the out. The Desolate Tundra enjoyed making a meal out of those foolish enough to think they could brave the desert and survive. The harsh, unforgiving landscape was ever-changing, a conundrum. No one knew why the land changed itself. *Like a fayhill. A circle of the fay.* The flat expanse stretching out before the ever-senseless or desperate traveller, suddenly becoming a magnificent range of treacherous dunes, impossible to scale and pass. Marble watched as the same also worked in reverse, far in the distance. The gigantic dune that another senseless, desperate pilgrim - a dark speck she squinted to see - was attempting to climb, disappeared beneath their feet, taking them with it.

The difference between the Tundra and the faycircles of the west, she mused, silently mourning for the lost traveller and praying for her path to remain steady. *No stones mark the Tundra's boundaries and anywhere in the desert is prone to change its form. The dangers not isolated to one spot, for the Tundra was a vast place indeed.*

Looking over her shoulder, Marble's breath came out in rough, furious pants as she took in the distance she had travelled. Not enough. The Palace and Garrison loomed too close for comfort, with the city itself lost behind the walls. The Queen's residence hosted a magnificent edifice once named for the ancient sanctuary of the Gods. The majestic structure was awe-inspiring and an incredible feat of craftsmanship and beauty. A solid stone monument in the rough shape of a square with plentiful rooftop sanctuaries intermingled with huge turquoise domes. Decorative arches covered the outer walls with artfully carved scenes filling each one. A great gate, a masterpiece of more elaborate artwork and structural and defensive integrity and ingenuity, guarded the main entry point to the inner sanctum of the grounds. The gate was seldom closed, easing access for all.

It was closed now. Raids on Selentis were a frequent occurrence. It grated on Marble that she could not be there to help defend the city, but she knew she had a much more important task to complete.

Reasonably sure that any guards had not spotted her, and due to the absence of visible raiders, Marble decided that she was safe to take her time and pace herself. She could not overtax her body so soon into her journey, and she had to remember that the water she had procured from the Quirsus fountain could only be drunk when it was an absolute necessity.

Blazing hot, the sun beat down, and the sand beneath Marble's feet was furnace hot. The muggy air scorched like boiling broth as the emissary tried to breathe, burning her throat and lungs with each laboured inhalation. Marble's signature scarf became suffocating when combined with the midday atmosphere of the Desolate Tundra. Removing it from her head, Marble used it to wipe up the sweat that had gathered and placed it back over her hair but did not cover her face again to protect the crown of her head from the furious light in the sky. Taking in the position of the burning ball high above, Marble corrected her course, south by southeast.

The day wore on, and time dragged as Marble focused on putting one foot in front of the other as she kept an eye on her direction to maintain her course. The sun and heat were relentless, and Marble was more than parched, but she refrained from sipping from the waterskin tied to her belt. The sun passed overhead and began its slow descent. Marble breathed more easily. A smidgen of the tension holding her shoulders tight and strained her muscles started to ease. With the temperature beginning to drop, Marble hoped that she could find a small measure of relief in her journey. *The peak of the day is the most frequent hour of change in the land and the most likely time to get caught in the Tundra's swift, deadly storms.*

Ahead of her, the way was still flat and easy, with the

occasional small range of rolling dunes scattered along the horizon. Marble hoped to not encounter any hazardous surprises throughout the dusk and nighttime.

With the cooling temperatures, Marble removed her sandals from her torn feet. The skin rubbed raw where the sand and skin met. The ground was still hot, but it was tolerable.

Day bled into night, and a kaleidoscope of colours saturated the sky. A breathtaking sight, unlike anything Marble had ever seen or experienced. Possibly made even more astonishing because Marble was beginning to experience the symptoms of her dehydration and sunstroke.

The city of Selentis was gone, having dropped off the horizon hours ago. Marble had not, would not, and did not stop. *I have to make the Outpost. If I stop, I die.* With the addition of her sandals to her pack, she slung it across her back and noted the difference in weight. Shivering as the last of the day's warmth bled away to join the light, Marble withdrew an extra top, this one owning long sleeves, and donned it over the top of her current one. A sunset, the colour and fury of crimson flame, was fast fading upon the horizon, leaving Marble with only hope that the stars would shine bright enough to aid in her navigating the treacherous land.

Night wore on, and Marble donned the other tops balled in her pack. At last, she succumbed to taking tantalising, rationed sips from the waterskin. Although shaky with fatigue, the emissary did not stop pushing on, pushing forwards.

With the sun already a distant memory, the sand had chilled until it was like ice beneath Marble's feet, stinging

41

and burning as though another sun were now beating down on it. Her breath fogged before her face, and she wiped away the snot from her numbing nose. Wrapping her scarf once more around her face, she hoped to stave off some of the cold and that her blurring eyesight would not interfere too much with her ability to navigate using the stars. The clear night sky was both a blessing and a curse.

Everything hurt and ached as Marble continued, stumbling forward in the cold, doing her best to keep her eyelids from drooping for longer than a second.

She was without a mount, but that did not bother her. *I can do this on my own two feet.* She needed the food and water most and felt the lack of them.

Then the desert changed, the land darkened, and the dreadblack lines in the sand moved. *Fuck.*

The land around her morphed into a different world, it seemed. The ground rumbled, shaking beneath her feet, tripping her. She rolled swiftly and violently down the massive dune rising evermore into the sky. Finally rolling to a stop, winded and with a possibly dislocated shoulder, though the pain was somewhat distant to Marble at that moment, she looked around.

The sand at her feet exploded outwards, and the pillar that erupted filled the world with its screech. It was too dark. She tried to move and couldn't tell if it was fear or delirium, but she stood unmoving. Beholding the thing, her eyes followed the shade in its sheer, horrifying size. The dark silhouette blotted out the stars. She breathed, and tried to stop the beating of her heart. It saw her. *Fuck.*

4

AUDEYRN

"…some other way. A rowboat, maybe? A logger's raft. Hell, I'd even settle for a coracle at this rate." Audeyrn looked into the tankard before him. Foam clung desperately to the rim, and sediment had settled at the bottom into a crescent shape. He stared hard into the dregs until spots appeared in his vision. He grit his teeth. It was either that or admit failure. He hated failure.

The inn was not the cleanest place the emissary had ever visited. Nor the friendliest. But it offered a hot duck broth full of potatoes, the cook even managing to surprise him by magicking some pepper to sprinkle into the rich mushroom sauce. They had loaves of baked bread on the side with butter melting on top, and to wash it down, they drank the strong brown ale that had made Vastiland famous.

Deri twirled the end of his moustache, quaffing his latest pint of Vasti ale. "We could go to the alderman. Not together, of course. Just myself, and ask for passage on the ferry. Cross that crooked bastard's palm with a silver or three, and I guarantee he'd be smiling 'til wintertide. I have been thinking it awhile, you see. We present ourselves as godmen, of the like that sometimes prattle in the foreigner's market in Low Castan. We could be Lar'garans! We go to the alderman. We let him know that you are some priest, and we will your bondservants journeying—"

Gregyn winced. "I've had my fill of bondservitude for a life, Hearty, even if I've to act the part. I've a better idea, anyways." He pushed his empty bowl away and leant forward. His voice was low, and Audeyrn noticed that he didn't stutter. The boy was currently gulping through his seventh pint. "We don't lie to anyone. Only *withhold* certain truths. We go to the nearest timberman along the river and tell him who we are. *Really* are. That we are… carrying… a message." He looked about furtively at the other patrons, but the place boasted few travellers and the locals appeared not to care or were too busy working on their own stupor. Greg leant over to Hearty, brandishing a long finger like a knife. "*Yar*'ll take care of the timberman if he has any disagreements. We'll pay him well, of course, but his silence should be guaranteed 'til we're well and good 'cross the river."

Audeyrn listened, but they were just words. He eyed the big door. *Nat should be back by now. I gave him leave for two hours at most. Where could he be? Probably married, the slipshod fool. Damn him.* His friend had been earnest enough in his request to visit the fancyhouse in Forlorn, and he could not deny that his men deserved some much needed respite after weeks on the long road. Yet his friend's absence disquieted him.

The booth was secluded, giving them a shadowed corner to themselves. From the sad-looking sign outside, they learned it was called the Happy Huntsman. The *happy* sort did not deign to appear as they bought their bed and board. Those that did arrive after them were hard-worn foresters and timberfolk, who wasted no time before lounging about, drinking and dicing and fondling the girls in their laps.

In their travel-stained leathers and heavy cloaks, no one would have thought that they had been sent by royal decree. *Good. Ignorance is safety to these people. Forlorn has seen enough horrors.*

The maps given to him by Hector the Gifted still named the town Furrowfield, the original name of its founding. When Audeyrn had passed through two years ago, it had seemed a pleasant enough place, but he had learned the history from the local crier. Straddling the great White Rush, it made its steady coin from logging the expansive forests that clung to the slopes of the Vasti Highlands, great limbed garwoods used for almost anything. The furrowed field, which it took its name, had long been given over to settlement, the meagre flatland that sat above the churning water of the Rush now dominated by the tall sloping roofs that were popular among the Vasti. It was pretty, but the lone bridge that spanned the river had been the site of a score of battles and a dozen twin pogroms. It had been a great carved wooden arch when he had crossed it, shaped and graven like a shoal of intertwining river trout. He had admired it then. Now he could not help but scowl. Riding into the north-side, they were confronted by the remains. It left a bitter taste in his mouth. *To think I had boasted of its beauty.* The locals had been busy collecting the debris from the storm, and upon questioning one such, they learned that the night before, the Rush had burst its banks and uprooted the bridge, dragging the structure and a dozen of the riverfront houses downstream. It had been over in an instant, if the local could be believed.

So they found board, and chewed on the next step of the journey. A ferry crossed the river several times a day, but the alderman had forbidden outsiders from using it, and allowed only his household guards to cross freely to collect levies. Audeyrn knew of Alderman Raynolf if only by reputation, and that was enough to know that he would not help. The alternative would be to tack upriver until they could find a ford. He had never travelled upriver of the White Rush before, though he knew that they would inevitably find a crossing on a smaller stretch of water. But doing so, would delay them no end. The cartographer who made the maps seemed similarly ill-informed.

The woman came back with another helping of bread and broth for Deri, two more tankards of brown for Audeyrn and Greg, and a shy smile for the former. "Hav'n seen you bowt *here* before." She said in a voice that was all for Deri. "Where's you and yours from, if I might 'quire?"

"Gorm's Town," the emissary shot in quickly. It was a safe answer. A town close enough to Forlorn to warrant some familiarity yet far enough to ensure a lowly serving woman such as her would have no connection to it. *And no prying questions.*

"Ah. You's travelled far, then. Don't get many from *Gorms* round here. Not since the troubles picked up again, anyway. And now the Bridge has gone a floatin'. It seems it gets worser every day. Soldiers abroad, talk of monsters, godmen hiding away. You heard about the dunny defeat at Hobart's Motte? " Before Audeyrn could answer, Greg blurted drunkenly, "Hobart's Motte? But Castan doesn't have forces that far east."

Her smile was innocent enough. She stood there, almost as though she did not understand his words. Then she collected herself enough to say, "Nah. Not Castan. Not them." Her eyes fell on Deri, and a suggestive smile broached her lips. "I see you's had no stomach for cook's broth, big man. He'll be awfully cross with me if I were to tell him."

Deri guffawed and plopped a large arm on the table. "Best not tell cook!"

She giggled at that, scooping up his empty bowl and giving a wave as she went. *Pretty*, thought the emissary. *A pity Deri is more enamoured by the food.* Her words swam in his mind. *Them?* He clenched his jaw, all too aware of whom she meant, the knowledge setting a bad feeling in his gut. *The Rowetts.*

He looked to the big man, who was making short work of his fourth helping, savouring little, quaffing his food and drink, clearly enjoying the few delights Vastiland had to offer. Audeyrn couldn't blame him. It was the first true meal they had had since their waterlogged way from Castan through the blackwood, and that had been a month ago. He waited for the words he needed to say but found his mouth dry. *The Rowetts.* Even the name put him on edge, and he thought he noticed a few of the locals sending quick glances his way. He felt all a coward, and needing the reassuring words of a father.

But his father was dead and gone. Coram, although capable, was never a well man, and it had been bonerot that took him in the end. Deri seemed the closest to a father now. Kind and stalwart, he was a follower first and friend second, and the gluttonous oaf was not one for consolation and would shrug off anguish in favour of a jape and a drink.

He swayed in his seat. *I'm drunk. Dark beer brings darker thoughts.* Someone had told him that once. Maybe it was his father. He could not say. He yawned, his eyes watering to blur his vision. If Deri and Greg had grievances, they kept them well hidden. Audeyrn stood. He dropped a copper to the table. "I'll retire. Wake me should Nat decide to appear. I'll be wanting a word with him."

"He probably turned the girlhouse red," sneered Greg, the drink making him bold.

Audeyrn eyed him coolly. "This is important. As soon as he comes back, send him to me. See you on the morrow." Not allowing time for either of the men to respond, he stalked across the common room to the ramshackle steps that led upstairs.

They creaked dangerously as he took them two at a time. When he reached the rented room, he turned the key and retreated within. The oil lamp was where he had left it, so he struck a flint to the kindling the innkeep had given him and lit the oil. A wan glow penetrated the room, banishing the shadows to their corners. Four straw pallets occupied the planked floor. On one wall, a window with clouded glass was a door to night. *The days are shorter.* He took off his cloak, placing it on a wall hanging. He peeled off his leathers, relieved to be free of their harsh groping. Those he folded and placed in a pile beside the pallet he had claimed for his own. The one furthest from the window.

His mind turned to the box, hidden in a travel bag beneath the pallet. Swearing under his breath, he brought it out, placing it gently on the bed covers. It wasn't much to look at. A strongbox, unadorned and bare. He ran a hand along its surface and found a creeping curiosity, an unbidden desire, winding its way across the surface of his mind. He suddenly wanted nothing more than to see the inside. The keyhole was almost obscene in the way it goaded him. With an effort, he brushed it aside, gathering up the box and replacing it under the bed.

"Still a long day," he said to himself. When he tried to laugh, he sounded hoarse and tired.

As he lay down, he found himself staring at the cracked plaster of the ceiling. His eyelids became too heavy, so he closed them. The darkness did not wait long. Soon he could no longer hear the hubbub of the inn, his breathing, the occasional creak of the floor as someone led a girl laughing into bed. After a while, he heard nothing at all. The dreams came to him. The usual absurd ghosts. The ones long gone. The mother he never knew. The girl…

The spectres fled as the door was slammed by a mailed fist. *Nat.* He thought angrily. *He is drunk, and means to wake the whole tavern.* It was dark in the room; the oil long burnt up. Instinct made him grab his sword, the hilt more reassuring than the strongest castle wall. He lay there, naked, still and quiet and waiting. He heard voices from outside the room. Unfamiliar and hushed.

"Who are you?" He shouted, and realised how groggy he sounded.

"His lordship's guards." Came the voice. Fear knotted in his gut. "Open the door, if ya please."

The forced decorum fooled him none. "A moment." He slid from the bed and donned his leathers. The darkness

49

had made him clumsy, but he still managed to get dressed quickly and soon had his sword in hand and poised by the doorframe. He regarded himself for a quick instant. His garb was much better suited to halting the elements than a length of cold unyielding steel. But it was all he had. *Better than being naked.* His thoughts went to Deri and Greg, wondering where they could be. He looked back at the window, seeing how useless it would be to try and squeeze through. Even if he did manage to get out, he wagered that he would probably break a leg from the fall.

The fists at the door again, and a second voice, nasal and simpering, said, "We said to open up. We'll not be liking havin' wait to wait. So open it, I say!" *Two, or more?* He raised the latch.

Outside, a big man and a small man stood in old mail and crumpled regalia and looked at him from hard faces. "Lord Raynolf is wanting to see ya." Said the big man, who Audeyrn recognised as the second voice. *The alderman gives himself the title of lord now?* He left the question unsaid, instead asking, "Where are my companions?" The big man smiled and shot a glance at the smaller man.

"Lord Raynolf said ya's to come to the River House," he said, a spare man with a pair of swollen lips with a sore at one corner. He jerked a thumb at Audeyrn's sword. "And ya won't be needing that."

The night was cold despite his cloak, and he shivered all the way across the White Rush. A barge made of garwood like most everything else in the town, square and wide, each corner adorned with beams carved to resemble stalking herons. They regarded Audeyrn with blind, unfeeling eyes.

The guards ignored him on the passage across the river.

They chatted with the bargeman, a stringy man who looked ninety and a day if one was kind. They did not have to consider him in the slightest. Not that Audeyrn thought of escaping. The river still ran high and rough from the rains, too high and too fast to try anything stupid, a torrent living up to its name. He needed to find his friends, and the surest course of action seemed to play the prisoner and head to the alderman.

He tried to recall all he had heard of Raynolf, from his father and Hector and the king, and all the stories he had heard along the long road. Most of it was half-remembered, and rumours besides, but what he knew for a certainty was that he was a vile, conniving schemer. A man of old blood in an otherwise impoverished noble house, who had ushered in the resurgence of the town of Forlorn through astute financial planning and nefarious subterfuge. Who had once refused to save his daughter from a band of marauders. *He claimed the price they offered too high.* He prayed for his friends' fate as he was led to the master of Forlorn.

The River House dominated the south-side of the river, its high, sloping roofs dwarfing all the homes and guildhalls and tavern-brothels that dared to encroach. It only loomed larger as the ferry reached the far-side. The alderman had ordered that work to repair the bridge be carried out both day and night, so the town was ablaze with torch light from oil lamps and lanterns, all flashing upon the gilded wooden beams of the alderman's house, and turning the night into a false day. Unlike the rest of the town, the River House was built with the golden deynwood that grew in the high passes of the Vasti snowmonts. Every shadow of a nook and column made the manor look like some spectacular golden skeleton in the dark, every recess an empty eye socket, every handrail and balustrade a row of gilded ribbons. Audeyrn realised that he had never seen the River House at night. Perhaps Raynolf knew what his home looked like in the dark. Perhaps it was some sort of game of the mind. Maybe not. Regardless, as he was ushered through a small servant's entrance off to the side, he knew there was no going back.

His guards had turned mute since setting foot inside. Neither answered his questions, nor looked his way. The guards that lined the vast walls of the River House were likewise tongueless and still. He looked about, hoping to glimpse his friends being prodded along by guards themselves. He was sadly disappointed. Besides the guards, the manor was deserted. No servants, maids, messengers, scullions, washerwomen, grooms, cooks, retainers, chamberlains, or wards. It was inhabited only by the men of stone, each one different in height, or build or beards, or baldness or pox-scars, but all dressed in the same watery livery of Forlorn, the same dinted mail, the same indifferent faces.

The corridors began to look the same after a while. Audeyrn was shown the way down a steep stair to a storehouse of a sort, up a stair, down again, a corkscrew that went higher than he would have dared guess, a trapdoor with handholds cut into rock. He was turned around so many times that he lost all sense of direction. It went on for so long that he wondered if he would be shown to a door that opened inside Castle Castan. He realised why they had not bothered to blindfold him, as labyrinthine as the warrens were. They were not only his arresters but his salvation too. Then he arrived at the cellar.

The door was heavy, and its hinges screamed as it was forced open. The under-cellar was four-sided and dingy. The air was stale, and the floor uneven. The ceiling was eight feet high, a cave of sorts carved from solid rock. Between a half-dozen iron wall sconces hammered into bare stone burned oily flames. The only covering on the bare stone walls was a thick layer of nitre like some mockery of a tapestry. Pressed flush against the opposing wall to the door was a floor-to-ceiling bottle rack made of solid deynwood. He could not help but marvel at how intricate patterns had been carved into the wood, and how fresh it appeared, even in that damp place. Each compartment was filled with a dark bottle, made darker still by the liquid held within.

His boots scraped noisily against the floor. He stalked into the cellar, his eyes darting to find an exit, an opening, something sharp to use as a weapon. *A broken bottle will do.* He swallowed as he eyed the wine rack. Blood swam through his ears. He chose a bottle.

"Leave us," growled a voice that echoed through the cellar. Turning, Audeyrn saw a bald man standing in the gloom of the tunnel. They left with their heads bowed. When the door screamed to a close, he heard a key turn.

"I would offer you a seat. Alas, I lacked the foresight to send for such." The man was heavy-set, yet the way he sauntered to the wine rack belied light feet and fluid, unhampered movement. His hands went from one row to the next, pulling a bottle out here and examining a seal there, always his eyes looking to the next row. Finally, he ran out of bottles and looked at Audeyrn the way a man chews on a piece of gristle. "You're late." His jowls wobbled as he talked, his mouth a small, lipless thing between two round red cheeks. He was bald, the baldest man Audeyrn had ever seen. He had no hair atop his head, nor eyebrows or eyelashes; his flabby hands were fleshy and hairless, and his jaw looked as fresh-faced as a babe. He wasn't an ugly man, but neither was he handsome. He was of middling height, and his shoulders and paunch did not seem overly large to the emissary. He would have taken him for a lout if he was not dressed like a peacock, and indeed he would have put even the most arrogant of those birds to shame. Fine silks flowed from him in vivid purples and maroons, burgundies and carmines. Over his breast, a deynwood brooch, shaped like a leaping pike, glared at Audeyrn with a ruby eye. His own eyes were a startling green, brighter than they had any right to be in that ill-lit cellar. He couldn't tell the alderman's age, perhaps because of the baldness or the fleshiness or the way his eyes glowed in the dim light, but he knew that he must be as old as Hearty, if not older.

"Why am I here? Where are—" The questions tumbled from him all at once.

The alderman made a dismissive flick of the wrist. "Your companions, all three of them, are contained and safe. For the nonce." His words did nothing to release the knot in Audeyrn's stomach.

"How can I believe you?"

The man's lip curled. "Because I have no reason to be false." He placed his meaty hands behind his back. "Do you know the contents of the message you carry?"

"I–" Audeyrn weighed his words carefully. His armpits felt damp, and his throat dry. "No. The message is for the Queen in Silentis. I am only the bearer of–"

"I know the oath of the Royal Emissary." His voice was a feral growl between small white teeth. "What I want to know is why you have been sent."

Present confidence. Give him nothing. "I could not say other than I am delivering a message."

"Don't be coy with me, Audeyrn, son of Coram. I know who you are, and I know why you've been skulking around my town." His mouth twisted in impatience. "Enough of the back and forth. You won't willingly divulge your mission. Fine. That is the way with you *emissaries*. I'll explain how I know and my motive. Is that good enough for you? Trust is built upon the foundation of truth." Audeyrn was allowed no time to respond, for the alderman continued on to say, "Your friend, the one that visited The Rose's Daughter earlier this eve, was titillating one of the girls when he started to boast of his position as a guardian to a king's messenger. Had I been a different man, I would have put him to the rack and had my way to wrinkle out his secrets. Had I been a different man..."

Audeyrn felt sick. *I'll kill that slipshod.* His mind raced. *If I live to see the dawn.*

"Turned out to be very talkative, when plied with the right wine and distracted by a pretty face. One of mine worked as well. Most of them are. The bed sheets hadn't a chance to dry before I was made aware that the king's royal emissary was gracing my town with his presence. You can imagine my fretting at hearing such pressing news. *And in the Huntsman too!*" He gestured at the room. "Hence our conference in my least favourite of places. I know the noble Royal Emissary is used to more illustrious halls, but be aware that my hospitality is not lacking."

55

A laugh somehow found its way to Audeyrn's lips. "You said enough back and forth. Tell me true. Are my companions harmed?" *The mission is always first.* "Where is the chest?"

Reynolf put a hand to his bald head as though he had forgotten that he lacked hair. "Safe, and safe. Your companions have been given apartments at the River House, the chest placed with them. I retrieved your fornicating friend and reunited him with the others. When my men deposited him with that fat man and your skinny boy, he was... drunk. Otherwise untouched, and nothing a night of sleep cannot remedy."

"And I suppose I will have to take you at your word."

"Yes." Something in those eyes flashed menacingly. "I have no interest in playing the falsifier."

Audeyrn looked at the wine rack again. "So why am I *here?*"

"I am not in the business of killing emissaries, if that is what you're worrying about. Such barbarous acts would irreparably sully my reputation..." Audeyrn hid a smile. "This cellar, however, contains my private stock of Loudwater red. Open one if you like. There are many foul calumnies that I hoard bodies and other macabre fancies down here. The truth is no less horrific. My forebears had the insight to create the warrens beneath Forlorn to hide valuables when the raiders from the snowmonts came a-calling. You're the first outsider to step foot here since the last twin pogrom a hundred years ago." Aud could see the flickering of something pass over the alderman's eyes. *Memories?* It was ephemeral, the briefest of moments, for then he gave a perfunctory shake of his head and was back in the cellar again. "But enough of history. We of the folk of Furrowfield dwell on it too much. Now, I rudely woke you and dragged you here to *talk*, if you choose to believe me. I don't care either way. I want to warn you, Audeyrn. You cannot go further. You have to return to Castan."

Something in his tone made him angry. "Because of the war?"

Reynholf sighed. "Because of *them*. No message you possess is worth being captured by them. Captured, or worse. We hear all sorts of things coming from the east, and all the messengers that bring us that woeful news are all skeletons with skin, deathly afraid, howling that we should flee to the mountain fastnesses and pray, pray that *they* do not find us."

Audeyrn was unimpressed."The dunnies can be avoided. I've travelled the long road countless times and learned to avoid certain troublesome areas. Even with the war, a group of four may be able to slip by. Anyway, I do not fear the men of Sora. They are not evil. They are people. Bad, good, apathetic, kind, cruel, passionate, sloth. They can be bargained with, reasoned, or bribed. They will let my friends and I through the lines. I've done it before. I speak the tongue of the road wanderers. I can be persuasive. My trade demands it. My king tasked me with delivering his message with all due haste, and I will not tarry or turn back. I will make the journey to Silentis. If I make it, I can stop the war."

Reynolf laughed. It was a cruel, throaty thing that rasped and grated, made larger through the under-cellar. Audeyrn heard the mockery reverberate around him. But there was something else too. Something like pity.

"The Sorans are just like us, yes. That is obvious. Any man who says such is a blasted fool. No. I talk of *them*. The *godless*. The burners. The blooddrinkers. Those who dwell in Godswrath-on-the-Rock. You truly are a fool if you do not fear them, boy. They cannot be reasoned with, haggled, bribed or bought, befriended or cosened... For they are not men like you or me. They do not love. They live only for their fucking Child-god. Born believing it in their cribs and living and dying bloody immolations for the passion of their dark idol. I *must* fear them. Fear is the sole reason why this cellar exists, why my town is not a midden heap of old stones, and why my ancestors were not killed or carried off for raping up in the fucking snowmonts." He looked to the messenger, his eyes drawn. *Is that true fear, or only what he wants me to see.* Audeyrn wanted to argue with him. He did. But the enemy in Godswrath had always loomed no larger than the childish fears of things that crawl in the dark. But sometimes, you see things in the dark.

"I understand," was all he said. Doubt clung to his throat like a bad humour. "But the Disciples of the Child are a cult long dead. A dangerous cult, yes, but they did not venture far from Godswrath, wherever the fuck it is. They are gone."

"Gone?" the alderman nodded gravely. "They are dead, but their ideas persist. Those that cling to their foul babe walk the same ground as both of us, and you know it. What would happen should a roving band of godless chance upon your merry little troupe? I saw that you carry weapons, and you probably have some skill yourself. But do you think it will be enough to stave off warrior-priests who have pledged their entire lives to the passion, their hearts and minds to perfecting the art of killing?"

"As I said, we can–"

He moved toward Audeyrn with unbelievable speed until he was close enough to smell the alderman's jasmine perfume. "I think not. You will be caught, messenger. The world is getting darker, and the horrors of the past will soon become the dreaded reality of the present. Godswrath has emptied."

Raynolf spun on his heel and made for the door. "Should court come calling for me, you were never here. I never met Audeyrn, son of Coram."

The emissary burnt with rage. A wordless, red anger. He felt the urge to smash every bottle of Raynolf's special reserve and destroy the deynwood. "You are wrong, *my lord*." He could not think. He coiled a fist, and dark thoughts passed his mind. "With my message, an alliance can be made. Hope can be forged yet. With that, we have the power to conquer all our enemies."

Raynolf shook his head. He went to the door, and Audeyrn thought he saw his shoulders droop for a moment. A meaty fist slammed against the door. Green eyes flashed towards the Royal Emissary, a mask of indifference on that hairless head.

"Open up. The dead man wants to leave."

5

NATOLY

The girl had known her way about.

Nat smiled broadly, gulping down the wine. He pulled his breeches from the carpets and tied himself back up. The candle on the bedside had suffused the room with a sweet aroma. As he was led into the room, she had teased him, and shared a secret smile. But now the scent seemed cloying and overpowering, as though it was trying to conceal an undercurrent of something foul and rancid.

She had certainly smelled sweet. *Ambara. Like the flower.* Just shy of twenty, or so Nat thought. She had been shy in other ways, too, until she wasn't. He watched as she slipped the wispy amethyst silk gown over her head, revealing all of her beneath. He liked her hair. Dark, the near-black of a cloudless dusk, that shone a burnt red in the flickering candlelight. She was not tall, shorter than Nat at any rate, and lithe and graceful with her long supple legs and slim shoulders. She was not the first one he had seen as he walked gingerly into the Rose's Daughter, but he was taken the moment she came to him. He knew why, and he was not long in quelling such interloping thoughts.

Ambara had now reposed herself in the high seat near the door, looking flushed and breathless. In her hand was a glass shaped like a swan, its winding neck acting as a fine handle for her little hand. She sipped at the wine, watching him curiously with eyes the colour of a river in torrent. For a moment, he thought he could have her again, but it was a fleeting urge, and he turned away in disgust. His cheeks burned.

The look did not go unnoticed. "Am I not to your liking? A moment ago, you professed all sorts of things to me… you liked me then, sure as day." Nat refused to rise to the bait, the playful flyting, all too aware that her pouting lips would make him think of nothing but lust and flesh. He collected his own glass, the one shaped like a river pike, with the eyes and fangs picked out in mother-of-pearl. He drained it and wandered to the decanter for another.

Is that all? The decanter was half full, yet it seemed like they had been drinking it all night. *Am I pissed already?* He imagined what Hearty would think of that. The older man would never belabour himself to visit a brothel. The man was renowned across Castan for his bottomless stomach, and the few times Nat had chanced to drink with him, he had outdrank and outshone the younger man every time. The girls never seemed to notice, so he kept drinking and spending coin, and wore his smile.

The Rose's Daughter had come by recommendation from the Happy Huntsman's dour landlord. There were a dozen in total in the town called Forlorn, each one catering to the carnal tastes of their patrons. He was not particular, so when he asked for a clean and discreet house, where the girls were good and not like to rob you and cut your throat, the man had seemed anything but dour when given the chance to talk of his favourite redhouse.

It was not an impressive building, as the houses of courtesans go, but still larger than some guildhalls. The renowned brothels of High Castan held host to the most famous courtesans west of the Ruell Sea, with high, fanciful facades and marbled terraces full of old sculptures of some goddess of love. He had been to such places before, so routing out the Rose's Daughter had just been a matter of being pointed in the right direction. He was sure that *someone* along the way would help. The locals he asked snorted derisively, but sent him to the Daughter nonetheless.

Perched on a knuckle of rock above the riverbank, the sloping roofs of the redhouse rose high at a rakish angle, shaming all those that neighboured close by. The tiled roof and doors were all painted a garish red… the badge of their trade. He was not disappointed, despite the place being smaller and less beautified than its larger cousins in Castan. The Daughter had a fair semblance. Atop the rise, it was safe from flooding and dominated that corner of town as though it was some red-clad castle. He approached the grand double doors, made of some foreign wood naturally tinted a slight pink.

The man out front was as big as they come and bid Nat leave his sabre. Reluctantly, he entered the redhouse, unarmed. He still held his coin, for which he took a mite of comfort, but a voice inside told him to be wary, that he wouldn't be the first to go missing after visiting a redhouse.

He touched the knife concealed at his hip, and went inside.

The whores that were not engaged were playing tiles or busy chatting or in the middle of adjusting their hair in a large reception hall. Low tables and wall hangings depicting carnal acts dominated the place, and around the room, several spiralling staircases led away to the vaulted rafters and the rooms. Far off, he heard moaning.

Castanni law had long decreed that redwomen, although not explicitly outlawed, were nevertheless required to wear a choker around their neck at all times, lest they be mistaken for a reputable woman. Usually about as wide as the last joint of a pinkie, the lace or satin ribbon was never to be removed, on penalty of public humiliation. The dictates were not taken seriously in Forlorn, Nat regarded with a sly smile. The few that did wear the red ribbon wore it askew or in elaborate plaits or used midnight-black silk from the Hellspine glass spiders. It was then that he saw an off-duty guard making a young worker laugh while they played a game of Faerl's Gamble. He decided then that he liked the place.

There were no windows in that hall, so he could not tell how long he had wandered and leered. Some time must have passed before she came to him wearing a smile that revealed nothing and clad in a dress that hid little. He liked her face, and her dark, dark hair. Something about her seemed familiar.

"Is Ambara your real name?" He asked now, sending a quick, perfunctory glance to the sultry woman lounging in the chair. She had one leg swinging over the chair arm, something that seemed terribly fiendish to Nat. The room was well furnished, with polished and engraved deynwood panelling covering each wall. The bed was also deynwood, an oversized bed that must have been made for a small whale, and Nat marvelled at the blood-red drapes that hung from each post carved as a myriad leaping shoals of fish.

Her brow furrowed for a moment, her mouth twisting in confusion. "Yes, of course. My ma named me it... Why ask that? You don't like it?" She wrinkled her little nose.

Nat did not know if that was sincere or teasing. He was uncomfortable. The initial urges he had felt fled, leaving him only with a sense of deep regret. "No. I mean, *yes*, I do. It's only... you don't usually hear that name where I'm from."

Her face lit up then, her shy smile returning, "Castan, you mean?"

"Aye. A beautiful name, truly. I think it means... 'flower of dawn', but I cannot be certain. The ambara used to blossom in the meadows beyond the high walls of the city. Now they don't. I couldn't say why. Hector the Gifted probably knows. I can still remember them though, the meadow in bloom just after wintertide, the way they looked so bright even among the snows, like tiny stars in the fields of a night... in my memory, they never wilt or fade. In my dreams, they're always in bloom." *What made you say that?*

"I didn't know that they grew so far west. I suppose you miss it, your home, I mean, being out here in a strange land. We Vasti live hard lives, especially those folks that live up near the snowmonts. Sometimes I wish I was far away, in the high retreats of Lar'gara or the dune seas of Sora... It must be awfully exciting on the long road. Everyone here hears tales of the goings-ons in the blackwood, and I don't think I would ever be able to go through it. It scares me, truly."

Nat filled his glass until the pike threatened to spill it over the rim. "The *blackwood* should be feared. I'm not ashamed to admit I have my fair share of dread… especially after seeing the wyrm, or whatever that thing was. I don't lend credence to portents or signs, but I saw how that mark put Aud on edge. When he thinks something's amiss, you should heed him." When he stared at the bottom of the glass, he poured it again.

"And you said he… *Aud*… he is the king's own messenger!" The way she smiled and shrieked with joy, it was beautiful, and he drank. He drank so that the words would not come.. *Her hair is all wrong. It should be longer, and the light should turn it hazel, not red. And her eyes…* "Ambara…"

"Natoly…" She said it with an impish grin, her voice low and dripping with lust. In a voice that was all for him. How could he resist?

"Aye, Aud's the emissary. But *I'm* his strong right hand!" He said, letting the glass fall to the carpets. She laughed, and it was high and sweet. She had dimples on her cheeks when she smiled. He had not heard a girl laugh like that in a long time.

She must have noticed how he looked at her, for she said, "What are you thinking, soldier?" Her gown slipped from one small shoulder. His face was the only answer she needed. His mind was a haze as he pulled her to the bed.

"I think you're lying," she whispered in his ear as she adjusted herself on him. "I think you're just some tenderfoot mercen boy looking to spend the coin he made from his latest offing." Nat was too busy at her neck to see the mischief playing in her eyes, but he knew it was there.

"Do you plan on returning to Forlorn soon?" Wordless, he pulled her mouth down to his own, and heard a tiny whine escape her mouth as they met. She said something, but it was muffled.

Eventually, she broke off to work at the laces of his breeches again, breathless and quick-fingered. *She sounds different. So different, yet so familiar. This is some cruel fucking joke.* Then he remembered that out of all the pretty notiviates parading around the hall, lounging on cushions and sending him suggestive looks, he had chosen her, and the shame overwhelmed him. He felt like a drowning man clawing for the surface that was too far out of reach. He couldn't even bring himself to say her name. *A fucking joke.* It felt wrong. He needed to get back. He swayed to the side, struggling to push her off him. "Leave off," he said, his voice sounding foreign. "I said off!"

"Oh," came her voice, sounding meek and shy. She slid away, sitting on the bed and tucking her long legs beneath her. Her dress had been torn. He could not remember doing that. After a hesitated moment, she placed a hand on his knee. "What's wrong, soldier?" That sweet sincerity again. "What can I say to make you happy? What do you want to forget?"

He wanted to believe it was real. *Nothing in this place is real.* Yet when he looked into her eyes, he could not read them. "I— I need to go," he said, shaking off the hand and rushing for the door. As he rose, he staggered and fell into the wall, knocking over the bedside. The decanter smashed to the floor, and Nat saw how greedily the carpets drank the wine. *Fuck.*

He was on all fours then, crawling to the door, and the

voices were all around him. The spectres seemed to appear from nowhere. They were harsh and questioning. Men's voices. When his hand went to his hip, he found his knife gone. "Oh fuck…"

The girl was saying something, but her words made no sense. When he managed to raise his head, she no longer smiled. A spectre picked up the broken decanter and said something amusing. Nat did not laugh.

His world churned.

The guards that made off with him had his arms swung loosely about their shoulders. His feet never touched the ground. They were strong, swaying but little as they moved with the sure steps of those well used to carrying bodies. The whole thing gave Nat a sense of addled buoyancy, as though he were sailing on some sea that stank of sweat and sex and Vasti beer long gone to staleness.

Talking was hard. And he had talked a lot at the beginning. Anything and all he said was slurred and nonsensical, the garblings of the wretches that he used to steal from in the wynds of Low Castan when he was nothing but a naked orphan boy. The memory forced a rueful laugh that sounded inane. One of the guards grumbled something. Nat ignored him, as he had ignored most insults thrown his way in life.

Wait 'til I have my knife, bastards. He left the words unsaid. Strangely, he found himself lucid, his thoughts coming coherently, if not slowly. At least, he thought they made sense. He tried to give meaning to his situation. His knife was gone, taken along with his curved *kje* sabre and the rest of his coin. They had not even permitted him his clothes, giving him only a rough wool shift to cover his nakedness.

They're a prudish people, these. What had Aud to say about them? Something... something about pogroms. Fuckers. I still have my breeches, at least... They had even thrown a black sack rudely over his head, turning the brisk Forlorn night into an implacable and impenetrable black and making the going even more unsteady.

His world was without light, and smelled of vomit.

His mind returned to that place. That lovely place. To a girl called Ambara. *No. A trick.* He balled his fists and tensed his shoulders at the realisation, but a smack to the back of his head soon remedied his moment of fury.

Fuckers.

He expected to be thrown into the river, but they disappointed him. After some time, he was ushered inside a building, the sound of a heavy metal door clanging shut behind him. He outstretched the fingers of one hand and managed to brush against a wall. It was covered in some sort of fabric. The material he could not tell, but it was woven and smooth, cool but not cold. He smiled under the hood. Stairs. Stairs. Stairs. He was being hoisted up one flight after the next, and he tried to count the steps, losing the count somewhere after a hundred.

When his gaolers finally stopped, the sudden jolt sent a bout of nausea to rise from his gut until he could taste bile. His eyes darted feverishly, desperate for some light through the black confines of his cloth prison. The men let his feet touch the floor, and it was all he could do to stop himself from collapsing. One of them snickered. At their urging, he disentangled himself and found his arms leaden and useless. A metallic scrambling sound came out of the dark, harsh and threatening. He knew what it was. A room.

A room for him to rot in.

A door opened on well-oiled hinges. Warmth spilt forth like the heated pools at the Hardranger Inn in Castan.

"In you go, drunk. You're lucky the Lord Raynolf was feeling merciful this evening. Count yourself lucky." He felt hands usher him within, and for a moment, he thought they felt almost gentle. *What a strange…*

"And what of our leader, eh?" A voice boomed inside the room.

"How the fuck am I to know?" Nat felt a hand grab his head and wrench the sack free, spilling light into his world once more. Before him stood Hearty, and he looked very angry. Greg was standing at his shoulder, but try as he might, his gangrel appearance did little by way of intimidation.

"If he dies, you will rue this day." Said the old warrior, his beard full of breadcrumbs and stained by beer. At his heel was the chest.

"As you say, fat man." The guards turned to leave. "Go back to polishing the plates with that dog-tongue of yours." To that, Hearty *harrumphed*, nursing his wounded pride. The door slammed shut behind Nat. A key turned in the lock. The room was spacious for a gaol. It boasted two large beds. In one nook there was a privy, and nearby a washbasin and high-fluted decanters full of water and some dark liquid he took for wine. The rest of the room was furnished as well as any castle, with walls covered in elaborated tapestries of fishing scenes and a strange screen portraiture of two children, one dark and one light, frolicking on a snowbound mountainside. There was also a large window, the glass clear and cut into an elegant lattice. Braziers roared merrily on opposing walls, spilling rich orange light to dance on the hanging pictures to make the scenes shimmer with a surreal movement. Nat had eyes only for the bed.

Hearty turned to him, his eyes narrowed yet glazed, seeing him for the first time. He crossed his arms across his huge barrel chest. "So. I hope it was worth the trouble."

Nat bristled at the way he said that. As though he were talking to a child. "So?"

"He has returned from his travails at last. Greg, have you ever seen such a sorry sight from one so young? No, don't answer that. You're piss-drunk too. Striplings, the both of you. Striplings and execrables. When Aud returns, he'll peel the skin from your bones, but you already knew that. *You*, in particular. You have compromised our mission. *The* mission. And for what? So you could tickle a tit for a time? There were girls inside the inn."

Nat's head swam. He wanted nothing more than to sleep, but he knew this blowhard would never allow him any respite until he had his fill. *And there's no filling Hearty Deri.*

"As I recall, Aud *allowed* me to visit the red-house, Deramun. I did not leave the inn looking for trouble. I just happened to find me with my breeches down. You have *your vow,* yes, but it doesn't mean we must all suffer the hollow sanctimony of chastity."

Hearty's face grew red. Under his whiskers, his lips twitched. Before he could bluster any further, Nat seethed, "Leave off, will you? Aud will have words enough upon his return from Gods-know-where. At least have the grace to allow me some shut-eye before our elan leader decides to give me his sodding death-glare."

No sooner had he said it, he felt the rage leave him. He

turned away, hoping that they would not see his eyes. He fell into the nearest bed, throwing the blankets over him violently and staring into the brazier until it hurt. He expected Hearty to continue his tirade but was surprised to be greeted by silence.

It had fallen to a dull ember glow, and the first pink streamers of daylight stole into their cell between the diamond-shaped panes. It was bright and very ruddy, but cold.

Hearty was sprawled passed out in the other bed, the bedclothes rising and falling with every prodigious breath. Greg sat cross-legged on the floor, basking in the rosy light. Nat thought he looked all a statue of marble, for he sat upright and motionless in the cold first-light, looking as though he was covered in blood.

Nat looked from one to the other, the grogginess of the night lacing through him like he was wearing a suit of plated steel, and his helm had just been hit by a monstrous warhammer.

"How long have you been sat there, eh?" He asked, and then remembered, "Did Aud come back in the night?" His voice did nothing to hide his hangover. Greg looked dazed for a moment before uttering, "What? Oh. No, he ain't back. I dunno where he is. I…" His voice trailed away, only to stand and stretch, all gangrel elbows and knees. "I was thinking, is all. Thinking of the road ahead." Despite everything, he looked excited at the prospect.

"Some would call that hopeful." Nat rubbed at his temples. Greg ignored him, going on to say, "We was makin' good time on the long road, 'til Harlan's Waypost, that is. If… when Aud rejoins, I think we should try to sail the Ruell.

71

Make up for lost time and the like."

The idea made Nat laugh spitefully. "The Ruell? Don't be a clod, Greg. Have you ever *seen* a sea before, let alone traverse one?" The Ruell Sea was a wide wet wedge that cleaved the continent in two. Bordered to the north and west by the imperious snowmonts, it was the most direct, if not most perilous route east, as the long road wound off northward to skirt along the coast. Leaving the hidden valleys of Vastiland behind, the bare strip of land that squatted behind mount and sea was the Knifedge Coast. The road was scribbled down as the *high road* on maps. It was also known by a more sinister name- the "bloody road". There it led up onto high granite bluffs that shouldered hard against the unruly sea below, with an unrelenting wind that swept down from the snowmonts. Wains and wagons were said to be thrown off the cliffs as though they weighed nothing, to fall hundreds of feet onto the spearstacks jutting above the waves. The lands of the Knifedge were also home to all manner of reavers and bandits that preyed on any fool enough to travel unprotected. Nat shifted uncomfortably, realising that he said spoken too soon. The Ruell had its own perils, but one was more likely to evade corsairs if they were aboard a swift ship. He rose and made water in a bed bowl. "The alternative is not much better, but sailing the open waters? *I* can't sail. We'd have to hire a ship, one with a trustworthy captain, I should add, which is a rare thing indeed. That's coin on top of coin on top of time wasted unnecessarily." He chewed on that for a moment, listening to his piss rattle in the brass bowl. "Yet the bloody road is a poisoned cup itself." Even in Castan, the tales of the Reavers of the Knifedge Coast were well known, and Nat did not think the details could be exaggerated. When he was done, he laced himself and went to the wine. It was warm, but it did not matter. "Should Aud choose to travel across the waters, we could make up the time, but we could also chance a blackboat, manned by reavers and mercen and worse. Then we would be treated to the best the Ruell *and* the Knifedge have to offer." The thought made him feel cold.

"What should we do, then, eh?" The lad asked, exasperation filling his voice. Nat shook his shoulders and grabbed the chest, pulling it towards the side of the room with the chair. He fell into the cushioned high-back, placing his bare feet atop the chest with audible relief. "A beggar's choice's still a choice."

"Never heard of that before." Greg sat on his haunches like some lanky cat.

A snort came from the bed, "It's a saying from Low Castan." Said Hearty Deri. He rolled out of the bedclothes, and to Nat's relief, saw that beneath, he was wearing a nightgown, albeit tightly. "Sometimes you're made to choose, even if the choices are shit." He looked tired and worn. Nat let the insults in mind go unsaid.

Servants came after a while, bringing fresh clothes and blankets, fried bread and oaten porridge, a flagon of crisp water and a fresh bottle of chilled wine. Hearty asked them a score of questions that all went unanswered. Greg set to the food but avoided the wine. Nat found that he had little appetite and eyed the servants as they left the wine. Hours came and went, and the sunlight shifted across the room. He wanted to say something to Hearty. To sing a song to lift their spirits. To share a drink and celebrate another day of living. But it only caused him to feel nauseous. Habit made his hand go to his knife more than once, only to be reminded that he no longer had it.

The day crawled on. The light filled the room, resolving onto the tapestries to give them a vigour they lacked in the wan blazier-light. He held little interest in artisan pieces, the only true craftsmanship he admired was swordplay, yet all the same, he found himself admiring the scenes that played out on the screen and tapestries. They were striking, the colours of reds and teals and pearl and tourmaline and beryl, all interwoven between artful borders of goldthread that shone gaily, as though it were, in fact, solid gold itself. His eyes kept falling on the image of the children.

When the voices came from outside, the sun had vanished behind the walls of their cell. The servants had not returned since the morning, and the coals had not been replaced in the braziers. With a chill in the air, they braced themselves as the voices became louder and louder.

Hearty and Greg were standing nearby, the anxiety making them restless to see their friend return. Greg clopped over to the wine that remained and drank from the bottle. Nat did not blame him. After all, he was young, and these things still scared him.

What fear Nat felt was for Aud and what had happened to him. He had been through too much to fear anything could do. The memories stung. *Better to feel the sharp edge of pain than be crippled numb and dumbstruck by fear.*

The key fumbled in the lock. Nat thought it slow and ponderous, as though an old done man were opening the door. He clenched his jaw at the sound. The death knell.

The man that stood in the open door was short and

spare, his only hair the thinning hedge that encircled his crown like a fur collar. Beneath a pair of pale eyes were large drooping pouches. His nose was thin and red, and his mouth held a sour look. "I am Vikken, the Reeve of Furrowfield. Come with me, if you please, sirs." His voice was even and without inflection.

Hearty, for once, held his tongue, so it fell to Nat to ask, "Where is Audeyrn?"

The Reeve's eyes fell on him then, and in them Nat could see a quiet malice, not unlike an animal long turned feral, making something roil inside Nat's gut.

He misliked the smile that curled upon those lips. "Oh, him. You'll be joining him soon enough."

6

MARBLE

Laughing, the little boy ran in circles, taunting the little girl. They were in a field. Long, tall grass tickled at their hips. The little boy jumped around and back and forth and poked the little girl, doing his best to entice her to play the game of his choice. To make her laugh. The little boy loved making the little girl laugh. It was his favourite thing to do. The little boy was always laughing and smiling, which annoyed the girl even as she loved to hear the sound and see the boy happy. When the little boy poked the little girl one too many times, she launched herself at him, and the little boy rejoiced in triumph. The gangly little creatures ran around the field chasing each other, playing their favourite game. They ran and laughed and tripped and fell and got back up and did it all over again. Their joy was wondrous and so, so innocent. The children were as yet unaware of the horrors of the world.

They tussled with each other in the long grass as their laughter and giggles, and joy raced across the land. The tinkling bell of their little voices, a beacon and light of hope for some, was an alarm for others. Bringing the two wondrous, innocent children onto the radar of those it would have been best for them to have remained invisible.

And so the beginning of their joyful existence would soon cease to exist. It was on a warm, dark night weeks later it happened. A ruckus and loud noises in the street alerted the children's parents of their imminent demise. They had known this would come, and so they were prepared. Without further ado, the parents ferried the children into the deep, dark bowels of the night, and as the children were separated, to probably never see each other again, they cried. They cried and cried, but they cried silently as they heeded their parents' warnings. They watched each other, doing their best to mutely express their goodbyes and take in every last detail they could of their best friend, who would forever be lost to them. When the little girl and the little boy were far enough away from the bad men and the bad place that used to be their home, their exhausted tears lulled them to sleep, and by the time they woke again, they were both different people. She was no longer carefree and happy. There was a piece missing, and they were lost in the world. Now knowing some of the horrors of the world, they began their education of evil.

Marble came too, the ache and hurt engulfing her whole person, dragging her from her restless slumber rather unpleasantly. The ground beneath her was hard and uncomfortable and cold, doing nothing to ease her pain. Head pounding, a vicious drumbeat echoed throughout her mind, bringing a new wave of misery and nausea with each reverberating blow. She did not dare attempt to open her eyes, not yet. They were crusted together, and she knew it would send her straight back into oblivion if she risked prying them apart. Her whole body observed a heaviness, weighted down. By her injuries, exhaustion or the weight of the world, it was difficult to discern. Each breath rasped agonisingly as Marble tried to keep them shallow and bearable.

The emissaries' pitiful groan conducted a whole cacophony of the loudest drums and percussion, and bile raced its way up her throat, desperately chasing release. The excruciating and sudden jarring of Marble's battered body brought a new wave of agony. The dizziness in her head multiplied tenfold. *I cannot afford to lose more fluids. I do not have much more to forfeit.* Doing her best to breathe deeply, despite what she suspected were some bruised, if not broken, ribs, Marble ignored the stench of her eject and valiantly blocked out the pain. There was no telling how much time passed while Marble cleared her mind and composed herself, but however much later it was, with the agony, a dull throb in the background and the rushing sound filling her ears muted. *What is that?* The sound was faint and distant, but it was a beacon calling out. *Drip. Drip. Drip. Drip.*

The emissary could hardly believe it. She did not know if it was real or conjured by the stress of her mind and body. *That does not matter. No. What matters is finding water.* She took a fortifying breath and braced herself, readying to shut down the torment she knew would come as soon as she moved.

Pushing up onto all fours would be the start. Her eyes could stay closed for a while longer. She wasn't ready to tempt fate. Marble did not know if she was being watched or if anybody or anything else was nearby. It hadn't seemed to be the case when she had been silent, but she knew her instincts could not be trusted at the moment. This quest to try and find water was foolish, likely to do more harm than good. Nevertheless, a necessary gamble she hoped to the gods would pay off. Marble grunted with the effort as she held back the nausea and twisted onto her shaky limbs. Unsteadily, the emissary inched forwards, taking her time. It was impossible to move any quicker in the state she was in. Breathing in through the nose and trying to control each wobbly exhale that left her mouth, Marble did her best to concentrate on moving toward the dripping sonance. The ground beneath her hands and knees was rough and cold, biting into her limbs.

The cold did its best to seep into her flesh. Staving off the shivering was hampered by the floor biting into her flesh and leaving a bloody trail to show her slow, stubborn progress. She would get there, no matter what it took. *No matter what I lose, I will get there.*

No person with a sound mind ever succeeded at the Garrison, or so they said. An inherent need to constantly push themselves, both physically and mentally, no matter what. A need instilled into them day and night by the instructors. It was expected to push oneself too far, too many times, and there would be that *one* time when they would be unable to put themselves back together again. The damage wrought by the training yard or harshing or mental conditioning breaking them until they were only a thing, no good to anybody anymore. When she reflected on her comrades in arms, many not even surviving their own making.

Drip, drip, drip. The sound grew louder as Marble drew closer, but despite its change in volume, the dripping noise was very close to being drowned out by her deep, shuddering breaths, pounding heart and pained grunts, the sound of her body moving along her bloodsoaked trail only added to the discord. She collapsed numerous times, her weak limbs giving out beneath her, but every time, Marble would merely compose herself once more, push the pain away inside. So far, Marble hadn't encountered any walls or obvious obstructions in her path. *That could just be me, though,* she reasoned, *crisscrossing myself to no end.*

She tried to open her eyes. It took some time, more than she was comfortable with, but gradually her strange surroundings became more focused.

Drip, drip, drip.

Open your eyes. One step at a time. Water first. Get to the water... well, if it is water, and go from there. Moving one struggling, shaking arm forward, she placed a hand on the biting ground, trying, in vain, to ignore the pain. *Drip. Drip. Drip. Splash.*

Marble jerked her hand back and gasped in equal parts relief, shock, and surprise. She had reached her intended destination. *Finally.* But she could not collapse in triumph yet. Thankfully, when her hand landed unceremoniously in the mystery liquid Marble desperately hoped was water, it didn't seem to burn. *Pain masks pain,* the saying went. She huffed and leaned closer.

There was no discernible scent indicating the presence of anything other than water. *What in the hells?* Worst case scenario, it wasn't water but instead something poisonous and deadly, in which case it would only bring about her demise more swiftly than dying of dehydration. Best, it was water, and she would live to suffer more. Marble scooped up a handful of the mystery liquid and sloshed it in her mouth before swallowing. The substance was cool and refreshing. It was not pure, for Marble could taste something tangy and metallic. It was revitalising all the same. Making a bowl with her hands, the emissary scooped up more of the mystery liquid from the pool before her and splashed the handfuls over her face a half dozen times before wiping it away and rubbing and cleaning with a particular focus around her eyes. Eventually, Marble had her fill of what she hoped was water and steadied her breathing. With her face as clean as it would get for now, Marble sank again to the ground. *Time to get out,* she thought, her eyes getting heavy.

Marble woke. She did not know how long she dosed. She was stiff and sore, and her body cried in agony. The shivers set in. She couldn't forget her mission. No matter how she felt, there was no time to waste... *and no rest for the wicked.* Breathing shallowly, she forced open her eyes. The dark place kept almost all its secrets. Some shadows, however, were darker than others. She noticed the slight flicker of movement in the corner of her eye. She was not alone in the lightless place. It could be the beginning of the fever dreams, she reasoned to herself. *No...* another flicker of black on black from somewhere in the gloom. The prickle wending its way along her confirmed her suspicions. Marble was not alone, and she was being watched.

Gritting her teeth with determination, Marble pushed past the weakness and pain. It would not do to advertise such things to some unseen adversary. No. *I'm strong. Capable. Let them underestimate. They won't be the first, or the last.* She needed to leave. Before the fever struck her fully, leaving her defenceless to her silent hosts.

If these *things*, whatever they were, had not brought her here, she knew the Tundra would have taken her. Whatever their intentions were, she did not trust them.

I've lost too much time already. She perceived it a miracle when she pushed herself to her feet and did not stumble, baulk, or falter. Maybe not so miraculous. The General had said her stubbornness was like to keep her alive.

Taking a deep, fortifying breath, Marble waited and watched for more flickers. When it became apparent her night-eyes were as sharp as they were like to get, Marble once again steadied herself. Her other senses soon followed suit.

Focus intent, she listened. She sniffed at the air surreptitiously.

It was some terrifying instinct that guided her motions. Marble did not want to harm these creatures right now. She was more than capable, but doing so would waste too much time. They may have saved her life, but now they were in the way of her completing the mission to which only she had been entrusted. She would not fail here and now, as so many would expect her to. She would delay no further.

Dropping to the ground, Marble blindly rolled and lept back to her feet, ignoring her body's protests and the wave of agony threatening to overcome her. Dodging instinctively, Marble continued, her instincts aiding her forward momentum. Marble could not see, but her movements were sure and steady. No hesitation of hitch in her step to be seen. No weakness. No stumbling. No pausing for any reason. Marble's movements were fluid. But she'd not trained as hard as she had for nought. Marble's blood was singing as the adrenaline pumped her full of much-needed energy. Another duck. A pivot to the right. Another roll. And so it continued. The blind dodging of unseen obstacles until, at last, she felt it.

It was faint at first. The breeze. A slight rustle of her hair. With that rustle, Marble realised the loss of her scarf and the direction of, if not freedom, at least the way forward in her journey. Her mission. It was hot and crisp on her tongue. The scent of it was both sharp and cloying. And the sound an ominous but welcome whistle beckoning her forward. And follow its call, Marble did.

The path was winding and long, but her surroundings eventually brightened. Slowly, at first, but the light soon blinded Marble's sensitive eyes. It was day beyond the caves. Marble pressed on with no sign of pursuit. She could only hope she would be able to figure out where she was and find some shelter and fuel even more swiftly.

Ever since Queen Salphyre impressed upon her the importance of this venture… everything seemed to go out of their way to try and stop her. As though fate was trying to tie her into a knot. Resolving to succeed out of spite, she marched on, towards the blinding light and scorch of the air outside.

Only when Marble stepped out onto the burning sand did she realise her feet were bare. *Where did my sandals go?* She took a moment to look behind her, no longer able to see the cavemouth. *Odd…* The questions she had went unvoiced. *How am I to get answers out here anyways?*

Ashen hair fell in her eyes, having escaped from its confines. It was all matted and dirty and full of unknown debris. Even with all of this shortening its length, the locks still fell to her waist. Marble would have to try and find a way to disguise the colour. She would have also tried to cut it, but knew it would do no good. She'd tried before, but it never worked out well for her. Her hair was an entity all of its own. It was just as well Bonebridge was the closest town. At least her bedraggled appearance was unlikely to raise many eyebrows there. Her clothing torn, feet lathered in dried blood, she pushed south and east and south again. Somehow, her feverborne journey through the caves and winding path had brought her close to the outskirts of Bonebridge. She laughed, if only to stop the tears.

Taking in the desolate atmosphere leaching from the place, Marble steeled herself and pushed towards the crumbling vista ahead. Her whole being was numb, the shock and pain catching up to her. She needed to find supplies and somewhere she could barricade herself. She didn't have much time left. Somehow, she quickened her pace.

7

GREGYN

The news left him thunderstruck and empty.

He had refused to accept it at first, and the longer he dwelled on it, the more he knew that he *must* be dreaming, that he would wake up, and he would be back in the Dun Vale and safe, and that he had never met the Royal Emissary. But when he did summon the courage enough to open his eyes, the emissary rode before him, and the snows kept falling on their dour ride through the snowmonts.

First appearing as a fine grey raking on the horizon north-east to the Vasti highlands, they only rose higher and higher, until they became the granite massifs of legend. The high precipitous peaks arrogantly thrust their way into the morning sky to rip through the clouds, each with a tarn wallowing beneath it, and mantled by a cold, white peak above.

It was summer, and it was cold, and there was *so much snow!* He found looking down less daunting than the hardscrabble path snaking through the narrow valley to fall behind the high spurs of rock, the frigid trek that awaited them. The frozen stream that passed as a track was iced here and there, passing freely over the ground made hard-packed by centuries of spur-horned goats and making little islands of stones jutting out. More than once, when it was too narrow to ride, he would trip and silently curse himself for being so clumsy.

If the others noticed, they said nothing. The fury of their reunion on the ferry had ebbed, but the frustration lingered like a puckered scar. Nat and Hearty exchanged little since that night in Forlorn, and Aud...

The emissary had always been kind to Greg. A gentle word of encouragement or genial smile at a jape, the aloof front broken so easily by Nat's quips or one of Hearty's rambling tales of gallantry. Yet there was something else. Greg would be the first to admit Audeyrn could be grave when it came to the assignment. He had always been a mite melancholy. He was worse now. Greg didn't consider himself a clever man, but he sometimes wondered if even the most stoneheaded dullard could see it in the emissary's eyes. Whatever the alderman had said, it had made the emissary unyielding, the feeble banter mustered by Nat received only by a clench of his sharp jaw. Not that he could blame him. Natoly was a staunch friend to have, yes, but his fits of lunacy only vexed their leader and infuriated Deri.

The bird that sings loudest oft has the shortest song. Departing Forlorn had been as uncomfortable as it was uneventful, a sombre ride without conversation. The words spoken between them sounding clipped and forced. More than once, his mind returned to his humble croft. As Aud had announced his intention to avoid the Ruell Sea entirely, and

Greg had felt the relief wash over him in waves. What he had heard instead, he did not like. The idea of travelling the snowmonts seemed a jolly adventure in comparison. The reality had hit hard as the snowstorms.

In their brief breaks out of the elements, he would find better conversation with his horse, the fleetfooted skewbald rouncy he had lovingly dubbed Muddy. He could not recall if the others had given their mounts names, and now didn't seem the right time to ask. He held his tongue, and suffered in silence as the snows fell and the mountains closed around them.

Greg had seen snow before. Of course he had. The High Forks had their share of it every winter, freezing the lands on the narrow green tributaries of the High Torrent until all turned into an ever-meandering circuit of cold-clad roads. As a child he had been enraptured by the eerie beauty of winter, watching the slow descent of the snowflakes from the porch, balling up the cold to form ranks of ice knights with their helms of old buckets and broom-handle swords and beards of long drooping icicles. It had been Lan who had shown him how to make snowfays, and who had taught him to skate on the pond at the bottom of the glen.

For a moon's turn, the Dun Vale would be transformed as though they had been sent to an icebound mirror of their own world. For the few peaceful years of guileless childhood, Greg had lived for brisk days when he would skive his chores to go with the other children, staying long after his fingers had gone numb. Old Mart always had something to say about that: usually that he would lose a toe or the end of his nose to winter's kiss, that his hair would turn white and brittle, that winter was when the wolves of the deepingwood took away naughty children, and that he must always wear his scarf.

His father had had no use for it, of course. If Garren was anything, he had been a practical man, his whole world being the family's flour mill. For when the days shortened and darkness crept in, he turned grim, his summer smiles melting away and freezing into the harsh rictus of a scowl. He was not a cruel man, was Garren, but life had made him bitter and obdurate. When he wasn't breaking the ice beneath the water wheel or cleaning the slush from the sluice gates, he worked the mill and cursed the gods for letting them suffer such unjust hardship, as he saw it. He had married Westa, a woman so unlike himself, and they had begot four unruly children, each taking their toll on her in their own way.

Gregyn was the first, born sickly and small, and Old Mart was wont to tell him that his mother had prayed every hour during the winter of his birth. Greg knew little and less about gods, so he had brushed off Old Mart's toothless wanderings and stories. His mother however, she had always been the face of charity and kindliness in the village. She had never enjoyed a sound constitution, even his earliest memories of her being the vague days of that winter when she was bed-bound and ailing after the birth of his sister. She had died in the crib, but they had named her Zoar.

Westa would have two more children. His younger sisters, Val first and then Drue. Talan Twins, called as such because of the legendary twins Bale and Dale, born not a year apart in the city Drukish of Talan. The whisperings spread through the Dun Vale, regardless, that twins had been born to the miller Garren and his wife, Westa. It was pointless to argue the difference. At the birth of Drue, the barber-surgeon Oldac had told his father that delivering the babe was a waste, and that the children would only live in shame. Garren had liked that not at all, taking the man outside. Greg did not know what his father said to the barber-surgeon, but Oldac looked shrunken and ashen-faced when they came back. The child came squalling into the world, but his mother did not survive the ordeal.

The boy had learned early that twins were ever an omen of ill-luck. He did not understand why. His sisters, all small and helpless and screaming for suck. He was told by one wizened old character that it was because of his sister that his mother had to die. The memory still seemed clear to him. The cracked knuckles of the bent-backed man leaning heavily on a stick. The sour stench of brown-toothed breath. The voice like a whip. "Kill the twin! *Evil*, I say! Soulless! Kill it! Kill it! *Kill it!*"

Their innocence could not ward them from the accusing stares and the hushed words at their backs. Were it not for the dreadblack shadow of Garren looming large over the Dun Vale, he could only imagine what would have happened.

The children were no better. Echoing all they have heard with the ignorant confidence of youth. As the years passed, he only seemed to get taller and taller, never filling out his scrawny frame. He soon towered above those that dare shame his family, casting a shadow of his own. It looked ever unsubstantial, the arms too long and spindly, the head overlarge and the neck craned. The children did not fear it…

On the rare occasion his father would let his heart bleed, he could instil words that stayed with Greg. Once, he saw a child push a much older and taller Greg to the ground, and Garren had taken his son aside. *All's need do is punch 'em here,* he told him, holding his colossal coiled fist to Greg's nose. *And never beg pardon for it.* Countless times the lanky boy would fall into bed bruised, his knuckles bloody. His father must have guessed the origins of his wounds, but he never asked. It wasn't in him.

In the end, when his father's hair was white and his chest was bad, he made a habit of sitting on the porch at dusk. It was a winter two years past. He was fourteen. Val and Drue had gone. Greg saw little of his father, being apprenticed to the forrester Huhtal. But he came back to his ailing father that winter. The mill wheel had not turned over years at that point. Garren was too sickly to work repairs and too crabbed to ask for help. Winter blossom grew between the paddles. He still remembered the way the planks of the porch had creaked beneath him like an old man's knees. Snow fell on the mill. The cracks in the walls and weathered wood were soon covered by a fine powdering. They had been transported to that mirror world again, and in that place, time stood still.

Garren sat there bundled up in blankets enough to make him whole again. For the first time, he saw the once-powerful giant of his youth reduced to a gaunt bent gransh. He had only seen forty-four winters. He scowled in his chair for a long time, or so it seemed to Greg, ruminating with the few teeth that remained him with a quiet air of respect. At least time had not robbed him of that.

"Ya mother loved the snows," was all he said. Then he

wept.

Time did not stay still but marched on regardless, with all the surety of dawn. The snows melted and the rivers flowed. The cracks in the mill deepened. Two years. A lot can change in two years. He never thought that he would travel to these strange, queer places. Through the unknowable blackwood to see a great white wyrm, or stay in the house of the alderman of Forlorn (albeit as a prisoner). Then again, he never thought he would end up serving the Royal Emissary.

"We'll make camp there," Audeyrn said now, calling ahead on his tall sorrel. He pointed up, off to a hanging crag of rock, to where a darkened recess loomed out from between the shelf above it and the scree below. Greg instinctively looked about, drilled by wise old Huhtal to appraise the land for anything that could be foraged. The land was all grey stone, the only verdance the tortured blackthorn rooted in what passed as soil here. The valley sloped violently until it reached a meltwater river. There were no woods to catch game, no fields to look for mushrooms or roots. A complaint formed in his mouth, but Nat seemed to read his mind. "And do what? Burn stones?"

Audeyrn's mouth was hard set. He pulled his mount about. "See the blackthorn? We burn that. We have salt pork enough from the alderman, so we shan't starve tonight." Then he was off, spurring the horse on violently up the scree slope.

"We should be quiet," Greg said. His voice was drowned out by the shattered stone falling towards them in streams. He felt a hand on his shoulder and saw Deri abreast on his old warhorse. "He will come round, lad. Once we have grub, all will be right."

The fire burned merrily. Nat worried at the old branches with a small wood-axe while Deri turned the spit. Greg had tickled trout from the river, so they ate more than the expected hard meat. The hollow was littered with shingle and goat pellets, but it was in the lee of the wind, so they were soon warmed up. Aside from Nat and Deri, who exchanged more lively talk since the start of that leg of the journey, Aud sat sullen and silent. His only contribution to the conversation was saluting Hearty for cooking their supper.

It was more than Greg could take. Fire coiled about inside, and he wanted nothing more than to unsheath his arrows and shoot a tree or a hare or something. He stood, not knowing what else to do. All eyes fell on him. "Why are you all so horrible? We aren't enemies! We're friends… All this– this feuding and brooding is makin' me mad. *Mad*!" He screamed the words. It was either that or cry. "Nat made a mistake. He's sorry for it. You know that he didn't mean ill by it. Aud, we need you t'be open with us. The mountains are dangerous… lead us, don't just let us march forward with nothin' but a whit. We…"

The fire crackled softly. It threw the shadows of the men along the rock walls, and for a moment, Greg thought he was speaking to a crowd of shades. Then Hearty gave a booming laugh, almost falling on his back. Nat was staring unbelieving at what he had just heard, but now he too laughed aloud. Then it was Audeyrn, a smile breaking across his open face. But he did not laugh at him.

The sun sank beneath a jagged arête, and someone broke out the wine. The skin was old, cracked leather, but the wine they gulped down was from the alderman's own private stock, a rich Caldland red. As the shadows crept in, the songs began, and for a while, Greg forgot that he was in the middle of that grey land.

They mounted at dawn, and despite all nursing their heads, they were in high spirits. From there, the valley only narrowed further, and they found themselves having to cross the river more often to find better footing for their mounts. The water ran low and slow there, so fording was not difficult. Not that they minded it. They kept up the conversation that day, and soon they had tacked onto a high plateau, the snow all around them.

Greg was beginning to see the beauty of the high places. He noticed the small silvery flowers that sometimes broke through the snowdrifts, the swifts that dived overhead, and even a stalking cat on the mountainside eyeing them warily. The alderman had given them fur-lined cloaks with thick hoods, so more often than not, the going was not taxing on Greg. Only when they crested a ridge, and the wind rose from the vale beneath did he feel the bite of cold on his ears. Otherwise, the tracker started to enjoy the bright, fresh days and clear nights of stars above the jagged peaks.

He found himself asking questions more often in those following days. Where before he had relied on the hope of others finding the words for him, he would pose the question himself. Oftentimes the answer was unfulfilling, but then again most of his questions sounded inane when voiced. He did not care. He thought he sounded more confident now anyway.

Audeyrn appeared to know which valleys to avoid. The maps from Hector were of little use up here, them being drawn with highways in mind. The tracker sometimes looked at them for a lark, having been taught his letters and map-reading by the adroit Huhtal. The parchment was crumbling in some corners, and the script seemed faded and illegible here and there. When posed to Aud, he had only shook his head, "Perhaps they wanted to be rid of them." Greg did not think that was funny, but he kept looking at the maps.

One day his curiosity proved too much, and he blurted out to his captain, "How do you know the way? I mean, direction with the sun and moon, and stars, I don't mean navigation, only... what I mean is. How? I mean..." Aud brought his mount astride Muddy. For a moment the emissary looked troubled, but then said, "Have you noticed how barren the snowmonts are?"

"Aye. Stone and snow and sheep shit." The answer seemed obvious to Greg. That elicited a sincere laugh from Aud. "Yes, but where are all the *people*?" Greg had wondered that. The lands they had passed through had soil too thin to farm, and given the option he would not choose to live there. He admired the beauty of the place, but to live there seemed a wretched existence. The emissary had made him uncertain, though. "So people *do* live here?"

He nodded. "Yes. Were you to ask a Vastiman, they would undoubtedly say they are all brigands, stealing from the heights to pillage and take women. It has happened, but to say that the lowest malefactor reflects a people is asinine. They did not always dwell here. They lived in the Vasti Highlands. The successive conquests of the Hyslanians of old pushed them further and further from the green lands, until they were debased and made the snowmonts their fortress." Greg scratched at the sparse stubble on his chin, thinking he had missed something important. "But if they're here… *where're they all?*"

"I'll show you." The valleys shallowed, and they came to skirt a high ridge exposed to the keening wind to put ice crystals in their hair. It only climbed higher. One shaded glen gave way to another, and they took relief in the many sheepback rocks that littered the stony ground like discarded building blocks. When they met the first true road in days, a zig-zagging stair, they climbed a gradual rise. It made Greg feel uneasy. Muddy seemed to sense it, and kicked nervously. He calmed the horse with a gentle word, and wished his fears could be quelled as easily. Aud led them onto a windswept escarpment. To their right, the earth fell away entirely. The snows gave way to basalt cliffs, falling two thousand feet to the valley floor. The skies were white, but enough light in the day for Greg to make out the mountain range that even these peaks cowed from, the ragged massif of black stone the Vasti called the Crown. And there, positioned centrally and looming above all, was the Fang, it's brooding summit shrouded by the clouds. Greg felt small, and very much a paltry thing compared to all that. But he looked up, and did not flinch from it.

Sheltering beneath those mighty sentinels poured forth a vast bowled cwm, verdant and sprawling, with only the lightest sign of snow cover. There was smoke rising from the dozen or so structures that hugged a ribboned meltwater tarn. *The nesting bird sees spring.* Straining his eyes, he could just make out specks going about between cabins. Nearby a group of them that Greg took for children looked to be running around a standing stone playing some sort of game. The mountainfolk did not seem so fearsome from up there. He said as much to Aud, and Nat conceited, "I agree. Let's see if they have some goat haunch to spare for hungry travellers."

"Best not. They are fiercely protective of their secret vales." Aud turned to Gregyn, looking at him sadly. "Not all the lands within the snowmonts are bleak. There's a reason why these have yet to be conquered by the Paydar or Vasti. The alderman is a cunning man, but I doubt that even he knows about these places. For true, sometimes you find a truffle in the midden heap." Greg could only nod at that. Not for the first time, he thanked whatever gods had made him.

They did not linger. Nat proposed that they piss off the edge, but a clip to the back of his head by the large hand of Hearty soon silenced that. "Don't you know of the Tagh bowmen?" He put to Nat as they made their way to the nearest col. The younger man laughed. "The *what*? Archers? From that height? Don't shit and tell me I smell roses, Deramun."

"No, it's true! You see, they use the updraft..." Long after they fell into a new, similar grey stone corridor, the wonderment remained for Greg. When his friends got tired of the subject, he talked to the horses. Muddy did not share his opinion.

That night, they chanced to shelter beneath a circle of sad-looking pines. The sky had darkened after their descent, so Aud thought it wise to use the canvas. So far, it had been overcast, but Greg could smell a turn in the air.

Try as he might, he caught no fish in that valley's tragic stream, so they boiled a stretch of beef in their cookpot to make a thin broth. Greg had found nettles and a handful of bog mushrooms earlier that day, so they added those to the stew. It filled their bellies at least, and despite the taste Greg felt satisfied. Aud set about a watch due to their closeness to the hidden valley. Luckily, Greg drew sleep first. When he pulled his cloak over him, he drifted off soundly.

He could not say when it started, but his dreams of mountains became twisted with wild screeching. Then Nat was standing over him, a finger on lips. The fire had died, only white coals hissing in their pit. Aud waved to get his attention, and a moment later he found himself stringing his bow and scanning the nightscape. The clouds remained, but it was dry. *Didn't need the canvas after all...*

SHKrkrkraaaa! SHKrkrkraaaa!

A dreadblack shadow flashed above them. It flew on great wings. Another shadow crept over his heart. "Greg, what is it?" Whispered a stricken Hearty. That old warrior would fight any man, but the beasts of the land he feared with an implacable dread. "I saw wings. Dark, almost black. The tail was wide, fanned-like."

That did little to calm his friends. "So *what is it?*" Came the shouted whisper of Nat. He wished that he could be certain. Old Huhtal had instructed him in most every bestiary west of the Ruell. The call made him want to say a shrieker, the batlike hunters of the Lar'garan heights. *But the shriekers don't have feathers. A Barrelwing, then? No. It's...*

"A roc. Can't be sure, but I saw a caged one—"

SHKrkrkraaaa! SHKrkrkraaaa! SHKrkrkraaaaaaaaaaaa! The screech was followed by a ripping sound, and through the dark they saw a half dozen long slashes in the canvas overhead. Audeyrn's eyes shone briefly. "Nat, rebuild the fire! Now!"

Greg skirted the pines, realising that the roc was too big to pass through the trees. Hearty stood with his greatsword in hand, the years suddenly vanishing from his figure. The bow felt damp in his hand, the drawn bowstring digging deeply into his calloused fingers. The itch was on him. His eyes darted about, and sound leeched from the world until all he heard was the thrum of his heart. *Steady hands set the snare.*

A pair of black wings came to bear before him, drifting low to the ground, only to sweep into the air to reveal silvered claws of its own. It screeched once more before Greg released the bowstring.

It all happened at once. The roc writhed in flight, and Hearty charged at it despite his fear. Then Aud and Nat were there, wielding fiery brands, waving at the creature as it crashed hard to the stones.

The beast was not so scary once he could see it. The one before had been in captivity for so long in the wanderer's troupe, scarred and wild-eyed, raking its talons against its bars and spitting at any children that came too close. What he saw was a great stretch-necked avian with feathers a glossy black. It had landed on its legs in the fall, which were now folded under it at unnatural angles. The firebrands shone hotly in its eyes, and it shrieked intolerably. Hearty laughed and said something to Nat, but Greg only felt pity. It was not in him.

Aud held his torch at a goodly distance. "So this a roc, then."

Somehow, the tracker had Natoly's knife. It was like he was dreaming. The screaming was too much. It wasn't right. For everything that Huhtal was, he had drilled into Greg that beasts should never suffer under a hunter. As he neared, it didn't seem to notice him, despite the eyes darting around in desperation. He pulled the knife hard across the beast's long throat. The edge glistened a bright red.

The moon came out, mused the tracker.

8

THE GHOST

The city in the sand bristled among moonlight.

He flitted between one shadow and another in the darkening approach of dusk. He was a creature born of the night. He melded with the dark spots, often appearing as though he travelled through the darkness, from one point to the next, seemingly without moving at all.

The raid alarm had sounded many hours ago. A mass of soldiers and warriors manned the battlements that surrounded the city, but not Reza. He was not a soldier, nor was he a warrior for that matter. No, Reza was something far more deadly. He was a ghost. As silent as the grave, as sharp as steel.

Not much observation of the city's attackers was required to determine that they were just a lowly group of bandits. *Outlaws, most like. Desperate, and oh-so deadly. Desperate... and daring. Daring enough to strike at the slumbering city. They don't stand a chance.*

Still, he drifted through the streets of the lower city,

stalking the night and hunting down any who did not belong. He could not allow his boredom to impact his vigilance. Caution was always the friend of those from the Garrison; it kept them alive, and hidden. Street after street he trawled, alleyway after ally, bazaar after bazaar, one after the other. Over and over again. Retracing his steps and changing routine frequently and suddenly. To fall into a pattern was to cosen with death.

As the tolling bells final ring echoed and dissipated into the greying sky, the ghost slipped from the city walls and disappeared himself, ethereal and phantasmal.

The following days had him stalking the creature. Reza was becoming impatient, which was not at all conducive to capturing one's prey. Not that he had an abundance of patience to begin with. Most others finding themselves in his situation would no doubt have been a mess of frayed nerves. But not Reza. This is what he did. And he was very good at what he did.

The sun was slowly rising, Reza observed with a grimace. Pushing the worry from his mind, lest it consume his thoughts, Reza continued to study and monitor his mark. *Caution is key. Caution is* always *key.* More time passed, the sun climbing overhead, beating down relentlessly, as it was wont to do.

The prey had not moved for quite some time, and neither had he. He was required to change his position slightly from to time, due to the direction the slight breeze giving away his position by scent. He was not tense, for it was imperative to keep relaxed and languid in body even as the mind and senses were functioning at the highest capacity and level of alertness. Ready to react without a moment's notice.

The day waned once more as noon gave way to dusk and in the twilight of the evening, Reza's prey moved on once more.

The missing dagger was a secret signal that she had once again got herself caught up in something. And so Reza had traced her movements into the Tundra, heading in the direction of the Bonebridge Outpost. He knew that Marble had never ventured there before, unlike himself, and he knew that if he had any hope of finding her he would need a bribe. Hence his rather unpleasant... detour.

In order for the contact to even deign to meet with him, let alone *talk*, he needed some fresh venom. The fresher and deadlier, the better. Venom was the infamous Soran drink that only the foolhardy attempted to survive, for it was poison. The toxic venom from the yappor of the Tundra. Sorans had different ways of consuming Venom. The first and safest, although not entirely safe, was served in a shot glass inside of a mug of ripe janburry juice, the fruit having properties that counteracted the lethality of the scorps venom when mixed together. The second way of drinking was to drink the venom and the juice separately, one shot after the other, this way came with a much greater risk. And so Reza continued to stalk his yappor through the deadly Tundra. *Damn it, Marble.*

The creature was a type of invertebrate native only to the Desolate Tundra. It is said that they just appeared one day, and it was assumed that they had stumbled into this realm during one of the times that the Gods had been angry enough to thin the veils between worlds and turn the sands to glass. It was a creature in the truest of sense, but not one that was now domesticated into society. It was still a beast, surviving on instinct and calling the wasteland its home.

About the size of an aurochs that inhabited the yappor boasted ten horrifying legs ending in vicious, deadly spikes, four grasping pincers and a long, thick, segmented tail ending in a venomous stinger. The large, clawed pincers were studded with extremely sensitive tactile fibres. The exact moment some prey finds itself in contact with those hairs, the yappor snatched it with a crushing force to kill. *Brute force*, the yappers preferred killing method, even though possessing the fast acting venom that would paralyse their prey for effective capture and consumption.

An extremely durable exoskeleton armoured the beast, making them nigh on impossible to stab or slash. As they grew however, they shedded their old exoskeleton, which made them vulnerable to attack while the new shell hardened. Such detritus commanded a rather exorbitant fee on the black market.

Twilight turned to night. Reza, a shadow on a dune sea, followed in the wake of the large female. With the night and the dark, the temperature plummeted. His intensive Garrison training allowed him to repress the shivers and ignore the frigidness of the air. The cloudy sky prevented the light of the stars and the moon to illuminate the landscape. The yappor was on the prowl for a meal, and the beasts were extremely swift on their spiked feet.

The sand muffled the sound of Reza's running steps as he navigated the shifting sands in pursuit. He tailed her a league or so before the mighty yappor came to a sudden halt, spraying up waves of loose sand as its spikes gouged deep trenches in the ground, ten uniform, parallel grooves.

Reza, too, slowed. *Caution. Caution is* always *key.*

The yappor hunched her forelegs and curved its tail over her back, to swivel slightly to and fro, opening and closing its pincers repeatedly both high and low, making sharp snapping noises that both echoed and disappeared over the land.

As it moved, Reza took the opportunity to lay himself as flat as he could on the ground behind a slightly raised hill of sand. He needed to blend in, and allowed no sound to bounce off of himself. Everything stilled, and the air suffused with a palpable tension. Reza hardly dared breathe. Head down, he listened. *Silence, click.*

Silence, click.

Silence. Click.

Click, silence.

Click. Snap. Crunch!

Releasing a steady breath, he began his advance as the yappor crushed its victim with its four deadly pincers. The breaking bones covered his own quiet movements, forward and forward again.

This yappor was the largest he had seen, and there was no indication of an imminent moult. Female scorps were fierce, female yappors lethal.

Reza's eyes followed the motions of the beast tearing apart its meal in the caliginosity. Whatever it was, not much remained already.

Now, he had the beast slow and languid from feeding, making it as vulnerable as he was ever likely to find it. Creeping closer, he catalogued the creature for the umpteenth time. The ten cruel spikes at the end of its ten stalwart legs. The four malignant pincers that pulverised with little effort. The savage chelicerae and virulent secretions. The stinger at the point of its very nimble tail.

Preparing himself, he retrieved the lengths of rope and twine from his pack. He removed his flowing outer layers, to better be agile for the dance ahead. Just as the creature slumped heavily, further into the ground, he charged. Launching himself as far as he could with each determined move, he moved as swiftly as he could to impede the yappor before it was alerted and began to fight back.

Sliding down the dune, using the loose sand to enhance his speed, Reza flung a loop of rope to catch the stinger. The creature lumbered to its spiked feet, and turned in his direction. Rolling between two of the creature's spiny legs, he managed to hold onto the rope as he went beneath its massive body.

He needed to hobble the beast, quickly.

Dodging and weaving, the yappor frantically stabbed its feet in to the ground in its attempts to stick the threat through. The rope slid through Reza's hands, burning his palms. It raised its tail in preparation to strike or free itself; he could not tell. The dance begun.

He memorised the rhythm and movement of the beast. He prepared to enter the dangerous open space, where a single misstep could result in a fatal sting or crushing blow. He counted the beats, readying himself– *THWMP!*

It collapsed, its full weight falling on him, to pin the man securely to the ground. He felt his bones creak as the weight and strain crushed him. *She wants to... bury me.* Reza held his breath and scrunched his eyes to the merest of slits. The smallest of cracks appeared in the chitinous weight above him, hairline fractures that betrayed an old shell. Relinquishing the grip of one hand on the rope while holding more tightly than ever with the other, Reza scrambled to retrieve a blade, *anything*, and thrust desperately. He touched the leather hilt of a dagger, unsheathed it, and stabbed at a crack.

It worked, and the beast moved upward and away from the pain. Gasping for air, he hoped that none of his ribs were broken, and scrambled out of reach of the legs as they made to stab at him. He was behind her, but he knew she could see him. Hoping against hope, he leapt.

Clambering onto the thing's back was stupid. Trying to *stay* there was moreso. Keeping the blade in hand, Reza heaved on the rope in order to pin the creature's tail down to its back. The stinger camp to a *thump* on the thing's back, and he wrapped and looped his length of rope around it a couple of times to help flatten it securely to the hard shell.

It jostled violently in its mission to dislodge the pest from itself. One particularly aggressive shake saw the man flung through the air. The only thing that kept him close was his desperate hold of the rough chord. His hands burned once more, shredded open as they slid roughly down the twined length. When his flying momentum ceased, he fell roughly to the ground and landed with a painful thump.

The sound of his impact echoed to the yappor, and it swifty stabbed down with one of its legs, catching the flesh of Reza's own leg as he did his best to roll out of the way. From there, it was a back and forth. He could feel the blood weeping down his leg and dripping onto the thirsty ground, the loss making him lightheaded, compounded by exhaustion, dehydration, and the unyielding speed of the huge scorps.

Then the beast slowed. Two pincers he caught and bound, before a third, while not crushing him, walloped him forcefully in his side, breaking a couple of his ribs for definite. He gritted his teeth, and carried on.

Fighting through the agony and nausea was increasingly difficult. Time served no meaning now, both man and yappor were weak as the sky began to brighten and the sun burned the eastern horizon a deep rose. It wouldn't be until the sun had made its presence fully known that the beast finally succumbed to his many ropes, woven in and out and around the creature intricately, hobbling it until it dropped to the ground hard.

He passed out soon after. He dreamed, but he could not remember what it had been about when he woke. Spitting a curse at the beast before mounting it, he allowed it to walk on a few legs as they made their beleaguered way to the Outpost. He would tap it gently on its flanks from time to time, to coax it in the right direction. It put up little fight. It was too exhausted, but he hoped it would see him the way.

Cresting a high dune littered with shattered stone, he squinted at a dark smudge far off to the east. *A storm, most-like.* Sandstorms here were incredibly deadly. Gesturing for the yappor to move on, he allowed himself a smile as he relished the thought of his arrival.

He hoped she was there, too. Safe, and out of the storm.

9

AUDEYRN

The war found them in the hills.

For the past three miles, men on either side of the muddy road diced and drank, a few shooting belligerent words of goading their way. The rest just looked on dead-eyed, silent and wary. *Ghost-men,* thought Audeyrn sadly. The sergeant, a man with skin pulled tightly over his bones, waved the riders through with a languid gesture. Audeyrn inclined his head in respect. The last thing he needed now was for them to provoke their own countrymen.

The camp sprawled out like a restive beast of iron and canvas. The army had stopped in the Hills of the Paydar, the grass churned up by footfall and mount until the lush greens and yellows and golds surrendered to a stolid brown. Even the crisp blue and green surcoats and cloaks of the Castanni forces were not safe, all suffering the inevitable filth of marching and combat. The Rowetts, the lords of these lands in their gaudy reds and blues and whites, were not in attendance, nor could he see any other Paydar. Only the

108

levies that owed their allegiance to the king, all hunkering down around their fires with what little booze they had brought themselves or taken with steel.

Up ahead, the commander's pavilion loomed large on a swollen rise. Audeyrn admired the sight. The tent was the only scrap of cloth that had escaped the befoulment of campaign. He braced himself as he led his ragged group up to the structure, the overlapping azure and jade silk slapping gently in the breeze of late summer. The zephyr edged past, a promise of the cold hard days to come. Lord Gergy Mansell was not a kind man; the few times he had met him had been brief and prickly encounters. He held caution close to his heart.

The thunder of hooves made him turn in his saddle just in time to see a column of dozens of armoured men gallop past, each wearing a midnight-blue cloak emblazoned by a snarling white wolf. Their standard flew above them, again the wolf lunging forward with hunger in its feral eyes.

"Make way! Make way for the King's Riders!" Cried the knight at the head. They did as they were bid. The man was huge and wore thick plated armour over mail, his great helm adorned with a pair of silver eagle wings. From an open visor, Audeyrn glimpsed a face regarding him with open malice. He must have thought the emissary's small train a detestable lot, with their weather-worn cloaks and haggard look, for he glanced briefly at them as though the mere act were beneath him.

Natoly made a mock salute at their backs. "Honour to thee, bastards."

A laugh erupted close by, "They make for quite the show, don't they?" Audeyrn had not heard him approach, but now he rode behind him and abreast of Nat. He was looking at the emissary, eyes burning with interest. His smile was wide and coy, as though he knew some clever jape. A strong clean-shaven jaw and restive green eyes were framed by a mass of dark lazy curls, a handsome face but for a faded scar over the bridge of his nose. He wore a black gambeson with silver fastenings, and embroidered over his heart was a cockerel spitting fire. The spirited young courser he rode was bridled with her silver clasps of her own, he saw. Audeyrn tried to place his age and decided he couldn't be older than himself.

"Do you ride with them, sir?" Asked Hearty, ever eager to meet new gallantry.

"I do, if not for choice. Despite their gracious disposition, they're nothing but the lowliest mercen scum. There is nothing royal about *them*."

"*You* are not yourself mercen?" Audeyrn reined in beside him.

"Thankfully not," the smile revealed a set of straight white teeth. He, at the least, had the grace to look somewhat abashed. "I am something of a tag-along. An adventurer, if you will." He jerked a thumb at the Riders. "Where the mercen curries the king's favour, he considers himself the very image of knighthood. We adventurers are of humbler stuff. We have no illusions of grandeur. We accept what is offered with head bowed, and thank you kindly." Hearty was so engrossed by the heraldry and pomp that he blurted, "Adventurer? We should be honoured to hear some stories, if you wish to share, that is. I am Sir De—"

"Messengers," Audeyrn broke in, sending a sharp look to Hearty. "On an important errand."

110

The spitfire rooster looked at each of the travellers in turn before turning to Audeyrn again. "I am Norther, at your service."

They were halted as they approached the pavilion, the perimeter surrounded by a freshly dug moat filled with fifteen-foot stakes. The sergeant here was a barrel of a man who challenged the newcomers across the gap. From his tunic, Audeyrn produced the Writ with the king's own seal for the man's inspection. The sergeant huffed but let them through. The man called Norther had fallen in between Gregyn and a verbose Hearty, and was regaling them about the time he fought for the King of Aitis. The sergeant regarded him for an instant, eyes flashing to the rooster, stiffening and alert. That was all Audeyrn needed. Norther ended the tale with his miraculous escape from the king's protectors after deflowering his daughter. *His face is too familiar, and smile too coy.*

The King's Riders had hobbled their mounts away from the tent, grooms having already given them their fodder and brushed them down. He tasked the others to do the same. When Norther made to follow Audeyrn into the pavilion, he turned on him with hand on sword hilt and a threat in his voice, "What's your game? I know you."

"I assure you, we have never met." He looked nonplussed, nodding to the guards at the tent's entrance. "I'm going to the commander's pavilion."

"What business demands you go there, eh? I saw you flitting past the sergeant. He recognised you. You're false coin."

"Falsities are sometimes necessary, Langholm. Step aside." *He knows my name.* The man barged past him, the emissary too stunned to stop him. Not knowing what else to do, he followed at his heels. His fingers itched on the pommel of his blade. The guards ushered them both inside.

A sea of bald heads stood loosely around a stretched war table. Unfriendly faces all, they watched the adventurer and the emissary. One whispered something into his companion's ear to make him snigger. At the head of the table sat a man with his back to them, reading something on a scrap of vellum that curled at its edges. A head shorn to a martial cut was all Aud saw. The hair around the temples and neck razed to the bone. *Lord Mansell.*

The big knight from the column was there too. "Norther brings the rabble to council," he boomed, eliciting laughter from all. He sat on a camp stool, crunching down on an apple loudly. Norther took it in good humour, plucking a glass from a nearby platter and helping himself to a purple wine from a flagon. "Something about a pot and a kettle springs to mind, Sir Vician." Muttered words replaced the laughter. The knight called Vician had a face made for battle, Audeyrn could not help but think. He no longer wore his greathelm, revealing a mouth full of shattered stained teeth, a nose that had been broken and healed crookedly, and hair held back by a scarlet headband, which accentuated his already prominent brow. Of all the men in their cloaks of darkness, he alone had hair. His eyes never left Norther as he plopped the apple core in his mouth and bit down hard.

"Terrifying," Norther said with feigned exaggerated horror. To Audeyrn's astonishment, Norther stalked to the table to look over the emplacements on the arrayed maps. He took a swallow of the wine, making a face in doing so.

"This is horrible. Good enough for Vician Redhand and his polished catamites mayhaps, but I thought we would have had better wine stores on campaign than this draff, Walt."

Walt? No, that's Mansell, surely. He can't mean... The vellum flew across the table at the adventurer. It was aimed at his head, but Norther lifted his arm in time, knocking the glass from his hand to smash against one of the Rider's shining heads. *"Why the fuck are you here?"* Screamed the commander, his voice drowning out the rider's screams as tears of blood and wine ran down his face. Sir Vician grumbled, rising to his full height to loom over Norther. "That's my brother by marriage you just blinded, Norther." Audeyrn thought his tone strangely calm.

Norther worried at a splash of wine that had fallen on his gambeson to stain the rooster. "I'll send the family bloodgold, never you worry... so you're married? Is *she* blind too?" Vician seethed, pulling free a monstrous double-edged axe from his hip. "You've a big mouth, whoreson."

"Enough!" Suddenly Walton was between them, not even registering Audeyrn a few feet away. The Walton Iddles he had known at Castle Castan was a podgy man pushing forty, a capable master-at-arms in his youth, who had had an unparalleled love of lechery, feasting, and ale, and would sooner wake up insensate in a gutter than train at arms. The man he saw now must have been an older, leaner cousin. He had shed five stone at least. His belly was gone, on a chequy vermillion and amber surcoat tucked tightly over a taut body was the elephant skull of his forebears. Beneath a mail shirt were arms corded with muscle. He looked almost naked without his long flowing hair and flamboyant sand-coloured beard and whiskers, that had been his habit

to twist and curl the ends until it looked like some tree monkey from Izar clung to his face. In its place, a closely trimmed chin-beard and moustache well salted with grey draped a lined face and angry mouth. "All of you out, *now!*"

The Riders did not move, but looked to Vician. The knight had the gall to say, "The captains have not finished with their reports." Walton closed on the hulking Sir Vician, close enough to count the blackheads on his crooked nose. "I said... fuck off, *Sir*." Walton stood a good head shorter than the mercen leader. Audeyrn tapped his blade, readying himself for what came next. Seconds stretched by until Vician slung his axe over a shoulder and strode out wordless. It was his men who helped his blinded brother-in-law from the tent.

Only when the last of the King's Riders had left did Walton move; a flash of steel and then his sword was at the adventurer's throat. "Why would you provoke the Redhand? No, riddle me this, *Norther*. Why shouldn't I gut you now and send what's left to—"

"You know why," if the adventurer felt fear at the naked steel, he hid it well, "and because I bring the Royal Emissary." Walton's eyes slid to Audeyrn, for a moment glazed and unrecognising. Then the scales fell away, and a familiar smile sent crow's feet to nestle around those sharp eyes. They looked strained. He sheathed his sword. "The son of Coram. Here! What news of our *glorious* Castan?" Audeyrn smiled at the unguarded ire in the commander's voice. *He named that blade after a redhouse girl, or I'm the Queen of Sora...* Then he saw Norther collect another glass of wine, and felt an uneasy feeling in his gut. "I would rather we discussed this privately, Sir."

"Oh, him? He is… one of mine." That prompted a brusque bow from Spitfire Norther, who was careful not to spill his drink. "My dear Walt, you flatter me oh so graciously," then he proceeded to sit at the head of the table, planting his feet on a map of Paydar. "Picture me a fly, my lords."

Walton combed fingers through his cropped hair. "You've been sent by Isambard, I dare to guess?" He poured a glass of the dark wine for Audeyrn, and water for himself.

"Aye. But I was told by the alderman Raynolf of Forlorn that Lord Gergy Mansell commanded the combined Castanni forces."

"He did, until the fool decided to go hunting in the hills for great elk. They found no elk, but instead, the strangest thing- a hoard of treasure laying unclaimed in the grasses. Solid gold, I hear. Plates there were, and coin, torqs, even a crystal Druke fertility idol. That night, they celebrated, claiming the goods in the name of Isembard. The Rowett nobles that had accompanied him, however, had other ideas. A son of Elmer Rowett, or maybe a nephew. They said that as it was found on Rowett land, that a portion in the least should revert to Lord Rowett and the Tor. He denied them their share of the spoils. Angry words were exchanged, a fight ensued, with one woodman planting a skewer in the lordly eye. A sad end, to an even sadder man. With his death, he lost the Rowetts." The emissary heard no sorrow in those words, not that he expected any. Iddles had a longseated and widely known hatred of Lord Gergy Mansell. Audeyrn considered the look of rueful splendour on the face of this changed man. "I suppose you were the first choice to supplant Mansell as battle commander."

A hoarse laugh broke through the care-lines. "Hardly.

Isambard was wroth that his favourite was killed, and from such an asinine death. No. The king wanted the *new* Lord Mansell, Petterick, a boy of fourteen and cousin to the late lord, to take command. Hector thankfully brought some well-wanting reason into the royal head. He suggested Sir Symon Stepp the Small to his majesty. No doubt a better choice than Gergy Mansell... but all that is irrelevant now. A horse fell beneath Ser Symon on the road from Harlan's Waypost. Poor beast, the man must have weighed twenty-five stone at least. It was *then* my lowly name came to the fore. I was thus relieved of my command of the outriders and given the boots belonging to two dead men. Gods only know I should be proud that the once great Iddles have been graced with such an honour, yet all I know is that it is fit only for a fool."

Norther looked up from his glass, "Some might call that cowardice."

Walton ignored the obloquy. He leant on the table. "An eastern wind blows. The war goes our way no longer. The forces of Silentis assault us asymmetrically. Our heavy horses are too cumbersome to pursue the firemane cavalry they employ. The flanks are endlessly harried, the supply trains plundered mercilessly. You must tell the king this, Aud. Tell him that this war is fruitless. We must sue for peace, before any more lives are given over to this pointless conflict."

The wine in Audeyrn's hand had gone untouched. *In this light, it almost looks like blood.* "I am not here to report back to Castan."

Doubt flickered in Walton's eyes. He crossed his wiry arms. "You've been sent to us by the king, no?"

116

"Aye, but I'm destined for the east." The realisation came to Walton in an instant. He hammered the table with his fist, and laugh lines surrounded his careworn face.

Walton "You carry a message of peace to Silentis! Aha! This is joyous news, my friend. It gladdens me no end."

It was Norther who ventured, "The chest is the message, no?"

The words caught in the emissary's throat. He forced them out, knowing it was not what Walt wanted to hear. Yet he owed him the truth, didn't he? *The mission is always first.* "My men are guarding it as we speak. A plain strongbox, the contents of which are unknown to me. The king bid me deliver it to the court at Silentis, for the eyes of the queen and her battle commander." King Isambard the First, if anything, was changeable. He acted on any given whim, fits of animated fervour and spirited elation, showering retainers and courtiers in offices and rewards. All to buy their loyalty. Buy their love. His grandfather, the fearsome King Odaric IV, called Maidenbane, had been butchered in bed with his mistress of the time, after years of taking the young virgin daughters of his nobles and disposing of them when he would lose interest. Hector the Gifted had seen to it that in the ensuing succession crisis, it was Isembard, a young and impressionable boy of ten, and legitimate besides, would ascend to the storied Tourmaline Throne of Castan. If the tales could be believed, the once gleeful child had become the paranoid and mercurial man he knew well; vindictive and vengeful, who yearned for the approval of his subjects and relied on his seneschals to undertake the day-to-day governing of the kingdom. He would suffer episodes of mania, accusing even the bloodroyals of some treachery or other. By the time Audeyrn had arrived at court, the queen had ushered herself away to the royal estates on Stony Lake, along with the king's son and heir. Years drifted by, and the royal moods darkened and fomented war. And war had bloomed into a flower that drank blood. *A changeable man, but unyielding in this decision. The box, the contents for only royal eyes to see...*

"Open it then," the spitfire suggested with a shrug. Walton made to say something, but it must have been a shadow in the tent, for Audeyrn thought his face drawn. "Maybe. Audeyrn, you are the Royal Emissary. I understand the charge you've been given. I do. Should you open the box, the knowledge will not leave this tent."

The suggestion hung in the air, an arrant incite to betrayal that lusted to be realised. But Audeyrn would *not* accuse Walton of that. He could not. His eyes turned to Norther. "Who are you, really?"

"Your salvation, Audeyrn."

"Don't play the helpmate with me, mercen. You are nobody to me. For all I know, you're just a rebel."

The spitfire cocked an eyebrow, pretending to regard the strategies on the table. The man who approached Audeyrn then was the old Walton no longer, but this stranger hewn by war. "He is an ally. That is all you need to know. The strongest ally the king could ever have."

He talks, yet his words are practiced. Rebel or no, they mean to compromise me.

Looking Walton in the eyes, he said, "No. That would be me."

He could not say much about what they talked of after that. Walton was angry, using his commander's voice much

118

like he used to drill the squires in the Great Bailey of Castle Castan. Norther let loose a ragged laugh. Audeyrn did not play with the palace intrigues, so all this talk left a bad taste in his mouth. He obeyed the king. *The mission...*

It was Gregyn who asked later on if Norther would be joining them on the road ahead. Audeyrn wanted to tell them what had happened, to lay everything bare to be purified by the daylight. But he could not. The sun was already low, setting over the dark, jagged impression of the Snowmonts to the west. By rights, he should report back to the alderman of Forlorn, but he gave no orders to do so. He only stood on the hillock, his friends around him japing about the bedside habits of the King's Riders. The light was dying.

He was given quarters near the commander's pavilion, his field tent overlarge in his mind, but he was tired of the day and sleep gnawed at him, so he accepted it for the night. The others were given tents of their own, but they were paltry things next to the fine silk-draped canvas he enjoyed. A featherbed was prepared for him, the silk sheets the blue and green of Castan. He grimaced, wondering if that was Walt's doing. He poured himself some wine to settle his mind but found he did not need it. *Maybe I should bathe,* was the last he remembered before the veil took him.

He could not say when it began, only that he came to realise he was there. A half-light surrounded him, a brume of grey haze that sent ghostly wisps to engulf the sheer inky blackness beyond. A feeling of weightlessness, and he saw that he was naked. Looking down, he saw his body shine pale-bright from some phantom moonglow. His lithe legs swayed lazily, along with everything in between.

119

"Where am I?" posing the question to no one.

The answer came belatedly from on high. What he thought of as the sky above suddenly burned a ghastly crimson, a dome of perennial fire edged by the darkness of a dreadblack horizon. Fear clung to his heart like a belt cinched two holes too tight. When he moved, his muscles groaned in agony. *What's happening to me? This is a dream. Nothing can harm me. I will wake, and all will be well...*

A shuffling from behind pricked his ears. Wide-eyed, he strained to turn his head at the oncoming danger. For it could only be danger. He struggled to find his footing, to somehow fight his way to the ground, or floor, or whatever counted as the bottom in this unseen place. *Where's my sword? Gods... I've lost my sword.*

The caress came unbidden, a gentle touch to his leg, and he saw her.

He did not know the woman who stood before him, only that her touch routed out the fear in his heart and the pain from his body. She balanced deftly on her toes to reach him, her lean limbs stretched and posed like some Warretumi boltdancer.

No, not Warretumi... her skin was lighter than the ebon-skinned peoples of Warretum. Not one of the Caldish peoples that populated the lands west of the Ruell either, who were usually fair of skin. Her bare arms and legs shone darkly, olive-skinned and alluring. *Soran, then?* She was clad in some strange shift that clung winsomely against her frame as she gently pulled him to her. Glancing up at him unsmiling, with an upturned pug nose in a heart-shaped face. Something danced and sang in her eyes that, for a moment, lit by some errant ghost light of the beyond, flashed a striking hazel to break his heart. Her unbound hair swarmed about her head in locks the colour of deep red ochre.

When his bare feet touched the false-ground, she was holding his hand.

"You're…" *gorgeous.* When her full lips parted in a smile, she raised his hand with hers. Their fingers locked together. The sky darkened, replaced by a coronal of stars and all the constellations. He saw the Blue Hawk and Ghost Mountain, the Colossus and Aelynyr the Archer, all surrendering to the milky gleam that ripped across the nocturne in ethereal splendour: the Palace of the Fay, named for the fortress-city of legend, where the First War had resulted in the victory of men over the fay-folk.

"Look," came a voice, the phantom of a whisper.

He looked to the woman, but she only pointed with her free hand to his right, where the rising sun silhouetted the landscape as it took on form, rising in billowing waves as a swelling ball of fury presided over a sea the colour of sand. *Sand, only sand.* A castle of pale sun-bleached stone rose in high domed spires and crowned towers, populated by shady gardens and columned atria. Long plumes of black smoke rose from the city beneath.

"Silentis." It must have been the city of the Sorans. He knew the place by sight, but he had never been there. Besieged by some enemy, the smoke crawling up its walls to shroud the Royal Palace in a death pall. "They're dying." he could see them. Men and women in battle-leathers wielding the slim bows of the east and operating the ballistas lining the high walls like rows of fangs. And the others, those too frail or old or crippled to fight, watching on in glazed anticipation. And the children, wailing. The sun dried the tears as they fell upon their cheeks.

"Yes," was her answer. He held her tight.

Silentis shrunk beneath the pitiless Soran sun. Very soon, it was gone. The only sight the shifting sands of those nameless lands to the east. Sands of ill repute. The desert stretched on for leagues, an unending ocean of heat and scorpions and yappors and then more sand. For a moment, he thought he saw something move on the dunes- *a person?*- or a drywood tree. Leaving the bloody road behind, the road left the coast of the Ruell and tracked inland, becoming the sand road leading into the Desolate Tundra, that lifeless expanse that meant only death. The sun sank at their backs, so he realised they must have been west of Silentis, to sands settled only by ghosts and vultures.

There's nothing there.

"No," she said. Her voice hard as fabled Lar'garan steel. "She is there."

His anger spurred at this sphinx. "*She? Who?* What does this all mean? I pray, tell me!" he grabbed her other hand, but her lips were closed, and her eyes sad.

The sands turned grey, and somehow the sun sank at their back again. *I didn't see it rise.* His gaze was torn from the rending visage by something rough in his hands.

Sand dusted his fingers, abrasive and uncaring. When he looked up, he saw the woman was shorter than before. *Sand.* A smile full of sorrow traced her lips. When her words came, her lips did not move.

"*Bring Norther.*"

When her mouth opened, a gout of sand poured forth. Only sand.

Darkness closed in.

.

10

MARBLE

As the outpost's limits came into view, the wanderer did not know whether to be comforted or disturbed.

No distinguishable path led to the outpost, but the ground became dry and brittle the closer she ventured to the ramshackle structures. The sand gave way to cracked clay, which gave way to the impression of a path. Marble was unsure if it was a blessing she could barely feel the pain in her broken feet anymore.

Time was one of many enemies that eluded her. Bonebridge was mostly unknown to the rest of the kingdom. All sorts of brigands could have made their home there. *Even those that are assaulting my city.* Yet she could not be sure. The threat of being apprehended loomed large in her mind. *Apprehended*, she mused. Just a prettier way to say kidnapped, forced into becoming a slave, used for pleasure out in the wastes.

There was only hope, at this point, such extremes would be unnecessary. Allowing herself to fall into their clutches would be a last resort. But, first, she had to make it into the town and find somewhere to stay while the fever passed.

The blinding sun seemed to reflect off every surface it touched to shine into Marble's eyes. Sunblind, she stumbled onwards, passing larger and larger lumps of stone and rock, and the gods only knew what else, until she reached the ruins.

Bonebridge was an education. Marble took time to marvel at the husks of homes that were no more. It was eerie, passing through a ghostly ring surrounding the desolate town beyond. Sand was slowly encroaching, what had been there before, known only to ghosts and scorpions. Nature was steadily taking back its demesne.

She thought it strange to be standing in the footsteps of those whose lives were now mere spectres. Once something much more and known by a different name, the outskirts of Bonebridge, at least, were a ghost town in the truest sense. The many voices of a once bustling community had been replaced by the desolate wails of the hot desert wind that swept off the Tundra, whistling through the bones of the once great pillar of society.

Shrugging off those thoughts was easier than travailing the rocks, the detritus growing larger, and the ruins becoming more whole. The outpost boasted no fortifying wall or blockade. Amongst the dead stones one moment, the next, vague impressions of avenues opened before her. Forms took shape, too uniform to be natural. It took all her will not to collapse in the middle of the town. The townsfolk were all about her, yet seemed too far away to hear. Beasts of burden trod back and forth, shutters creaked, a signpost swung wide, and the door opened. Barging inside, she demanded a room, food and water, though she had nothing to pay for it. *They are talking to me.* Walls bent and the floor wobbled beneath her.

She woke in an unfamiliar room. The chamber replete with elaborate furnishings. She occupied a featherbed. Her stomach gnawed painfully, and she soon discovered a plate of cold cuts and bread on the bedside table, accompanied by a pitcher full of water, at the far end of the room. Marble failed to take in any more detail as she scrambled out of the all-too-comforting embrace of the bed and fell upon the meal, devouring it, despite knowing she may make herself ill. Feeling bone tired and weary, she wasted little time crawling back into the comfort of the feathers. Sleep took her before her head hit the pillow.

The cool cloth against her forehead a balm to the senses. She was hot and cold. Shivering terribly, her teeth chattering against the ice while burning up from the inside and drenched in a sickly sweat. The realisation of comfort was slow but certain. It unsettled her, but she could not say why. Her mind wandered, and then she saw it.

Blue and monstrous. It was huge and ugly, and it scared her. Indistinct, the only clarity she had, it hungered for her. *It's going to eat me.*

It had caught her. *Trapped her.* She had been tied down, she couldn't escape, no matter how hard she flailed and thrashed.

It was dark. Dreadblack. The type of dark no light has any hope of penetrating. It was the kind of darkness that consumes and devours. It was the darkness of oblivion, of nothing, of despair. It was never-ending and soulsucking. There was no sound. There was nothing but darkness.

126

Darkness and pain and anguish and hot and cold and the end.

No matter how desperately Marble tried to wriggle free of the strong limbs holding her in place, there was no relief. She was weak. Always weak. Never strong. She would fail; she was destined to fail. It was all pointless, but Marble didn't care. She would push and push and push and break and break and break until there was nothing left of her for those mighty limbs to hold on to until there was no purchase to be gained on her being, and then she would be free. She would break, and she would fall, and she would escape, and she would survive, and she would try to take as many of her broken pieces with her as possible. She would drag them and carry them and kick them along ahead of her, and then she would puzzle herself back together with what remained and patch in the holes as best she could, and she would carry on. She would endure.

The tree stood tall in the twilight. A menacing feature on the desolate landscape. It called and whispered, and it seemed to pulse and move. It was not a normal tree. It swayed in the nonexistent breeze, its branches rustling on a whisper and clawing at the air, ground, and anything that dared move into its reach. The night came closer, the sky grew darker, and the tree *glowed*. Then it burned. Afire, it began to wail in agony. Still, it clawed at its surroundings, but now it was more desperate and violent. A vulture of some kind got too close. The tree snatched the creature, tearing it from the sky and ripping it to pieces. No mercy. No escape. It howled and howled, and the inferno raged on.

The cold was inside her. So very cold. But it was nice.

She liked this cold. And floating. She was floating in cold water. Someone was there. *How did I get here?* Sleep.

Sunlight streamed into the room and onto Marble's face, rousing her from what had finally become a restful sleep. The emissary felt lethargic. Not the worn-out, awful kind of lethargy but the lazy, comforting type that succeeded in a night of true rest. Head still a little fuzzy from the fever she knew she had suffered, Marble luxuriated in the bed, stretching her sore limbs under the thin sheet covering her. The room warmed with the day's heat permeating the building. Wherever it was. Marble blinked her eyes as she turned her face away from the sun, adjusting them to the relative gloom inside the room thanks to the heavy curtains covering the windows, blocking out the full might of the daylight. Marble allowed herself the time to take in the details of the room, orienting herself within her surroundings and absorbing all the information she could gather of her staggering into that strange place. The fever broken, leaving only the recollections of lost youth and the already fading image of a tree. The memories, pieces of a woman that, try as they might stop her, was still there, in a room where the sun shone golden.

Looking about the place, Marble began to doubt she was even at Bonebridge. It seemed more and more improbable the more she took in the room. Maybe the outlying ruins had been a fevered hallucination, and the sickness had taken her far sooner than she had anticipated. If that was the case, then it was highly likely the Tundra's changing landscape, the night creature and the caves were all in her head too. But Marble quickly dismissed that train of thought when she attempted to push herself sitting and her body cried out in protest.

No. Those hardships had all been real, and she was paying the price for them now. Her pained groan, impossible to hold at bay, echoed around the plush space and Marble was once again entranced by the view. She stumbled her way out of the cloudlike mattress and tripped over to spread the curtains wide open. She needed the light. She needed to see the room in the bright light of day to be sure her mind and eyes were not devious and playing tricks on her still battered and weary self. Standing before the now unobstructed window, Marble could hear the hustle and bustle of everyday life loud and clear. It was a wonder she hadn't noticed the noise before, for it was hardly an unobtrusive sound but rather quite the ruckus.

Maybe Marble had heard it, though. Perhaps she was aware of the noise but pushed it to the back of her head and drowned it out with her thoughts. Maybe Marble was more broken than she had thought. *How could I have ignored this racket?* She would be dead within seconds of leaving the room if she wasn't careful, and there would be nothing spectacular, brave, courageous, or worthy about it. She would likely just trip and break her neck, and nobody would know what had happened to her. Marble would be dead and branded a traitor to Sora and would have died of pure stupidity.

Marble observed people coming and going, watching without seeing. She looked down onto the street below, realising her room was some stories above ground level. Looking at the building opposite gave the impression she resided on the fourth floor. *The Garrison never trained for defenestration. What a terrible oversight.*

The buildings opposite were alien to her. Shorter, the walls were of clean grey stone charmingly placed between weathered wood. Timber beams protruded, sprouting diagonally to support the overhang of the upper stories. Windows bore storm shutters, pushed back to welcome the day's sun. To crown the podunk's queer buildings were rows and rows of warped tiles, stuck cunningly together, all of them faded to a burnt orange.

An odd site for the middle of a desert. *Am I not in Bonebridge?* If this was indeed the hub of criminality, it hid its true face well. Then there was the grime. There wasn't any. From her vantage point, she saw the well-dressed townsfolk walk the swept road free of muck and filth. Their clothing was in good repair and *clean*. When she raised her eyes to the next street over, it was spotless too. She liked it not at all and felt her hackles rise.

Anywhere else, there would be feuds and fighting in the streets, she knew. There was something strange about this place. Marble observed the friendly, happy, carefree way the residents of the bizarre little town carried themselves and moved and greeted each other when they passed on the street. Children laughed joyously as they darted precariously through the heavy foot traffic, and not a one of them looked to be picking any pockets.

Yes, a strange place indeed. Marble collected her wits. *It is an illusion, or artifice. Some trickery.* Turning her back on the disconcerting scene displayed through the pristine, clear glass, she scanned the room out of habit.

The bed boasted four posters of rich, sturdy oak matching the foot and headboards and startlingly white sheets. Marble refused to feel a smidgen of guilt for sullying with her unclean self. A trunk sat at the foot of the giant with an amethyst-coloured velvet cushioned lid, with its body a sibling for most of the furniture in the room, that luscious oak, carved intricately with odd scenes Marble had never before seen the like. The space larger than Marble had ever seen a suite of rooms at any other inn boast. Spacious and ornate. *Definitely not an inn*, Marble admitted to herself. She pondered what in all the realms she had gotten herself into in her delirious state, with a growing sense of dread and grim acceptance.

Draped in a thin, so thin it was sheer, russet sheath, Marble belatedly wondered who would have dressed her unconscious self, especially who dared to clothe her in some outdated whore's fashion. Irrational, she supposed, the reason the gown offended her. It was not the thought of somebody presuming they had the right to touch her body and wrap her up in their choice of attire, nor the sheerness of the fabric that left hardly an iota of her body to the imagination of any who dared a glance. Not the liberty some person had taken to dress her like a woman of wares, ready to sell. *No.* It was the fact her apparel was not at all seductive in the way it fell about her body. It would be not at all appealing if it were not so indecent.

If I am to be dressed as a worldly woman, the least they could have done was outfit me in a more flattering style. No cinching in at the waist or shape to the garment. No tease of more covered areas, no show of skin. Tied around her neck and wrists and falling lamely to the floor, it billowed around her so not a slice of material would touch her skin. *It is truly monstrous.* Marble was not usually one to become so conscious about her attire, but, she supposed, she had never

131

had to wear something as ghastly as her current outfit.

Pushing aside her dismay at the gown, Marble finally admitted to herself what she had been feeling and had thought all along. Despite the pain, she was almost fully healed. She guessed this outcome had been inevitable in the end, and no matter how contradictory life appeared here at Bonebridge compared to its well-cultivated and clever reputation, she had still been acquired by one of the many criminal guilds. She guessed the outfit made more sense now. Almost a prison guard unto itself. She supposed, for many, if not most women, would not dare venture out into society dressed so indecently. Unfortunately for whoever her captors turned out to be, however, Marble was not an ordinary woman. She was a resident of the Garrison of Selentis, and she did not have the same qualms or mental barriers of a perceived well-adjusted person, which would suit her well about now. She refused to venture out and begin her reconnaissance without making a few alterations to her habit. A resigned sigh escaped, *I am more similar to Cliada than I wish to admit.* She shucked the monstrosity over her head to transform it into something much more flattering. Marble could see the other woman's smirk as she began her adjustments.

11

NATOLY

H is knife pulled the crud from beneath his fingernails. The Paydar sun reflected off the naked steel and into his eyes. He did not mind. The hills unfolded before them like a grassy sea, leagues of wild barley and wheat blowing in airy currents, and here and there, fingers of rock poking shyly through the shimmering grasses. He had thought the Snowmonts unending and eternal, their imperious summits lording high enough to banish the light of day from the frigid valleys. It had been exhilarating for a boy from the mean wynds of Low Castan. It seemed almost like a story of heroes from a long-forgotten age had come to life. The roc had come for them in one nameless vale, and Nat had been dumbstruck at the meek Gregyn ending it so swiftly. Upon his return to Castan, no one would best their tale, he knew.

He had no idea his knife was gone until Greg came about with blade in hand, doing for the beast as they stood gawking. The boy's eyes had glistened wetly in the moonlight, but he destroyed them before they fell. *Not just a boy after all, then.*

After that, he continued to jape with the young tracker and take his sleep in the bedroll next to his, but there was a feeling, something unsaid and well hidden, he thought, in those large callow eyes and halting speech. Yet the more he thought on it, the less certain he became. *Gregyn of Dun Vale.* Bringing the lad's name to mind brought forth nothing but the quiet string of piss he had grown fond of. *Thinking leads to trouble,* that's what Maarten would say...

...and talking too.

They had been warned. *Norther was not to be trusted,* Audeyrn had pressed on them. They were not to speak a word of their mission or destination to their unlikely guide. The man seemed amiable enough to Nat with his amusing tales and lightning wit. If Audeyrn had reasons for mistrusting the man, he kept it to himself.

They stayed apart from the Castanni soldiery in the camp. Breakfast had been bacon and goldenbread, washed down with brown ale and Hearty recounting his drinking contest with The Belly. No sooner had Audeyrn returned from the commander's pavilion, his jaw hard and his mood harder, than he announced that he was off to practice his sword swings. An hour later, as they broke camp and saddled the horses, a certain swordsman fell in beside them, and matched Hearty yarn for yarn. In a quiet moment, Nat had asked the emissary why he had relented in allowing the man to come. Audeyrn had answered him cordially enough, but his causting gaze lit his mood. *He will be useful in Rowett's Town,* he promised, disquiet edging his voice. *He follows us no further.*

The man was certainly easy to like, and if his sagas were to be believed, a favourite of maidens high and humble, having travelled to the lands of the Ruell Sea, and to the Azure Coast north of Castan, and even beyond that, to places with names that sounded queer and hard to pronounce. The villains in those tales always seemed to resemble Audeyrn, which did not go unnoticed. Very soon, the emissary was refusing to call Norther by his name entirely, opting to call him the *spitfire cock*. It was a small company, so it wasn't long before Norther jested with the others that they followed Audeyrn "the Emisery", vexing their leader no end. Hearty had almost choked on his laughter.

The gods, wherever they were, smiled on their journey through the gentle hills. Despite the prodding by Norther, the emissary himself was in high spirits, Nat could see, after a time finding the humour in the newcomer's tales and bawdy jokes. There was something else too. The lingering melancholy that plagued Aud. He chanced to see him looking off a few times, as though dreaming. He wanted desperately to ask him what occupied his thoughts, but never had the heart. He knew that he burdened himself heavily. He knew there was something he kept from even his friends.

As they left the army behind, the land knew man by the toiling of the earth by scythe instead of sword, the hills were soon covered by farms and crofts, hugging the easy slopes and surrounded by levelled terraces for grape vines. Here and there, they even glimpsed a water mill working the low rivers, and Greg would perk in his saddle and regale them with everything there was to know about that trite trade. They saw no one, but he knew they were being watched by wary eyes.

It was on a crest of a nondescript knoll that the adventurer bridled his pitch-black mount beside Nat. The smell of silverleaf preceded him, chewing it habitually. He had fashioned a wide-brimmed hat for himself on the road, the like worn by peasants as they worked the fields. "A kje sword is something of a rarity in Castan," he said, a blade of grass sticking jauntily from his mouth. His calm demeanour was reassuring to Nat, and he found himself in easy conversation. "Aye, Sir. I find greatswords and claymores clumsy, and lacking elegance. A kje, though, they say that the Warretumi wield them as though they were a part of their arm. Truly, an artform to behold."

The man whistled beneath the shade of the hat. "Warring is a gruesome art, yet I understand your meaning." Nat did not know if he heard mockery in that voice. He was about to make his argument when Greg broke off from the line, galloping down to appraise the ardent stream that beribboned a shady glen ahead. *He took my knife like it was nothing...*

Norther must have sensed that, for he said, "How does a lowly boy from the High Forks come to serve the Royal Emissary?" It was not the first question he had asked him or his company. Over the past few days showing that he had almost the inquisitiveness of a child. Then again, he had told Nat and the others a plenitude of stories about his eventful life. A voice inside told him otherwise. *Why so interested in Gregyn?* He shook the thoughts off as silly. He looked ahead, where Audeyrn was talking quietly with Hearty. It seemed almost churlish that he should spurn Norther for something so anodyne.

"Oh, Greg? Two years past, he was poaching from

Mornswood. Pilfered buck and urca and halcyon, I believe. Even moa when he could. Where sporting is concerned, Greg is peerless."

Norther widened his eyes, "You claim our young Greg is a master at his craft?"

"Yes," *Our young Greg?* He realised his error too late.

"The doyen poacher stalks the Mornswood no longer. The only conclusions I can draw from *that* are: either he was apprehended, thence handed over to the Reeve Arran for bondservitude, or, our roguish scofflaw saw the error of his ways and repented to a godman, to be reborn into the light of the virtue of the gods. My coin favours the former, I fear." When he laughed, his white teeth shone.

"I thought mercen only spent their coin on redgirls and ale, and wagered what's left on basilisk fights."

"Mercen do many graceless things, Nat." He spread his hands in all innocence. "Can you imagine *me* going to a basilisk fight?"

Fool. Aud is right. Nat would give him little after that, answering non-committedly and giving no banter. Norther sought conversation elsewhere soon after, leaving Nat with his thoughts.

Thinking leads to trouble. I know, Maarten. I fucking know.

He tried to avoid Norther the following days. That was easier said than done, him being their guide through the Paydar and all. Audeyrn assured him that the man was not a mortal threat, and that for the nonce, their interests were one and the same. Nat wanted to feel as relaxed as his friend, but sometimes he wondered if the emissary's lordly upbringing blinkered him to certain things. For one, he knew a threat when he saw it. Long before his deliverance by Maarten and the Guildcorps, he had endured sleepless nights without count, naked in the stinking gutters, vigilance his only shield from the men that walked in the dark looking for little boys. In his mind, Norther trying to wise his way with questions about the lad was far from subtle. The message was clear: *I'll find out who you are.* He did not think himself a scholar, but his first life in Low Castan had been a ceaseless education into the angry hearts of men.

The fantastical stories seemed all the more spurious, and the humour was lost on him. He rode alongside Audeyrn more and more, finding the usually serious talk a balm to the pinpricks of his incessant anxiety.

"Tomorrow should see us to Rowett's Town," the emissary said, after his customary lapses into silence. Nat nodded in approval, "Aye. Will this be a stopover, or…" Audeyrn had been tight-lipped about their checkpoint, with Nat fearing to broach the subject before now.

"I wish I could be certain. Our garrulous friend promises me that the need will prompt an explanation. The need for secrecy I can understand, but he must be a fool if he thinks we could not guess the reason why we journey to the Stonehall."

Nat was nonplussed, feeling like someone looking for a feather in a dark room. He ventured, "We go there for allies, surely." Audeyrn *hmm*ed at that, saying, "Not exactly. The Rowetts are on uncertain terms with the Kingdom of Castan. The esteemed Lord Mansell did not help. When he shamed the Rowetts on that hunting trip of his, he incurred the ire of the Lord of the Paydar, Elmer. Then Sir Symon the Small came broken and dying into the camp from his midnight ride, and the Rowetts took that as affirmation King Isembard rules a weak kingdom, his followers being only lickspittles and cravens. Lord Elmer Rowett had had enough, and he marched his soldiers home.

"Castan is now on the backfoot, Nat. The loss of the Rowetts brings the war effort to a standstill, and presents them with the opportunity to enter into alliance with Silentis. If that should happen, they may cut off the long road, assault the Castanni landings on the Ruell, and augment the already formidable Soran army. These Paydar may be ferine in the eyes of the Castanni nobility, but when all's said and done, we need them. So that is why we go to Rowett's Town. We go to mend the rift between Castan and Stonehill. I *am* the Royal Emissary, so my presence seems appropriate. How Norther fits into all of this, I fail to see. Walton seems to trust him. He may prove to be of use."

Nat was not so sure about the Rowetts and this *Lord Elmer*, whoever he was. He had never seen a Paydar before, let alone Rowett's Town and the fabled Stonehall that towered above it on the Tor. But what he knew was people, and he knew that Norther was false. *He's too clever by half. We trust him overmuch.* "I mislike this, Aud. He's meant to be our guide, yes, but he thinks himself one of us now. He bought into Greg's confidence early on, and Hearty... you'd swear they've been firm drinking friends for years."

Audeyrn snorted derisively. "He is bold, and comely, and dangerous. He's a braggart, yet I don't doubt his skill at arms. I'm beginning to believe the stories he tells, the way he tells them... almost mesmeric." He turned and looked Nat in the eye. "I think him almost regal."

Nat was aghast, "What? *You?* But, you despise the man."

He was careful to keep his voice low. "I– But why?" And the emissary laughed. It was long and loud, Nat noticing that the others had fallen silent at the sudden gale.

"Fuck you, Aud," the chagrin pouring over him to burn his cheeks. *Devious bastard.*

"What?" The emissary managed between howls, "I thought it hilarious."

"No. This is hilarious." With a flourish, he brandished his kje, holding it aloft to let the sunlight dance on long curved steel. Then, the solid metal turned to a flash as he brought it downward, the flat of the blade slapping the emissary's mount hard on the hindquarters. The horse bolted as he had hoped, with Audeyrn grasping the bucking neck hard as the reins flapped about his head. The frenzied mount galloped further and further ahead, the thundering of the hooves punctuated all the way by a string of obscenities.

It felt then as though they were nothing but boys back at Castle Castan, showing all and sundry the fuzz on their cheeks and wanting knighthood more than anything. *Take me back. To the days of quintains and ponies. To boisterous Walton Iddles outdrinking Hearty in the King's High Hall. To stealing away to the lakes with Rhyrn.*

"Oho! He will be mighty wroth with you, lad," came the voice of Hearty, a bellyful of joyous giggles making his paunch bob up and down. "Well, when he regains the mount, that is." Greg scolded him for hitting the horse, but it was half-hearted, and he did so with a smirk. "Well played," said the adventurer, his hat shadowing his eyes, "Almost artful."

The tracks they followed became a road, yet it was unmarked on their maps. Not that they needed direction.

They met fellow travellers more often then, and Nat wondered why they had so little up until then. *The war has come to their doorstep. The peasants fear the hills.* The Paydar had been ruled by the Rowetts for thousands of years (to hear them tell). From their seat at Stonehall, they demanded fealty from all that dwelt in the Hills, from the snowmonts to the west (called the Western Wall by the Rowetts) and the Grassy Road to the east. These were no Vasti, he learned as they came on the town. He did not like the Vastimen, with their milkblood attitudes to putting trade above war. He could not understand how a people with mountain savages at their gates could be so cowardly. The thought of that night in the redhouse still made him feel queasy.

Seeing the Paydar, though, he was entranced. *These are Vasti with steel in their blood.* The men were tall, gruff folk, who spoke in that lumbering tongue of theirs. *Qellish?* They had supposedly mingled with the blood of Old Qell, from that fanciful kingdom to the far north. Some scholars even debated whether they were related to the Lar'garans. Nat could not disagree. The women themselves looked mannish, for it was their custom for men and women both to wear their hair long and braided. Many had bosoms all muscle, with little breasts to speak of, with arms and legs to shame the men. *They even dress like men.* He wondered how often the mountainmen raided these people, and decided he already had the answer.

They saw the Tor first. A naked thumb of rock thrusting from the town proper a thousand feet high until it was crowned by a ring of bright white stone- The Stonehall. A set of stairs had been carved around the rock thirteen times, before meeting the ante-castle on the summit. *A blunt name for a blunt people,* he thought.

The legend being that the titan Argere, while striding through the snowmonts, trod on an exposed spire of hard stone. Howling with fury, he plucked it from his foot as though it were a splinter. In his annoyance, he flung it high and fast, landing far away in the Paydar. In time, a daughter of the gods was placed atop the upright rock to be safe from the lusts of men. This did not stop the mighty hero Ro Rowett however, who climbed the sheer face to claim the maiden for his own. The gods had vanished by then, so fortunately for Ro he did not see their vengeance, but went on to establish the Kingdom of Northmarch, with the Tor as his citadel.

The town itself was a mirror to those that dwelt within. The buildings that had sprung up around the base were like grey mushrooms, each from quarried stone to make large blocks that fit together adroitly, all topped by roofs of grey slate. Even the larger buildings, which he took for guildhouses or houses of old blood, were hewn from the same bricks, albeit crowned by sculpted stone beasts. And everywhere, from gatehouses to barbicans and between cobbled streets and gables and hanging from the crenels of the curtain wall that encircled the town, were the striped red, white and blue banners of the Rowetts.

Do the redhouses hang such pennants, I wonder.

The drawbridge was down and the western gate, called the Mountain Doors, was open. They were solid hardiron, the gift from some ancient Castanni king. They were swung inward, flanked by two massive roundtowers. Passing beneath the archway topping the threshold, Nat stared up at the murder holes and portcullis, the metal red with rust, yet sharp and heavy enough to cleave a man in two. *Let the mountainmen try that.*

Men-at-arms were inspecting the flow of traffic, all wearing long suits of mail, a long stretch of red white and blue fabric wound across their chest and over a shoulder. The captain, a tall woman even by Paydar standards, stood regarding each visitor with an acid gaze, beneath a polished silver helm with a sunburst encircling her head. On a breastplate, a titan's face stared out in challenge. Nat thought her the most terrifying woman he had ever seen. A scar from some old wound gnawed its way up her chin, the left side of her face and through her eye, dead and white-blind. It had healed tight, a scowl lashing out angrily on that side.

She stood out, to say the least. He was about to make some jape to Hearty when Norther came up beside the emissary. "That's my contact."

"*Her?*" Nat blurted. *She is more like to gut you than talk.*

Norther took the peasant hat off and untied his hair, letting the lazy curls dance about his comely face. "I thought you liked women, Nat."

I thought you liked living, he thought, but said, "I prefer not to look *up* at mine."

Audeyrn silenced him with eyes like a squall. "Enough banter. Spitfire, make the introductions." The adventurer gave a loose bow in his saddle. His mount, so like her rider, whinnied lightly. "As you say, *my lord.*" Nat expected him then to dismount and lead his horse to the captain. Instead, he pulled a silver disk of some sort from his gambeson and held it at arm's length in the direction of the guards. The woman noticed him, producing a selfsame bauble. Nodding in approval, she sauntered over. She was there in less than a dozen strides. *She has long legs, at least.*

"Password?" the scarred sun sounded as though she chewed iron filings.

"*Statue.* And yours, fair lady?"

"*Haven.* You are early, Castanni."

"Good. I'm never late," he gave a lazy flick of the wrist to Nat and the others. "They're with me. Now, if you would be so kind, captain, we are famished. Stonehall has good wine, I hope?"

The guards appeared from nowhere and everywhere, falling in around them to create an escort fit for a king. The Scarred Sun led them afoot, roaring at any that came too close or blocked the road with wayns selling meat and fruits and trinkets. The avenue was well kept, the cobbles here in good repair and swept regularly. Those that scrubbed the stones were brawny, with scarred arms and hard faces. *They are warriors...* he realised, and looked to Audeyrn for an explanation, only to see the emissary with the same expression. Norther laughed at them both. "Curious, I know. They are *Unblooded.* Those that have not yet proven themselves worthy of the battlefield, or procreation. Until such time, they serve their Lord Rowett in other ways... not excluding public sanitation. I can only wonder how old Isembard would fare if he tried to implement such policies in Castan." They all knew the answer to that, but it went unsaid.

The road criss-crossed open squares and markets, an overabundance of red and white and blue hanging in bunting across the wide streets. They soon lost their luster however, for as they reached the Titan Gate, the sun began its slow descent beneath the verdant waves of the hills beyond the walls. The Titan himself watched the sunset. His stone eyes followed them as they approached. The gate, in place of an archway like on the walls, bore a strikingly hewed Argere, rising above the cobbles. He strode between the roundtowers, frozen in rank ignominy, as teams of donkeys passed beneath his legs and through a pair of hardiron doors twice as tall as those on the Mountain Door. Argere dwarfed the towers and doors all, reaching nearly a hundred foot above the cobbles, a hard foot planted arrogantly on the flat roof of each, his right arm outstretched and clawing at the air. Nat thought he would be taller.

The Scarred Sun advised them to leave their mounts at the Titan Gate, saying that the donkeys employed on the stair were more sure-footed here than their wearied warhorses, and were used to the terrain besides. Surprisingly, it was Hearty who was the most opposed to the idea, exchanging rough words with the scarred captain. *Maybe he fears the donkey will collapse under him.* Everyone knew what had happened to the grossly fat Sir Symon Stepp. Hearty was no Sir Symon, yet the donkeys that plied the steps were lean beasts much smaller than the great warhorses he was accustomed to riding.

It was Norther who resolved the debacle. When an ox cart passed them, laden with vittles going to the summit, the man jerked a thumb to the cart laden with foodstuffs and asked the Scarred Sun if it would be permissible to let Hearty ride in the back of one. The darkest smile crossed the captain's face, the scar tissue twisting and the blind-eye shining brightly. "An ale cart will come soon. He can ride that. Those oxen are used to carrying kegs." Hearty scoffed, but waited for the cart.

In twilight, they climbed. The Scarred Sun relieved her men; she was the only member of the honour guard to continue their escort. Mounting a donkey of her own, she said little and less on the stair. They started, the gaunt mounts edging toward the edge. A good two foot of crenelation had been carved in case the way needed to be defended from above, yet he would have preferred a chain-fence, or a true wall. The world emptied beneath them.

Their new mounts needed little encouragement. They went single file at a gentle pace, each one having traversed the steps thousands of times before. *Perhaps they've lived their whole lives on the stone. How big can must their world be, if all they know is a stair?* Nat's jenny in particular proved to be a sprightly yearling, whickering now and then and seemed to prefer when Nat did not try to correct her line of travel. It felt unnatural, riding in failing light, on an unfamiliar mount, on an ascent that seemed to go on and on.

He did not think that he feared heights, but as they climbed, each revolution bringing them back into the dusklight, the sky painted salmon and speckled with wisps of cloud, the ground fell away, and soon Rowett's Town shrunk to be no larger than a hand's length. *How high does this thing go?* Talking became impossible after a time, the winds picking up to whip at their cloaks and sending the donkey's ears flapping endlessly. It ripped at them from the north, from the dreaded legacy of the ice fortress at Qell.

Higher they went, and higher, and higher some more.

The Scarred Sun, then Norther, Audeyrn and Nat and Greg. Once they spotted an ox cart carrying a shamefaced Hearty, but they were slow-going, and with the height and deepening gloom, it became impossible to pick out one cart from another.

The inexorable mantle of darkness fell. No amount of praying from Nat could stop it. With the sun gone, he soon lost count of the turns they had made. It seemed to climb forever. Did it climb forever? The stairs, not built by man, but by some insane god that hated reason and time, living only to trap those foolish souls that dared try to climb his lofty ziggurat. He tried to laugh such sad notions away. When he tried, the keening wind stole his breath, to leave him brooding in silence. It would not end. It could not end. Higher and higher. *Why is no one speaking? The dark.* Even the drop had vanished, the only reminder that nearly a thousand foot of emptiness lay before them the way the wind skirled cruelly up the rock.

When the gatehouse finally appeared before them, Nat thanked the gods, if they could hear him. The twin towers overhung the solid stone of the Tor, the stair bending sharply to angle directly onto the pair of huge hardiron doors that he thought must have been the largest yet. *Let us in*, he pleaded.

Scarred Sun dismounted. She led her donkey to a row of metal loops hammered into the bare rock that anchored one tower. Giving the beast the gentlest pat on the head, she stormed towards the doors, and hammered on them with a fist to make the pugilists of Low Castan wince. The *thwang thwang thwang* cut through the wind, but only for a moment, until the sound died away, giving them over

147

to the ululating gale once more. When the doors opened, it seemed as though some hell had come. Gleams of fire spilt from inside the keep. Servants came too, taking the donkeys in hand and leading them all into the fire.

With a great *clang* the doors closed. The antecastle smelled of smoke and donkey shit, but at least it was warm. Scarred Sun ordered food and liquor be brought, and very soon, they were all warming by the great fireplace covered in urca pelts and lapping up the last of their thick potato and leek broth. *Not bad for hell.* It was only after he was done and he was well into his mug of mulled wine did he notice Audeyrn was talking intently to Norther.

"Welcome to the Barbican," Scarred Sun announced with pride.

Norther used his spoon to point at the doors at the far end of the gatehouse. "No doubt it has a formidable history. We would see the Lord." The scarred captain only nodded, and bid him and the emissary follow her. Depositing their weapons, they vanished to meet the lord of the castle.

They had a second helping from the kitchens after that. And a second helping from the wine cellar. Hearty must have smelled the liquor, for he arrived just as they rolled out a keg of red beer. Soon he had forgotten all about his shameful ride.

Nat found his eyes going to the house guards manning the inner doors. A pile of shawls had been hastily shoved aside on the table beside Aud's longsword and Norther's silverhilted hand-and-a-half. Cloaks, or at least, Nat thought they were cloaks. The kind worn on the arid prairies of Warretum to ward off the merciless southern sun.

A corner had been pulled by the weight of the blades atop. Something bright shone in the hearthlight. He saw it now. The third blade. It wasn't Warretumi.

Gods save us.

It was Soran.

12

AUDEYRN

amn this war...Damn Walt...Damn Symon and his fat arse.
Damn them all.
They were escorted into the castle proper along a series of boardwalks and moats, creatively named the Stonehall-on-the-Tor, or more commonly just the Stonehall. Audeyrn quicked a glance to the Spitfire beside him, the usual knowing smile riding the adventurer's lips. If he had any sense, he would be wary. Lord Elmer had been shamed by the Castanni, the dishonour brought to the Rowetts would be raw and bloody. The last thing he needed now would be Norther the gab rubbing salt into the wound. Desperation made him say, "What do you know of Lord Elmer?"

"Oh, he's a merry fellow!" The emissary gave him a long look for that, so in return, Norther produced a small piece of silver, flicking it curtly at Audeyrn. He all but caught it, bouncing from clasped hands to his chest. He maintained composure enough to keep it from falling. The adventurer snorted. It was not a coin in truth. It was too large, and concave besides. It was the trinket that he had shown the captain. On the depressed side, a relief bearing the image of two figures holding hands, the details rubbed smooth from handling. What remained were a pair of silhouettes in a silver world. He gestured to the scarred captain of the guard walking briskly before them. "One of two?"

Norther clicked his tongue, "Nothing gets past you. I can see why they made *you* emissary."

"So what is it?"

"Something old," a look of solemnity passed his dark face, and for a moment Audeyrn almost believed it. "Something true."

"What the fuck does that mean?" Why did he think that all of this was some sort of a game? "Speak plainly, damn you."

"The occasion warrants the explanation. Trust must be earned."

Audeyrn felt his jaw tighten. *That's rich.* He couldn't shake the feeling that he knew his face. "Who are you really?"

When Norther smiled, his teeth shone.

The emissary tried to think what his father would do if he were still the emissary, and not dead and buried in the crypt at Langholm. He would probably know how to deal with the Spitfire, for one. And the Rowetts...

They came on the hall too soon, his thoughts still a jumble. He would have appreciated an hour of sleep before meeting the lord, the day's ride had been wearing and the winds that battered them as they climbed had chilled him. *A bed. Some wine. Maybe even a girl...* but he knew that wishes were never granted. His dream at the camp had left him troubled. He didn't know the girl in the desert, even if he felt he ought to. It gnawed at him.

It was poison. Like the wightbloom, the flower that grew in the High Forks and the hinterlands north of Castan. It was an alluring thing, delightful, bright and pleasing to sight. The wightbloom is beautiful, and deadly. To smell the plant will cause a man to vomit and convulse with needles in his gut. If you were to eat it, death is a surety. Even peering at the pale elongated petals too long causes the head to throb unbearably. Scholars debate about why. Audeyrn only knew it had something to do with adaptation. *Life and love, then, are flowers that kill.* He did not let Norther see his tears.

The Grey Court opened before them to the clangour of hardiron. Warm light suffused the room, the circular drum of the hall of the Rowetts, a round room within an even larger circular fortress. There were no windows here. Even day could not penetrate walls twenty feet deep. *Deeds done in darkness are oft whispered*, Hector liked to say.

A fire burned high in the centre of the hall, the smoke rising until it was lost to the shadow of the rafters. A few men stood around the fire, talking in voices contorted by the shape of this fabled hall. *Sorans.* Their garb made them stand out, even if they tried to hide their talking. *They came before us.*

Others loitered in loose groups, wearing the red and white and blue and talking in the drawling accents of the hills. Cousins, guessed Audeyrn. The Rowetts were an old and fertile family, and many of the hulking men and women looked alike to some degree. They all bore the same hard eyes, for one.

Standing sentinel in gloomy alcoves bordering the walls, the decaying marble remains of the gods looked on with blind eyes, the only indication of who they represented the crude glyphs that marked their plinths. He noticed an elderly woman before one such likeness, her bone-white hair done in the Paydar style and leaning heavily on a stick.

A dais was raised near the opposing wall, steps of solid slate rising six foot above the carpeted floor to the throne. The Throne of Northmarch, cresting the rise, in all its glory. Black granite it was, black and veined with pearly lightning, all hard square edges and high-backed, and incised with the old runes of warding that the Kings of the Tor thought would keep the sword-sorcerors of Qell at bay. Not that it helped. The Qellish Empire had beat them into submission and scorned their magicks. After that, the Rowetts were reduced to mere feudal lords, yet were still permitted to sit the seat of the Northmarch Kings. That was a thousand years ago, and the throne had outlasted the power of Qell, the fury of Zahyr the Aeromancer, the Thaumaturge Cataclysm, the Rowetts had outlasted them all. A people forged in war, that dwelt in a land watered by the blood of a thousand thousand battles.

Audeyrn made himself look at the man seated on the throne, anxious that his firelit eyes regarded him coolly. Instinct made his hand go to his hip, only to be reminded that his sword was not there.

The lord had eyes only for them. Motionless, he watched as the emissary and Norther were escorted around the fire towards the dais. Those huddled close to the flames exchanged glances at one another.

Lord Elmer was forty, and then some. A large man, with

bull shoulders and thick arms. His chest, too, was heavily muscled, his stomach and waist slim. Woolly hair the colour of mud and iron fell about his head in elaborate braids, bound with gold and silver and bronze rings. They were incised with runes too. Around a thin-lipped mouth, he had cultivated a closely-trimmed beard, which only seemed to accentuate a nose like a hook. He wore a tabard bedecked in red and white and blue, striped on the chest and swirling on the sleeves. A ruby the size of a babe's fist swung from a chain of white gold snake-links around his large neck.

A herald announced, "You have the honour of audience to the Lord Elmer of the most celebrated house of Rowett, Prince-Triumphal of Stonehall-on-the-Tor, master of Rowett's Town, and overlord of the Paydar. My lord, I present Audeyrn, son of Coram, the Royal Emissary of Isembard, King of Castan. I also present the adventurer–"

"Norther." Lord Elmer boomed, his voice sonorous despite the thick Paydar accent. He stood, outstretching his arms in a sign of friendship. Norther inclined his head, and made to climb the steps.

"No. You shall stay." A wrinkling, wicked smile swept across the lord's mouth, exposing teeth with runes of their own. Lord Elmer sat on the highest step, making an overexaggerated sigh as he leant on a knee. Audeyrn chanced a glance at Norther. *Is that surprise or fear I see? Or both?*

The lord looked to the scarred captain of the guard, "Cousin Sere, that will be all." The woman saluted and like that was gone, her long legs carrying her out. Hardiron opened and closed, and the lord seemed to wait until the noise fell to regard the Spitfire. "Ah, Norther. These must be glad tidings indeed if *you* return to our loving embrace. Who sent you to treat with me? Forgive me, but you Castanni change battle commanders so often these days I scarcely find the time to learn their names." Laughter erupted from the Rowetts in the Grey Court. Their lord stroked his beard mockingly. "Mylton? No, no. Dreygart? I think not. Am I close, Norther? I must be close to the mark!"

"Sir Walton Iddles is the commander of the combined Castanni army, my lord." There was the slightest edge in the adventurer's voice. Again, Audeyrn's hand went to his hip.

"*Iddles*? What peculiar names the Castanni have. I did not linger long enough to acquaint myself with your quaint argot, I fear. The sight of dying whales has always soured my stomach, so I was not loath to return home. Tell me, what could you say to sway my heart? I've heard you sing *many* a redolent tale in this very hall. Ballads of adventure and daring, saving the sweet from high towers and vanquishing the evil ne'er-do-wells… Why so silent now? I'm *sure* the aplomb Norther of the North can make me pledge my good men and women to your war again. If you have the words for it. You do lovely things with that wagging tongue of yours. No? Very well, perhaps…" Lord Elmer shifted his gaze to Audeyrn. *Ready yourself,* came the voice inside. *He is trying to provoke you.* He made himself match the lord's gaze. He saw the crow's feet at the corners, the restive twitching of the left, the rust-coloured sclera from *nhere*. The emissary had his back to the fire, so his eyes would not burn as bright, but he needed to do *something*.

Lord Elmer only glowered the harder. For a moment

malice charred lustily in his blood-shot eyes, then temerity, and then a flicker of something more furtive and hidden. *Speak,* Audeyrn screamed inside. *The mission comes first. Do it. Say it!*

The sound of metal striking stone cut through his thoughts. "Enough, enough. This gets us no place, Elmer. No place at all." The voice came from a shrunken thing beside Audeyrn. A ghost in skin. She must have been ninety, the firelight made a shining of her scalp through silky thin hair, and shadowed every wrinkle until they became canyons. She hobbled up the steps, her hardiron cane slamming down on the slate. "*Hphfff,*" she grunted indignantly. She turned to Audeyrn. "You, Castanni. Help an old woman, will you. Yes, you. Are there any other Castanni here? I see Norther, that I do. I am not blind. I will not have that sordid *braggart* touching me. That I will not! Come, help me now!" She was lighter than he would have guessed. The Grey Court fell into a weighted silence as he aided the beldame, each blow of her cane seeming to reverberate around the drum of the hall until it resounded a dirge.

She was the woman he had seen by the statue, he realised. She was short, not even reaching four and a half foot, made shorter by her bent-back. Her limbs were spindly, all bone and veins and liver spots, and when she moved, her joints creaked like hinges more rust than metal. Yet arm in arm, Audeyrn could feel the quiet strength in the aged woman. The comfortable authority she enjoyed over her kin.

"Ah. Gentle hands. Sorely lacking in the Paydar. Only hard hands and harder hearts. Ha! That's the way of it. Now shove off. Back to your friend, that's it. I have to take my chair." Lord Elmer had not shifted from the step. Now he looked up from steepled hands. "You err, mother. The seat of the Northmarch is mine."

She plopped her diminutive frame on the throne regardless. "It was mine before you crawled out from between my legs. It shall remain mine until you give me to the crows. Now, Elmer dear, we must end this farce."

Lord Elmer did as he was bid, his fists clenched hard as he scoffed. As Audeyrn replaced himself next to Norther, he heard him whisper, *"I did not see the Lady Cyrinne. This changes things, Aud. Make sure–"*

"The hour is late, and this chair makes the arse ache most abominably," Lady Cyrinne Rowett announced to all, her voice commanding and shrill. "This meeting will be brief. We receive the honoured dignitaries from Castan. May they have... I forget the rest. Forgive me for misremembering the formalities, for I am very old. Now. My son had the meat of it. However, he has always toyed with his food, so he neglected to mention that we had a prior offer."

The lord laughed, "You hurt me, mother. My jesting is nothing to what the Castanni have inflicted upon our honour." The old woman slammed her cane thrice. "That they have."

"My lady, you mentioned a prior offer?" Norther glanced to the men about the fire, his face flushed. "You can't mean–" He was silenced by a shrivelled hand. Her moist mouth made a throaty chuckle, and Audeyrn thought he saw something of her son flash in her dim eyes. "I meant what I meant. We sample the banquet, to ascertain the good meats."

"The right choice my lady, to be true." The liquid tones of

Sora drifted through the Grey Court. They emerged from the fire like the phoenix of legend. *A pity these won't turn to ashes.* The speaker was a tall, rangy man in bright salmon-coloured robes, here and revealing the brightly polished Soran scale armour beneath. His olive skin glowed ruddy in the firelight, his amber eyes hooded. Long hair lustered in a tight knot behind his head.

Audeyrn noticed the clasp that secured his robes at the shoulder. A rearing yale done in mother-of-pearl, the tusks and horns and hooves glittering gold. "Lyonis of Ves."

"Captain-General Lyonis of Ves, if you please. I've found that titles are important in this part of the world." The Soran sauntered to the foot of the dais, bowing with a flourish of his satin cape. Norther crept closer to Audeyrn, whispering, *"What did Coram tell you of Lyonis?"*

"Enough." The man was a born leader, and the very soul of guile if the rumours were true. His father certainly had reason to believe them. Eight years prior, old Coram had been sent to mediate the Steppes Crisis, where Silentis had claimed sovereignty over land controlled by the confederation of the Ikteti. The talks were to take place in the city-state of Seaton, a maritime kingdom perched on the Ruell Sea. The deliberations had been a disaster. On the first day, a guardsman in Soran finery was found murdered, his throat cut, with a Ikteti dagger through his heart. The chief of the Ikteti claimed to know nothing of what happened. Lyonis had announced that the murder was a declaration of war. Coram had returned to Castan defeated, the Ikteti Alliance crumbling as each tribe accused the other of instigating the killing. All the while, the Sorans annexed the Steppes of Iktet entirely. *Subtle,* that was what

Coram had to say. *Subtle, and dangerous. A snake lying in the grass, fangs dripping with venom.*

"My Lady Cyrinne and Lord Elmer," the Soran began, "What the Kingdom of Sora can give you is far more than paltry *words*. May I be so bold as to enquire, what did Isembard of Castan offer for your alliance?"

"One hundred thousand Castanni reals," Lord Elmer said, his voice raised for all to hear. "Along with the spoils of war and choice lands of the Desolate Tundra." A wave of outrage met that, those in the hall raising angry fists and slamming their chests to Qellish curses.

Lyonis of Ves nodded gravely. "The Desolate Tundra harbours little resources, I will admit. Even we Sorans bear a healthy distaste for the foul wasteland on our doorstep. Nothing lives there, nothing survives. An empty reward, if I may say so. It appears that the Castanni believe the Rowetts worthy of nought but a hundred thousand reals. How very complaisant."

"It was not the gold that bought us," professed Lord Elmer, spatting. "Affable words and the occasion for martial glory made our blood hot. Our friend Norther managed to stir me and the cousins present into a battle frenzy not seen since the Roc King invaded over a hundred years ago. How surprised we were then that we would be commanded by birdbrains and fat men. No, we bent backs to the Qell once, for they harnessed the magicks of the realms. We shall not follow weaklings. The Rowetts follow strength."

When his mother bobbed her head in agreement, the skin folds beneath her chin wobbled. "My noble son speaks true. The Qell were gods upon earth. You follow a man. A man with a bit of metal on his brow, yes, but a man all the same.

And what we hear of Isembard we like not." Lyonis of Ves stroked his chin. "For he is a tyrant, my lady of the Tor, and these men follow the will of that tyrant like lapping dogs stroking their master's cock."

Some took that as a jest, others as an accusation. The result was a harsh clamour of disdain and mocking laughter, filling the ancient hall of the Rowetts with raucous noise that seemed to shake the very foundations of Stonehall. Even Lady Cyrinne gave a strident cackle, her son showing his runed teeth. The emissary fumed. *Damn the Rowetts and their braying. The Qell were fools to let them live... The mission comes first.* He clenched his fists, hard enough to feel himself draw blood. *Let them laugh. Let them talk. Let them... wait...* It came to him.

He was surrounded by the derision of men who loved him not as he placed a booted foot on the first step of the dais. The reaction was what he expected. The Lady Cyrinne held up her hands for silence. It was not needed. The tumult had already ebbed until only the few too slow to comprehend what was happening remained laughing. *Talk.* Lord Elmer guffawed, calling for a cup of wine. Norther pulled up, as close as he dared. "What are you *doing?*"

"My duty. Now shut your mouth." The emissary did not deign to wait for a response, but bowed his head in reverence. A few errant mutterings stirred behind him, but the Grey Court was otherwise quiet but for the fire. After a moment, he raised his head, looking the old woman in the eye and keeping his posture. Her face was guarded. "My lady. My lord. Noble men and women," he bowed to the Soran, "esteemed Captain-General." He removed his foot from the step, careful to make no sudden movements.

160

"What can I say to mend the rift between the Paydar and Castan? Lord Elmer, I was not present when you discovered the treasure trove in the hills. Nor was I there when a whale arrived to take up command." A few chuckled at that. *Good. Now let's see...*

"I say this not to unburden myself of guilt, but to show you that we of Castan are not all Gergy Mansells or Symon Stepps. You say that you departed soon after Sir Symon came to camp. Have you perchance met Sir Walton?"

Lord Elmer gave a curt nod, "Iddles, you mean? The leader of the outriders? No. I know the man by reputation, I cannot say we have ever met. What of it?"

"Then you would know that he is a warrior to the bone, my lord." the lord grumbled at that. His mother was not so persuasive.

"So you would bandy words for this new lackey of Isembard? You disappoint. What would you *offer* us, eh? Tracts of sand and scorpions last time. What now, strips of water in the Ruell?"

"No. I regret we broke your trust, my lady." *Do it now, damn you.* "Words cannot deliver restitution for that. Words are easy, after all. We can try to–"

"No, no," when she waved her hand, it was a harpy claw, "You say words are of no use, yet still you jabber on and on... what can you do, eh? What could you do to show us Rowetts that Castan deserves our respect, and alliance?"

The Soran gave a laugh, "My lady, they have no such argument for that. For they–" He did not have a chance to finish. "You had your chance Soran. You will be quiet, or you will feed the winds. I would hear the Castanni now."

Audeyrn did not know. He struggled for words. The very

effort made his throat feel strangled and seized. They all expected something from him, he knew. Something they would not expect. When he heard the sound, it was too faint to hear. He turned, seeing Norther mouth something. What did he say? Again. There. A word. A word, and the beginnings of a plan. Audeyrn prayed to gods far away that he had it right.

Sword.

It was like the phantom fingers loosed their grip on him, for he said, "I wish to prove to the Rowetts that we are not what you think of us. I shall prove that are blades are true." *They follow strength.* "Where words fail, perhaps the song of steel will prove my kingdom worthy of your alliance. I challenge the Captain-General to a test of arms."

The hall erupted to roars, the Rowetts stamping their feet in approval and hooting with atavistic anticipation. Audeyrn felt giddy. He reeled unsteady until Norther grabbed him by the arm. "Easy, *easy.* I was hoping you would choose me to fight for you, but what's written is written. The gods know why you did that." His laugh was rueful. "This will help us regardless. I can find my true contact now that the Rowetts are forestalled. Nothing gets them harder than the smell of blood."

"You could have told me this before now." Audeyrn noticed Lady Cyrinne beckon the herald forward, the words drowned in the sea of Paydar howling.

Norther scratched his stubble, grinning secretly. "All in time. By the by, how good are you with a sword?"

"I'm no Silver Knight, but I can hold my own."

"Good enough to kill him?"

"*Silence!*" boomed Lord Elmer. His voice was a thunderclap in a squalling seastorm. "We are not done." The smile he sent Audeyrn's way was all for him, and it was all malice. The Lady Cyrinne stood, slamming her hardiron cane thrice. "A challenge will be a most pleasing display, emissary. Do you accept, Soran?"

Captain-General Lyonis of Ves, commander of the Sorans, merely nodded his assent. From his belt he pulled a supple leather glove, which he threw at Audeyrn's foot. "The gods shall decide, then."

The matriarch of the Rowetts slammed down her cane upon the dais once again. "On the morrow, we shall see who desires our friendship more. Midday. The Pit shall be opened, ready for the contest!" Chants of assent eddied around the hall. The mood was high, except for Audeyrn. *Have I just killed myself?* He chewed on that, glad he wouldn't have to face it until the new day. Then came the words he dreaded.

"Emissary, your company numbers five, yes?" *Dear gods no.* Words failed him entirely. The nod he gave was strained and weighty.

"Good. It appears the Soran also has that number." Norther cursed, and Audeyrn did something much worse. He did nothing.

13

MARBLE

S he smirked at her reflection. It wasn't often she indulged in admiring her body, dressing it as though a gift. The scars littering her taught abdomen left bare with the gown's new design. They told a story of her battles.

Marble felt no remorse for the liberties she had taken with the contents of her silken prison. Gladly taking what she needed, dismantling and tearing apart several undoubtedly precious items. She had managed to fashion a skirt that sat low on her hips and gave the impression that the lightest of movements would dislodge it from its perch. The sleeves were removed, used instead to bind her breasts somewhat; it was always an annoyance when they moved about and bobbed in a fight.

Cleaning up using the washbasin in the corner of the room, Marble also helped herself to a comb, doing her best to wrestle with her hair. She missed her scarf dearly, for if she could cover it, she wouldn't have to expend any effort trying to make it look presentable to realise the distracting appearance she was hoping to achieve. Eventually, she managed to tame it into a long braid that she wrapped around the crown of her head. Hoping the colour would not draw too much notice, at least not enough to draw speculation.

Staring at her reflection, she looked hard at the person staring back at her. The memory came unbidden. The half-remembered face of her father. Sometimes, when she looked at her face, she saw him. Other times, she was sure she imagined the similarities; she had only been small when her mother had taken her. She saw the high cheekbones and strong jaw, the slight tilt of her eyes, the cushioned lips and the button nose, and her heart ached a little.

Clenching her teeth, she steeled herself. The raid on Silentis was likely quashed by now, and no doubt her comrades from the Garrison would be searching for her. It would be her luck if, of all people, Cliada found her here. *The look on her face would be golden.*

Turning swiftly towards the doorway, her skirt flowed freely, and the assortment of beads and trinkets she'd strung together and wrapped haphazardly around her body tinkled lightly. Then, head held high, she opened the latch.

The two goons standing guard were surprisingly alert. They didn't even seem to flinch when the door opened unexpectedly. *Impressive.*

They stood as tall as any hero from the tales, and just as fair. Things were not starting out brilliantly. *Damnit.* While she would have relished distracting the men with their rugged handsomeness, broad shoulders and clever gazes, a cooler head prevailed. *These men would not be swayed by* my *looks.* They only had eyes for each other. Though she wagered her attire would become of use sooner rather than later.

The man on the left was slightly taller than his companion, but not by much. They were both towering beasts. Though no hard feat, given the woman's diminutive stature. Dark skin, and still faces. They looked no more than ten years her senior but were clean-shaven, so Marble could not be sure.

They stood silent and steady, barely moving an inch as shrewd eyes observed Marble. The emissary admired their finely tailored clothing. Well made and close-fitting. The man on the left wore crimson, and the man on the right was garbed in a vivid emerald. Sandal-clad feet, long airy tunics and bell-shaped trousers, a nice light colour. Of course, the henchmen's garb was much more ornate than Marble's unusual plain block colours with no adornment to be seen. The stitching decorating the uniforms before her were some of the most beautiful and intricate patterns Marble had ever seen.

Neither of them made to stop her. Neither did they move for her. She reserved herself to inaction. There would be no retreat. Only holding her ground. She would be the urca, planting itself and facing down the wolves as they eyed their prey.

Then the noise came to break the silence. All three persons stood to attention, their gazes alert for any form of threat that may be approaching. The men relaxed before Marble allowed herself the same luxury. *It's their home, after all. I am the outsider here. The alien.* Obviously, they could recognise the approaching insurgent's gait, but Marble would do well to keep her guard high and mind and body on alert.

The twin smirks adorning the chiselled facades of her guards certainly didn't help. She wouldn't let her nerves show. She had been in more precarious positions than this. Yet, when she tried to recollect them, her mind was blank.

Her body acted when her mind failed. She shifted her body in the doorway. The guards leaned backwards to prop up the wall behind them, simultaneously folding their arms over their powerful chests. Marble mirrored the movement. Turning sideways to prop up the door frame, keeping a seductive angle to her torso. The provocative twist of a hip was subtle, yet enough to make notice. Their smirks grew. She plastered one of her own across her face making it as innocent as possible.

A sharp intake of breath, and all eyes fell on her. She could only imagine what they thought of her. It took her all of a moment, but then she realised the terrified young woman wasn't Cliada. A serving girl, and only that.

Damn fever. The guards, alert and wary, watched curiously as Marble forced herself to relax from the fighting instinct the maid had inspired; she cleared her throat awkwardly.

It appeared the route Marble was destined to take would be stupid recklessness after all. She would not be able to charm herself out of this situation, not after that performance. Again, leaning back against the side of the door frame, this time not in a carefully positioned pose but one born of frustration, lingering fatigue and resignation, Mable tilted her head and banged it on the wall behind her, eliciting a raised eyebrow from Mr Red while a perplexed frown drew together Green's brows.

"Something wrong, miss?" He rumbled surprisingly eloquently. His voice was deep and rumbled like thunder, exactly as Marble surmised it would. She shook her head wordlessly in response but then thought better of remaining silent. She was already a prisoner, after all, and perhaps if she voiced the reason for her peculiar reaction to the maid, the other woman may unfreeze from the stilted and startled way she held herself terrifyingly still at the end of the hallway.

"Thought she was someone else." Marble managed to rasp out through her dry throat. *When did I get so thirsty?* That, more than anything, seemed to stir the maid into forgetting her reservations about approaching the prisoner. The woman who was *not* Cliada bumbled forward efficiently and quickly took charge.

If their positions were reversed, she would not have been so quick to offer her aid. Caution warded her, weary this was some ploy or hoax.

"Come on, miss." The maid's lyrical voice cooed softly into the emissary's ear. "Let's get you sorted."

She gently ushered the waif back into the room to the chair next to a window. "One of you, fetch water," she commanded the guards, and after sharing an intense look, Red disappeared from the doorway, and Green took a step inside the room himself.

Marble's throat, though still sore, was feeling scores better, thanks to the water the maid had procured.

"So." She broke the silence, "What now?" Marble forced herself to assume a relaxed and somewhat carefree posture leaning against the chair's backrest, slouched lackadaisically. The maid looked confused, but the guards both bore calculating expressions. The green guard seemed to be the designated talker for the two, and as he opened his mouth to respond, Marble's empty stomach interrupted whatever he was about to say. An amused glint entered his eye at the gurgling sound.

"You eat." His low rumble of thunder came in response.

At his declaration, the maid turned to leave, assuming she was required to fetch said food, but the guard's next words stopped her. "Come then, miss. I imagine you would like to stretch your legs."

"Grenn!" The maid gasped in shock. "You can't possibly mean for our guest to wander in company without proper attire!" The poor woman looked scandalised. Marble smirked. "I will -"

"Don't trouble yourself, ma'am." Marble interrupted. "I am more than eager for a turnabout. I can't bear to be cooped up longer than I must." While the Green Guard... *Grenn*, she corrected herself, nodded and preceded Marble out of the room, enjoying himself, his companion merely looked concerned as the trio left the spluttering and aghast maid in their wake.

The corridor and stairways were full of twists and turns, designed to confuse. The one called Grenn seemed to make it his mission to disorient her by doubling back and taking a pointlessly circuitous route. He almost succeeded before she caught the scent. Tantalising, it immediately aromas made her mouth fill with saliva. Her stomach clenched at the promise of a hearty fare.

She knew she would have to restrain herself. Yet she was *starving*. Even now, she fought against her desire to sprint toward her bounty. The raucous calamity of sound that betrayed the kitchens just ahead, muted somewhat by the doorway, reached her ears.

There were plentiful muffled conversations, laughter, and the wonderful sounds of pots banging around and food bubbling and sizzling away on stoves. Marble, distracted by her stomach's fantasies, took a moment to realise Grenn had walked past the kitchens and continued down the corridor. She looked back dismayed at the heavenly gateway she was forced to bypass, and the Red Guard's eyes crinkled at her forlorn expression. "Don't worry. You'll be feasting soon." He chuckled, encouraging Marble along. She dragged her feet down the pathway petulantly, not caring she was a prisoner in enemy territory any more. She wanted food. Her pitiful display of protest was brought to an abrupt halt when she entered a dining area behind Grenn's large back. The room was packed full of people. Hardened men and women all turned curiously towards the new arrivals.

Oh, Marble thought privately. *This is going to be fun.*

14

GREGYN

The Sorans were waiting for him, he knew. Sharpening their blades for the blood of the Castanni. In his mind, they all wore the same snarling face, the same oiled beards, the same teeth filed into points. He tried to pull his perturbing thoughts from the dunnies. He focused on the sights and sounds of the Paydar.

The town he had liked, despite the bellicose Paydarians that swaggered through the streets and eyed any ignorant into putting up their steel. It had been a wonder, with its gaudy banners and pennants flying from every rooftop and gable, crossbeam and trave, parapet and turret, lintel and crenel. And above all, the monolithic Tor overtopping every building, an upthrust fist of rock lost to the skies, the greatest banner of any lord in any land on the continent. Rowett's Town sat on the roots of that mighty promontory, filling Greg with a perverse fascination. At first. Even the lowliest squatting stone hovels had shown some ragged scrap of red white and blue to blow listlessly in the gentle

171

summer breeze. They all seemed paltry when compared to that colossal bluff.

What happens if they don't fly a banner? he had mused vacantly. From what the others had told him and from what he had heard so far, he would rather not know.

That fascination had turned to fear quickly enough. These Paydar did not love the Castanni. The tracker had not lived a gentle, coddled life up in the High Forks, for comfort was a luxury enjoyed only by lordly in High Castan. He could tell these Paydar were different. They sought out pain. They basked in war and revelled in the glory.

The bruises of his past had faded over time until nothing remained. The hurts inside were different. The lessons from his father and those continued by Huhtal the Forester had allowed him to find some measure of solace for a boy from Dun Vale. It had served him well. That was, until he was caught.

He had known fear. Fear was what kept a poacher alive. It was not always evil. The night they found him in the Mornswood with a brace of halcyon slung over his shoulder, he had felt fear then. Alone and deserted by Huhtal, he was taken. His skills useless against the probing words and cruel tools of the Reeve Arran in the dungeons of Mornfort. He could not think of that now. Not while death was so close.

"You're not going to die," Nat assured him, and not for the first time. The fox stuck another spoonful of buttered duck in his mouth, without waiting to swallow saying, "The dunnies are craven. It's well known. They fight with bolos, the edges poisoned with scorpion venom and hemlock and gods-know-what filth."

"For a man that fights with a *knife*, you're quick to accuse someone of being craven." Hearty belched through his second helping of peppered swan, attacking the huge platter as though he were a man starved. He swilled it all down with his fifth mug of Paydar blackwine, that drink the Rowetts brewed atop the Tor, the making of which was a secret to all but the brewmasters, and the Lord Rowett himself. Just thinking of the man sent an icy finger down his spine. He shivered despite the stifling heat of the Hall of the Masons.

Their lodging was well furnished and roomy, the Hall itself fit to sit four hundred comfortably on the wide trestles and benches. Large iron candles lined the slightly curving walls from bases shaped like titan's heads gaping wide in agony. The hearths had been lit, the meals prepared, and the wine flowing, yet only the Royal Emissary and his company were present. Audeyrn had said Lord Rowett decreed that it was only fitting for the Sorans to have separate lodgings, for, in his words, "Should a melee happen before tomorrow, there would be no audience to witness it." For Greg, that was all he needed to know about these Rowetts. Putting aside the thoughts of the Paydar lord and his implacable mother wasn't easy, so he tried to eat some more of the duck. His stomach roiled at the cloying sweetness.

He wondered if the Sorans were as afraid as he was for tomorrow. If there was a tracker with their party too, someone who didn't want to hurt anybody. He knew it was foolish to think such a thing, so he kept it to himself. As for the Sorans, they had been put in the hall on the far side of Stonehall, within the Hall of the Smiths. In his mind, it was identical to the Mason's Hall, but he had no way of knowing.

"Why defend the honour of the dunnies, Hearty?" Nat

pointed his spoon, a lump of greasy meat sticking out all but threateningly. It earned him a look of adamant loathing from the ageing knight. "Defend? Pray never say that again, Natoly. The Sorans are my enemies, do not mistake it. I only ask for an honourable fight of them. More than they gave Noyon anyway. Poor bastard. After the Battle of Kande's Mire they took him and a hundred others. He must have gave them some insult, for they tied him strappado high up in a silver birch so the wolves wouldn't get him. We found him, that we did, but a month had come and gone, and there was hardly anything left. Still had his surcoat, though. The sand devils let him keep that. Probably so we would recognise the body."

"Evil bastards." Nat spitting a mouth of gristle to the flags. "*Savages*, to treat a knight so. Not surprising really, for those that lie with sand-dogs and boas. My kje itches to gorge itself on dunny blood."

Hearty thumped a meaty fist on the table, sending platters and mugs to jump. "I'll kill them on the morrow, that I will. See that I don't. Noyon deserved better! A good man, treated like a common brigand!"

Audeyrn had been silent until now, and Greg saw something move across his face like he was in pain. When he talked, it was low and deep, as though he was only half awake. "Focus on the tomorrow. I know that you all have reason to hate the Sorans. I do not doubt that. But we cannot change the yesterdays. The tomorrow, however, that is untravelled, virgin, unknown." Greg saw that Nat and Hearty still held themselves tense from bloodlust, yet they listened all the same.

"These Sorans will taunt you, beguile you, dig under your

skin until all the defences are broken, and then they'll kill you… Unless you keep yourself from falling into their ploys. These are no mere Soran levies looking for plunder and an easy raping. These are the Headhunters. Trained from birth in some guild or another, from what I've heard. Each specialised in the art of killing. Educated. Single-minded. Strategic. The moment they see that they have picked at some old war wound or opened you up to derision, they will strike. I say this not to scare you," the tracker could not help but see Audeyrn's piercing eyes fall on him then. He did not know whether to feel proud or shamed. "But to make you all aware of the true dangers these Soran Headhunters present."

You're not going to die, Nat had told him. How could he ever stand a chance against these stalwart warriors, these *Headhunters?* He felt his supper rise in his throat. He suddenly didn't feel hungry. Oddly, he heard himself say, "What 'bout the leader? This… Lonnis of Vez?"

He could not read the emissary's face. Looking to Nat and Hearty, he saw that they too had lost their appetite. "*Lyonis,*" corrected Audeyrn. "He's mine."

The tracker slept little, knowing what was to come. Sounds of lovemaking drifted down the hallway outside. He had been given his own bed in a chamber of his own, but he would have traded all the plush furnishings and featherbeds for a room together with his friends. It was probably his last night; he didn't want to spend it alone.

When someone knocked at his door, he ignored it. He thought of home.

Sleep took him eventually, the sun ripping him coldly from formless dreams. The light slanted through the oblong window of his chamber to bathe him in warmth. It felt tepid upon his skin. The fires in the Hall of Masons had been allowed to die during the night, and a draft filled the air. The bench made his arse cold, and he suddenly missed the muggy smoky heat of the night before.

They talked sparingly, breaking their fast on eggs and porritch with honeycombs, while comely serving girls came and went with the morning's beer. Greg did not think they looked Paydar, but then again his mind was not on them. Nat was in his oils though, looking at one tall willowy girl with straight flaxen hair in particular, who seemed to enjoy his sideways glances and wandering hands.

So that was the noise last night.

Audeyrn led the conversation, what little there was. He talked to them all in turn, joking and making plans and remembering things they had forgotten. He was trying, Greg could tell. *He's afraid too.* Of Norther, there was no sign. He had risen before all of them if the chamberlain of the Hall was to be believed, and had business at the gate. That was strange to Greg, but then again, Norther was a strange man.

Hearty had eyes only for the broadsword laying across his knees like a loyal hound. *A blood hound.* The big man gave only non-committed responses between licks of whetstone upon blade, or just nodded. The strokes became rhythmic, softly rasping in the funereal hall. The tracker thought the movements gentle for a man his size, tender and thoughtful. It was out of place, in his mind, that something so pleasant and genial should precede a battle. Even the weather outside befuddled him. Why should it be so fine when men are destined to die? In the stories, the day of

176

war was always squalling, the winds howling in their grief and the heavens weeping for the fallen heroes. Why were the stories so untrue, if men must face the real with hard hearts? He only hoped the sun wouldn't shine on their confrontation with the Sorans.

It didn't.

At the tenth bell, the chamberlain appeared, letting them know that they were summoned to the Pit. They were led out of the Hall, along a walkway into a sheltered garden blooming with hightubers and golden aubades, arbours running with creeping vines where the flowers bloomed bone-white and spotted with red. Their escort was two burly Paydar in the livery of the household guard, who only spoke Qellish. They led them into a small keep in an old part of Stonehall, where hardiron doors opened to reveal a stair. Down and down and down it went. So they descended into the Tor.

The guards held torches and offered none to their Caldish guests. The steps changed direction for a time, then seemed to circle, underfoot the steps changing to bare stone worn smooth by rogue streams of water. Whichever direction it went, it always went *down*. So they trod on, encumbered by their weapons and watching their footing by the flickering of two torches. It was not long before they reached the bottom. Or whatever end this tunnel seemed to have.

The walls ran with saltpetre. Here and there, an iron sconce set into the stuff to send light to flicker across the frozen streams and made them almost seem liquid. It was round with a low ceiling, the cave floor covered in a fine sand that scraped at his boots. It could not have reached twenty foot from one end to the other. They were beneath the Stonehall, yet he wagered they were still a goodly height above Rowett's Town. He stood there with his bow slung by his quiver, a dozen arrows with their yellow halcyon fletchings within. He looked down at the dirk in his belt, as though it would disappear if he did not keep his eye on it. *I should've practiced more. Bow I can shoot blind, but the dirk...* Then he shot a glance at the fletchings and remembered he was caught for poaching halcyon. He made a sign of protection against the omen. He didn't think it would help. He could not let himself show how afraid he was. Isn't that what Aud said? Across the chamber the Sorans stood tall and dark, the shadows playing against the folds of their cloaks.

When Greg looked at the emissary, he may as well have been made of marble. The shadows under his eyes seemed sunken, his hand planted on the hilt of his fine sword, and his eyes fixed on the slim Soran leader, who was talking lightly with his men. And women. Greg saw that two of his four companions were female, no older than Nat, despite their slight frames moving with all the sure deadly grace of vipers. One of them caught him staring, the one with long legs clad in tight-fitting mail and with almond-shaped eyes that left him flustered. She turned to the other women, buxom and shapely, and whispered something to make her laugh. Greg failed to stop the blood rushing to his cheeks, and realised his hands were soaked with sweat. He could not have been more relieved as Lyonis of Ves said, "How long must we wait for the rooster, I ask again?"

The tracker realised that he was asking one of the guards, who said something in Qellish. The reply seemed to satisfy the Soran, readjusting the knot behind his head. "To think that Norther would turn out to be craven. The surprise has shaken me, sir." His amber eyes darted to Audeyrn.

"I am not a knight." The emissary's voice was flat and even, but even so, Greg did not like the face the Soran made.

"More's the pity, then."

From the entrance to the stair came a flash of white. *No, silver.* A Paydar nobleman came sauntering into the stone chamber, descending the last solemn stone steps to leap into the cave, prancing around the Caldishmen and Sorans alike and bellowing laughter. Greg heard Hearty mutter, "…and who's this fool now?"

The fool was dressed in a tooled brockade that, until the other Paydar, was cloth-of-silver, shimmering in the wasting light of the room. His hair too was not in the Paydar style, but instead cut to a razor's breadth on top, his crown hidden by a floppy wide-brimmed silver bonnet with a peacock feather rakishly placed on one side. His chestnut-coloured beard was split into three prongs and tied together by silver wire. When the man finally stopped pirouetting and tumbling, he stood between the two parties, hands on his hips and wearing the widest grin Greg had ever seen. He even saw a silvery glint from one tooth. "You have the honour of meeting Hollis Rowett, nephew and ward and blood-ward to Lord Rowett. I am a warrior, bard, *lover…*" He sent a lecherous glance to the female Headhunters, who only looked at him disdainfully. "I have been given many epithets by my loving and cherished uncle: Bastard-born, Hollis the Rollick, Forkbeard, Alebuckets, Moon-Lover, Hollis Howl, Thunderbum. But the one I prefer is Silvertongue. So I am Hollis Silvertongue, if you please. Yet the honour of meeting such prodigious guests is mine. The warriors of Castan, fighting the warriors of Silentis... I quake at the very notion! And very soon, you shall meet your onlookers. You shall fight for the allegiance of the Paydar, and Stonehall." His voice had a lilt, or so Greg thought. It was the sort of voice used by singers in royal courts and gutter taverns alike. The ones that always had their eyes down the bodices of serving women. For an instant, it seemed he would break into song. "Soon, the gallery shall be replete, and the contest shall begin." He finished with a flourish.

Nat snorted, "Where has this one been hiding?"

One of the Headhunters, the one with the wicked halberd in gnarled hands, grunted. "Gallery? Ain't no gallery here, fool." Lyonis quietened him with a hand. "Lomas speaks true. This is no fit arena for a contest of arms, and with an audience set to arrive? No. This... *Pit* is a poor field, my lord of Rowett."

Hollis Silvertongue scuffed his grey calfskin on the loose rubble littering the floor, appearing to notice the cave for the first time. With a sharp intake of breath, he exclaimed, "I do believe you are right, revered Captain-General. How dreadful! How could such an error have occurred, and under my watch too?!"

Audeyrn stepped forward, "When will our fifth arrive, Silvertongue?" The way Silvertongue glanced about as though he was as nonplussed as them was frightening to Greg. Under the heavy silvered fabrics, he could faintly make out arms heavy with muscle, and his eyes hid nothing of the malice that shone through.

"This ain't the Pit." Greg heard a voice say. It took him a few moments to realise that it was his own. Silvertongue looked his way, slapping his knee with a bejewelled hand, saying, "Oho! The Castanni has a sage among them! But will it save them against cold Soran steel? Let us see." The rompful Rowett grabbed a nearby torch from an obeisant guard. He capered over to a shadowed length of wall. With a satisfied *Ha!* he thrust the torch into the wall, revealing a hollow not unlike a garderobe. He let it fall, and the torch vanished, plunging him into dim-light and turning his brilliant silvers into sombre greys.

"Welcome to the Readying Room, my friends of Castan and Silentis." Said the living shadow, his silks ruffling softly in the gloom. For a heavy second, Greg could only hear his heavy breathing, the realisation hitting him square in the chest. *The signal.* The Sorans seemed to realise this too.

"This chicanery is ill-fitting for one of your station, Rowett," The iron tone of Lyonis echoed through the Room. The laugh that exuded from the dark was mocking. "The toad calls the frog warty."

Then the world filled with thunder. The walls and floor shook with a grinding scream, sending the sand on the cave floor up in great gouts as the whole cave became the inside of a drum. Greg clenched his jaw hard, trying to stop his teeth from chattering. He felt one crack under the pressure. He could not remember jumping, but one moment he was trying to keep his footing, and then the next, he was nearly a foot above the sands, crashing down as light swamped the cave from between the walls and floor.

The floor of the Readying Room lowered slowly, the chains holding it aloft stretched taut and a sullen red from age. Four there were, each fastened to the stage by a loop of hardiron the size of an aurochs. Each link of the chain was just as large, the grinding of the mechanism high above deafening all looking about in bewilderment, as they sunk down into a gargantuan arena carved from the very rock. "Behold!" Silvertongue was silver again, the light of a thousand oil braziers dying the silks a brilliant orange-white. He had one hand upon his hip, the other thrown out over the side as the titan frowned down upon them. "The Pit! The grand arena of the Northmarch Kingdom!"

Argere did not seem pleased to see them. His out-stretched arm was melded to the ceiling of the colossal cavern, revealing that the Room had been *inside his hand*. Greg had no words. He could only look on. The stone man was naked, his only covering a newly woven shoulder cape the colours of the Rowetts. It failed to hide his manhood. Greg decided to look up instead. His physique was carved cunningly to resemble tight muscles, corded and packed along with chest and limbs like the roots of a great stone tree. He looked so lifelike. *No, it's just stone. See the eyes, fool.* From empty eye sockets the light of day shone through, giving the titan a truly inhuman appearance as the twin suns blazed through the rock. No one could boast that they could look him in the eye.

"Impressive, is he not?" Silvertongue needed to shout above the scrape of metal, and a sound like the battering of the sea beneath. "He is nine hundred years old. Not as old as the *real* Argere, mind you. If you believe the tales, that one would be more than nine thousand years old if he still lived in the snowmonts." *Why is he saying this to me?* He nodded to the noble. Then he leaned in close, "You know, there is a certain story of another titan... I forget his name, but he was supposed to be tall, even by the titanic standards.

182

Yet in this story, a younger titan managed to kill him, after discovering his only weakness." *Only weakness? Younger titan?* "One such titan present here has the same weakness." Greg felt something being pressed into his hand. It was a glass vial, no bigger than the last joint of his thumb. The label had been ripped off, but the liquid inside was dark and oily. "Just a thought, eh." With a hard clap to Greg's shoulder, he was gone.

The stage kept a steady pace. Greg saw that the Sorans were looking at something over the lip of the platform, and succumbing to curiosity, he also went to the edge, finding Nat whistling as he peered warily down. "Somewhat larger than Fydor's Amphitheatre, don't you think?" he asked, wide eyes meeting Greg. The arena was twenty times the size of the theatre in Castan that hosted plays and dramas and frolics on feast days, and could host a mere five hundred on its ageing steps. To his eyes, it looked as though the Pit could host ten times that number. The seats encircled the walls of the cave, stone where Fydor's were wood, all arranged in orderly rings of decreasing size as they descended closer to the arena proper. The stone seats were barely noticeable, for they were packed cheek by jowl with Paydar. Thousands to his eyes. A living sea of red and white and blue, and here and there more drab colours, moving with all frenetic discordance and anticipation. The shouting and howling was louder now, brought to a harrowing crescendo as the stage came to the last hundred feet above the floor. *The Pit.*

Do it. Do it now. He fumbled for his quiver, managing somehow to get his bow stuck between it and his arm. When he finally managed to untie that knot, he pulled the arrows forth and proceeded to scrape off the wax that sealed the vial. *Poison? Some trick of Silvertongue to make me think I got a chance?*

He dabbed each steel arrowhead in the concoction, cautious not to touch the liquid himself, or breath in the fumes. A dozen arrows newly anointed, he replaced them in the quiver, anxious of the rows of seats that were appearing over the edge. The rows of faces calling out in Qellish voices for Caldish blood. He tried to focus, thinking of the next thing to do. To ready himself for battle. For death. His fingers touched the dirk. He placed the remainder of the philtre along the blade. Then he noticed Nat. His eyes shot from the blade to the now-empty vial. Words choked him. "It– I– I mean– the *younger* titan... he told me, I mean– He said the weakness– He– He– "

"Weakness? What are you talking about?" Nat must have been the oily sheen on the blade. He knelt, for a moment Greg was afraid he would take the dirk, or call him a craven, no better than the dunnies that put hemlock and other shit on their dreaded bolos. He didn't. He grabbed the empty vial, and after a moment's glance pocketed it. With a hand on his kje sabre, he said, "Will it kill?"

Greg shook his head. "I don't–" The ground slammed up beneath them, making Greg jolt backwards and collapse. Across the stage he heard a foreign tongue. He did not need to speak it to know that they were insulting him. "Up you come. Easy there," said another. He was about to thank him, but just then he came face to face with the Soran. He had seemed taller to him from afar, and up close he noticed that he had an inch or so on the Captain-General. The smile on his face was not unkind. "Back to your camp, lad. Now, if you would." His accent betrayed him as a noble, so Greg instinctively inclined his head and tugged at a forelock. He refused to look at his countrymen, Audeyrn's words filling his head. Turning on heel, he briskly walked back to his friends.

It was Audeyrn who came close, speaking above the din of battlecheer, "What did he say?" Greg swallowed, suddenly fearful of the hard face of the emissary. "He– He called me lad." The tendons in Audeyrn's neck stuck out like fine catgut on a fiddle.

"My Castanni friends, I believe your fifth and final champion has deigned to appear!" Silvertongue walked off the stage, and onto the blood-red sands of the arena. Greg had thought them at the bottom, but the titans shredded his hope. The four stone giants, half the size of Argere glowering above, stood at the compass points. Two male, two female. Their heads were bowed, their arms upraised in front of them. From those hands, the giants each bore a different device. A bronze cornucopia, a hardiron war helm, a quartz skull, and a silver chalice. Chains poured forth from all, each securing the arena of the Pit securely in place. *If this is not the bottom, then what is?* Norther stood a few feet away, his gambeson bloody and one eye swollen shut. "Now, if you would all kindly enter the red, we shall commence in short order." They did as they were bid, the Sorans directed by the guards to the opposite end of the suspended arena. The guards themselves remained on the platform, along with Silvertongue, who proceeded to steal the other guard's now guttering torch. Waving it above his head, and after a moment of inaction, the stage began to ascend. It seemed to Greg as though it was quicker going up than coming down.

"Farewell, warriors! I hope to meet those skilled enough to survive very soon." Even from a great height, Greg noticed the flash of a silver tooth.

Norther was in no state to fight. That was clear. Along with his eye, he had a fresh cut across the bridge of his nose, and his knuckles were bloody. When Hearty noticed his injuries, he raged, crying that the Paydar were dishonourable to injure one of them before the contest. Norther explained that it wasn't the Paydar, "...but a true enemy I was sent here to combat. One that I had hoped would be unaware of my presence. The element of surprise has been ripped from me now. I was discovered, I underestimated my opponent, and my contact was killed. I can only assume that the killer will go underground." When he spat, his blood mixed with the sand. "If it wasn't for the Lady Sere Rowett, I'd be dead, and you would be facing the Sorans without my handsome mug."

Audeyrn was unimpressed, "You can still fight? Even with one eye?"

"One eye is better than none, son of Coram. I came for blood today. Not Soran blood, but it will have to do. I have a fury that seeks the blood of my enemies, and the gods help those that get in my way." Hearty slammed a mail-clad fist on his chest. "Yes! For blood! For Castan!" They made their oaths of bloodlust, all except Nat, who drew Greg aside. In his hand was the dirk. *I dropped it. Fool! Fool boy!* "Give them no quarter, Greg. I don't like what you've done, but if it lets us live, who can argue against that?" His grin seemed more wolf than fox then, and Greg returned it gladly. Maybe the bloodlust was on him too, for the fear had gone the first time that day he felt hungry, and not for food. Looking down, he liked the way the daylight dappled on the poisoned blade.

"Silence!" came the voice of a landslide in a thunderstorm. Greg looked for the source, and saw the man with long braids standing in the lowest ring, the nearest to the arena, that boasted the greatest views of the sands. He stood next to a seated beldame upon a raised section of the gallery, a frieze chiselled in the rock beneath them into a myriad depictions of combat and coitus intertwined until Greg could no longer tell one from the other. When he spoke, those gathered hushed, the remaining hubbub dissipating until even the echoes faded to nothing. "Paydar! Kinsmen! Countrymen! Friends of the Tor! Today, we shall bask in the glory of a contest which has not been seen in living memory. Indeed, for the first time in nigh on two hundred years, champions shall fight in the Pit. Their screams shall fill the Halls of the Craftsmen with song, their blood shall water the roots of Stonehall, their bones will be ground for meal. Today, we shall witness the mortal arts. The gods may not see it, for that is their shame. *We* shall see it! The sport of a yesteryear born again! Glory to the Paydar!"

"*GLORY TO PAYDAR!*"
"*GLORY TO PAYDAR!*"
"*GLORY TO PAYDAR!*"
"*GLORY TO PAYDAR!*"
"*PAYDAR!*"
"*PAYDAR!*"
"*PAYDAR!*"

The lord of the hills produced a bow from someplace, a gilded deynwood recurve, incised with Qellish runes picked out in goldleaf. A servant brought him an arrow, the tip blazing soundly with purple flame. He took the arrow, pulling the drawstring back until it brushed at his braids. The fire hissed almost too loudly.

Norther ripped his sword free of his scabbard. "This is it. Ready yourselves. May our blades strike true." They all repeated him, but Greg mumbled his words, and was in turn drowned out by the masses of Paydar war cries. A purple comet blazed across the hollow within the Tor. Argere looked on with a grim fascination, his aureate gaze transfixed on the sands that yearned for a blood rain. The cheering reached an ululating height, the initial chant replaced by the roars of a beast covered in mouths that screamed for blood. He tightened his grip on the dirk.

From across the arena, the Sorans stood watching. Lyonis paced forward leisurely, as though he were in the garden atop the Tor and not in the Pit. In his hand, he held a delicate blade that curved toward the end, the hilt crafted to show white and purple yales. His cohorts stayed back, as though they awaited some sign from the Captain-General. The slimmer woman and a man wielding a pair of hook swords came forward to Greg's right, while the larger woman and the man named Lomas came on the left.

Hearty stepped forth, raising his greatsword before him one-handed as a sign of respect. Greg slipped his bow free and reached back for an arrow, letting the halcyon feathers brush his fingers for luck. *I'm gonna need it.* Nat pulled his kje free and then planted it in the sand, leaning on the crossguard as he said, "Maarten, my father. All my fathers before me. Grant strength to my arm. Grant me patience and virtue. Grant victory to us this day…" Norther gave his sword a few practice swings, trying desperately to appear stronger than he was. It looked unfamiliar to him, or so Greg thought, and he feared it was a replacement given to him by the Paydar armourers.

"Friends," said Audeyrn, with steel lining his fist and his voice, "Now we fight. For Castan, and for ourselves. Greg, you know what to do."

Words weren't needed now, which was fine by Greg. He loosed his first arrow as easy as breathing. Then a second flew. And the third.

The Sorans charged.

15

NATOLY

Everything was a blur of steel and stone and screams. Every instinct told him to lunge forward, as his boots ground hard against the scarlet sands of the Pit. His movements seemed slow, the Sorans that bolted towards him spellbound within molasses, their motions curbed to an impossible lethargy.

He felt the change come on him then. The red rage. He held his kje upright, ready to swing as his enemies neared. They were near now.

His boots felt tight and uncomfortable, his knife clanged annoyingly at his hip, his bowels loose and the need to piss an intrusive wisp of thought. He quashed them as soon as they were borne: it was only the anticipation of battle, and it was well known to him. Every morning, an hour before sunrise, he had trained with sword and lance and mace in the practice yard of the Guardcorps. Every morning, the feeling had taken him. Long before he could grow his fiery beard, he had gone to bed too bruised and battered to sleep, but as the years slowly passed him by, he would become the one who dealt the blows. He was as good as any knight, even if he didn't yet have his spurs. He adjusted his grip on the sabre, the soft leather of the hilt reassuring, the feel between his fingers as soft as a woman's thigh...

Natoly felt good. This was what he was made for. Not delivering messages for tired old men on their fancy thrones or keeping watch for feathery monsters in the godsforsaken snowmonts. No. Such tasks were beneath him, and they all knew it. Even Audeyrn, lovely loyal fool that he was. *His* place was on the road. This, not running on the whims of kings, was life. With a blade in his hand, a girl in his lap, and the whites of his enemy's eyes before him. *Give it to me!* His war cry seemed disembodied, and it was hard and guttural. *Try me now!* His long steel claw glistened in the light of the Titan's fixated glare. He found his opponent.

The Soran leader, whatever his name was, was stalking unhurriedly towards them, apparently unaffected by bloodlust. *What a queer fellow.* Aud had claimed him already, so Nat angled off to the left, setting his sights on the woman that pounced forward with the deadly feline grace of a razorcat. He felt his groin stir at the way she looked at him, dark eyes lined with charcoal. She was garbed in leather scale armour, lightweight and versatile, her only hard form of protection the mail covering her long comely legs. Her arms were bare, scars and sweat shining coolly in the brazen torchlight.

She wielded a broad cutlass, held in a reverse grip. He liked the way she held it. The way she held her jaw, tight and scowling. Even the way she had tied her hair. *Shame she has to die. These dunnies can be quite appetising when they make*

191

the effort. She moved quicker than he could have believed. One moment she was sizing him up with the cutlass held high; the next, a length of rope was swinging towards him. *No, a whip.*

He hated such weapons. Not that he wasn't prepared, tucking and rolling beneath the oiled plaited leather as it cracked where his face had been a moment before, blowing the gentlest kiss to the hairs on his neck. His footing was good, and he sprung up just as she had begun her slash of the cutlass.

Steel met steel with a deafening *CLANNGGG.* She had momentum and the advantage of a heavier weapon, and for a second the kje was pushed back. For only a second. He soon overpowered her, bearing down on her with his height and weight. *Don't underestimate her. Finish her quick.* The voice in his head was almost foreign. It sounded like Aud. He pulled back with his kje, angling for a downward strike that demanded she parry the blow with an upthrust of the cutlass. Nat brought it down.

The cat caught it, a silver-white spark hissing off the dancing blades. Forced to drop the whip, she held the cutlass two-handed. Nat's strike was halted, the downward force held at bay by the surprising strength in the woman's sinewy arms. A baleful look flashed from amber-coloured eyes. *Pretty eyes, too.* The knife was in his hand. It was razor-sharp, he had honed it everyday, sharp enough for a close shave. When it entered her between the breasts, it was noiseless and quick, the only sound the shuddering gasp that erupted from the woman's open mouth.

She died, and Nat pulled his knife free. He thought about using her hip sash to clean the blade, but found himself hesitating. Cursing, he brusquely removed the worst of the heartsblood on his own breeches. A man entered his field of vision.

"You, halberdier! Come and face me!" The olive-skinned man pulled back his lips to show pristine white teeth, eyes bulging fish-like from his skull. He held an eight-foot long shaft of ashwood, topped by a head of dark steel another two-foot in length, shaped like a double-headed battleaxe. He twirled it around his head and behind his back as he came, bearing the staff as though it were nothing but a reed. It made for a pretty sight, but it cost him his speed. Nat spurred himself on, not twenty feet from the big man. Nat measured himself against his enemy. The big man wore leather, chainmail tucked away beneath. His legs were coated in bronzed greeves, his forearms vambrace clad, and his chest protected by a sturdy breastplate, all delicately filigreed with sandthorns of topaz and peridot. Nat himself wore a mail hauberk and coif, his borrowed gambeson (unadorned and scratchy) hastily bleached to white to remove any hint of the Paydar colours. Armour was clearly on the side of the dunny then, but he knew that speed and longevity favoured him. That's how he would win.

All the feelings of turgid qualmishness moments before turned frenetic and frenzied. The air itself seemed to shimmer above the head of the dunny, alive with energy and heat. Nat thought he heard voices calling him, but they were marred and unrecognisable. His kje called for blood. A hollow ringing took to the air, a heavy dissonance as apparent to him as the sun in the giant's empty eye sockets. No doubt his friends had engaged the other Sorans. *The other woman, no doubt.* He lamented that he was fighting amidst the tumult of the sanguinary Paydar, their howls seeming to give the statue of the giant a voice all thunder, all terror. It was not a field upon which men of honour fought, but it was a field regardless. *No matter. These hillfuckers want a show. I'll make them a show.* The halberd came round, again and again, each cycle slicing the empty air an inch from the sand, now at head height, now in the stomach. The Soran knew this craft well.

Luckily, so did Nat.

The double-edged axe swung a few feet away. He didn't slow down. He plucked Maarten's knife from his belt. He considered throwing it, but shook it off. *If I miss, or he dodges, the knife's as good as gone.* He palmed the blade. The axehead swung round again, a foot from his face. Inhaling sharply, he sprinted within the halberd's ring of steel. The dunny's eyes bulged even more, and Nat could see the veins sticking out on the warrior's shorn temples. Even with his strength, it must have taken a great force of will to bring the axehead about in time. *Not quick enough though...*

Then the spear butt shot out an inch from Nat's face. Before he could knock it off-balance, the Soran retracted it lightning quick. Nat shot out with his kje, using the curved sword to hack at the man's open side. He wore mail and leather, yet the links under his arm would be weaker and prone to break. He never got the chance. The halberdier bulled forward, using the momentum of his spin to slam into Nat, the ash shaft pushing deep into his chest and taking the wind out of him.

Grunting, and knocked back onto a knee, he slashed with his knife. More instinct than thought, it connected, but screeched harmlessly off the breastplate. The Soran bellowed a cruel laugh at that, and shifted his grip one-handed to plant the staff in the ground with a spray of red. He made to back-hand Nat with his fist. *Now.* Nat dived forward, close enough to smell the Soran's breakfast beer, and hacked at the outstretched hand with the kje. The Soran stifled a howl, coming out as a harsh growl promising vengeance. Nat did not wait for him to bull again, so he swung the kje with all his weight at the shift of the halberd. The wood was dense, made harder by some kind of lacquer, and the kje stuck. *Oh shit. Oh shit. Oh shit.* With movement that belied the man's size, he swung the staff with sword and all. Sounds of snapping filled his ears, a battleaxe shot out, and the world turned black.

From the shadows came a memory he thought he had shut away, the face appearing before him, the one it hurt to see. Her hand extended towards him. Her hair tousled all about her head, weightless as though submerged in water. In her eyes he saw the love they once shared, and sorrow, mostly sorrow, for the end that had to come. When the fingers brushed his chin, they became iron and unyielding, and he struggled to breath.

His ears rang as he came to, a crimson fist gripping his throat. "Castanni cunt!" Came the hard voice above him. His chest throbbed, and a man was lying on him. The axe had taken him in the chest... He felt his eyes pound hard with every second, and he wondered if they bulged as much as the dunny's. He tasted blood, his or the man that lay on him, he did not know.

Hands probed the grit around him, coming up empty. His sword was around here somewhere, his knife... his fingers rooting desperately until he thought his nails had been ripped off. Thought escaped him, replaced by the exigency to survive. He needed to live. He had to. Fingers clenched, he flung a fistful of sand in the man's face. Through watering eyes, the large fingers around Nat's throat tightened like a fleshy noose. Spittle dripped down from a Soran mouth, Nat too desperate for air to close his own. *Help me, you gods, help...* Fists were sent flying into the face of the big man, each more feeble than the last. An iron grip found his left arm and pommelled it into the dirt, followed by a lance of pain. His vision blurred. *Help me...* The words were a silent prayer, pleading, begging... Something hard brushed his finger.

A whistle cut through the pain. The hold over his throat loosened, and air rushed into Nat's lungs, sweet as honey. The man was looking to his right, a look of black fury furrowing his brow. Something looked funny about the man's left arm. It was jerked upwards, as though pushed, and a stick protruded from his armpit. A stick with yellow fletchings.

Pulling his head back, Nat saw Gregyn standing about twenty feet away. The world was upside-down and filled with agony, and he couldn't be sure of the distance. *No. Should have gone for the throat.* He tried to speak, only for a rough croak to wheeze through his cracked lips. The young tracker looked shit-scared. *Run... Boy! Run!* But he stood his ground, reaching back to his quiver to find... nothing. Even from that angle and distance, Nat saw the boy's arms shake like a shitting dog. *No. Like a lamb at the abattoir.*

Something pale caught his eye, the thing he'd touched. Long it was, and jaggedly sharp at one end. It was not far.

If only he could reach…

The Soran laughed at the sight of the arrowless archer, rising to one knee to give the arrow beneath his arm only the most momentary of glances. Grasping it with his maimed hand, it came free, a steady stream flowing down onto his breastplate to paint the sandthorns a ghastly red-black. He even snapped the arrow in two using one large slicked hand. Fast-acting poison or no, Nat doubted it would take effect before he smashed Greg's head in.

The man had eyes only for the tracker. Pain hindering his movements, Nat positioned himself closer to the pale thing… Some vigour filled him, and he pulled whatever it was free of the sand. Some tickling its way down his back, he rose, the thrumming of blood in his ears. It felt more like falling than striking. Maybe it was. He drove the staff through the throat of his would-be killer. Five and a half feet of ash sprouted from the Soran's neck, tapping into the fountain that spouted and gurgled and sprayed Nat with life's blood. The top half lay strewn further away, the axehead resting neatly in the sands that now drank the blood of Silentis insatiably.

The sombre grey of the ash planted in the jugular turned dark, rivulets streaming down the length of the shaft, to become a mockery of bloody roots.

The big man turned his fish eyes to the wood, the realisation setting in slowly and surely. Some curse formed about his lips, but he fell before it passed them. He lay convulsing, bubbles erupting sickeningly from both mouths.

It was quiet. Maybe the battle had moved elsewhere. Nat found that he could not look away from the dead man, who was quickly turning pale and cold. He did not know how long he watched, his knees sodden from the damp sand, when the shadow fell across him. He looked almost a giant then, did Gregyn of Dun Vale, the true giant of stone high above them, looking on with a mien all grimace, all morose. "The poison don't work," the boy said, his shoulders hangdog and slouched from the weight of his mail shirt. "The man– that Silvertongue fella– he said t'was their weakness. Summin' 'bout a titan an–"

"We'll discuss the how's and why's later," Nat's voice was raspy and thin, phantom fingers still coiling tight around his throat. "Shame you don't have more." The boy nodded his agreement, then turned wide-eyed and pulled his blade free. A straight piece of steel about a foot long, it was plain and crude, but would do the job as well as any other. *Long and sharp, and poisoned too.* No doubt it was poisoned. The look he had seen on Greg's face before the fight had been proof enough, the liquid that had run its edge, unlike any blade oil he had ever seen. "Where are they? The Emissary? Hearty?"

Greg's brows knitted together in confusion. "They– They're right there." Nat followed his pointed finger to the other end of the arena, close to a hundred feet away where the sands gave way to the abyss, some fifty feet below the lord's box. Light was playing off the dance of steel to add a metallic complement to the discordant song of the crowds. *How could I think it had gone quiet?* The deaths had only inflamed the crowd, it seemed.

A body lay sprawled in the fray, two towering figures standing over it as their blades exchanged furious strikes. A little ways off, he saw a man that could only be Hearty fend off two of the remaining Sorans. His blows came heavy and laboured, and he was giving ground.

Fuck. The fallen man had blond hair.

"Hurry! He needs us!" His left arm hurting abysmally, he collected his knife and then snatched up his kje, knocked free of the halberd as it snapped in two. "Oh, gods…" was all Nat heard the lad say before breaking into a run.

The sands gave way beneath his feet, as though the arena in its rancour was refusing to let him save his friends. *Fuck the arena, and fuck the Paydar.*

Dread filled his mind, and he would have given anything for a horse or one of those asses they used on the stair, or anything else, as long as he reached Audeyrn in time. In his haste, he felt sand being kicked up behind him. When the other's footfalls came behind him, he silently thanked what god had taken pity on him. *You should be thanking Greg, not the gods. May as well make a shrine to Gregyn the Merciful for all the praying you've done.* The distance from the onslaught was swallowed up soon enough.

Even the pain seemed to dissipate, vanish, as though he had found some panacea from death. The realisation was much more glorious. The lust was on him again. Not to kill this time, but a need to save *them*, even that arse Norther. He will be the one to save them. He had to believe it. He came to bear before him. The hiss from his kje as he pulled it from its scabbard was the sweetest sound in the world. Even sweeter than the look on the Soran's face as he swung it into the back of the man's head.

He was not as big as the halberdier, but large enough for Nat to call it a worthy kill. The twin bolos he wielded fell to the sands from limp fingers twitching spasmodically.

The she-Soran that swung her twin hook-swords beside her countryman broke off her attack, distracted, a broad look of horror crawling across her pretty face. Her dying compatriot fell to his knees. Yanking the kje free, Nat saw Hearty striding closer, giving ground no longer. For a second, he thought he saw the dying Soran turn his head to the woman. He could not have been certain, for he moved away quickly, as Hearty came on and swung his monstrous broadsword high above his head.

"CASTAN!" he bellowed, the sword a flash as it connected with the Soran's crown. Bone and brain gave way to steel. It cleaved the man's skull in two, right down to the shoulders. Nat felt his breakfast rise in his throat. "Die, bastard!" Screamed the knight, to the man that was already dead. Nat was not so consumed by the red mist now, and he turned to Greg, who stood poised uncomfortably with his short sword. Nearby, the blows were still being met by Norther and the remaining Soran. The fray had moved away from Audeyrn's body, and for that, Nat was thankful.

Wordless, he gestured to the woman with his kje. Greg was quick to obey, and trotted off to help Hearty engage her. And with that, he ran.

He had a plan, or what passed as the beginnings of one. The woman would soon be defeated, he knew. But until then, he needed to help Norther. Help him enough until Gregyn and Hearty could outnumber General Whatever-His-Name-Is. His competition was now before him, and his back was turned. The one that needed to die today. He ran with kje in hand, the sound of sword-on-sword more than a summoning, as gentle as a lullaby, as sure as sunset, the kiss of a lover and smile of a friend. He was breathless and haggard, but he laughed. He didn't seem to hurt much then.

Norther was holding his own, to his credit. His eye was still swollen and closed, and a new slash had opened the right sleeve of his gambeson. His borrowed sword shook in an arm that struggled to stay aloft. Slick with sweat, his dark hair was plastered to his once comely face. The leader of the Sorans looked fresh by comparison. His lustrous long hair was still held tight about the back of his head, the armour of gilded scale and festooned robes unscratched and unsoiled. He had not even broken into a sweat.

That only enraged Nat. Norther faced him as he chased towards their duel but was either too intent on returning blows or couldn't see him together from being half-blind. It made no matter. The Soran had his back to Nat, and that was beautiful. Some mad urge wanted him to scream out, to grab his enemy's attention. It would probably give Norther the chance to deliver the killing blow.

He hesitated again. A voice inside told him it would not work, that the man wouldn't hear, or he would easily parry his strike. Doubt filled him. *Why should Norther get the killing blow, the glory, anyway?* It should be his, and he knew it. He caged his tongue behind clenched teeth and pulled his kje back, angling for the chink between the scales that overlapped near a Soran elbow. He would take off the bastard's arm. Then dispatch him clean. More than he deserved. It would be easy. The kje swung out.

He was so close, and then Norther saw him. It was nothing, a paltry flicker in his remaining open eye. But it was enough. The Soran saw it and turned, meeting the kje with his own bejewelled longsword. *Gods, he's strong.*

The fulcrum turned, knocking Nat off-balance, reeling off to Norther's left. "Fuck." By some miracle he kept his feet, and nearly bowled into the one-eyed man. He had no time to marvel at that, for the man came charging forward, meeting both his and Norther's blades as easily as though they were one man, with only three eyes between them. The edge came worryingly close. Nat tried all the tricks he had learned, the feints and misdirects and pirouettes, even fingering his knife to distract him, in the hope Norther could find an opening. It didn't work, and with each blow, the pain returned to him harder than before. His ally was dead on his feet, his defence dropping under the weight of his blade. He was done, as the Soran knew full well. The rangy Soran's attacks became gestureful and empty, playful even. Nat thought of it like a dog given a pair of kittens. It would have it's play with them, but after a while grow bored and then shake them in its jaws, until it heard that satisfying crack.

Something glinted out of the corner of his eye. He held his kje high, ready for the next blow, and chanced a look to his left. *Yes.* A snort of derision came from the Soran. He halted his attack and stalked back and forth.

"You truly believe *that* will work? What are you? Some trash from a Castanni gutter?" He could not have known. Yet when the flush came to Nat's cheeks, it was all the admission he needed. "Aha! You are? I must say, you fight well… for an urchin from a shithole. Who are you, pray? A tanner's whelp? A bed-boy from a redhouse? A bastard in a basket?"

Norther edged close. "Don't listen to him. You know what he's—"

"Oh, shut that cock hole, Norther. You lack for sport, so I must look elsewhere for competition." Nat heard the leather of his hilt creak hard in his grasp. The Soran's amber eyes looked into him, and he said, "You *do* fight well. That is a fact… Say your name, urchin, so that I may honour the gods with a true warrior's death."

"*Don't.*" Seethed Norther. The clangour of the crowds screamed for blood. How could Natoly deny them?

"I am Natoly, son of Maarten. I am of the Guardcorps of Castan… and today is your death."

The look the man gave him was almost condoling. "Natoly… How laudable. How foolish." He drew his blade in a reverse grip over his heart, and then flicked it into a forward grip to salute Nat. *So the man has some honour, however scant.* Norther shambled between the two men like a drunk. "Lay off, the man is mine," Nat growled, surprised at the vehemence in his voice. *It* caught his attention again, and his heart lifted. Then *he* walked forward.

Like some hero from the stories...

The longsword was bloodstained, which confused Nat. *Who's blood is that?* The hand that wielded it was also bloody. His face was worse. Audeyrn had a deep gash running across the leftside of his jaw to his chin. Covered in a fine smattering of red sand, he looked like something out of Seratyn's plays. It poured off of him like a fine spray of bloodied ashes, his features obscured by a curtain that looked closer to silk than grit. A demonhead or fiend conjured up from the Hell Unending. He looked half-dead too, but it could not have been a more glorious sight for Natoly. His look must have been something, for the Soran leader himself now turned to regard the emissary, something strange glinting darkly in those eyes. The yales on his sword hilt glittering menacingly, to mimic their master. The sands chimed softly as it cascaded down his mail. "No, he's *mine*."

"The errand boy lives," Lyonis said, Nat now forgotten. The emissary spat out a gobbet of blood. "No one is to interfere. *No one*." Nat happened to look him in the eye, and he saw the fire swell and consume the grey, until all that was left was smoulder and smoke and white-hot coals, the laughter burnt away until only the cinder remained. He wanted to object, to say something, but his words failed him. He was not even looking at him, and something in that voice compelled him to obey.

Then he was stepping away, and Norther likewise heeded the emissary. *Did he see the fire too?* Hearty and Greg were there, but he couldn't have said when they arrived. Their blades were fangs freshly coated in the blood of foemen. The Soran saw them.

"Ah, so Tenniel and Lija failed as well. For shame, the garrison promised me that they were among the best. Today has seen the deaths of too many good men and women." He said it sincerely, or so it seemed to Nat. He could remember their faces.

"You're alone now, Captain-General," the longsword shone ruddily as Audeyrn poised himself. "That trick you used was ignoble, Lyonis. Effective, I will grant you *that* at least, yet you failed to finish the job."

"Aha! Who is to say I did not want you dead? For all your bluster and evil eyes, you are at best a mediocre swordsman, and at worst consumed by self doubt."

The emissary dropped his sword an inch. Nat saw the

words cut him deeper than the slash on his face. *No, you know what he's...*

"Enough. If you would goad me into fighting, you need only ask. I'll show you my skill, truly, I'll give you an intimate demonstration." The delight sparkled a bright purple on the Captain-General's face, but it could easily have been the torches. *Purple?*

He turned to watch the arrow shoot across the face of the giant, the head blazing heliotrope. The Paydar lord was standing with bow in hand once more. Nat thought he looked different. He had no time to scrutinise, for he disappeared beyond the lip of the viewing box.

"The– The purple arrow. The lord fi-fi-fired one when we began." Stuttered Greg.

"Indeed, your stammering friend is right," Lyonis said, his face indecipherable. "We are not done yet. I believe our host has more games to play." *More? What does he–* Nat had thought that the assembled men and women of the hills could not cheer any louder. He was wrong.

PAYDAR!

PAYDAR!

PAYDAR!

PAYYYDAAARRRR!

They all seemed just a writhing wave to him. Some chthonic beast miners claim to live in the depths of the earth. In his mind's eye, he could see them all, the frothing mouths and pumping fists and faces contorted into a rictus of arousal. They saw something that he could not. Something above them. He adjusted his grip on the kje, palmed his knife. He was ready, wasn't he?

The hardiron beam jolted into view, extending out from

the lord's box with crazed movement. It came on until it was a third of the way across the Pit, straddling the gap and the emptiness below. The thing must have been a good four foot wide, and the shadow it cast upon the sand made it seem wider still. Looking up, Nat noticed the giant's frown change slightly. He thought he imagined it, but it seemed as though the bouldery lips had curled at the edges to make a simpering smirk.

Nat gave a sardonic chuckle, more cough than anything, "More planned, ya right there, dunny." Lyonis turned to him. To give a rebuke or withering look, Nat could not say, for the sound of rampant metallic caterwauling engulfed the Pit. It came from the metal beam, which suddenly grew a dozen wings, splintery metal bars of equal length, equidistant, and bearing a loop on the end of each.

He knew what was about to happen, even before the three figures ran across the length of the beam with loops of rope slung about their bodies, and the crowds abruptly changed their chant. The cries of *Paydar* remained, but were supplanted by many different bawls of *Death* and *Glory* and *Stonehall*, yet above all, the one that humbled them all in a tide of furoric voices was for *ROWETT! ROWETT! ROWETT!*

Their movements were well-practiced, liquid even, making for the ends of the furthest bars. *This is nothing but a game to them, truly. A game of death.* They were all armoured but without helms, their Paydar braids dancing freely about their bearded heads. They continued on, rapidly changing direction as they lunged onto the smaller bars, the ends bending precipitously under their weight.

As though they shared a common mind, the three of them

leapt in the empty air, hooking something through the loops as they did. Then came the fall. The rope unfolded, and they glided down to the sands with a rakish flourish.

The noise of the Paydar was delirious, giddy, an ecstasy that Nat could not share, as they watched their lord and his champions join the fight.

16

AUDEYRN

Lord Rowett was dressed for war. *Or a war game.* His braids were freshly bound, each gold and silver rings in his hair and beard glittering and tinkling against the steel gorget at his neck. His fellows were similarly clad, all bedecked in plate armour embossed with images of titanomachy.

"You do realise our situation has changed a mite," Lyonis said to him, an edge of nervousness creeping into his speech.

"I have. Seems we're like to be bedfellows for the now." Audeyrn made his most savage smile. "Tomorrow will be different."

The Soran commander laughed, as loud as it was bluff. "For tomorrow then. Good luck, Emissary. The gods preserve us all."

The crowds were fanatic, roaring as though their lord had already bested these outsiders. Something about the way Lord Elmer sauntered and saluted the onlookers gave Audeyrn pause. His hands twitched, and his head jerked about all too quickly. His eyes were glassy, and bloodshot. *Nhere*, it had to be, his mind pulled back to the Grey Court. The stimulant was from the nherej root, and when ingested in large doses, brought on berserker strength and ferocity. The pugilists in Low Castan were wont to use the stuff, and other, less savoury denizens too. He told the others what he thought.

"Huh, that'll make him deaf to reason and thought," pointed out Hearty.

"Aye. he'll be in all a rage and fighting only for himself," added Nat.

"And the others?" enquired Norther, his words strained from his hurts.

The champions of House Rowett did not look frenzied to Audeyrn, but he did not want to think them easy prey either. Both were men, large ursine warriors with deceiving agility, both pacing furtively at their lord's heels, eager to begin. He considered the trio, lapping up the thunder that seemed no sign of abating.

He told the others his plan. Even the Soran seemed intrigued.

"That was entertaining, you know. The fight. I was surprised that so many of the *celebrated* Headhunters fell, to be sure. I put a lot of coin on them besting your lot. But then again, you came awfully close to succumbing to a Soran blade yourself, *Audeyrn*. The mighty royal emissary of Castan! Do you think Isembard appreciates your skills of negotiation?" They both knew the answer to *that*. The Lord of the Hills smiled at his own wit, wielding a warhammer as tall as he was, the head as big as an anvil and wrought in the shape of a face that writhed in agony. "But you live... I fear I thought you dead, so I collected my men and sought to extend the sport. Much can be said for you and yours fighting the Sorans, yet my people did not come here for an afternoon's diversion. They came for the makings of history."

"All you do is talk," Audeyrn knew all too well the reputation of Elmer in battle. *I should have expected this.* A man that preferred to command his troops from the front, he was never one to hide if he could smell blood. His men arrayed themselves to his left and right, both wielding greatswords incised with Qellish spells. He was apprehensive to begin, and he told himself that was only reasonable. Yet the more he waited, the more he felt the dread touch his bones.

"My lovely mother says the same thing…" And with that, the lord roared, striding forward with the wailing hammer on high.

The lieutenants flanked him, and strafed off to the others with likewise blood-curdling screams on their lips. The Lord Rowett had his wasted gaze dead set on Audeyrn. *I should feel honoured my Lord graces me with his attention...* Every instinct told him to run, but he could not. He plunged forward, the sword not as light or beautiful as the other one he had held, but it was sharp and hard, and that is all that mattered. The warhammer slammed into the sand to massive spouts of red. The emissary squinted from the spray, just making out the tragic face stare at him with mute appeal as it was ripped free.

They exchanged blows. Prodding, probing, strikes that Audeyrn knew were just the lord taking the measure of his opponent. He could only marvel at his prowess, even with something as maladroit as a warhammer of that size. Between clashes, he even wondered if he could fight with something like that, but then collected himself, silently thanking Walt for putting a sword in his hand. *Even a man on nhere has to tire eventually.*

He was not much shorter than Lord Elmer, but weight went in the Paydar's favour, having being about five stone heavier, and all that being hard muscle. Soon Audeyrn was giving ground, forcing him to dodge widely as the warhammer came at him diagonally, here and there a diagonal feint that turned into a side-slash, then a downward hammer smash that was pulled inward instead of striking, only for the lord to repel it out immediately after to cause the emissary to make a brash dodge backward.

The ceaseless attacks made it difficult for Audeyrn to get in close enough to make a worthwhile assault. He knew that he needed to get within the line of defence. He needed to find an opening. He needed to tire him out. He tried *something.* "I must say, my lord, I am impressed."

"Do you intend to kill me with flattery?"

"I intend to gain your allegiance." He jabbed with his sword. The slim blade was promptly swatted away by a mailed fist, with a disgusted look from the bearer. "You *must* try harder, Castanni. I'm like to die from old age at our current rate of battle."

"At least the good people here will not want for entertainment."

"Indeed." The next strike was a savage thing. The hammerhead swung low like a pendulum, only for it to overextend and turn into a lunging one-handed swing of a club. Audeyrn nimbly danced away, but scolded himself for retreating further. On the periphery of sight, the edge of the Pit loomed large and dark. His mind rang to the sound of steel as his blade glanced off the warhammer. It did not help the throbbing in his head, the gift from Lyonis. The villain had seen to him quickly, striking the pommel of his garish sword into his temple before he could parry.

The ringing in his ears had not gone away, long after he knew he was dreaming. At the least, it felt like a dream. It had been dark, but he was not afraid. He could walk, even though the ground beneath him was a litless featureless cold that made his feet ache. And he was naked again.

Lyonis hit me so hard my armour fell off.

The dream had had no beginning that he could tell. A hollow noise came rattling from some far-off place. *The Pit,* a voice inside whispered. It said something else too, but it was muffled and too quiet.

She came to him, as he wrested with the shame of being outwitted by the Soran. Hours passed as easily as moments there, she could have been standing there all the time, coaxing him to follow her. He wanted to know where, why must he follow? He did not ask, but dogged her heels anyway.

It seemed much the same, on the unlit path that only she seemed to see. The girl that looked Soran had a long stride, long enough to match his own. She was wearing leathers in place of a dress now, the sort that allowed one to carry all sorts of weapons and pouches and gods know what else. It clung to her body tightly, and the stuff was supple and made no noise. He was not unimpressed by the change of attire, much the opposite, but it disquieted him to see the girl walking before him, wordless and solemn. She had

212

disembodied into a heap of sand when he had dreamt of her back at the camp, and he had wakened in sweats and screams. He eyed her cautiously, fearful it would happen again.

"River," came her voice. He almost thought he had imagined it. Hadn't he? He loped ahead and grabbed her arm, forcing her to face him.

"What did you say? River? What *river*?" He released his grip, realising how tight it was. The girl had not even flinched. Her mouth was closed, and something in her eyes gleamed hotly. The hazel that had been so rich and alluring the last time was supplanted by unblemished white. He could feel it behind him. A voiceless call beckoning to him. He could not resist.

The light was blinding in that gloomy place, an intruder to this dreamscape. It called, and he answered. It took all a moment for his eyes to adjust. The light never ebbed, or faltered. It was solid and unyielding, a star brought low and wrought into the shape of a sword. It held itself there, suspended with the blade thrusting upwards, the hilt at shoulder height. Audeyrn made his movements slow and deliberate. Yet somehow he knew it was safe. It was for him after all. The knowledge disturbed him.

His fingers brushed the hilt. It was soft white leather, burning blazingly white-hot like the rest of the sword, the pommel and cross-guard and blade all. The leather gave way beneath his grip, and he found that it was exquisitely balanced, light beyond belief, and cool to the touch. The straight edge was about four foot long, perfectly outfitted for him. He gave the blade an appraising swing, as he did so hearing the lightest of *thrumms* cut the air.

What is this?

"A gift," she said. The confusion must have been plain on his face, for she returned it with a mischievous grin. "Funny. Seen as you're talkative now, maybe you can explain why I'm here." But she didn't answer, the smile flickering until she looked sad. Her head shook side to side, brief and halting, as though it hurt to move. She turned away, walking unhurriedly on the same unseen trail.

He followed her. What else was he supposed to do? When he saw how far ahead she had gotten, he quickened his pace. He could not keep up. Soon she was nothing but the vaguest impression of a person, a speck on the edge of sight, an imagining of an already forgotten dream. He shouted and hollered, but she was gone. Then came the shadow. A dark figure on dark. A creeping mass moving languidly through the outward. The sword felt the presence, and pulsated rhythmically in his hand.

Eyes appeared where there had only been glooming before. A set of round pallid yellow things that bobbed ceaselessly, prowling beyond the reach of the sword's coruscation. *It hates the light. It's anathema.* If he thought it would stop the beast, he was wrong. Suddenly a vague quadrupedal shape detached itself from the mother darkness, extending long claws that shone darkly like jagged chunks of obsidian. It was big, bigger even than that pale wyrm in the blackwood, and it was coming for *him*.

He knew it was a dream, and nothing can hurt you in dreams. Yet… A sound almost too low to hear muttered in a dozen discordant voices. *Betrayer*, they hissed. *Deserter, traitor, renegade.* Above the rest, one seemed stronger and stuck out. A petulant tone dominated the chorus, full of power, full of fear. He knew that voice.

The sword felt right in his hand. His nakedness did not feel so disarming then. As long as he held it steady and true, nothing, not even this *thing*, could harm him. The fear fell away like an old scab, to reveal the new skin beneath. He poised himself, waiting for the monster to attack.

It didn't. The shadows shred and dissipated, a caul ripped apart until the titan loomed over him. He stood, the iron stink of blood suffusing the air. For a moment, he thought the Paydar cheered for him.

"You say you would win my favour," Lord Elmer asked now. "So show me that Castan breeds more than weaklings and fools!"

"Who trained you in arms? I've never seen a weapon wielded with such deftness. I—"

The noise Lord Elmer made was the same as if he had stepped in dog shit. "My father of course, the Lord Rutger Steelfist. He who was taught by his father, Lord Rigard Bloodaxe, the son of Ransom the Mightygrasp, grandson of Rodigan. And so on and on, unbroken, until the sire of my sires, King Ro Rowett, who bested the gods, fucked their daughter, and conquered the Tor." He grunted as he pulled the hammer across the sands, making a tight revolution around his head and swiping where Audeyrn had stood a moment before. The emissary forced out a laugh. "You seem to have inherited your speech from your venerable mother." *Take the bait, take it, take–*

"What of *her*? She is nothing. A tree clinging to a windswept crag."

Audeyrn hazarded his response. "She rules the Tor."

It was heedless, and it elicited a snarl from Lord Rowett.

"Her words have pith because of *me*! Cyrinne has little to no Rowett in her blood. That is, not since the old man died. She is a Warsash, the daughter of Tagg Warsash, Tagg the Craven he was called, the Lord of the Jade Reach, who fled from the mountain chieftain Olryc One-Eye at the Battle of Sheepback Rock. There's some drop of Rowett there, from some ancient union to bind them to the Tor, no doubt. Little enough to warrant any pride. She is nothing. When she is dead, all shall pass to me."

I have you, bastard.

"Then why haven't you killed her already? You're a strong man." That caused the next strike to fall short, and for Lord Elmer to look at the emissary with pink eyes and a look of scorn. He kept the warhammer planted. "You're a fiend. Howbeit, you'll be a dead man before the Titan goes blind, so know this." He released his grip on the shaft, cracking his knuckles as he did so, never blinking and ever twitching. "I love my mother. Dearly. I fear that it is unseemly, and sometimes she makes me think corrupting thoughts. Were the gods still here, I would be sent to the Hell Unending I have no doubt, the things I've done. A son must love his mother, especially in her advanced age. But I want my throne. I want it dreadfully. So much more. Whether from a fall from the Tor or a chill in the night, she will die, and I will rule."

The admission was not what Audeyrn was expecting, yet he kept himself composed all the same. Fresh blood dripped from his fingers. From the wound he had given himself. In his mind's eye, the white sword still shone blindingly bright. He could feel it, and it gave him comfort.

"Now, it comes to me that a blow from my hammer would

be too... *swift.* Why don't we settle this properly, eh? With flesh." He pulled his massive fists before his face, pulling his lobstered gauntlets free and letting them fall to the ground. The calluses criss-crossed his fingers like a pale web. The emissary resisted the urge to drop his sword. He was no fool. Should he disarm himself, he was as good as dead he knew. He could never hope to match the lord's strength, even without *nhere.* He wondered. Just how far could he go... The edge could not have been ten feet away now.

"I admit that you are formidable, my lord. It seems to me that your victory would be all the more sweeter if you were to defeat me barehanded." Something moved along the bearded features. Audeyrn could not tell if it was because of his words, but he had to believe it. *He yearns for it. He needs it.* A scream split his head.

It came from the melee ahead of him. A good distance away, a Paydar was holding his own against Hearty, Nat and Norther. The man must have realised that he was on the backfoot, for his movements were wild, always putting himself between the three men. Audeyrn did not concern himself with that fool. *The scream did not come from there. Look!* Closer to hand, the other Paydar was standing over someone, smacking the fallen man with the flat of his sword, against his knees, his arse, his head. Greg screamed again, slashing blindly with his dirk. All the while mocked by his foe, aping his cries of pain and movements. The noise caught the attention of Lord Rowett, who turned away brazenly to glimpse at the fight.

I should go, Audeyrn told himself. *I should stay. The mission...* A gruff snort came from the Lord, just as the emissary saw a figure leap into view.

The next swipe aimed at Greg was caught flawlessly by the yale sword, the beasts crowing as he twisted the Paydar blade away. It looked effortless. Lyonis danced away, laying into the Paydar despite having a lighter weapon. Lord Rowett *harrumphed* in disgust, his shoulders tightening in chagrin. Audeyrn seemed to wake from some dream, not for the first time that day. It could not have been easier. His enemy's back was large and protected by thick plate. But the rest of him wasn't. He grabbed his chance.

The sword seemed weightless as he brought it to bear, tight to his right, an upward strike aimed at joint at the knee. *There.* The scream was all beast, hardly human at all. Metal crunched, and the sword went deep, sliding through plate and mail and flesh and bone with a sickening grating beneath his fingers. The crowd gave their cries of anguish, howling in the Qellish tongue obvious insults at the royal emissary.

Audeyrn was away from his mark as quick as he had struck. Fresh blood ran down the length of his sword, making the titan's reflection awash in crimson. "Fucking cunt! Coward! Striking a foe while his back is turned?" Rowett limped forward. Each step on his right leg was laboured, the pain dulled to a tolerable level by copious amounts of *nhere*.

"Now you die, *dhereda*!" He hobbled straight past his hammer, forgotten in his wrath. "Fucking *dhereda*."

Audeyrn spread his arms wide, allowing himself a moment of satisfaction. "Now we dance."

"*Yaaargghh!*" The lord frothed at the mouth, pink spittle running down his lips and into his beard. Audeyrn planted his feet shoulder length, his blade held steady before him.

Another warcry filled the air with rosy slaver, and then a fist the size of a haunch of beef veered at his face. It was Rowett's right fist, so Audeyrn ducked and rolled beneath that side. He pulled the sword tight across his chest as he did, landing, and rising onto a knee, he swung out the long stretch of steel back into the knee again.

Lord Rowett dropped to a knee now, albeit much less gracefully. Audeyrn ensured he was clear of any back-handed swipes before circling the man. Facing him, he saw a face red with exertion, intoxication, and shame. *"Dhereda."* The curse was laboured. "I offered you a fair fight."

Now it was Audeyrn's turn to scoff. "I would have thought someone like you would know better. War is not fair. War is life and death. Not... *this."* He gestured to the baying crowds with his free hand. Lord Elmer shook his head. He spat at the emissary's feet. "Well, I am at your mercy, *Audeyrn.* Finish it, boy, and revel in glory."

"I told you. I want your allegiance, not your death."

"You have shamed me. How could I possibly hope to hold the loyalty of the Paydar with what you've shown them, eh? Without loyalty, without fear... to live as a sheep among wolves... that is no life for a man." Audeyrn could not help but pity him. He strained his hearing beyond the tumult. Hard as he could, he could no longer hear the clashing of blades, or the screams of wounded men. His initial relief was replaced by a darker thought. *What if the Paydar won? What if they're waiting to put a steel tongue through my throat?*

No. If that were the case they would have done so already, to save their liege. Either they fear what I will do, or they're lying dead in the dirt.

"You hesitate. Do it. Send me to whatever hell awaits me.

219

Here! I'll make it easy for you." His hands ripped at the fastenings of his gorget. The steel clattered to the sands. The lord yanked his braids back, to expose a thick bull neck. He had dropped to both knees now, the action clearly sending lances of pain through him. That close, Audeyrn could see his dilated eyes, how the colour was barely visible at all, the pink of his bloody sclerae the only colour to be seen.

"I will not kill you, lord." He could not say where his courage came from, but just then he had extended his hand. His sword hand.

Lord Elmer merely looked at it, his face pure scorn. But then something changed. One side of his mouth twitched, his dark lightened, and then he was looking at Audeyrn in the eye. His mouth broke into a pained smile, lines forming at the corners of his eyes.

The emissary returned it on instinct. When Lord Elmer opened his mouth, the ghost breath of words were swallowed by a new chant from the crowd. It was a flood tide that came from nowhere, a word repeated over and over, a Qellish word. *Swyai! Swyai! Swyai!* Audeyrn did not recognise it. He did know the speech of Old Qell.

"What are they saying?" He asked the supplicating lord. He did not notice that he had looked away, but when he saw Elmer's face, the smile was gone. Beneath the bloodshot and swelter, a cheerless face brooded. "Glory…" His knuckles cracked loudly.

The man became a beast as he pounced on Audeyrn, his rune-carved teeth dripping slaver as hands like claws flew at his face.

Swyai!

Swyai!

SWYAI!

Everything happened lightning-fast. One moment the man was mid-flight, the braids suspended around his head like the mane of a western lion. The blade seemed to glow almost ghostly as it came up.

SWYAI!

Something moved beneath the emissary's foot. Blood? Viscera? He did not know, only that he was slipping, and the beast bore down on him. He slashed in front of him, and saw that his aim was off, his arm pulled back too far. Shrill screams assaulted him.

SWYOOOOOOH!

The Paydar howled with their lord, who lay clutching at the end of his left arm that now ended in a red stump. He held it, hysterical, trying to staunch the bleeding with his own fingers. Audeyrn had aimed for both. *Guess one is good enough.* All screamed bloody murder, the outrage of maiming their liege apparent in the curses hurled at Audeyrn. He spat into the sands. Looking at the lord clutching his now shortened arm, he found that he wanted done with this farce.

She could not have read his mind. But then suddenly she was there, standing alone and proud atop the lord's box. The Paydar had quietened at her sudden movement, anxious to see what the venerated Lady Cyrinne was about to do. The silence was louder than any incessant gabble they could have made. Even the titan was ogling on agape, deep shadows collecting in the hollows where his eyes should be.

Lord Elmer's sobs were intolerable. Audeyrn knew he

should keep a keen watch on the downed man, lest he tried something stupid again. Yet his gaze was pinned to the shrunken woman on high. He expected her to speak. To condemn him and his, to give the signal for the rest of House Rowett's champions to come flooding into the Pit to finish what their lord could not, for archers to make them pin cushions, to declare that they would be treated and tried and judged and condemned as the outlaws that they were, to harm a Rowett so brazenly.

He felt his wits had left him then, as her ponderous slow clapping echoed through the hall in the earth.

Then all he heard was his name.

17

MARBLE

M arble and her entourage wove between the tightly packed rows of tables and benches. The emissary tried to emphasise the sway in her hips, embodying the outfit she wore. Stretching as tall as she could and walking with confidence to border on obnoxious, she met the eyes of many she passed, to be greeted with a plenitude of emotions. Those gathered were harder and more jaded and cautious than most of the street goers.

A lot of guards for little ol' me, Marble amused herself with the thought.

The smirk that twisted her lips caught the narrowed, critical gaze of a larger woman. Tall and buff and stronger than most men in the room. The frown marring her worn face tightened it into a scrunched-up thing obscuring most all her features so it seemed one was looking at an old battered ball of skin in bad condition from repeated pummelings. Marble allowed a revolted expression to cross her own face, knowing it would rile the woman. The scrotum face snarled audibly, drawing the attention of her companions. With an obnoxious smirk directed at Scrotumface, Marble gave a snide chuckle and obvious side-eye towards the large woman. The immense warrior hauled one trunk-like leg over the bench after the other, rising to an enormous height and blocking the forward path.

"Scuse us, sir!" The emissary hollered, leaning around Grenn's bulk, "I believe that's the way we are headed. Do you mind, moving out of the way?" She ignored Grenn's aggravated sigh. They continued forwards even as the woman stood resolute before them. "Sir!" Marble hollered again as they came ever closer. "Oh!" She exclaimed as Grenn came to a halt, unable to continue forwards until Scrotumface moved.

"So sorry, madam, such a terrible mistake on my part. It was difficult to tell from the distance. From the door, I could've sworn you were a Griffpatch, clearly you came more into focus as I got closer. I like what you've done with your hair though. Very Felnarth-like." Scrotumface turned redder and redder, becoming an almost violent shade of purple as her outrage grew exponentially. Quivering with barely suppressed rage.

The Red guard muffled the continuation of offensive babble Marble spouted with a large hand covering her mouth. Grenn, standing between Marble and Scrotum face's roiling fury on the verge of eruption, stood ready for mediation.

With a quiet word spoken softly into Scrotumface's ear, Grenn convinced the woman to retake her seat. *That will not do at all.* The emissary pointedly sniggered and raised a brow in challenge as she sauntered past.

The large woman charged, and Marble slid away. She turned quick enough to see the bull slam face first into the table behind her. The table that had been packed high with food.

Others, seated too close for comfort, did not take being covered in delicious dishes well. Outraged, they leapt to their feet as though of a single mind. A mind to punish this outsider. The one closest to Marble was average height, portly, with fine wrinkles covering his bald pate. Dark eyes glittered above an even darker beard. His knuckles went white. He glowered at the woman sprawled on the table.

"Jus what do yas think yas doing!?" The bald man rasped, his tone soft and quiet but lined with malice. Scrotumface stepped closer to him, trying to use her indomitable size to intimidate the smaller man.

"You's gots a problem?" Her voice was unexpected. High and nasally and unexpectedly feminine.

"Aye, sir. I do gots a pro–" The fist flying at his face cut him off. Marble watched with barely contained delight. The brawl took over the place, all fists and feet and faces of shattered teeth. Marble's escort tried their best to calm the others. It didn't work.

Marble slipped through the carnage for something useful. Ducking and dodging and weaving and twirling through the anarchic masses, she deftly clambered over benches and tables. She browsed many a potential armament, tempted by a few offerings and discarding many more. A fairly long, thick, jagged blade made of steel held by a grip wrapped in strange, leaf-green leather caught her eye, as did a dual-edged and razor-sharp weapon perfect to slice, dice, stab, and jab. Another blade with a barbed, curved crossguard, adding just enough weight to ensure the blade sat firmly in the owner's hand, protecting those same hands as well. The crossguard had an elaborate claw on each side, a unique design for a unique weapon.

A thick pommel marked with the sword maker's symbol, a symbol of true greatness was yet another arresting option. An axe, the blade engraved with presumably the symbol of the owner's house, like a blessing, to protect the weapon's owner in battle. Another usually the type to be used only during celebrations. A particularly wondrous staff was also an incredibly tempting possibility. A hundred and sixty six whits of extraordinary fiddlewood formed the base of the grand staff. The entirety of the staff had been decorated with gilded patterns, only leaving the handle wrapped in reptilian leather, untouched. The bottom ended in a mirrored marquise shape made of crystal and decorated with a mosaic of rough, multi-coloured crystal shards of various sizes. The top was made out of elegant wood and had been crafted into a lantern-like shape, carved with curved bladed shapes, positioned together in a fan or wing-like pattern. But then Marble saw it.

Oh, it was perfect. Truly. She couldn't help but gasp in delight when her eyes fell on it. It was clear this object had stood the test of many battles. Dents and scratches made by who knows what had left signs of perseverance and power. Its edges were emblazoned with large metal studs. The scores and scars leaving a legacy told of a well-served life. Not the work of a mere amateur, made from hardiron which offered a tenacious barricade, especially against slashing and lunging attacks. It wasn't near, however. And so she danced.

The emissary joyed in the thrill and excitement of dodging through the uncontrolled skirmish. She hopped over fists, twirled around brawls and slid aside of many missiles, all the while managing to avoid becoming entangled in an altercation herself. The path Marble trekked was winding and convoluted. This way and that, Marble traced its path as it travelled a mean journey itself. Under benches and over tables, disappearing behind behemoth louts and unconscious folk til it came to a rest at the edge of the room, leaning wearily against the solid wall. A few more ducks and skirts later Marble finally reached her prize. An enormous grin pulling at her lips, the emissary wasted no time. Reverently, she picked up the fine, sturdy metal bowl. Turning triumphantly, weapon now in hand, Marble was more than ready to engage in the frenzy.

Observing the frey she watched, carefully choosing her targets. Marble tossed the hardwon bowl. It knocked her first victim over the head, rendering him unconscious and returned neatly to her hand with the rebound. She continued leisurely in the same vein for a time, throwing and catching the bowl when it bounced back to her off the heads of casualties, til a group of rowdy fighters took note. They began to amble angrily in Marble's direction, though their progress was slow going. Drawn as they were into more scuffles on their way.

Marble kept an eye on their progress as she continued downing louts. The first combatant of the approaching ragtag group wasted no time throwing punches as he charged towards the small but vicious woman. Marble deftly dodged the flying fists, spinning around the lumbering body of her assailant. Smooth and quick were her movements. The lumberer was positively slugabed in comparison, his clumsy feet and wild movements looking amateur next to the lithe agility of the emissary.

Marble waited patiently for yet another flying, beefy fist, meeting the offending projectile on its path towards her face with her trusty bowl. Marble's arms jerked with the strong impact, but she held strong and planted her feet.

A crunch, simultaneously satisfying and stomach-churning, echoed closely. Before the man could howl when the agony of his now crushed hand registered, Marble efficiently sent a quick jab to his throat Enough to wind but not permanently damage, choking and silencing him as he collapsed in a useless heap at Marble's dainty, bare feet.

Wasting no more time, she leapt over the downed man to avoid the figure approaching readily from behind. Turning to face her newest opponent Marble took a fraction of a second to observe the carnage that was the rest of the food hall. She could see Grenn holding his own, rather impressively, the same as the Red Guard. *I really must learn his name*.

Quick and clever, but lacking their predecessor's strength and brute force, her new opponent was much more skilled than the last. Marble smirked. She was having fun. They both stood for a moment weighing the other. They charged. Marble dived into a roll as the other woman threw a smythstar, aimed perfectly for where the emissary had been, just a second before. Marble stumbled a little as she righted herself to standing before the woman with a shorn side of her head, as she narrowly avoided losing her skirt.

She raised her bowl and used it as a shield, blocking the

striking attack of another smythstar, this one still in her opponent's grasp. Marble parried continuously as the other woman set about on a vicious assault of repeated strikes. High and low and slashing sideways. They danced around each other and obstacles in a decent fight. In between countering stabs, Marble reciprocated a few blows for the small scratches the fighter managed to land that had drawn blood.

A quick look over her shoulder was all the tell the emissary needed to end this battle. Marble took the unguarded opportunity to underhandedly swing up the bowl and throw the woman insensate, just in time to fall backwards onto her arse and raise the bowl above her head to shield herself once more from a sneaky attack from above and behind. Marble grabbed the wrist attached to the offending fist and used the leverage to knock her newest attacker off balance.

She pulled the assailant forward over her shoulder, tripping them over her body and used the momentum of their fall to propel herself on top. Turning swiftly on one knee, she unstraddled them, and twisted to see her would-be attacker's face, clipping them upside the head with the bowl as she went.

Marble threw the bowl once more towards another oncoming attacker. As soon as the projectile left her hand, she threw herself forwards, kicking up a leg behind her to trip whoever she felt coming from the rear. The emissary lost track of her weapon as her newest opponent pulled her off balance using her outstretched leg.

Marbles' crashed landing into a swarm of other fighters was rather unceremonious. They all went toppling over, and by the time the emissary managed to untangle herself from the frey, the hulking figure of the one that had thrown her was there with grabbing hands that did their best to crush Marbles' head in their enormous paws.

As the giant lifted the emissary off of her feet by the crushing vice wrapped around her head, Marble desperately grabbed at the wrists of her assailant in the hopes of relieving the pressure of her whole body's weight hanging from her neck. Marble kicked out with violent intent. She made feeble contact a few times, her legs seemingly unable to reach their target. *How bloody big is this lout?*

Finally, when the pain was almost overwhelming, Marble managed to stretch and wriggle enough to bring the lout stumbling slightly closer and connect her barefoot furiously at the juncture of their thighs. It would hurt man or woman, a common weak area. Marble landed heavily, crashing to her knees with a jarring impact that had her gritting her teeth and blinking back a light sheen of salty fluid from her eyes.

Breathing raggedly and mindful of her now pounding head, she launched forwards at the blurry figure in front of her propelling her body over the louts shoulder but hooking their neck with an arm as she flew past. As she was airborne, Mable spotted her bowl once more. Before she could head to retrieve it, however, she needed to finish off this lug that had decided to mess with her hair. As she landed, she stooped low, swiping a butterknife, one of countless that had fallen and was strewn carelessly about the ground. Arm now squeezing the lug's throat with deceptive strength Marble thrust the blunt blade into their side, breaking past all barriers excruciatingly painfully.

Ignoring the howled agony of the opponent, Marble ducked and dodged and wove around the downed bodies and the much smaller but much more violent fights that still raged on. The emissary was a little bloody and beaten, but she was in much better shape than most, she observed, looking around for her next target. *As is only right.* She thought even as she despaired at some of the more clumsy mistakes that she knew better than to make.

Reuniting with her trusty weapon again, Marble smirked gleefully as she set eyes on her next victim. She had been pondering who to take on, but as soon as she saw Scrotum face's mean mug, Marble was delighted that the angry woman was still going strong. She watched appreciatively at the vicious takedown of Scrotum's current opponent. She watched with amusement as the woman's face twisted into an outraged snarl when she noticed Marble swaggering lazily in her direction. As if by agreement, both women begin to charge towards each other within the blink of an eye, dodging and leaping wherever required without missing a beat. Closer and closer, and Marble launched her bowl at Scrotumface's face when the other woman took her eyes off of the emissary for just a second. It was all she needed. *Does her face always look like that? Does it know no other expression?* The women were close now, almost within striking distance.

The sturdy bowl connected solidly with the side of Scrotum's head, knocking her balance and momentum. Marble jumped and propelled herself using a bench to catch the bowl from where it hung suspended in the air and brought it down, so it landed on the larger woman's head like a helmet. Marble climbed swiftly onto Scrotum's shoulders and began pummeling the outside of the upside-down bowl with another random utensil she had collected on the way, like a hammer.

Clang. Clang. Clang, sounded the metal on metal. The large woman stumbled, disoriented from the cacophony and the emissary's jerky movements jostling her whenever she started to steady herself.

Several strikes later, Scrote managed to grab a secure hold of one of Marble's legs and tossed the emissary from her shoulders to land heavily on her back. Swiftly regaining her feet, Marble charged at the woman once more, only to be greeted with a cracking fist when she failed to duck in time. The powerful impact sent Marble's head spinning and her body crashing into a weakened bench, the emissary's fall breaking through the kindling-like timber and depositing her directly onto the floor in an ungainly heap of rubble and splinters.

Scrotumface gave the emissary no time to try and rise to her feet again under a continuous assault of punches and kicking raining down on the smaller woman's person. It was all Marble could do to shield and guard herself to minimise the damage caused by the impressive blows. The harsh, vicious impacts suddenly ceased, and it was with a still disorientated mind that Marble saw the Red Guard defending her. He had stepped up to Scrotumface and appeared to be attempting to arbitrate a parlay on Marble's behalf. The ugly woman watched as the emissary staggered unsteadily but still cocksure to her feet and declined the Red Guards' offering of a detente by butting him in the face with her own hard head. As the Red Guard stumbled back a few steps, disorientated, Marble threw her bowl once more, but this time Scrotumface managed to avoid its impact. Marble was tiring. Her body lagged from such physical exertion, not being completely rested and recuperated.

Kicking up a wave of debris at Scrotumface's head, Marble used her momentary distraction to skirt out of punching range and devise a plan. With her energy lacking and body weak, Marble knew that she had to finish things quickly and most efficiently or else she would make another stupid mistake that would lay her abed for yet more time that she couldn't afford to be diverted from her mission and journey. The Red Guard glared at Scrotumface even as he clutched his bleeding nose. It looked to be broken. The emissary paid him no more heed as she ran through a list of possible moves and contingencies, quickly calculating her best course of action to bring this battle to its inevitable close. When Scrote turned to face the emissary once more, Marble could see a few splinters sticking out from the larger woman's face as her angry eyes glared. Scrotumface was flagging too, Marble gleefully interpreted in her sluggish movements. And so the emissary led her on a merry little chase around the food hall, jumping close and delivering precise hits to Scrotum's weak spots and lunging away again before the larger woman could react and retaliate. In and out. Duck and dart. Hit and dodge and kick and hit. Pivot and lunge.

Scrotumface stumbled, her breath coming in heaving, heavy pants and a sheen of sweat gathered on her forehead. Dripping. Marble allowed herself a short reprieve, downing a half pint miraculously untouched atop the table nearby.

Drink finished, Marble's own breath coming in pants; she wiped her mouth with the back of her hand and threw the metal tankard with perfect precision, nailing Scrotumface in the temple. Knocked out soundly, her face looked just as ugly.

18

GREGYN

Muddy wickered nervously as he was led down the slope. It was too steep for the rouncey, and Greg did not want to risk breaking a leg, not after having gone so far. The Paydar mounts were not so skittish, their fearsome riders forced to dismount and muttering in their hard voices, no doubt worrying that they had lost the scent. Greg could not blame them. They were frustrated and angry, fuming at the mere notion that the Godless had established a toehold in the hills. Perhaps they blamed him too.

"Stop feelin' sorry for y'self," he said under his breath, as much to himself as to his horse. He was oft berating himself since leaving the Tor, the party of the Royal Emissary nursing their wounds and drinking blackwine with their newfound allies. Nothing he said seemed to serve to make him any less apprehensive. So he had waited with the rest. Waited until Norther had told them.

The Paydar that comprised the scouting parties given to him were not as bad as he had initially thought. They were big, like the rest of their hillborne countrymen, and each had their own mop of dun or mud-coloured hair that they elaborated into streaking braids or bundles. Even their firemane mounts had braided manes and tails. He had come to know them all, some more than others in the five hundred strong group. The stocky ranger called Crispin was brilliant with a double-curved bow, and always had a kind word in accented common for Greg. The siblings Hellion and Heloise were stoic and guarded, yet when piss drunk would talk with him as though they had been friends for years. The axeman Arne the Mute was taciturn, and the balding Kete was boisterous and of a height with Greg and sang deep thundery songs in the Qellish tongue, no doubt about the glory days of the old Northmarch Kingdom. They seemed to be sergeants, as far as Greg could tell, each commanding a hundred rangers and foragers and foresters that scurried across the rolling glades of the Outer Qell in search of their prey, hirsute mice with steel teeth that rode fiery horses. The Rowett colours were not flown this far from the Tor. It was only sensible. Should *they* see the bright banners, their mission would reach a premature end. They all wore nondescript armour, bore no escutcheon, and even their hair and beards lacked the rings they were wont to wear by the dozen.

And at their head was a boy from the High Forks. Greg hated it. He would have been much more comfortable if he was with Audeyrn, or Hearty, or Nat. But they were far to the south, captaining boats up the Wolfswater River that cleaved the land in two and emptied hundreds and hundreds of leagues to the south-west into the Ruell Sea at Wolfsmouth. Norther was farther still, east of the river and leading his own hunters alongside the scarred captain of guards called Sere Rowett.

The plan was all Audeyrn. Two sweeping arms to scour the lands of the Wolfswater, in the hopes of finding the Godless and their lair. Gregyn was on the western arm, riding north-east and eventually south. Land in the Outer Qell was less hill and more swards of wide pasture, steppe that usually went unnoticed, and the riding was usually swift. Audeyrn had been adamant that the river was the answer, his tone all authority, with none of the soft words that Greg had grown used to.

It had all come to the fore after their battle in the Pit.

The Lady of the Rowetts, Cyrinne, had declared that the victor was Castan, and that the alliance would be restored. The now one-handed Lord Elmer was collected by healers and taken to his chambers high in the towery Stonehall. It must have been by some mistake or oversight, for Lyonis was escorted to the Hall of Masons with the Caldishmen; instead of his previous accommodation at the Hall of Smiths. No one complained of this. No one raised a hue when Lyonis brought the remainder of his escort from the base of the Tor to the apartments. Greg no longer saw the man as some dark and evil foreigner, his swarthy complexion that once held dread replaced by a feeling that only two men who have fought together could feel. He even struck up conversation with the Captain-General, and gushed when the man happened to mention that he had a love of hunting urca in the grasslands surrounding Ves. The other Sorans were given places in the Hall of Smiths though. Everyone, including Greg, guessed that that was wise.

They were all bloody, yet Norther had been the worst. The healer tending to him had said he could lose his eye. The adventurer laughed at that, saying that the swashbucklers of legend always wore an eye-patch into battle. Greg had broken an arm in the fray, a souvenir of one of the champions of House Rowett. The healer told him it would heal cleanly, if he rested and took a sleeping draught every night. The concoction came in a tiny bottle, the same type that had been given to him by Silvertongue. He worried at the thought. What peace they had hoped for then was dashed when a herald arrived to summon them to feast at sixth bell.

The Grey Court was transformed. It seemed full of life despite the day's bloodletting, and all had a good word and smile for the champions of the Pit. All that is, except Lord Elmer, who sat to the right of Lady Cyrinne at the head of the lord's table, a stump wrapped in thick linen placed unceremoniously on the table and a leg held together by splints beneath it. He sat and drank and glowered, and said not a word. The bloodroyal Rowetts of Stonehall-On-The-Tor assembled, along with the lesser Rowett cousins: Lord Elusendy of the Rowetts of Spikemont, and Lord Rodane of the Rowetts of Eldargat, and their own cousins, and relatives of less importance, and bastards and adoptives and ankle-biters and dogs. Gregyn was ushered in with the rest of the guests of honour. They were placed on the lord's table too, at the expense of the other bloodroyals like Sere and the mad cousin Barwell, and sat as to flank the Lady and Lord upon the lower steps of the dais. The tracker felt his heart enter his throat as he was seated immediately left of the Lady Cyrinne.

Speeches were given, toasts were made, and oaths were sworn. It was Cyrinne herself that pledged the blood and steel of the Rowetts to the Kingdom of Castan, placing Audeyrn's hand on her forehead and swearing to fight bravely and loyally beside the army of Castan, against Sora. There was blood on her wrinkled brow and amongst her wispy hair as she returned to the high seat, and Greg thought that he was the only one who noticed, for others said nothing or ignored it completely.

It was not long after that Lady Cyrinne turned to him, commending him on his courage in the arena. His words sounded garbled, yet she talked to him lightly and politely all the same, and after getting comfortable (or perhaps with the help of the bittersweet blackwine reserve) he was regaling her of stories of hunting and how best to skin an aurochs. Even as the wine kept flowing, he made no mention of the blood on the brow. He was just a lowly son of a miller after all, and shaming a noble would not do.

Hours fleeted by, yet the sunset was hidden by the walls. Torches gave the round hall the feel as though the walls were an ever-changing mosaic of molten gold, and the fools that capered around wore their motley in bright red, white and blue. It was Hollis Silvertongue who made the most thrilling site. He was bedecked in silver, his dress and girdle and mantle and wide-brimmed hat all variegated in hues of ash and pearl and smoke and dusk. Only his tooth shone true silver though, and it shone often. By that point, the hall was awash in drinking and song, most of which were led by Silvertongue himself, who plied the crowd with old favourites and even one he swore he had composed within an hour of the contest, about the daring and heroic deeds of the Castanni Emissary and his captains against the dastardly Sorans and their impish lord. It was funny, and the master of ceremonies could sing well, and Greg laughed along with the Grey Court. He just so happened to notice Lyonis, who was seated at the far end of the dais beside Natoly. From what he could tell, he did not look insulted by the song and its scurrilous descriptions of the Sorans and himself, but something of a simper lit his face, now and again sipping from his cup. The torchlight made his amber eyes flicker brightly.

His brow furrowed remembering that, careful to lead Muddy around a deadfall. *Silvertongue was the one that gave me the poison, but it was Lyonis that saved me.*

The morning following the feast, he had a head that felt too large and a stomach full of lead. Breaking fast was an empty affair, anxious to distract himself from the wine demons with the talk of the road ahead. It had been Lyonis that was talking however, so he sat abashed in silence and listened.

"The hill road is well maintained from the Tor to Wolfsmouth on the Ruell. A good five hundred leagues." The Soran speared a slice of bacon with his knife. "It is straight and largely unimpeded. The hazards presented by bandits are high, however, since the rangers whose duty it is to patrol the road were recalled to Rowett's Town."

Audeyrn stroked his stubble, looking as though a dusting of sand coated his face. "We must go to the river first."

"The river... The Wolfswater, you mean? Travelling due east is the most direct route, yes, but the way has smaller roads. Then there's the river itself to negotiate, and the 'water is wide and fast, and you'll need to find a crossing that hasn't been destroyed by my countrymen. I say you use the hill road. My escort will be ample protection."

"I do not intend to go due east, as yet. Nor the hill road. There was a vision. Or... a dream, I think..." The hesitation made Greg's ears prick, and he did not fail to see that even Hearty had put down the half dozen boiled eggs ready to enter his gob. "A... dream?"

"If truth be told, I am not sure about any of it. But the night before we struck out from Walt's camp I had a waking dream, frightening, in a dark place with scenes of war and sand, and a woman I have never met before telling me to take Norther with us. Against my better judgement, I agreed."

"This dream lady of yours has good taste," whistled Norther, who's face was now half-swollen and already bruising, making him look like the plum left at the bottom of the sack.

Audeyrn ignored him. "And when Lyonis did for me, she was there again, only now she was saying 'river'. Do you think it could be this Wolfswater?"

Lyonis steepled his long fingers, "Maybe. It's the largest river between Iktet to the east and the Snowmonts to the west, the principal waterway not including the lesser tributaries like the Wolfcub, Longscar, Greenrun, the Hillwinder, Rushie, among others. I knew at the war's start that a valuable natural barrier would be paramount for installing a buffer zone should the conflict reach a stalemate. Again, if you wish to reach the far side, you'll have to find a viable ford or a crossing not reduced to kindling. Sora has secured the Halfway Bridge. But crossing *that* is out of the question."

241

Hearty *hmm*ed with all the grace of a fat man eating a whole leg of lamb. "But if you were to come with us, your countrymen would recognise you. They'd recognise the Captain-General and fall over themselves to obey your commands."

"That is so, if I was the one commanding them."

Audeyrn leaned forward, "How do you mean? They're not your men?"

Lyonis rapped his hand on the table. "I advised on the strategy to capture the Wolfswater, but command of *that* campaign was ultimately given to Darge Pirellion." The name sounded strange, and meant nothing to Greg. He looked at the others, hoping they could explain or know something. Then it was Norther who said, "That complicates matters."

"Why? Who's this Pirellion?" When Aud clenched his fist, his knuckles cracked.

"A rival," answered Lyonis, the disdain playing clearly across the sudden lines in his face, "The Pirellions are old blood, countless generations of the house having been elevated to the Martial Circle, and like myself, Darge is a master within that Circle. I cannot boast of a lineage so grand, despite my family ruling Ves for countless genera-tions. But we are similar in some regards... for one, we are both ambitious, and untrustworthy." The mordant made Hearty snort, and Nat managed a thin smile.

"Should we arrive at Halfway, and should I present myself at the bridge, the guards would undoubtedly make Pirellion aware of my presence and ask whether I can cross."

Audeyrn tentatively rubbed his jaw. "How can you be certain he hasn't delegated command of the crossing to a subordinate? Perhaps someone you know?"

"Halfway is the largest town in fifty leagues, likely the only remaining crossing for thrice that distance, and it is safe. It enjoys being the centre of trade of the Outer Qell and has a strong keep with stores, cisterns, battlements, and moat. Likely, he believes I am still in negotiation with my lord of Rowett, all too aware that my forces occupy the Paydar. He also feels wary at me being in such a position. An eventuality in his mind is that in allying with the Rowetts, and together with my twelve thousand, combined with the Paydar eight to ten thousand, I will have an army that vastly outnumbers his. With such a force, the Torrins of Wolfsmouth must let us cross. Such a prospect frightens him no end. So he waits on the other side of the 'water, thinking and whoring and clearing the land of fare and fodder. He will be there. I'll stake my life on that. To give ground entertains the possible that we will lose the crossing and risk invasion, and to cross himself would allow for enemies to destroy the bridge and route him. So no, should he see my face, he would likely deny me entry, or put an arrow through my skull. Either is probable, but if coin was to be placed on it, I choose the latter."

He was met with a wall of silence as impregnable as Stonehall. The braziers spat now and again, but otherwise they sat at their table, their breakfast congealing before them. Eventually, the servants came to clear it away. The flaxen-haired girl was back and flushed when she saw Nat. Another, a girl that must have been two years older than Greg at the least, yet nearly a foot shorter, sent lingering glances his way. Something shifted in his breeches. Her hair was tied back, the locks that were too unruly to contain playing across her pug nose and green eyes. *Her hair looks soft...* She left with the others but kept shooting looks of promise to him, and her hips swayed widely.

"Will they be patrolling the river?" Audeyrn posed to Lyonis when they were alone.

"Aye. I imagine they will lead mounted patrols on the eastern side, spying the river for anyone daring enough to ferry themselves. What are you proposing?"

"I don't know what we will find on the river, but if it is hostile–"

"I have an inkling," Norther broke in.

Audeyrn did not seem annoyed by the interruption but curious, "Go on."

"Before my contact died, he said he was investigating the bluffs to the north-east. Specifically, a ruinous fort by the name of *Bagman's Bluff*. He told of wayns suddenly appearing on the small roads, and that the once abandoned stronghold rang to the sound of hammers and winches and orders spoken in queer tongues. They were the Godless, he said, and they had extended themselves beyond Godswrath."

The Soran was incredulous, "Godswrath is a fay-tale, something that mothers scare their children with, like sandwights or the Darklady of Dunevale. The Godless are nothing more than mad godmen now, like the Sungazers, the only difference being that *they* can claim to number more than a hundred. I would not concern yourself with such rabble. They'll destroy themselves most like, like all the other moon howlers before them."

Norther frowned, and winced at the effort. "Whatever the case, they will be emboldened by our war. *They were deicides once*, lest we forget. My guess is that they wish to carve out a kingdom of their own from the carnage and spread their fucking filth quicker than cockrot."

"Colourful. What do you hope to do? Ride the length of the 'water until you find a castle full of witches and wargs?"

Audeyrn saved Norther the pain of moving his lips. "This could be the place... *could* be. If Norther is right and the Godless are posing to invade, it will take precedence over our war. Over my mission. And if *you're* right, Perillion's forces will be focused in and around Halfway, making the upper river free to roam for us... and the Godless." Greg remembered thinking that he didn't like sailing. He didn't even like rafts, the dark night in Forlorn all too vivid when he thought they had killed Audeyrn... All that talk of Godless brought back memories of Old Mart telling him of how they had ripped Quirsus apart for the crime of being a twin. When the command came down that he would not need to brave the river, the relief was more balming than the ointment on his broken arm. That was, until Aud told him he was to command Paydar warriors of his own. He had sworn, and the emissary had given a chuckle and put a hand on his unwounded shoulder. "You have nothing to fear."

I have everything to fear.

Arne the Mute was the last to lead his group down the pass. His Paydar firemane followed him closely, her snort a grunt so like her master. He had never seen horses like them. Larger and more powerful than the coursers and rounceys bred by Castan or Vastiland, they were bad tempered and aggressive, biting and kicking at the slightest provocation and never shying from the smell of blood.

They're warmounts, after all. Greg made sure to always hobble Muddy a goodly distance from the horselines as they made camp. He noticed early into the journey with his troupe that a Paydar never groomed or fed another man's horse. Indeed, they would not dare to even stroke the fiery mane. Even these bloodborne warriors balked at such a truculent horse. Crispin had warned Greg not to touch a firemane. His advice was gladly received, for four days later, a Paydar forester had his nose bitten off for straying too close. Crispin was a man who seemed more hunter than anything and often rode ahead with Greg with his levies. He was preparing a duck he had downed that afternoon as Greg came on, having given over Muddy to his squire Jephro Rowett, a son of Lord Elmer. The man gestured with his knife to a tree stump.

"Sit, sit my friend! I saw you watching for Arne and his stragglers. Is the Mute well?" Crispin was something of a lesser noble, to hear him tell, a Moss of the Unquiet Tower, a modest fort that occupied the heart of the Northmarch. A cousin to Lord Markun Moss, he was not as hard-mouthed as Paydar went, and Greg came to find himself thinking of him as a friend.

"From his scowl, he seemed content." That made Crispin laugh, but it was hushed. He knew as well as Greg that they could not risk alarum for the enemy. They even cooked with smokeless oil, as they would not chance a single wisp of smoke being spotted by watchers. Such a thing would be louder than any scream, he knew. *Secrecy's key, that's what Aud said.* "Game was good today?"

"Sweet as wine, *roqyi*," he drawled, every syllable elongated into a runon. Greg thought it strange. When he heard them talk Qellish, it seemed a quick, chattering thing, punctuated by broad hand gestures. In the common, it somehow stretched, as though the words were chewed out like bad jerk beef. "Though t'is a shame we can't find the fowl we set out to capture. A shifty bird is man."

"Aye, that's true," he agreed, remembering Arran looking down at him from where he had tried to hide in the gully. The pride that had washed the Reeve's face had made him look flushed from drink. He came to know that face well. Crispin said something, pulling him out of that dark place. "Huh? Wha d'ya say?"

"I said we tacking east tomorrow?" He made short work of gutting the carcass and placed it upon the spit.

"To the river, yea." *With some hope, we can reach it 'fore Aud and his river hunters. With hope.* "We bed down t'night, early some. Get there for the landings." His companion stroked his face in thought, where the densest coal-black stubble Greg had ever seen coated the man's cheeks and jowls like a wire brush. "A month come and gone already, eh?"

"Aye, a month." *And what have we got to show for it?* They ate well that night, the tracker taking second watch alongside Crispin. When he was finally relieved, the leaden sky that had beleaguered them shifted to the west, allowing a shy crescent moon to rise from the low-lying horizon, the jewel in the celestial crown of night, accompanied by a vast horde of silver dancers of the Palace of the Fay, that streaked across the dome above like so many faycups and wightblooms and pale narcissus. He did not remember his eyes closing, but sleep took him some time later, lulled by the secret language of stars.

He was woken by a cruel zephyr of cold, as it made its

247

way down his throat. *Too cold*, was his first groggy thought as he sat up, the last watch already busying themselves with the fires for the men to break their fast. *It isn't summer no more.* Crispin was up not long after, complaining that he had slept awkwardly again. Greg smiled, lifting his cloak to shake the morning dew from it. Then Jephro was there, offering to do it for him. Gingerly, he surrendered it, and found himself thinking not for the first time how strange it was having a squire doing his menial work. The lad could not have been more than twelve. He *hmm*ed and went off in search of grub.

He has the look of his da. The same dun hair, the same square jaw and deep-set eyes. Son of the Lord Rowett. He tried imagining having a grandfather like Lord Elmer, and remembered that he had never known either of them. *Perhaps they were like him and I'd never know.* Jephro Rowett had proven to be diligent and intelligent on their travels, always sensing when he was needed and never under the feet of the large Paydar or Greg himself. A quiet child, he did not often speak, but Greg knew that he was always listening. *And learning too.* His hair had been shorn to the bone on the sides, and that which was allowed to grow atop was unbraided. The strangest thing of all was the marking he painted on his forehead every morn, using the blade of his dagger as a mirror. It was a six-fingered hand, done in red paint, which made him stand out among the other squires. He had raised this with Crispin a week or so prior, and the sergeant had nodded gravely while taking a swig of ale. "Mark of the *gevh*, or blood-rite. Were the boy born a peasant and made blood-adoptive, like the other squires, he would be considered unblooded and set to scrubbing the flagstones in fair Rowett's Town, or sent to rid the sewers of armourfangs. Yet he is nobly born, *and* of the blood, the Rowetts, and it is expected of him to be greater than a mere fighter. So he serves as squire. Like the rest of his young kin, he marks himself with the six-fingered hand of the mage Havadar, who betrayed the Qell to fight for the Paydar. When he was killed in the Battle of Sundered Peak, he left behind a legacy of a thousand Gifted, taught in the ways of Qellish magicking. Not that we still have kid wizards at the Tor! With the gods gone, we lost the magic, or so the storymen would have us believe. Yet the tradition lives on, and the Rowett boys and girls live each day hoping to be the next Ransom Bearskin or Redda Snowhair."

The boy had been playing a game using dice. Greg asked, "And when'll he stop making the mark?"

"When he has taken his first kill," the ranger said, taking another swig.

Breakfast was a serving of bacon and potato broth, which he gladly spooned up, glad for the warmth of the bowl as he walked to Muddy. He gave the horse some oats, receiving a grateful rub of the great long head at his shoulder in return. "Looks so much like Lord Rowett, yet could'n be more diff'run." Muddy snorted, which Greg took as agreement.

When they rode, the urgency of the weeks before seemed forgotten. They forded the lesser Tumble River, an offshoot of the bedevilled waterway named the Ghasthaunt. East and south they went, making for the spot the Greenrun bled into the main channel of the Wolfswater, where they were to meet with the river hunters. Zoush, one of the rangers under the command of Crispin, hailed from this part of the Paydar, and knew the land as well as the back of his hand. Or rather, his own back, for every inch from nape to buttock had been artfully tattooed with the entirety of the river system, each tributary and rill tracing its long way down his spine, filled with the myriad beasts and monsters that were said to inhabit those courses. Here a drik, there a cockatrice, and everywhere the great ophidians of the waters coiled and hissed with bloody fangs. It made Greg glad that he was not on the boats. The ranger was jocose and boyish and made for good company, his many japes witty and usually at the expense of the Mute. And riddles. The man had a queer fascination with cunning wordplay.

"I have a crown and a tail, am brown but gold within, I travel wide but have no legs. What am I?" He asked Greg as they rode. The wind picked up to bite through their gloves. He had knitted his eyebrows to frown. The answer came soon after.

"A coin."

Zoushe clucked. "An easy answer for easy challenge. Good. How about another? Something difficult. You carry me everywhere you go, not in hand nor on back. I am given from sire to son, but not the either way. I am without weight, and only used when you know me."

That took him a little longer. *Everywhere I go.* He mulled it over, anxious of the eyes waiting for a response. *From sire to son. Weightless... It's something I can use when I know it...* He knew it.

"A name."

Gales of laughter erupted from his group. One of them in particular gave a hoot of glee, she who had caught his eye on the first day out of Rowett's Town. A tall girl an inch or so shy of his own height. *Mayred.* She had a small chest, and her nose had been broken, but she had long strong arms and legs, and her smile was the wickedest thing he had seen. Her hair was likewise braided, yet those always seemed to come loose in the saddle. It made his breath come ragged to see her smile. *Or maybe that was just the wind.* He did not know. He found himself stealing glances at her more often after that.

The sun was a shrouded candle as they came into view of the Wolfswater, the streaming lines of cloud-like bandages unravelling from a wound. It concealed the sun now, with only faltering light coming intermittently as it chanced between the ribbons of vapour. Even when it was permitted to shine through, there was no warmth to speak of. It was late morning, the spirit-light giving the day a delicate feeling, as though it would break at any second, with night edging in to replace it. The water reflected what little light met it, the high and wide flow flanked on either bank by thin copses of golden cottonwoods and willows of yellow honey that dipped their long fingers languidly in the shallows. More trees spotted here and there as the river valley rose around them, but these seemed paltry and undergrown compared to their lofty cousins manning the shore. A mile or so ahead of them, they saw the fork in the river as a wide knob of land split it in two. The once great Wolfswater journeying off north-east, as the Greenrun snaked high into a narrow valley far to the north. At the confluence, on the arrowhead of land between the two rivers, a thick ring of trees stood three to four deep as it circled a stark imposing hill that rose above the valley in arduous ridges, dwarfing the valley around it. The summit was flat, sheered clean as though the titans had carved it for a stool.

"What is *that?*" Greg realised how young he sounded.

He expected Crispin or Zoush to answer, but it was Arne the Mute that suddenly found his tongue. *"Dhun.* Magic place." *A fayhill. Must be six times the size of the one in the blackwood. Six hundred feet, or more.* The memory of the great white wyrm settled in his mind, lifeless eyes staring deadly at him while maggots erupted from its fanged mouth and smoking nostrils, and the mark between its eyes burning like a firebrand. Greg shot a glance to Jephro, who rode close behind on his firemane. He was looking away, at something on the river, yet Greg could still see the hand on the boy's forehead. The symbol on the monster atop the hill was queer, not anything he had seen before, and not a hand. Even so, his heart thumped hard in his chest. He stretched his half-healed arm, hoping he could use it soon.

The boats arrived two days later. Gliding up the course on banks of oars, the men that pulled them moving with a single mind. *Four, five, six...* Greg counted them, coming to a sound twelve. They were long and sat high in the water, each measuring a hundred foot long and half as wide. At fore and aft great carved wooden faces rose sternly, the faces of some giants no doubt. At the bow of each was placed a nasty piece of steel fashioned into a ram. *They don't need to use those, surely?* The double masts reached high and swayed each time the boat rocked in the currents, and atop each a crow's nest was crested by a beast or lucky charm of weathervane. Greg's party had spied them a long way off, and now the anticipation was high with the prospect of news of the river hunters' exploits. From their impromptu camp, Greg found the forester Den Loudmouth and told him to hail the boats. The man raised his long hunting horn to his mouth and made the signal: three short blows, followed by two long and then two short. The answering call from the lead boat was sweeter than any maiden's song.

"Ahoy, there!" Shouted a red-haired man at the side-rail of the nearest boat as it edged the shore. Greg recognised the man instantly. Nat was not that hard to miss. "How goes the hunt?"

"Found nothing! Good fishing to be had, but the Godless alluded us."

Nat made his easy smile. As his boat dropped anchor a few feet from the shingle, the fox-face jumped the portside to land knee-deep. The splash sent river water to drench his breeches. Again that easy smile. "Apologies Greg, we've been two days a-river, and I needed to feel dirt beneath my boots." *But you needn't get the whole river on me.*

The thing on his new surcoat caught his eye, "What's that?"

Nat looked down, making a face as he did so. The surcoat was coloured ivory, and near his heart was embroidered a raven with outstretched wings, one of its legs raised so as to drink from the golden chalice it held in its talons. "This? I thought it apt, given my command of the *Merry Raven*. The boys of the *Raven* seem to like it too, and they have even called me the Red Raven a time or two. Although a fox would be more appropriate, I accept. A knight must have a coat of arms." Greg thought it only sounded half-joking.

"But you're not a–" the sudden squall of trumpeting horns erupted from the next two boats to near shore. A gangplank was lowered, and Audeyrn greeted Greg with a wide smile. He was flanked by two men he did not know. A Paydar was one, betrayed by his hair and armour. The other was cloaked, a deep hood all but obscuring his face. Greg nearly didn't recognise the Emissary himself: Audeyrn had allowed his beard to grow since they parted ways, a wiry-mass of blond and brown hair that made him look years older. Despite his rugged appearance, his eyes were aglitter with delight as he embraced the tracker.

"What? No hug for me?" Nat had his hands on his hips, pouting.

Audeyrn huffed, "I heard you get enough embraces from your captain. And there I thought even *you* could manage sailing a river that only goes in one direction without help."

"Up and down?" He smiled darkly. "Sibyl can navigate more than that, I can assure you. She can also raise a sail very well." Greg could not help but feel the hooded man looking at him, despite the cowl that fell across his eyes. Audeyrn seemed to notice his discomfort. He laid a hand on the Paydar's shoulder to say, "This is Captain Arodyr Rowett, master of the *Leviathan,* nephew to Lady Cyrinne Rowett." The mention of Lord Elmer's mother instead of the lord himself eased some of Greg's apprehension. He made himself say, "Hail, my lord of Rowett. How was the 'water?" The captain's braids extended down to his belt and his beard to his groin. His armour was fine leather, dyed a deep teal and shaped and tooled to resemble the interlocking segments of a lobster's carapace. "Hail, Gregyn of the High Forks. My new friend Audeyrn has told me much and more of your exploits… your skill with a bow in particular. You must show me soon." His teeth were stained and his breath heavy with rum, and he embraced Greg's outstretched hand.

"Now if you would excuse me," Arodyr said, already off

254

and barking orders in his quickest Qellish. Then Audeyrn turned to his other companion, and his face lost some of its vigour. "This is–"

"Govier," shot the man, throwing back his hood to reveal a handsome, if not drawn, face. His brown hair fell to his collar formlessly, with more than ample ash settling in his stubble. Audeyrn nodded as though his name alone was explanation enough. He explained nonetheless, "He is known to Norther, who with hope will not be long in arriving. It was Govier who guided us as we portaged the boats over land. With his insight, we avoided the Soran mounted patrols on either side of Halfway. His aims align with ours."

Aye, but to what end?

"Lyonis told me of you," the man Govier said curtly. The mention of the Soran made Greg's words catch in his throat, allowing only for a squeaked "Aye… where…" His head spun. The man seemed to look *into* him, hard and unblinking.

The Emissary caught his meaning. "The Captain-General will regroup with his forces on the Ruell coast. He has pledged to forestall the Soran campaign, making token attacks on Sir Walt's men to feign aggression. Thus the illusion of war to our sovereigns is maintained, for now. The younger brother to Lord Elmer, Commander Yestyn Rowett, is accompanying him. Lyonis himself will ensure his loyalty as they travel south together… Still, I would not trust him."

This Rowett, or Lyonis, or… ?

Govier crossed his arms, revealing strange garb beneath his cloak, all brass trinkets and miniature curios. "Wise choice. This war isn't done and won yet."

19

NATOLY

When Norther finally arrived, a full two days after their landing near Flattop, their numbers swelled to nearly two thousand. He could say this of the Paydar- they could organise a war camp. It remained hidden from view, as the Merry Raven worked through the orneric currents spewing from the Greenrun as it merged with the 'water. The camp lay behind the brusque knee of stone he knew, trying to spy it out in vain. It was perched within the hidden valley at the base of the promontory. The fayhill itself loomed large before him, an earthen affront frowning down on his hopes.

He had been tasked with taking the *Merry Raven*, *Lady Cyrinne* and *Ardent Valour* to the east bank, to await there until the remnants of their army arrived. Upon the beleaguered arrival of Norther's five hundred, they would ferry them to the western side of the headland between the two rivers, within the arboreal ring that encircled the fayhill like a palisade, and where the path led to the camp. It *was* a fayhill, there was no doubt about that. Here a ring of stone was not to be found. Instead, the rise was garrisoned by ranks of trees tinged by the oncoming autumn, the leaves having not yet fallen. And they were huge. He had never seen trees this large. He had heard of the great redwoods that grew south of Castan, on the jagged spike of land men called Sunset Point in the lands of the Druke. He had never seen them however, so he could not say. He wondered if they were even taller than the ones he saw here. One birch must have raked and stretched until it stood a hundred and fifty feet. He almost wished he could put them to parchment like Hector the Gifted to capture the scene for eternity, unmarred by time, safe from the ravages of wasting memory.

Talk on the *Raven* as they had journeyed upriver had been consumed by the great spur of rock and its supposed magical properties. Nat had listened to the stories, finding some more interesting than others, and many that would make even that braggart Norther's stories seem almost believable. There was some common thread woven amongst every yarn the crew spun, however. It being that you must never climb to the summit. Never. To do so would only bring a terrible curse on you and your kin, pestilence to your kith and lameness upon your cattle, the foundations of your house will be crooked, rain will never touch your crops, the very earth you tread accursed and poisoned. *Dhun*, they called it, and it was forbidden to man.

It had been a chore to hide his smirk every time a Paydar had regaled him with some parable about the Flattop, of this person or this time, of wandering bards that came here looking for inspiration or warriors seeking some bargain to become impervious to harm. His nods came easily and solemnly, and he treated their trite with some modicum of respect. After all, they outnumbered him, and he did not fancy taking a dip in the 'water.

Still... He sometimes found his hand reaching for his kje, as though he felt some imminent danger. The crew liked him well, so it could not have been them. A voice inside assured him that it was the Flattop, a worrying presence, not easily ignored if you happened to be sleeping and shitting on its slopes. Sibyl had made those nights easier, to be sure. Her appetites in bed matched only by her appetites at the table. In Wolfsmouth, he had volunteered to be the navigator aboard the *Raven*. Nat was not a sailor, so it had fallen to Sibyl Hillborn to order the crewmen. *What sort of captain can't even command his own ship?* He had long since swallowed his pride, admitting that without her, without this hard beauty whose life was sailing, he would have been hopelessly lost aboard this strange longship full of strangers who hardly spoke the common. On the *Raven* she was captain, crewmate, and lover. Nat tried to busy himself throughout the days spent on the river, to take his mind away from the lusting thoughts that occupied his mind. He would be topside, watching as the river slid past, listening to the slow rhythm of the oars cutting the water. He threw himself into taking the inventories with the little quartermaster called Hobart Hobb, or studying over maps and charts of the great Wolfswater system until his eyes ached, hell, even flyting with the fat, toothless cook lovingly named Rabbit. Yet when the sun made its slow but sure descent to set the west ablaze, and as night drew in, he had no such diversions. He would go to the captain's quarters tucked away at the stern, the cramped room made homely by the light of a single taper. There he would find her, waiting, for him. It had been the same every night for nearly a month.

Thinking leads to trouble. I know Maarten, I know.

At the bow of the *Raven* now stood Norther with the brutish Sere Rowett, leisurely leaning against the crank of the forward scorpion. The disfigured captain of the guard that had greeted them upon arriving at Rowett's Town. He pushed away the thoughts of his sleepless nights as he shimmied through the crowds of travelworn warriors. A hundred and eighty stinking and swearing Paydar. The *Raven* bore the most due to her being the largest, with the *Lady Cyrinne* and *Ardent Valour* picking up the rest. He regretted it almost instantly. Some were almost as ugly as *her*. She was hard to look at, yet as he approached she was giving a harsh chuckle, by some jape of the adventurer by her side he did not doubt, puckering the scars to turn her face into a demon mask. The injuries on Norther's face had healed well, leaving only the hint of a scar at his temple, that only seemed to compliment the one on his nose. *Of course it would.* Nat brushed down his new surcoat, making sure the raven over his heart was clear as clean water for all to see.

"Did you find your quarry in the Qell?" He asked, realising then that his new boots made him taller. He also did not fail to notice the wear and tear of the adventurer's gambeson, the same one he had worn at the Tor, bloody spitfire and all. He shrugged. "Unfortunately, no. Our forces were relentless in the hunt, but the lands to the east are ripe only with the last of this year's crop, apples fall in the fields aplenty, and starlings swarm in murmuration, yet we found not one adherent of the Godless. A folly, really. I doubt we would have found any even if we had an army of ten thousand to comb the entirety of the Wolfswater basin from Old Qell in the North to Wolfsmouth on the Ruell."

His confidence knocked Nat, and he could not help but say, "Why would you say that?"

"Because we overestimated their range." Nat had never much liked Norther using "*we*", as though he was one of the Emissary's chosen few and not just a mercen tacked on by that old drunkard Walton Iddles. The brute Sere eyed him, hard. *If you want me that bad, just ask, woman.* "You think the Godless are a threat, even if they are… fucking about at Bagman's Bluff."

"I'm sure of it. Though I don't think 'fucking about' is fair. I'd say they're consolidating their position. Building *up*, instead of *out*."

"How?"

Norther looked absentminded, as though the question bored him. *Pretty haughty for a mercen. You're someone, and I'm going to find out who.* "Suring up defences, piling stores, training, planning. I cannot be sure. I merely speculate. Yet there are known unknowns in our quest. One such joined you on the river… What do you make of Govier?"

"Aye. Odd fellow…" *That made him start.* "How do you know Govier found us?"

Norther laughed, but there was no joy in it. "He has ways of finding things, and people, that otherwise wish to be hidden. You would be wise to heed his words. He knows things."

Don't command me aboard my own fucking ship, mercen. Don't think this gruesome bitch of yours could save you, either.

You had your chance to capture that Godless agent in Rowett's Town, and you fucking failed, nearly compromising the contest in the Pit. Fool! Do you think I would have failed? He hoped his thoughts did not surface, making his ruddy cast even redder. He kept his smile, and he promised Norther he would consider it.

Two days they had waited at camp. With the arrival of Norther and his lot, preparations could now truly begin. Not that the Emissary had been idle in the meantime. Mounted patrols rode the length of the hill, massive wooden stakes were erected and ditches had been dug at the entrance to the hidden valley, and drills were well underway. Anything to keep them busy. It was Arodyr's suggestion. After all, he was Paydar, and he knew how restless his people could be if left to their own devices. It had been a wooded dale before they had come, bordered by high spears of exposed granite that made a ragged curtain wall to the north, west, and south. To the northeast, the cliffs of Flattop rose unyielding and unconquerable. A path caught his eye, more of a sheep-track than anything, impressions in the rock switchbacking on itself higher and higher. *Huh, so they do go to the top. The poets and the madmen.* The only access not requiring grapples and climbing was a narrow refile to the south-east, a water-carved gully that followed the bones of a dead stream into a wooded vale. It was starkly different to two days ago: where once trees covered the bowl of the valley, now it was bare and well-trod and slick with mud from men and horse alike. Walkways had been placed along the makeshift avenues using planks from the trees. After all, there was ample wood to be had. Soon there were roads connecting the neat rows of campaign tents, the latrines and the horselines, drilling yards and mess halls, a secret town of canvas dyed in bright Paydar tricolour and muddy wooden colonnades constructed overnight.

Organise a war camp indeed.

"What did the Paydar have to say about *that?*" Norther asked as they passed two abreast through the gulley. It would not permit anymore without causing a bottleneck. The vagueness of his question irritated Nat. "That?" he shot back.

"The trees. This is a spiritual place for them. They would not willingly fell ring-trees of Flattop." The ugly woman was eager to agree. "Yes. They are sacred. To the gods. That which is taken must be replaced, else the balance of the land is disturbed." *How insightful.* It was accusing, accusing *him* no less, despite him having played the footman and not touching a single tree of that godsforsaken hill. It was a field camp, and wood was needed for nigh on everything from walkways to stakes to firewood. Luckily, the answer to their gripe was sweet as honey. "It was Govier that suggested we use the treeline bordering the fayhill." The look on Norther's face was gold, better than that, a salve to ease Nat's burning frustration. *Take it up with the stranger. You seem to like him so much. Yet you don't fully agree with his methods. Curious that...* "He assured us that the trees grow in soil unlike any other in the realm. Full of nutrients and... other things, I forget what he called them. The losses will soon be recouped. In six years, it would be like we were never here."

Norther was unconvinced. "And what if they don't grow back?" *An answer for everything, yet ears for none. The mind of a mercen is a fickle thing.* He let it go unanswered.

He had been tasked with bringing Norther directly to Audeyrn, and so he did just that. Audeyrn's squire, the sixteen year old Nyle Rowett, had told him that Audeyrn would sleep only little, and ate sparingly. The Emissary had confined himself to his cabin, he said, what time he had outside of rumination was spent training on the aftcastle of his ship. *What is it called? The Kraken? No, the Leviathan.* The burly Paydar sailors that tried him were left bruised and insensate. He had asked them to come at him two or three at a time, and he had bested them every time. Nat dreaded this meeting. Those that came to greet them did not share his misgivings. Soon, they were clapping the latecomers on the back and handing them horns full to the brim with dark frothy beer. *Two days. And if the squire is to be believed, Aud has been like this all the way from Wolfsmouth. The man does not sleep. He talks endlessly of dreams and visions, prophecies of sand and death and dark. And we aren't even heading for Silentis yet...*

The tent was the largest in the camp, a triple-peaked canvas castle tipped by the Paydar colours and the banner of Castan: on a horizontal field of blue and green a winged lion roared in its ferocity. The autumn wind whipped at the silk until it looked like the lion was writhing, eager to escape the fabric and rip apart the enemies of the king. The guards before the entrances flap were Paydar, but they uncrossed their tall halberds as he approached. They recognised him, or he hoped, they recognised the raven that bedecked his surcoat.

Inside, it was funereal. Arrayed around the great carved war table, atop of which lay an intricate map of the upper Wolfswater on vellum. The captains of the ships and lieutenants of the hunting parties were there. Audeyrn stood with his hands across the table, Gregyn looked like he wanted to be anywhere but there, and Govier, his hood pulled up even inside, sat off to the side on a camp stool looking on all with his deadman's stare. Nat had hoped to see Hearty here too. He was one of the Emissary's chosen few, after all. Yet the old bluff pisshead was nowhere to be seen.

The Emissary looked up at the newcomers, only the slightest smile making his whiskers rise a mite. *How strange...* His new beard made him look more rough-faced, yet he did not look like a man lacking sleep and obsessing over dreams. His hair was washed and combed, freshly cut. "Thank you, Nat. Welcome to Flattop, Norther, Lady Rowett. You are weary I know, but there is much to be done." He beckoned for refreshments. As the servants hurried about handing out cups of lemonwater, Nat searched the faces assembled in the tent. Most of the Paydar were wide-eyed and fitful, shambling from foot to foot and murmuring in hard-edged Qellish. *Restless, and itching to fight. It's soon, then.*

"While we waited for your group to make camp, we formulated a plan for the assault on Bagman's Bluff. To-morrow." *So we'll attack. Good. How–*

"How far is the fort from here?" Asked Sere Rowett, before Nat had the chance.

"Nine leagues north-north-east, on the Greenrun. It shall be a three-pronged strike, with our naval group commanding the river and preventing any hopes of them escaping via the water. Our cavalry shall assault them on either bank. They will be forced upriver, and to their doom."

264

The conversation was translated for those that did not speak the common, and only then did the majority of the Paydar notables thump their chests in assent. *Why do they do that? They probably already know the plan.* Norther stood shaking his head. "I disagree. We should wait until my hunters have had time to recuperate. Rest. Natoly told me that you have been here two days. My men have only now come." *And who's fault is that?*

Audeyrn considered him before saying, "I understand. I do. But we have to move now, or risk being discovered. *They* know, Norther."

"How?" the adventurer leaned on the table. "How can *you* be sure?" The Emissary gestured to Greg, who left the tent in a brisk trot. Not a few moments had passed before he returned, only now he was accompanied by that black-bearded ranger from his party… and a prisoner. The man was half-dragged across the fine carpets in iron manacles binding his hands and feet, blood dripping steadily from a broken nose and smashed lip. His garb had been taken from him, so now he came before them naked, his hair one ragged knot and his skin covered in grime and filth. *This is not even a man. It's a ghost.*

"Name?" Audeyrn said, the voice so much like it had been in the Pit. "Answer me, or we will give you back to Gentle Gaff." The man made a slight sound, too faint to even be a whimper. *"Please, no… not again."*

"It speaks!" Nat exclaimed before he could catch himself. Aud sent a sharp look his way, but he said nothing. The Emissary walked the length of the table and came about to kneel next to where the ghost hung in a dead weight from his chains. "Name, I said." His head was drooped, but he

265

raised his eyes to the Emissary now. Nat was afraid that this Godless would spit at him, or bite him, or something. One final fight to spite his captors and leave them bloodier than he.

"Preiki. My name is Preiki."

It was easier after that. The tent was silent as the ghost called Preiki spilled his guts before Audeyrn and the assembled war council. It lasted the whole of three hours: admissions given reluctantly, yet given all the same. How far were they from Bagman's Bluff? How long have they occupied the place? How many were they? How strong are the defences, what state of repair? When did the scouts leave? Who was in the scouting party? How many got away... and when he had nothing more to give, he knew it. He broke down and wept, pleading for someone, anyone, to kill him. His answers came, but they were mostly useless. Many of the questions asked of him were answered candidly, but blurted with all the desperation of a man who knows he is going to die. He was terrified, and they all knew it. *How can someone live among others, yet know so little about them?* The ghost had been able to give details of the scouts, their identities, their number, and provisions, but aside from this, he was almost a child, offering up only hedging and dull imploring glassy eyes. He was taken away after that to the music of jangling iron chains.

"*That* is why we must attack tomorrow," Audeyrn said as the others were dismissed. Nat was permitted to stay, along with Norther, Greg, Sere Rowett, and Govier the shadow, who had remained silent throughout.

"Torture is unsound, emissary." Norther made it sound like a scolding. Audeyrn, to Nat's surprise, sat down heavily on a stool and ran a hand through his sandy hair. "I... I did not want it to come to that. He was unyielding, man! His fear of his masters runs deeper than his fear for us. What would you have done? Eh?"

"Asked him nicely, of course," Nat shot in.

"Shut your mouth!" Audeyrn rounded on him. The sudden outburst made Nat's hand go to his kje. "Why do you think this is a lark? I had a man tortured over the best part of a day, by a man called *Gentle Gaff*. How gentle do you think he was? You didn't happen to see how many fingernails the Godless was missing? Did you?" For a moment, it was all Not could do not to storm out. He forced himself to stay. "No, I didn't," he spat through a clenched jaw.

"Then I advise you look more often, and keep your smart mouth shut." The rancour lessened in his voice until he spoke more evenly. "You have command of three ships. I have been told by Captain Arodyr that they are among the fastest we currently possess. Can I rely on you to lead the first line?" *Command of the vanguard.* He was not expecting that. It passed his mind that this was some sort of joke. Then he looked into the Emissary's eyes and saw how they burned. There was no joke there. "Yes, I am. I mean, you can rely on me."

Audeyrn made a satisfied noise, then moved to the table to refill his cup. From the wine decanter this time, not the lemonwater. Nat was about to ask him to pour a cup from him too, but found his throat choked by anger. Sere Rowett helped herself to the decanter, not a cup, and sloshed the blackwine about her chops sickeningly. "And us?" The Emissary gave his beard a tentative stroke. "You and Norther will share joint command of the cavalry that will assault the eastern gate." For a moment the woman held the decanter high, as though in mock salute. "I agree. Though it must be said that Norther is an awful distraction. He tells the most amusing tales." *And all of them false, bitch.* The leather grip of his sabre creaked, loudly.

"Was that your doing, Govier?" Norther asked, the talk of command and delegation seemingly unheard. A look of distaste curled his lips. The man in question looked not to hear his words either. The steady rise and fall of the stranger's chest was the only indication that he was alive. *Answer the man, gods damn you.*

"If you refer to capturing poor Preiki, then yes. The methods by which your information was attained, however, were yours alone."

Norther spat to the carpets. "*Our means?* Horseshit. You knew what would be needed to break him. *Any of them*, should we capture more." That earned him a derisive snort from Govier, who produced a hip flask from his cloak. He proceeded to take a long swallow from it. "I offered to lead you to the Godless and their enclave. I have done this."

Audeyrn set down his drink. "No. You haven't. Not yet, anyway. Tomorrow, we shall find out if your help has been worth the secrecy and the frustration, *Govier*, or whoever the hell you really are. Tomorrow we shall find the Godless, and destroy them. The truths you have oh so begrudgingly betrothed will be tested... and the gods are my witness... if you lied to me, I will let you join the Godless in the Hell Unending."

"So be it." Govier's smile was unflinching.

The sun still had not sunk by the time he finally left

Audeyrn to his brooding. *Or whatever the hell is going on in his head these days.* The sun was stronger than it had been for the past few days, and he toyed with the whim to go back to the *Raven* at her anchorage, and dice with the crew and lie bare-chested atop deck and listen to the rigging move lazily in the breeze.

Best not. What about...

Instead of the anchorage outside of the camp, he remained within, and headed for the barracks. The mess was heaving, full to the rafters with Paydar that must have gotten wind already that they would be breaking camp on the morrow, for they drank with a lust for living, a need to drown in blackwine and ale and cider before meeting their fates. A familiar voice was singing a familiar song. He initially thought he had misheard, but then the lyrics came through the rumble of the drinkers to dominate the clamour.

"I was once a boy, young as I was proud, ever toiling old Da's field.

My castle a hut and broth my sup, and a grasshook did I wield."

The old knight was standing on a new-made trestle, his raucous words punctuated by the rough rhythm of Paydar slamming their cups and tankards and horns on the tables where they sat, trying to stay in time despite being in various states of drunkenness. He was flushed, his hair was mussy, and there was ale running down his beard, but his words were strong and commanding. *A good voice for singing 'I was once a boy', but a better voice for battle.* "All together now! Ready? Aaaaaaa...." A chorus of Qell-accented voices took up the cry, and Nat could not resist joining as they

269

sang the refrain that was well-known throughout Castan. *"A sword! A sword! Put a sword in my hand, so I may fight for lord and land!"* He could not help but feel a perverse sense of pride at having the famous song sung in the Qell, so far from home. It almost made him miss it. Hearty did not have his lute, Nat noticed, wondering if it had been misplaced somewhere. *It would be drowned out anyway.*

The knight spied out Nat as he filled a half-clean tankard from a nearby optic. "What are you doing, you damned reprobate? Just 'cos the bird on your breast is always drinking don't mean you need to be!"

Nat feigned shock as he said, "I'll stop, when you do!" Hearty Deri laughed, slapping his thigh. He plunged on:

"I was once a boy, one day 'pon happenstance, a man came riding through the trees.

He was a knight you see, all beaten and bloody, then died upon my knee."

Nat felt overjoyed. The bickering with the Emissary seemed a trifle now, and he found that the more he drank, the less concerned he became. A laugh broke his lips into a broad grin, the one that Aud liked to say made him look vulpine. *Joyless bastard. He laments as though he were an old woman.*

"A sword! A sword! Put a sword in my hand, so I may fight for lord and land! A sword! A sword! Put a sword in my hand, so I may fight for lord and land!" To say that they were in time with Hearty would be generous, and to say they were in tune would have been a barefaced lie.

Drink sloshed as cups clanged and downed, the men and women hectoring those they viewed as not drinking enough. One such was a hefty woman that came lurching over to Nat. "You, Red Raven! You want a challenge of drinking?" He vaguely recognised her as a crewmate aboard the *Lady Cyrinne*. He couldn't think of an excuse, so shrugged and offered up his cup to be filled.

"I was once a boy, the knight's chattel was sold by Da, but blade I kept secret and buried."

With years I grew, fell in love with fair Syw, 'til Vig's Rogues came prowling with steel."

The liquor was strong, he could tell just by smelling. There was a thick head on top, and so the blackness beneath was obscured by a golden frothy crown. *"A sword! A sword! Put a sword in my hand, so I may fight for lord and land! A sword! A sword! Put a sword in my hand, so I may fight for lord and land!"* The *Lady*'s crewmate shook her hand and cursed in Qellish. "No, no. Bitterale not for the smelling. It for the drinking. Like this, you are looking?" Without waiting for a response, she threw the contents of her cup down her throat, not a drop able to flee the fleshy abyss.

"Impressive. Might have to match you then."

"Less talking. More drinking. Yes?"

These people. "Yes." She refilled her cup and presented it before her. He mimicked her gesture, and then opened his gob ready for the drink. It was bitter, and then some. Considering it was given to the rank and file, it was of good quality, heady and thick, the aftertaste a sweet lemony tang. "Another!" Cried the crewmate. "Another for Red Raven!" Nat tried to hide how wet his eyes were, and handed back his cup for a second round.

"I am now a man, the Rogues they took my love, killed ol' pa and left the farm all rubble.

In cinders lay the blade, I spurned life a staid, to dare live a

271

life of trouble."

All knew the refrain was coming then, even those who could no longer stand or see. The mess tent felt muggy and hot, and all bore a fine sheet of sweat across his brow and spittle on his lips. *"A sword! A sword! Put a sword in my hand, so I may fight for lord and land! A sword! A sword! Put a sword in my hand, so I may fight for lord and land!"* The second one went down more manageably, but he did not taste it, his mind filled with his nights in Low Castan where a pint could be bought for a copper. *And the girls were more expensive, but what is coin for, if not for spending?* His favourite haunt had been the *Hardranger Inn*, a lopsided ramshackle alehouse off Isor's Street, far from the judging eyes of the Castle. At the *Hardranger*, he had been a lord of night. In his fine guardsman mail with livery emblazoned with the legendary winged lion of Caldland, and the kje on his hip, men would offer up their seats, even call him *Sir*.

"I am now a man, cutting down my foes; trouble cannot withstand me!

They stood no chance, t'was a frightful dance, and Syw cried a dashing knight is thee!"

"A dashing knight is thee," Nat said, not realising how loud he was. He saw Rhyrn in his mind's eye, almost as clear as though she was really there, dancing, her skirts aswirl as she sipped from a chipped clay cup and held out her hand, beckoning to him. She wanted him to dance. *You'll be a knight someday. I know it.* The crewmate cocked her head like a dog, saying, "Eh, *roqyi*? What is you saying?"

"Nothing. Nothing." *Rhyrn. Forgive me.* The woman swayed as she cocked her wrinkled lip in dismissal. The light had dimmed, the scuttling light of torches painting all with a lambent orange glow. *How long have I...*

The song came to an end, but not before Hearty led them once more in the refrain. They were pissed and elated by then, and they roared with deafening ardour. *"A SWORD! A SWORD! PUT A SWORD IN MY HAND, SO I MAY FIGHT FOR LORD AND LAND! A SWORD! A SWORD! PUT A SWORD IN MY HAND, SO I MAY FIGHT FOR LORD AND LAND!"*

The crewmate held friendly talk with Nat, and their competition petered out quicker than a mayfly's cavort. They continued to drink, the bitterale running out a goodly hour after Hearty ended 'I was once a boy' with a flourish and a dangerous pirouette on the table. It was swiftly replaced by a Vasti ale, which was somewhat less choice than the previous drink brewed by the Paydar. *Might have to steal their secret. The Vasti could learn a thing or two from the hillfuckers. About brewcraft, and living with more than milk in their blood.* Sometime later he lost his newfound friend, both lost in an ale-flavoured haze as many others he barely recognised invited Nat to sit with them and share in their talk of the battle to come.

He found Hearty eventually, who was well and truly now a keg with legs, with as much beer in his beard as there was in his stomach.

"Deramun, it seems to me that you've outdone yourself."

The affront layered even more red in those big rosy cheeks. "Outdone how?" His speech was slurred.

"Your drinking, of course." The High Hall of Castan was often filled with Hearty going drink for drink with Walton Iddles or Symon the Small, to the singular joy of Nat. It was worse when the man would pass out, for none could move him or wake him. Nat pitied the sods that had pitched their tents neighbouring Hearty. *Poor bastards.*

"I have outdrunk every colt and filly here that dared think they could best *me*. I'm glad you're not so foolish, fox… or should I start naming you raven now?"

"Either is fine. What do you make of the men, and women?"

Hearty stroked his beard, "The Paydar are a strange folk, but gallant and loyal, once you look past the arrogance. There is kindness there, among the ruthless iron." Nat raised an eyebrow, and elbowed the bluff old fool. "Good luck with the hunt. I've seen many here tonight that aren't half too bad."

"Aye. That they are. Might be my tent will be loud tonight." Hearty Deri had a devilish grin on his broad features. *I don't doubt that.* "When will you be heading back?"

"Soon."

Soon came quicker than he would have liked. His walk to the anchorage was wandering and bothersome, and he lost his way five, maybe six times. He was pissed, he had to admit, and the planky-road vexed him no end as he plodded along to the sound of nailed boots on wood and the fading sound of merriment behind him. He found the ship in the end, the lanterns swaying from the masts to make him dizzy. The watchman voiced a challenge, but upon seeing who he was, tugged at a forelock and let him aboard.

It was quiet on the *Raven*. Strange, considering how blithe it had been on their voyage up the Wolfswater. Even in the dark fogbound nights on the river, there had always been a dozen or so whispering seamen that would hunker down beneath the gunwale and dice or take their rum ration or ritualistically whet their weapons. Now he felt all alone (but for the unlucky sod that pulled the watch), and he found that it had gotten cold. Or maybe he was sobering up.

The double doors to his cabin were windowless, but he saw the wink of light bleed through the keyhole. He braced himself, and then scolded himself for being such a craven. Even so, he evened out his rumpled surcoat. He opened the door, and he saw her.

"A vision," he said, trying to hide the crook the drink had left in his speech. Sibyl Hillborn looked up from the chart she had been studying. Her laugh was husky and rough. "What's this, a corsair drunk on ale and glory come to steal me away?" She had been reclining in the captain's chair, her feet thrown onto the table with boots hiding most of her body. Her braids were tied back with a bone brooch allowing the taper to throw warm light on her face, long and sharp and keen-eyed, with a smattering of freckles across her nose and wind-burnt cheeks. Without moving, she said, "Fetch me the wine would you?"

It was on the table, a pewter goblet with inky liquid within, and she had been using it to pin down the dog-eared corner of a nautical map he could not make head or tails of. When he picked it up, the map curled inward, guarding its secrets. *Not that I could make out the Qellish scribbles anyway.* Handing the wine to her, he placed his hand on her leg. She was wearing sea-stained breeches, which always looked too tight in his eyes, along with a loose-fitting sailor's vest. The pelt is what caught his eye. The pelt of a western lion he had bought in Wolfsmouth. He thought it would look good on him, being a Caldishman, after all. It looked much

275

better on her, draped over her shoulders, the opaline fur being large enough to cover her and keep off the night's chill. "Would you command me on my own ship?"

She scoffed, making a noise that many a Caldish lady would find savage. He only found it wicked. Between healthy sips of the wine, she said, "Your ship. Of course... *Captain*. Do all Castanni find women so intimidating?" Her teasing made him blush. He hoped the light of the tapers hid his colour. Why had he wanted to stay away from her? As much as he tried, he couldn't seem to remember.

"The captain wants to know what you're perusing."

She regarded the parchment, yellowed and crumbling from age. "It's a discourse on the advantages of clinker-built oceangoing vessels over those built in the carvel method. Written by Lodestone Locque about fifty years ago during the reign of King Odaric Maidenbane. He makes an otherwise interesting subject dreadfully boring. I know you won't be interested in that though."

"Lodestone? Wasn't he some sort of pirate?"

"Something like that." She rose abruptly, thrusting the wine at his chest. "Hold this." The turgid treatise she rolled up and placed within a leather map tube. He was about to take a measure of the drink before she said, "No, that vintage is too good for the likes of you. Besides, I see you've sampled enough of my countrymen's liquor tonight." *Do I truly look that drunk? I don't feel it.* "I don't think so."

"You are so. Did you find out about the battle? Hobart claims we're to attack on the morrow. I trust the man with numbers and stock, yet he's as bad as a fishwive when it comes to gossip." He was surprised at how fast news had travelled in the camp. "It's true. We sail first thing tomorrow…" He put a hand around her waist. "And I command the vanguard."

She did not pull away, but snatched the goblet from his hand. The lion pelt slipped from a freckled shoulder. "How pissed are you?" Her vest had fallen even lower.

"As you can see, I can stand."

His hand wandered downward. She made that noise again. "I don't want you standing. Now undo my hair."

20

GREGYN

The ramparts were alive with featureless heads bobbing between the cracked and crumbling merlons, to fire down on the besiegers. Crews of the similarly black-clad Godless struggled to operate the half-constructed trebuchets and onagers and ballistas that sat hunched like rocs, ready to strike the invaders that came up the river on their ships. Now and again came the low *thrrrum* as stones twice the size of a man's head crashed into the river to send up massive spouts of white-water, or strike the deck of one of the ships that choked the Greenrun, or rip through the ranks of oars. Greg saw one stone collide with a man running to the forecastle aboard a ship in the first-line, his head exploding in a gush of blood and bone until the once-braided head now covered his crewmates. Otherwise a rogue missile would strike home and explode in a fountain of splinters taller than a ship's mast. They rained down to kill a few more, making them pin-cushions of shredded wood, screaming in agony.

It was a grey day, and he thought it might rain. The

sun had raised its golden head just long enough above the east for the first furtive sunlight to dance about Sere Rowett's sun-ray helm. At least, he had thought it was her. It was hard to make out, with their five hundred being on the other side of the river and all, some seven hundred feet away. Norther was there too, he knew, commanding the assault on the east gate. The sun secreted itself soon after, shrouded by a nebulous slate sky that stretched from horizon to horizon, unbroken and unswayed. A dismal day, and one he knew would only get worse.

He stretched his arm, feeling the tightness that came with it. It had healed, but he knew it would never be as supple or strong as before. He just hoped it would be strong enough. He cursed, thinking about what his father, old Garren, would make of this. He would likely grunt, spitting, to declare what a waste it all was. When he thought of his mentor, cowardly Huhtal, wherever he might be, he could not easily say what he would have thought. That road led only to what had happened in Mornswood, and the way the Reeve Arran had licked his lips when he found him. "What have I here?" the Reeve had said, voice dripping in mock innocence. His guards had laughed, and one had prodded Greg with his spear. "Looks real fresh to me, lads…" The sound of a belt buckle grated against the inside of his head.

No. Don't think bowt that. Not now. Not ever. Focus on now. Now. Now. Now.

The Paydar aboard the first-line sang a battle chant, but the sounds of war made the words all ephemeral and dim. Whatever bolts and stones that managed to hit the ships were few, and the damage to the vanguard was still minimal, the scorpions on the fore and aft sending volley after volley of bolts in return. The already weak southern curtain wall and the tower that warded the way already becoming cratered and cravitous.

Bagman's Bluff occupied a large river islet rising from the stolid water of the Greenrun. Roughly diamond-shaped, and comprised of knuckly rock, the bluff had been built upon over time so that now tall walls came to claw up from the living rock a hundred foot high. To either end of the islet, the North Tower and South Tower stood crenellated and twice as tall as the walls, warning beacons atop both, the whole length of them riddled with arrow slits and leaded windows that gaped empty and dark. Connecting the fort to less watery ground was a pair of matching bridges in various states of disrepair. A pair of smaller guardtowers a mere ten feet taller than the walls seemed to bolt the bridges in place from riverbank to islet, with a portcullis barding both entrances to the bridges and the fortress proper. Everywhere, patches of new stonework pockmarked the walls and towers, and crawled with scaffold and cranes as though it were the web of a colossal spider.

"They are not organised," observed Audeyrn's squire, Nyle Rowett, as he shifted the Caldish Winged-Lion banner to his other shoulder. Greg regarded him briefly. Broad and stocky, with thin pale blond hair that he wore short and limed, with always a word to say and a joke to make. *A blond fox,* he thought, even though he looked nothing like Nat. The squire could not have been more different than his family too, with his fair cast and hair that seemed to stand stiff and straight, the boy was cocksure and able, and had ingratiated himself with the Emissary. The closest thing to being Paydar was that he rode a firemane, but even that beast was unique. The hair from poll, withers, and tail were coloured a fiery yellow-white instead of the common crimson. He didn't have the six-fingered hand on his forehead like his younger brother Jephro, a few feet away. *The gevh. Blood-rite, that's what Crispin called it.* Greg supposed that meant he had already blooded himself. "No discipline, neither. We've caught them with their breeches 'round their ankles." *Gods, he even speaks with a Caldish accent.*

"You're wrong," Audeyrn shifted in his saddle. "They knew we were coming." Greg had been there when Arne the Mute had arrived triumphant into the camp, a gagged man slung across his mount's rump. They had come across a Godless scouting party while outriding, and aside from the man, who they had later found out was called Preiki, they had killed two others. Another two had escaped, retreating to Bagman's Bluff to spread the word that the Paydar had been roused, and were coming up the river.

The ride was hellbent if there ever was one. The leagues were covered swiftly by Greg's group to the west and Norther to the east, making a mad gallop and swallowing up the distance to reach the Godless enclave before the surviving scouts, or at the very least, before they could raise the alarm and escape. No one could know how much information the Godless scouts had gathered. The Mute was acerbic, bitter that they had slipped through his grasp and dusty from the ensuing chase. He claimed they had been a goodly five miles northwest of Flattop, and if they knew anything it was paltry, if not picayune. All of this the Mute managed in two sentences, leading Greg to marvel at such a taciturn fellow. It was the most he had heard from him than the entire month they had spent together. They failed to find the surviving scouts, and came upon the fort in dreadblack night to await the ships. The first came with the shy blush of dawn.

The *Steel Kiss* had beached on the western riverbank and the *Tyger* on the east, and were busy offloading battering rams and crossbowmen. The Mute commanded the assault on the western gate, his Paydar busy traversing the hastily dug moat as arrows rained down on the great curved square shields emblazoned with screaming titans. The far bank was the same, Greg figured. It was difficult given the distance, and hidden by the Bluff besides. They knew what had to be done- to attack the Godless on all fronts and deny them any outlet for retreat, to break open the portcullis (if possible), while the ships destroyed as many weapon emplacements to allow for siege ladders to be erected on the walls. If that could be achieved, the attackers could scale the walls with rope and grapple, fight their way inside and raise the portcullises themselves, routing the bastards from within.

A miller might build a mill... the saying was meant for humble folks, but it applied just as well here. Every plan had its risks. It would not be easy, Greg knew with what little experience he had of warfare. For one, the Godless were not just going to allow them to break the fort. The arrows fired sporadically from the gatehouses, and atop them he could see smoke rising steadily. *Tar, most like. Liquid death.* The Paydar were being cautious, staying away from the gate proper until ordered to, attaching hooks. To sit beneath them would mean a slow agonising death, as the tar (and other nasty things) would be poured from the murder holes above and cook the besiegers in their own armour.

"Either way, they can't escape us now, Lord Emissary."
Nyle said, seeming to raise the banner higher with a puffed-
up chest. Audeyrn looked at him, the end of his hair curling
out from his mail coif. Greg thought he saw through Nyle,
as though he was regarding a riderless horse with a talking
war banner astride it. *What you's thinking, Aud? What's
amiss?* The emissary was armoured like a Paydar, in thick
mail and plate clinking softly as his mount moved beneath
him. His helmet rested on his saddle horn, a gift from Lady
Cyrinne, a great-helm and visor with the crest fashioned
into a rampant golden lion, with his wings extended, from
which hung streamers of Castan blue and green. *Lord
Emissary, aye. Sometimes easy to forget, that.* For all that
Audeyrn could be, he was his friend. So why did he not
recognise this stranger wearing his skin?

"Perhaps... Numbers seem to be in our favour, at any rate.
Even if we cannot encircle them, they remain trapped, and
soon the fort itself will betray them." Audeyrn clenched
his gauntlets tight about the reins. Govier had stated that
the fort was in a weakened state, but Greg would not have
thought it would be this bad. It remained strong where
it mattered, however. The bridges were still standing, for
one. The Emissary had hoped that both bridges had long
collapsed or been replaced by walkways made of wood,
the plan being to fire them and surround the fort from all
sides with the ships. A ring of fire would have spread out
the Godless forces and made it much easier to break the
defences. But the bridges stood, and despite being built to a
gentle arch, they were too low to allow for even one of their
ships to pass beneath. Audeyrn had proposed removing the

masts, as he argued that they would be using oars upriver anyway. *That* was met by disapproval by Govier, who claimed it would serve only to waste time, and by outrage by Captain Arodyr, who said the crews would see that as nothing less than sacrilegious to purposely damage the Bloodroyal Fleet. So Audeyrn had mulled it over as the fleet drew up before the Bluff, and with a curse, ordered the assault to proceed. The bridges barred their way, and the masts remained untouched. Greg kept thinking about it. It was strange that they would still be standing.

On their hillock overlooking the fray, they arrayed themselves around the Emissary; Nyle Rowett at Aud's heel, along with a few men-at-arms with their visors down; Hearty who carried the Paydar tricolour, looking ready to hurl; Mayred, who always seemed to be near the tracker and always had a smile for him; further back was his squire Jephro, attentive and timid; and behind the rest was Govier, who sat his horse and fiddled with some gewgaw. Greg found it unbelievable that a poacher from the High Forks and former bondservitor would be here with Audeyrn Langholm. Here, fighting the Godless amid fearsome warriors and intrepid travellers, beneath the king's banner too. It was unbelievable, but he made himself believe it. He believed–

An ear-splitting crash barrelled over the river, tearing at Greg's attention to focus on the river. The initial thundercrack had been a hail of brick and shattered stone as it was sent flying by a scorpion bolt, lodging itself in the South Tower. Deep fissures grew like creeping vines along its base, tracing a fault in the foundation where masonry met rock. The entire tower grinded with a noise like a thousand rusty wheels struggling to turn, like bones snapping, like a mountain collapsing. Those aboard the ships sent up a ragged cry, but it was cut short. With a groan, the South Tower began to lean... away from the fort. Greg could see figures jumping from the top. They knew it meant certain death to remain atop the turret, so they chanced the rocks below over the evitable crush of mortar and stone.

From behind Greg came a sharp intake of breath.

"Gods, it's going to..." Nyle said in a cracked voice. Muddy must have felt the fear that suddenly effused the air, for he snorted and retreated a step. *No, it's the sound. It's falling, and getting louder.* The South Tower was a broken finger, lurching outward towards the river, towards the vanguard.

"Backwater! *Backwater now!*" Shouted Audeyrn, but they could not hear him. It was too late, anyway. With a thunderclap, the drunken tower slammed down hard on the ship desperately trying to steer clear. Greg briefly saw men abandoning ship before it vanished, consumed by stone, pulled under as a gush of river water sent plumes of howling spray hundreds of feet into the air to douse the rest of the fleet. There was nothing left of the boat that went down, so heavy was the Tower wreck that it weighed down any flotsam that lay beneath the tonnes of rubble. The four remaining ships in the first line were sent reeling across the channel, turning about as the men aboard scrambled to prevent collision with the riverbanks, or each other.

"Nat... *no...*" Was that his voice? It sounded callow and lost.

"A spyglass! Bring me a spyglass, damn you! *Now!*" The

Emissary barked his orders to no one in particular. When someone did find one, he snatched it from their grasp to scan the debris. Hearty cantered his horse forward. The look on his face was grey and grim. "Are there… any survivors? Aud?" For a long moment he said nothing, now and again adjusting the lens.

Greg had seen how glory-hungry Nat had looked when Audeyrn offered him command of the vanguard back at camp. He was boastful and puffed up, yet Greg knew what he had wanted, beneath the ambition and bravado. To anyone who asked, he would have said it was his destiny to be a knight of Castan. That was not a lie. Nat did yearn for knighthood, but it was only a means to an end, a route to what he saw as a comfortable and respectable life. A life where he did not want. Greg knew what it was to want so badly, making them do things they were not proud of. The memory of the look the fox had given him in the snowmonts came to him, then. It had been full of repulsion. Roc blood had covered him from fingers to elbow, with Nat's knife shining darkly in the moonglow. *That's what I do t'survive, Nat. You knew it too, that's why you don' like it. 'Cos you saw it in y'self. I'm sorry, Nat.* The look had been a flicker, a momentary thing, a shadow of a shadow, replaced thereafter by the swelling pride as though he had caught his younger brother trying to shave the fluff off his cheeks. *An older brother.*

"Ha!" Audeyrn's laugh was bitter, tossing the spyglass underhand to Greg. The tracker made sure to catch it with his good arm. "The *Merry Raven* was on the left flank! There, along with *Charmian* and *Stormcloud*! The vainglorious bastard disobeyed me. The *Merry Raven* was for centre command, but he placed himself and the ship on the flank!"

Greg looked through the glass to the ship's banking oars to correct themselves. "Which boat sunk?" he asked.

"The *Lady Cyrinne*. All hands... gone."

"My noble grandmother won't be pleased with that," intoned Nyle, grinning upon seeing Audeyrn so relieved, and then making it disappear when he realised no one was smiling.

Hearty seemed less gloomy now, yet his face was still colourless, "Wherever the gods may be, let them be merciful on those dead. And for all those that will meet their fate here today."

The ships were angling away from the downed tower, the refuse rock so much like freshly piled earth on the ship's grave. The crash had brought a momentary halt to the battle, yet now the ballista fired again, as though nothing had happened. A half-dozen riders broke off from the assault on the western gate to climb the Emissary's hillock. The shields were slung across their backs, many littered with arrows. The leader dismounted when they closed on the party, nodding to Greg amiably. Audeyrn saluted them, "You are Crispin?"

"Aye, my Lord Emissary. Crispin Moss." The bewhiskered sergeant went to a knee.

"No need for all that. Do you have a report?"

"That I do, lord. We have managed to dislodge the portcullis from its frame. Bloody old it is, near as old as the Bagman itself. Put up as much a fight as the twats above it, that it did. But it's near done now. A strong rend using a few firemanes will free it, opening the way across. Well... the

287

lads were wondering... do you intend to lead the charge across the bridge?"

"No." The single word spoke volumes. The Paydar all made the same confused face at the Emissary. Greg heard mumbling from one of Crispin's riders. *Questioning if the Caldishman has no stomach for war?* Crispin collected himself enough to ask, "My lord, if you do not wish to, might someone else?" That brought them out of their stupefaction quickly enough. The riders and the Emissary's entourage all asked for the honour of leading the charge, humbly and brazenly offering themselves up. Nyle, ever eager to please, edged closer to Aud to say, "My Lord Emissary, I would do it. Give the banner to your man Gregyn, and let me ride down any faithless within for the glory of Castan and the Paydar."

Your man Gregyn? He thinks me a manservant.

"Something is off." Audeyrn did not even look at Nyle. His gaze was fixed on the *Merry Raven* as they made ground on the islet. A good fifty yards either side of where the tower had once stood, whole sections of the battlements had been ripped away, as though the South Tower had clung on to life before collapsing, and had brought down the walls in its death throes. The crewmen from the ships were leaping ashore, grapples to hand and pulling up the siege ladders as those still atop the walls tried to stop any that made it ashore. The rocks ascended thirty feet above the water before meeting the wall, and there was a plenitude of newmade cover for the attackers. "The Godless expect us to cross. We will not."

Hearty slapped his thigh, seeming to realise what Aud was saying. Nyle moved the banner between shoulders again, shaking his head. "I do not understand. We won't cross the bridge because the Godless would shoot at us?"

The Emissary's jaw set hard. "The question you should be asking, Nyle, should be: why did the Godless not collapse the bridges?"

Crispin nodded, a tight smile making his beard bristle. "The tricksy bastards. *Dhereda*, the lot of them," he said, though he offered no explanation himself.

Greg looked at the western bridge, dilapidated yet still firm. The closer he studied it in the spyglass, the more he felt deep apprehension fill him. "Pulleys, Aud. Ropes and that, weaving in and out of the walls… It's a trap."

"A trap?" Nyle gasped. "We can't cross, then. We just can't," he said, stating the obvious.

Greg's heart was a hammer in his chest. "The east bridge!" Audeyrn's mount whickered at the shout, so the Emissary yanked the reins hard. "They've rigged them both, yes."

"We 'ave to do summin! Norther is there! The people, they'll die!" And then Govier was there. His presence was anything but reassuring, him being all hooded and with his knowing eyes. The Paydar riders parted before him, edging their firemanes away as though he were infected with the malaise. Crispin gave Greg a wary look. He had told him he did not trust the man. Not many did.

"Norther is aware of the situation." The shadow's words were calm and even, unrushed. Greg thought they even sounded bored.

Audeyrn spurred his horse on so that he and Govier were at arm's distance. "Tell me how you know that. I *warned* you, if you led us down a knifed-alley, I'd kill you. So tell me. Prove that you're the ally you claim to be." Govier laughed, a brief but full roar that made Muddy shy away. When it subsided, he held up his hand. A fingerless glove pulled tightly at his fingers. One pointed at Greg.

"I'll tell you, if I can borrow him."

Greg's muttered objection was overrun by Audeyrn, "You're mad. Crispin, take him into custody. Don't mistreat him, though. He will be put to the question in due course."

"That shan't be needed, Audeyrn." The shadow put up his hands. "I meant no ill intent by it. By any of this. We waste time by jabbering, but I will allow a moment to explain."

"Then talk." Audeyrn laid a gauntlet on the hilt of his sword. The threat was plain to see.

Govier began, "In my line of work, ignorance is the most stalwart of protectors. I merely wish to say this, and I will use what brevity I can muster. I was able to inform Norther because I have been *here* many times. I know the layout intimately. I saw the Godless as they set their little snares. Given that Norther was to be sent across the water, I told him ahead of time. You, however, needed to be persuaded." Audeyrn bridled at that but kept his tongue behind closed teeth.

"Gregyn is a proficient hunter, and can be clandestine when it suits him." *Not in Mornswood. Not there. That's how I was caught.* "I shall enter through an outworn yet hidden postern gate on the north-side. I will need a spotter, and he fits that need quite well."

There's another way in. Why say 'bowt it now? Curiosity brought a thousand questions to mind.

When Audeyrn looked at Greg, his eyes burned. "What do you say to all this?"

There was only one thing he could say.

"Yes."

The northern tip of the islet seemed deserted in comparison. The North Tower stood high and dark. For a moment, the tracker had an uneasy feeling as they passed beneath it in their boat. That was another thing that worried him. The small rowboat had been there, ready, in the spot Govier said it would be. As though he put it there. *The man's a sphinx.* The questions he had posed to him were either hushed or dismissed with a flick of a wrist. Even he was not so stupid as to talk when they neared the islet, though, quieting himself at the looming. There, Govier took the tiller while Greg was told to row. Not that he needed to. The currents were strong there, and the shadow knew exactly where to guide them.

A door appeared from the bare rock twenty feet above the waterline. "That'll be the Thief's Door," Govier said, leaping gracefully to the rocks despite the slime and wet that covered them. Greg could not help but laugh. " S'pose I'm not intruding if it's named after me."

The smile on Govier's drawn face was wry and all coy. "I suppose that's true." He tied up the boat and made their tentative way upward. The door was locked, unsurprisingly. What frustration Greg felt was replaced by a strange joy as the shadow set at picking the lock. It took less than a minute, his hands were sure and deft, and he swung the door outward. Within, a dank cellar sprawled with saltpetre and a peculiarly loud squeaking. And it was dark.

It only became darker as Greg eased the door shut. "Shit. We've forgot torches. We haven' got–" The cellar blazed with a yellow-white light. It took Greg all of a moment to realise that it came from Govier, from something in his hand.

"No need for torches, then. Where we going now?" Govier led on, and Greg followed. They went deeper into the cellar, littered with barrels and crates that crumbled into splintery dust at the touch. The bones of dogs lay in a half dozen rude piles, serving their masters loyally even in death. Backed against one wall was a shock of timber and rubble. The light revealed an empty space behind, a threshold to a disused room. Careful to move enough detritus to slip through, without causing it fall on their heads, they passed through. Somewhere along the way, Greg slashed open the back of his hand, the blood flowing fast and free. The room proved to be the threshold to a staircase, winding tightly upward in a corkscrew. The steps danced in the light. Greg eyed the thing Govier held. A crystal atop a brass bar of some sort, with two arms attaching the two. The light did not flit and falter like a candle, but held an amaranthine light. *I want one.*

Up and up and up, they followed the stair, not stopping at the many doors they met along the way. When they did finally halt, it was so sudden Greg almost ran into Govier's back. A double-doors barred a broad corridor ahead. The stairs continued upward, but Govier shone his light away from them so that they fell away into darkness. These doors were unlocked, and budged after putting a strong shoulder into them. Beyond was a windowless colonnade, high-ceilinged and freshly swept. It extended for a time, until Govier made a sharp left, coming to face an old bronze door stained a deep green. When they opened it, he thought the noise was loud enough to wake even the dead in the crypts. At least, he thought there were crypts there. "Loud,

I know," conceded the shadow, not stopping to talk but striding through the door.

"Too loud, aye. Wha–"

"About the guards? They shan't trouble us here."

Greg didn't believe him. He stretched his bad arm. "Why not?" But the man was already heading down a large vaulted room full of gargantuan steel barrels. What looked like brewing equipment lay aimlessly over the lip of the vats and on tables beneath them. They all shone with a focused sheen, not a spot of rust or dust to be found and polished enough for Greg to see his reflection. *These are new...* Govier led him between two of the huge vats, where a small door stood, dwarfed by all. It was steel, with a panel above it bearing a string of letters neatly written in chalk. The door was half open.

"This is where I leave you."

"Whe– What? No!" All the words came tumbling out at once. Somehow he knew that nothing would sway this stranger. In the end, he said, "Fine. But why lead me here, only t'abandon me?"

"I cannot go any further. To do so would be... troublesome." When he saw the startled look on the tracker's face, he pulled back his hood. "Listen, Gregyn. You will not come to harm here. I promise you that. Make me swear if you'd like. On the gods, my dear old mam, my life or honour, anything. I'll do it, if that would make you feel safe. Just know this. You're meant to be here. You're a good man... just not a very good poacher." When he smiled, there were deep crow's feet in the corners of his eyes. "Through the door is another stair. Climb it. *Do not* enter the first three doors you encounter. Only the *fourth*. You'll find it unlocked. From there, you can end this."

"How d'ya…" But Govier backed away, and when he pulled up his hood the smile was gone. "Goodbye, Gregyn…" He looked down at the light, and with a flick, it was gone, and Greg was alone and surrounded by an inky darkness. However much he called out to the shadow, he got no response.

The bastard's gone. Hells… He's… He's gone and left me in a castle full of Godless. Shit.

Maybe it was the sense that he had come so far, or maybe he did not fancy negotiating the stairs in the dark, but he felt his way to the door. Cold metal kissed his fingers, sending gooseprickles across his skin. He needed to find some light. There could be anything in the dark.

The faintest impression of a stairway appeared before him, a vague shape lying below the surface of that tenebrous sea. It only got stronger as the stair ascended. Unlike before these did not spiral but led straight ahead. His footing was uneasy, yet the steps did not give under his feet, and he was soon taking the stair on his long legs three steps at a time. The doors came and went, just as Govier had said. The light was still too weak, so he felt them more than saw them. One was barred and nailed tightly shut, the next rotted and rimed with something like frost it was so cold, the next after that reinforced by iron stanchions. The fourth came soon after, an ordinary wooden door. The light pooled from some unseen flambeau further up the stair. He could not see the source. *How high does this thing go?* Govier had told him to go into the fourth. Only the *fourth.* Doubt gnawed at him, but he saw no other choice. There should have been, yet he found his feet carrying him to the door, his hand reaching for the latch and turning it upward, to the creak of old hinges.

The light of day rushed into his eyes, forcing him to squint. Some instinct made his good hand reach for his bow. Then it was all hard hands grabbing him, pulling him inside.

"Get in 'ere, fool! Don't make a noise! Fool. Fool of a boy." The old man smelled foul, as though he had been bathing in wyrm dung. His black tunic was torn and grease-stained, and the boots and gloves he wore looked two sizes too big.

"Hands off a'me!" His hand pulled free his dirk, and brought it under the old man's chin to shear at some of the stringy hairs protruding from his unwashed beard. "Get back!" The touch of steel caused all resistance to go out of the stranger. Greg used his bad arm to grab at the scruff of that dirty neck, to scan the room quickly.

A large window dominated the far wall, a hook and bucket hanging despondently from an overhanging gable. The room was rounded. At its centre stood a solid metal plinth, atop of which lay a mangled pile of metal clawing its way off the floor in an orderless sprawl. It looked like it had bent, melted even.

The others stirred at the uproar. Greg counted twenty, twenty-five or more, raising their heads slackly and blinking dimly. Greybearded and yearworn all, they sat or squatted in their own filth, and looked at him with rheumy eyes. "Wha… Who are you?" Greg forced out, then turned to his captive to scream, "Tell me!"

The man shook like a shitting dog in his grip. "We're the faithful. The chosen blessed of the Child. They told us that they'd come back, to save us. But they never did. They

295

said–"

"You are one of *them!*" Shrieked a thin voice. It came from a bent old woman, white hair stretching down in wads from a balding scalp. Her rags barely covered her as she rose from her spot near the plinth, all bones wrapped in tight leathery skin. "Ignore her," said the man, trembling as he put a gloved hand on Greg's shoulder. It was old leather, cracked and heavy. "She's mad, you see. Her boy fights outside."

"Aye!" Said the woman. "Six summers he's seen. Six, is all! Yet still braver than those heartless demons beyond the walls!" *Six. He said she's...* A terrible thought passed his mind. His throat felt dry, and he felt his bad arm ache. He released his grip on the old man, to make his way to the window. He heard the fellow collapse behind him, falling into a weeping fit.

It can't mean... The wind hit him as he reached the window. He was *in* the North Tower as far as he could tell, a good fifty feet above a protected bailey. A strong wall separated it from the rest of the castle, itself a good thirty feet above the great courtyard, where ramshackle buildings and a well stood witness to small soldiers struggling to carry wheelbarrows full of stone to the ballista crews atop the curtain walls. Most were concentrated at the far end, where the courtyard narrowed at the breach in the wall. They were short, all of them. "They…" He could not think. When he looked back into the room, he expected to see Govier. But no one was there, except for the stinking jetsam. His eyes found the old man, gloves covering a blubbering face.

He looked from the old man to the bucket, swaying from its rope.

"Up with ya, quick." The old man weighed almost nothing as he pulled him to his feet. "I need something from ya."

"Wha– What are y–you doing?" Fear was etched onto those aged features. Greg yanked at the hands so hard the leather creaked.

"Somethin' stupid."

The gloves were loose, but that couldn't be helped. He threw his bow, quiver, and dirk to the filthy floor. The bucket he unhooked, letting it fall with a whistle. Too soon after that it slammed on the broken cobbles with a crash. *Shouldn't 'ave done that. Shit. Shit. It's too high.* He pulled the hook on its rope down to use for a toehold, and wrapped the slack around his waist. Dread filled his limbs with lead, his movements were heavy and slow, his wits turned to molasses. His eyes found the ramparts, where we saw a short black-clad man running with crossbow in hand. A bolt skewered him. The child was dead before he hit the ground.

He held onto the rope, and jumped.

Voices shouted at his back, but the skirling wind drowned out the words as he felt the cobbles calling to him, rushing up with speed. He hoped with a fool's hope that the rope had been tied off at the bottom. It looked like it had, but it could have just been knotted or piled on its hasp. The coils leapt past him, snakes hissing with hempen fury. He prayed, and he held the rope tighter.

The loop around his waist constricted, pulling tighter and tighter, until it threatened to bisect him. The shock of stopping jolted his leg on the hook, and he could feel the burns on his hands despite the gloves. He was fifteen foot or more from the flags now, the rope tensed and the knot on the hasp below groaning from his weight. There was nothing else for it. He pulled his foot free, trying to catch the hook in hand on the way down to somewhat lessen his fall. It didn't work. His foot crumpled under him, and he let loose a cry as the sharp pain flared through his left leg. *First my arm, now...*

He forced himself to rise, each step filling his mind with angry fire. He needed to get to the breach. He needed to warn them. Warn them all. *They're jus' children. Jus'*–

The drawbridge to the bailey was lowered, and a couple of infants ran past him carrying a scorpion bolt four times their height. *Please... stop...* Crumbling steps led down to the courtyard, steep and slick with mud, offering a commanding view of the tumble-down outbuildings. It seemed to take an eternity to take the steps one at a time, the lancing in his leg only getting worse by the moment. Slumping his shoulders, he resigned himself to what he had to do. Throwing up his hands to protect his head, he made himself fall again.

His world spun, stone and sky everywhere, the steps making him impact and bounce, impact and bounce, crashing down and spinning, spinning. The lip of each had been gratefully worn by centuries of footfall, but it still hurt, hard. He was not halfway before something sharp snagged his leg, ripping his breeches. Every stony punch sent his mail shirt to slam into his chest, driving the air from his lungs. *Shoulda taken off my mail. Fool.*

The ground was as unyielding as it was hard, and he rolled a few more feet before he came to a stop, the leather of his jerkin's sleeves ripped to ribbons, the skin beneath looking like the pelt of a Warretumi stripecat. His head throbbed, and his knee screamed at him. Cursing between mouthfuls of blood, he shambled to his feet, throwing himself onward, nearly managing to crash into the well. His body begged, pleading to rest, to fall down and never get up.

I... can't...

The *thruuum* of trebuchets were ceaseless, a siren call, and he followed the direction of battle with his ears. His vision became hazy, tinged with crimson and nonsense lights. He saw little people stream past, there was crushed stone underfoot, and he heard a cry of triumph come from over the collapsed wall. *Too... late... I'm...* He willed his eyes open wide, but there was a gleam in the sky to blind him, and something wet dripped in his eyes to sting. *What's...* Iron-shod boots screeched on stone, and he heard the wailing of babes.

They're children... The.... "Children!" His arms were upraised, but he could not say how. He felt weightless and dizzy. He had to tell them. The Paydar, Aud, Norther, Govier... Govier! Where was he? He could help... He...

"Stop... The... *THEY'RE CHILDREN! PLEASE!*" Voices surrounded him. Harsh and indistinct. Someone laughed, and then came the whistle, that sound he knew so well. The arrow took him in the thigh, and that knee slammed onto the stones. Still, he tried to stand. He waved his hand madly. *"I'M GREGYN! AUD! IT'S–"* The next arrow took him in the chest, punching through mail to gorge flesh.

"It's..."

Someone called his name.

II

Part Two

21

THE TOWNSMAN

"No one's coming to save us."

The tears had run like salt rivers down Hodder's face, to mingle with the blood in his scraggly beard. There was blood on his coat too, to adorn the old brown wool with fresh crimson.

He had all but fallen from his horse. Now he was on his knees, hands upraised to the sky as though in prayer, beseeching those banished gods. The words that came through his cracked teeth were far from what Reeve Cole remembered of Hodder of the strong voice, the booming tones that often dominated devotions at the capelion. The man was broken now, like his teeth, his nose, like the body of his daughter slung over the rump of his horse. Deathflies covered the exposed hand and legs as though bees to the honeycomb.

He remembered the old man being fervent in his prayers at the moontide, when the Hierophant Tar-Ru-Yah had come up the river from Wolfsmouth. It had been the summer before last, and Hodder had been the first to receive the Blessings, and had laughed a rumbling laugh when the Hierophant had joked that the tall god Oxruer himself had returned. The Reeve did not like how freely the Hierophant joked about the gods returning to the land. A few of the other townsfolk made disapproving faces, but they knew better than to be disrespectful to the living representative of the voice of the pantheon. So Tar-Ru-Yah bumped his gums and jested and made blasphemy, while an enraptured Hodder bobbed his head, his grin revealing all his horse teeth.

The rest of the congregation had done their best to fill the small building. The Holy One had come to Home-upon-the-Rise to visit their famous capelion after all, and this was not an occupation to shirk. So they had all squeezed into the Riverhome, who those in far Wolfsmouth called the River Dome. Cole guessed the renaming was to make it sound similar to Wolfsmouth's own great capelion, the Dome of Life. *You would think the Torrins would leave us be, but no. The woman makes no friends here. That's why she sent that charlatan Tar-Ru-Yah, to appeal to the pious hearts among us.*

Now it was common for most in the town to call it by the name their southern neighbours had given it. Some, like the one-legged Dimitrak and witsaddled Joss Jumpstick still clung to the original name. The Reeve sided with the southerners. After all, he was the one that collected the taxes for Lady Torrin. It was only right that he should adopt their ways., even if he did not love the lady or her lordly family. If he looked into his heart, he found that he was loyal to Lord Myddle. His pa had made it plain that every riverman in Home-upon-the-Rise owed his allegiance to the Myddles of Halfway. For a thousand generations it had been the same, his pa had said. Then it had all changed in the spring before, when the godsforsaken dunnies had made Halfway their own. Lord Drury Myddle was dispossessed, his seat occupied by a swarthy Soran arse, who to hear tell had allowed his lieutenants to rape his virgin daughters. When news finally reached the dainty ears of Lady Torrin, she had decreed that House Myddle and Halfway was effectively in the possession of the invaders. So in turn, all their demesne and incomes were to pass to House Torrin, including the tariffs owed by Home-upon-the-Rise. The Torrin messenger had been quite forthright with the proclamation, even bearing a fancy parchment with scribbles and stamps and the like. Cole had looked over the document, pretending that the lines of ink made sense to him. He was the reeve, and it fell to him to uphold the law. With that, he had gone from being a Myddle man to a Torrin man. The banner of the Myddles atop the guardhouse had been lowered. It was purple, and for as long as he could remember it had borne the arms of House Myddle: a prancing man dressed in black, prancing across an arched silver and gold chequey bridge. In its place, the green seadog on white fluttered angrily on its pole, snarling this way and that as the autumn winds snapped at its tail, as though it were a weathervane that leered for blood.

Cole had scant time for politics, and even less for gods. Their stories had always fascinated him as a boy, but now they made him huff and spit. It was the same with the visit of the Holy Hierophant. He was blessed along with Hodder, and Elgin the smith, Bothy with his boys, ancient Dimitrak the Cripple, who claimed to have the golden rings of a hundred fallen foes buried for safekeeping. He made the same pious chants and made the sacred signs as the rest. If not for himself, then for Dyge. For Cole, the gods were a bothersome presence, as the capelion was the highest point of the town, and was never out of sight. He told the others to regard all of the sorry business of gods with a heady suspicion. *Stories, that is all. Stories we tell each other to keep our souls warm against the chill of life on this river.* He would never tell them any more than that.

That was a job for Auriel the drunken capeli in the capelion, or for his beloved Dyge. She always told the stories with such belief. He loved her for it, even if he could not love her gods. Little eyes full of wonder met her words of triumphant gods and dreadful monsters, listening to the tales of Ro Rowett of the Tor, the sword-sorcerers of Old Qell, even the legend that they were descended from the twin god Quirsus.

The white marble walls of the capelion were limned with lastlight as the sun sank below the turfed rise. The structure was small compared to other houses of the gods found in the lands that encircled the Ruell Sea, and it was old, here and there the huge pale bricks splintering into jagged knives, the floors within were welling where thousands of feet had stood and prayed and lamented, and one leaded strut in the crystal dome had begun to leak, letting the water plop on the pisshead capeli's head when delivering a sermon. The priest was called Auriel Hillborn, but he never went by his family name. Noble-born capeli's hated it if you reminded them of their heritage. He could drink and he could preach, that Cole could admit he did well. He had whinged terribly at the last town meeting, beseeching him to order all the townsfolk to give up their worldly valuables to pay for the repairs to the dome. The request had been denied of course. Something about seeing Auriel flush from the embarrassment had cheered up the reeve no end. Up until then, the meeting had been bone dull.

The reeve smiled despite himself. No one noticed. It was a glad change. All eyes were on the poor bastard that had rode into town screaming bloody murder. It had attracted a few curious glances from idlesome townsfolk. Someone had called Cole, and he had found the man there at the foot of the Riverhome, shouting that men had rode through his enclosure and killed his sweet Sanda. *Bandits,* thought the Reeve. *Or dunnies.* He would have to send word to Lady Torrin. The thought made his hairless head furrow deeply. Before the war came, any trouble meant sending the news to Halfway and the Lord Myddle, who would send a justiciar to sort it out. It usually only took a day's ride on a swift horse. Now complaints were to be sent all the way downriver to Brinewater Keep, to bony little Torrin on her sea-rock throne. He would have to choose someone, or otherwise go himself. The ride would take five days if the rider rested but a little. He did not envy the poor bastard the journey. Perhaps he would send Auriel.

It took both Strong Savin and Logero Longsword to remove the grief-stricken Hodder from his place. Savin had his nose broken for the effort, and would have had worse, if the Longsword had not knocked the old man to the ground with the butt of his blade. Then it was only carrying the weeping mess away, to be placed in the guardhouse until Cole decided what to do with him. Then he was alone, the capelion fading above him, the marble growing darker by the moment. Dyge said that it had been Ezdona herself who had raised the hillock, to best see the vast dome of night and first calculate how best to navigate the moon across the sky. It was there that the incisive goddess had grown frustrated with the way the Wolfswater would flood the plains, soaking her in her meditations, leaving her plans half-made and impossible to continue without further interruption. After one particularly wet season she resolved to free herself from the beleaguering waters and command the mortal men and women that fished the flats to raise a hill a hundred and thirty feet high, and to dredge the waterway, and to build their homes upon high foundations so that no one shall ever have to wake to find their homes filled with dirty river water, and their possessions floating down to the Ruell.

The stories were nice, and Cole could allow that they gave him a warm feeling inside. But he knew the truth. Ezdona had never laid her godly feet in their little damp patch of the river. The Riverhome had been built by lowly flats dwellers, yes, and they had dredged the river, and made their homes on high foundations a good twenty-five foot off the ground. But it was just that. The flats would regularly flood, making the land incredibly fertile and offering up unfailingly bountiful harvests. That was why Home-upon-the Rise had always been favoured by Halfway, for they had always delivered their tithes. As for the river, the deepened waters from the dredging had been for the settlers to build huge arrowhead-shaped fish-traps on the riverbed, and reap all manner of creatures for their summer-tide feasts. Their homes were veritable towers, the streets turned to canals when the floods proved too ungainly. Leading to the entrance to each was a long stretch of steps, the lower dozen or so always stained by the high water marks of floods years past.

The wall hugging the town was ever in disrepair, often appearing in a more sorry state each time the floodwaters had ebbed. That had always irked the reeve, especially now that there were dunnies abroad.

Walls, bloody big high stone walls, with hardiron on the doors to the guardhouse! We could dig around the town, make a moat even. Come flood season, the river will protect us, as it always has. Then we'll see these bloody bastards try and take the town. Hope they can bloody swim.

He could only laugh at his own thoughts. "Are you to organise the building works?" *Let the dunnies be content with Halfway.* "Besides, who's gonna pay for it all, eh?" *The Bloodroyal Fleet likely scared them shitless.* He had seen them. A dozen warships out of Wolfsmouth. A dozen ships! The Rowett tricolour had flown high and bright, and everywhere armoured men like the fabled knights of the west filled the decks and chanted all the old war-songs. They had even stopped for a respite in Home-upon-the Rise that fine afternoon, and Cole had made sure that they were given all necessary provisions. They were Torrin men too, he supposed.

The war fleet was headed by the famed Arodyr Rowett. He was even taller than Hodder, and his braids fell to his waist in the most incredible display. The reeve felt shame, his envy turning his cheeks the colour of beets, and he did have large cheeks. He had lost all his hair from a sickness as a child, and stood at only five foot flat, so the great Arodyr had a whole foot and a half on him. Along with Rowett, some lord from the Castanni Kingdom had come to fight the enemy. The way he ordered the Rowett took some getting used to. *Aurden? Adirn?* It was a queer Castanni name, and he could not find himself trusting a Castanni. His grandfather had lost his head to one.

They had left as soon as the tide began to rise, the waters in their wake looking very empty and very sombre in the dusk after the pageantry of the day. Cole had waited at the quay a little longer after the others lost interest. Days later, they returned in the small hours, but they did not stop, and by the time he had been roused the ship's hulls had dwindled downriver until they became no larger than the last joint of his pinkie. Then it became too dark to see anything at all, let alone the distant war ships of his liege lady. He had gone home, to tell his family what he had seen.

He was heading there now, before realising that Hodder awaited his pleasure at the guardhouse. If he knew the man, he knew he could be terribly stubborn. *Make him wait. Perhaps the night in the cell will calm the codger off a mite.* As appealing as that was, he found that he pitied the old man. *He's lost his daughter, after all.* The reeve was bracing himself for a long night of questioning, when someone came right up to him and grabbed his forearm.

"Cole! Please, come... I don't know how... I..." Dyge dug her nails into the hard hairless flesh of his arm. When he tried to pull free, she only tightened her grip.

"Wife, what is happening?" He tried to sound calm, all too aware of the eyes of those nearby. A team had been moving bails of hay, but they stopped now, fixing on the source of the commotion. *Nosy bastards would do well with a fortnight in the cell.*

With a smile, he laid a gentle hand on his wife's shoulder. The touch only seemed to enrage her. "He's gone, Cole. Gone! I don't know where." *Ley.* If the reeve had hair, they would have stood on end then. *Gods be good.* He felt frozen, but could feel his face burn, and his armpits were drenched. Heavy-footed steps came close from behind. "Reeve, what is it? Is Dyge sound? I heard shouting, and I thought maybe it had something to do with Hodder."

The sight of the old man with the mutilated body of his daughter across his horse was all he could see, his mind's eye drenched in the blood that dripped from the girl's thighs. He heard nothing but the buzzing of the flies that surrounded her.

"When I couldn't find Ley, I went out, but I wasn't thinking. I must have left the latch open, because when I came back..." She fell into his arms. Something dark fell across his heart. It was formless, but he knew what it was. The faces were looking at him, and he wished that his fist was big enough to pommel them all in one sure punch. "Listen woman," his voice was a growl, hard enough to get through to poor Dyge. "We'll find him, and we'll find..." *her.* It stuck in his throat. It must have been a long time, or maybe just a moment, but when he looked up, Strong Savin was there. "Reeve, little Ley is missing, is he?" His nose was still bleeding, the bridge shifted into an awkward angle and one eye darkened. Or perhaps it was just the evening.

"We get nothing past you, do we? Is there a reason why we don't all call you Clever Savin." Insulting the guard helped steady Cole somewhat. Savin gaped at him with his mouth open and eyes scrunched up, as if he had been presented with a riddle.

311

"Are you trying to catch some flies? Yes, you, Savin. Close that mouth. Don't forget to breathe now."

Cole found that Dyge was clinging desperately to his shoulder. She was taller than him, most people were, but he was still the stronger one. If he couldn't force her off him, he could at least bring her. He made for the guardhouse, while ordering Strong Savin to go to the Reeve's house and watch out for Ley's return. *Or hers...*

He trudged up the steps to the doors until he stood above all the other houses. The steps rose until forty feet here, only for the guardtower proper to climb a further fifty feet. It could boast to being the highest structure in Home-upon-the Rise, if one did not include the capelion on its high hill. He sounded the alarum.

Above the interior doors of the guardhouse, an old weather-stained and wind-eaten stone titan head looked out menacingly in the direction of the river. The features had shown a titaness once. Now, only a vague impression of the once fine masonry remained. Blank unseeing stone eyes, nubs for ears and a stub for a nose. This titaness was blind, deaf, and ugly. He could hardly tell that the face was meant to be female. But her cry was still fearsome to behold. From her gaping a mouth a long serpentine tongue lolled forth, falling out from between jagged teeth, downwards a good ten feet before coiling tightly to grasp the ring that held the bell fast. Cole rang it now.

All in the town knew what the sound warned of. *Peril! Foes! Woe! War!* The clangour was high and loud, the discord making Cole wince each time he pulled hard at the length of hempen rope attached to the hammer, causing it to crash and roar, a metal scream that knew no end. He kept on, the rhythm a song of despair in his ears and in his heart. He held onto it with a sure callused grip, sounding the alarum until all were in attendance before the guardhouse. Only then did he let go of the rope, the final reverberations sounding more and more like a dirge.

Two hundred townsfolk stood in the dark. Some had come armed already. Here a stave, there an old nicked axe or dirk. Old hard iron all, like their bearers. Dimitrak had a hardwood cane with nails driven through the top, hobbling forward and leaning heavily on his crutch. The eldest of Bothy's boys was there with one of his father's butchering cleavers. Even Anneke the midwife had heeded the call, carrying a yew bow and a quiver bristling with arrows. The reeve noticed another, too. Holding up his free hand, he called for silence. Then he called to the brawny man in front.

"Elgin! Come, if you would." The smith gave a nod and a grunt, and climbed the steps to the tower. When he reached the top, Cole pressed a set of keys into the smith's large hand. Dithering mutters permeated the crowd. Cole could feel their agitation. *They saw Hodder in his heap. They think we go out looking for trouble. I won't be having that. Trouble is best left far off, not brought home.* It must have been as though they heard his thoughts, for then a stick of a man, eighty and a day, stepped forward. "Is it war, Cole? Don't lie to me. I could always smell when you or your friends lied."

The old man was Rhadyr, a sharp and venomous scarecrow who had been brother to the old reeve. "It is not, venerable Rhadyr." The accusation made his brow furrow.

"You lie worse than your father. We heard that trouble with goodman Hodder. You expect us to go chasing outlaws

313

now? That's work for Lord Myddle and his justiciars."

We are Torrin men now, old man. Best you remember it. "Hodder's half mad. I haven't a chance to question what happened to him yet. But I ring the bell because my chil–" *You only have one child, fool.* "Son is missing… we will organise into search parties, find my son, and bring him home safely. Or do you believe me lying, venerable Rhadyr?"

Many of the others looked at the old man, judgement in their eyes. "A nasty situation. I wish to help any way I can, Reeve," he said, in a tone that suggested he would rather do anything but.

It was good enough for Cole. If these people cared about anything, it was the gods, their crops, and their children. For that bastard Rhadyr to countermand him for raising levies to find his missing son, it would be as though he were to admit that the gods did not exist. He may confuse who his liege was, but he would never be fool enough to forget *that*. The others were starting to mutter again. Cole raised his hand again.

"Elgin and myself will run a count of the armoury. Where is Logero Longsword?" a rangy youth stepped forth. He was capable and intelligent, and the ugliest man Cole had ever seen. Then he remembered that Strong Savin had broken his nose, and was never comely to begin with.

He shrugged off such impish thoughts angrily. "Logero! You will separate the townsfolk into groups of eight. Each posse will be given a steel sword from the armoury. You will determine who shall wield the weapon. Understood?" The man saluted Cole, then turned to his charges. "Aye, Reeve! You heard him. Move yourselves! Whatcha looking

314

at me for. Move! Eight was the order. Don't wanna be separated from your friends? Tough!" *He may be hard to look at, but the youth is capable.*

The reeve pulled at Dyge, only for her to break into a fresh fit of sobbing. He shouldered through the guardhouse doors, greeted by the squat Savin. "Reeve, why is Elgin looking at the armoury?" A pair of fat greasy sausages hung hot over the brazier in the corner of the room. They had caught him mid-supper, it would seem.

"To find the magic sword." Cole could not spare the time to explain to the dolt. Maybe he would work it out for himself. "Guard the doors and let no one in." *That* at least he couldn't muck up. *Then again, there's a first time for everything.*

The armoury was found in the deep foundations of the guardhouse proper. The heavy barred gate leading to the sword-cellar was open. Elgin knew what had to be done. The steps were hard and rough, the walls slick with saltpetre. The cellars contained the grain, the blackwine, and the swords: the most valuable goods in the town. It had been another reeve who had installed the locked gates, when there had been some trouble with pilfering some years back. Such thievery and low cunning always made Cole frown.

They halted at the lowest gate. The large barred door at the bottom of the hollow had been swung wide, an entreating gesture to dolorous parents. Inside, the room was aglow from the light of a single torch. Cole drew his wife inside. Beside one mortared wall stood a rack holding a few dozen spears, flanked by two hangings bolted into the rough-hewn stone. Swords hung from them sharp and shadowed despite the torchlight. On the opposing wall were similar racks, holding axes and mauls, pikes and bags full of caltrops, boarding hooks for combat upon the river. Some were covered in a thick layer of dust and mildew. Some had not seen the gleam of sun for decades. Above the man sitting on a dangerously small work stool was the old banner of the Myddles, the once proud golds and silvers of the bridge turned into dismal green and greys. The prancing man still pranced, though, despite his mouldy new attire. His features could still be plucked out in the thread. To Cole, it looked as though he were mocking him.

"Lahe is missing too," Dyge said, disentangling herself. Cole watched her go to the nearest bracket holding a brace of daggers. She sounded distant, as though she were absently mentioning the spots of rust on the flat of the blade. Elgin the smith eyed Cole hard. "I will watch for her. That I will. But what of Hodder? Is it true that raiders killed his daughter?" *Gossip travels faster than the clap in this town.*

"Aye. Deserters from the dunny army, most like. They will be starving and cold, and probably looked to Hodder's homestead as easy pickings. They will be trained and armed, but we can overwhelm them with our numbers." No one could hear them here, yet he hushed his voice all the same. Whether Elgin agreed with Cole, he could not tell. The gnarled smith was of an age with the reeve, but the years at the forge and the heat of the smithfires had made him as unyielding as hardiron and as craggy-faced as a Wolfswater bluff. To outsiders, he looked all the brute, which made him a terror to those that tried to cheat him. It was like some cruel god had molded his face after the mastiff, with jowly cheeks, a small, squashed nose, and dark

316

beady eyes. His thick hair was always lank from sweat, and his shirts always seemed to have dark circles beneath the arms. But this was not a cruel man. Far from it. Cole knew him well, but even he had fallen victim to thinking that Elgin was nothing more than a pit pugilist. That was before he came to know him. That was *before* everything that had happened. The way he had laughed when the babe came forth, minutes after his sister.

"What d'ya want me to do, Cole?" The question was meant to sound kind, the reeve knew, but with the smith's grinding voice, it always came out grudging.

What do I want? He felt his brow beetling hard. When he looked to Dyge, he saw that she had slung a belt of small knives around one shoulder, contrasting hard with the shift she wore. The tears had dried upon her cheeks, her eyes instead filled with a dark fury. The light in the cellar hit her face just right, and he could see the hard line of her jaw, the strong nose and full lips. The strength was quiet, but it was there. If his children were not missing, he would have fallen in love with her all over again. "Well, Cole? I thought you were the reeve."

"I am, woman." *I'll get them back. But Hodder must be revenged too.*

Cole had always wondered how his life would have turned out had he made the journey north. His father had always complimented him on his cleverness, and he was always outsmarting his brother's friends. He even made a habit of tricking the old Reeve Eistir, only getting caught the one time. Then there was that summer, he must have been nine or ten, when the journeyman had come. He was a wizard, some claimed. When his father presented him before the stranger, Cole did not think him particularly magical. He tended to hurts and gave out ointments, but he was young and gaunt, and only a learned man bartering his skills for a hot meal. *Take him to Lar'gara,* his father had said.

There had been tests. Tools were presented to him, puzzles on parchment, and counting exercises. In the end, the journeyman had *hmmm*ed until he pursed his lips and said that he was able, and that he would take him off his father's hands. *Five gold pieces,* came the offer from his father. *I saw how you like his smarts.* He travelled barefoot, the journeyman reminded him glibly. It seemed to annoy his father no end. He had always hated being made the fool, not that it took much doing. He had drawn his knife, the nasty one he kept on his hip. The journeyman left any further witty remarks unsaid. He avoided Cole too. When he had exhausted his welcome, he had left on the same lame donkey that he had arrived on.

Take him to Lar'gara. The words rang hollow in his ears.

Dealing out the weapons to the townsfolk, the rattle of the swords around him making his hand itch. It had been too long since he had fought. *Too little practice. You're slipping up.* He tried to banish the nasty thoughts by cricking his neck, eliciting a very loud and satisfying crack. Elgin gave his most gruff laugh.

"I feel it too, Cole. The bloodlust. Makes me wish I were twenty years younger. These striplings couldn't tell a cock from a couter." Laughs erupted around them. A tall man older than Cole and Elgin clapped the smith heartily on the shoulder. "Well put, hammer hand. Let us show these ducklings how we deal with rogues." Others laughed at that, including Strong Savin, who laughed at every joke, not realising that most were directed at him.

Cole could not share their mirth. He had left most of the roustabouts to search for his children, in Home-upon-the-Rise and the fields beyond. Logero Longsword had been given the command. He trusted him. But he had also tasked Dyge with organising the parties. Aside from them, he had taken the most able with him, Elgin the smith and Strong Savin, Bothy and the two sons old enough to wield swords, Rhadyr with his scowls, even Dimitrak and Anneke.

They trudged along the old dirt path that cut north by north-west from the riverbank and into the low grassy hills. They all carried weapons now. Liberated from the armoury only to look even darker in the night. Now and again they shone dully in the flickering torches. It would take them half the night to reach Hodder's homestead, so he encouraged them to sing to keep them awake in the nocturne.

Then dawn came too early. It was Savin of all people who noticed first. A dirty orange fulgor stretching low up into the eastern sky like a weal. They knew what it was. Daybreak was still hours away. The ghost light sent a cold finger to pluck at the reeve's heart. Words were not needed, yet the oaf among them still voiced the horror that they all felt.

"Fire! Fire! The town's on *fire!*"

The march back turned into a hellbent sprint. They covered the ground between them quickly and did not stop for Dimitrak or Rhadyr, who could not keep up. Each footfall drew them closer to the town. Very soon the wind changed, and thick smoke engulfed them like soup. They lost the path, but they could not lose the town, for it was ablaze, and now half of the hazy world was billowing out orange light. Then the guardhouse was before them, huge gouts of fire spitting from the gutted windows like tongues of some giant wyrm. Cole heard the screams.

At the top of the steps, he saw what was left of the doors, hacked away by some axe. Within, he heard a man's pained voice. But it was the queer words he heard shouting from the doors to the town. He looked out, and felt the need to make water. Men in black were mustering the townsfolk in the square before the guardhouse, some afoot while others rode huge horses that kicked and bit at the scent of blood. A hundred or so were herded together. Logero was a few feet in front of the rest, on his knees before a man with his back to Cole. At the sight of the reeve and the posse, Logero Longsword breathed in hard. *"Run!"*

Cole took a step back. His legs were stiff, and his throat was dry. The man now turned to face the newcomers. He had been smiling, Cole saw, but now the look was replaced by a look of mischief. In his hand was a long rapier, its slim serrated edge dazzlingly bright in the inferno. The dark man said something incomprehensible to Cole, and then he found himself surrounded equally by men on foot and ahorse. "Run! *Run!*"

The man with the sword spun, his sword making a sleek whirring noise as it cut through the air. Then Logero was choking on the blood, his neck gushing a red stream as he clawed feebly at the wound. Something stirred in Cole. His hand was on his sword, his own sword, not a rusty old one from the armoury. Ripping it free of its scabbard gave him heart. The others had their swords out too, and they made a loose circle on the top step to the burning ruin of the guardtower. They could not jump. When Cole turned, he saw how the same black-clad men had somehow got inside the guardhouse. They would have to fight. He would fight. He would kill if he had to. They would win.

Time runs differently in battle. One moment he was standing shoulder to shoulder with Elgin and Bothy, hacking at men who cursed them in a foreign tongue. The next, he was on his knees, in the same spot Logero had been. The dark man was asking him a question, and he forced himself to listen. The survivors depended on it.

"You are the commandant?" The dark one said the words in Qellish. The man was not tall, but neither was he short. Long dark hair framed a pallid face, made paler by the black ringmail he wore. But something strange stuck out to Cole. Over his armour, the man wore an apron not unlike what a butcher would wear, the cracked brown leather spattered with blood old and new. *I've died.* He thought, wanting to weep. *I've died, and gone to the Hell Unending.*

"Deaf then. I shall let you join your ugly friend now."

Fear made him speak. "No. I mean, I am the Reeve."

A thin eyebrow raised a mite on that pale face. "Reeve? Huh." The rapier was sheathed now, but Cole did not like the way the man played his fingers across the pommel. It was a skull, and it grinned at the Reeve.

"Where is the gate?"

Cole could not help but shake his head. "I don't… gate? Pray forgive me, I do not understand."

"Should have known better. All of you! Now… where is the gate? The place of power. It will *call* to you… Even make you see things. So where?" The fires were still blazing, so silence could not fall on the town. Instead, the wood screamed burning and the stones creaked and cracked.

"I know…" Cole turned at the sound of Rhadyr. The scarecrow had a cut above one eye, and from the way he looked at the reeve, one would swear he had given it to him. "It is in the reeve's house. I saw it there. He hides it, you see." Again the dark man unleashed a stream of foreign noises to an underling, who went off with a few others to the largest house in the town, among the other kindling houses. A long finger then aimed at Rhadyr's nose. "If you lie, you will die slowly. I will do it myself." The sad old man realised his error, and then he broke down.

"And you." Cole knew it was directed at him. He was staring at him. There was something in his eyes. It was unfeeling, yet inflamed by nightfire and rage.

A huge man with whiskers covering most of his face trotted forward. In each meaty hand, a small child squalled and shrieked. "No." *If they found them… then where's Dyge?* The dark man saw his open mouth, the way he struggled to breath. Words were exchanged, and suddenly the children were tossed unceremoniously at the man's feet.

"What are your names, little ones?" He squatted, his hand never stopping the fondling of his sword. "You can tell me."

Cole could only watch as his daughter told the man. She was hugging Ley close, and she did not seem to even notice him. "You are a very clever girl, I can tell. My name is very long and complicated, but you can call me Skinner."

Cole felt bile rise in his stomach. "Don't fucking talk to them!" The man called Skinner kept his eyes on the children. They flickered back and forth. An eye twitched. Then lightning fast, he leapt away as a man recoils from a viper. "They are… twins."

No. Gods no. Please no. Please… I tried to protect them, Dyge… I'm sorry…

It was a nightmare. Hell was real, and he was living it. The sword at his throat was razor sharp, the hand that held it unflinching. "They didn't know, did they?" His laugh was cruel. The reeve could not bring himself to look at the townsfolk.

"Secret's out. Where I come from, It's a mortal sin to harbour twins. You people will taste true justice, and I will be more than happy to administer it. Now…" His boy looked at him, his eyes big and brown and afraid. He could remember the day well. Anneke had been away, sleeping with Hodder when she told everyone she was tutoring little Sanda with her weaving. Elgin happened to come by, and it was his brawny hands that brought forth first Lahe, and then Ley. The smith was dead now, his head crushed by a maul on the steps. He did not know where Dyge was… but his children lived. He would always have his children.

"Choose." The word cut him deeper than the axe that had left his arm a red fountain. "Choose which of your children will live." *No. No. No. No. No. Never. Never. No. I won't. I won't. I…*

"If you don't choose, then they both die."

The reeve could not bring himself to look at his children. He had to choose. He always had a choice. Somehow, the life he had never lived at Lar'gara came back to him. He had to choose. What choice was that? *A beggar's choice… I have to choose for them now.* They all looked at him for the answer. The answer he knew he could never make. Until he made it.

"Ley. The boy…"

Skinner stood up. The fires had died down an inch, the blaze silhouetting him like he was wearing a mantle of fire on his shoulders, a crown of flames upon his head. "What a loving father." His rapier flashed, and suddenly the reeve's children were grasping at throats bearing bloody necklaces.

Cole heard himself scream. Laughter mingled with the roaring of the burning town as his children bled to death before him. He clung to Skinner's apron, feeling his blood, and the blood of many others between his fingers. Then he begged…

Skinner was more than happy to grant his wish.

22

MARBLE

The crowded room was very warm, and Marble was almost thankful that she was barely clothed. Looking around at her disgruntled companions and their less-than-polished exteriors, Marble still couldn't bring herself to feel even an ounce of guilt for starting the fight. It had been exactly what she needed to dispose of the remnants of fog clinging to her mind. The blood pumping and the adrenaline and the excitement of the brawl had certainly perked her up. And now she would be meeting with the Mistress.

Her madness definitely had a method behind it. Oh, she was feeling *good*. The food that she had managed to nab as she was dragged from the dining hall and subsequently stuffed her face with had been divine! A deliciously creamy Mogvi broth packed full of the most tantalising spices, the tender meat melted in her mouth, and the heavenly crust of the fluffiest, lightest bread that Marble could remember tasting was a fine accompaniment indeed. She knew the noises that had escaped her person as she devoured her stolen meal were positively obscene, but she honestly couldn't have cared less about the uncomfortable looks that her unfortunate and discontented companions kept shooting in her direction.

As Marble slumped indulgently and languidly in one of the few cushioned armchairs, her limbs spread out to make herself very much at home. The withering looks of her guards as they stood to attention around the perimeter of the room, furnished with the finest materials, craftsmanship and richest of colours, told of their desire to wipe the smug satisfaction from her with a thorough hiding. But their wish was not to be. Watching through heavy-lidded eyes that gave the impression of slumber, Marble hoped that their lips would loosen and tongues would wag. *Knowledge is survival, caution is key.*

The click-clack of approaching footsteps simultaneously stiffened spines and comforted her companions' demeanours. The incoming stride was confident and powerful and boasted of the owner's absolute self-importance. The heavy alckwood door, intricately carved with scenes so small one would have to use a looking glass to discern, opened without preamble or fanfare. *The Mistress.* Or at least that was who Marble supposed the stately figure to be.

The first thing that commanded Marble's attention, even as she forcefully kept up her rouse of indolence, was the glorious crown of obsidian curls that surrounded the woman's striking face like a beacon or coronet. Smooth skin boasted a pureness and unblemished youthfulness that contradicted quite completely with the sharp scrutiny of her brown eyes. The set of her strong jaw was almost indulgent, Marble thought, as was the snide smirk twisting her full lips. She was tall. Toned arms were bared by her fitted leather vest and a damp sheen of sweat covered her skin with an ethereal dew. The well-worn clothing and the comfortable way in which she caressed the knives adorning her thighs spoke of a deadly woman. Marble was suitably impressed and in more than a little awe.

The woman released an exasperated, heavy sigh that reminded Marble so much of a certain friend that it was all she could do not to laugh. The ability to express so much in just one small sound was truly an impressive skill that Marble had thought belonged only to one person. "Come on." Said a voice that was both honey and rough sand. The melodious sound limned with power and calm, ran over Marbles' being, lifting the hairs and prickling the skin as it caressed the flesh. "I'm not so easily fooled, although your act is rather impressive." The voice fondled Marble again. *Damn,* Marble thought. *That voice could bring even the hardest of men to their knees, begging for relief.* "I believe you requested a meeting?"

"That's a dangerous voice you have there." Marble stated as she launched readily to her feet. She ignored how her flimsy covering slipped precariously, and the way her guards startled at the sudden movement, flinching forward to protect their Mistress.

"Hmm. So I've been told." Replied the woman before demanding, "Who are you?" Without preamble.

"My name… is Marble." The emissary stated, blowing some hair out of her eyes. "I'll reserve judgement on whether making your acquaintance is an honour, just yet. I'm sure you understand." The woman smirked, and amusement danced in her eyes. There but gone in a flash, so quick and fleeting was the expression. But Marble saw everything. The slight wrinkle of skin around the eyes, the smallest of twitches and creases at the corner of the mouth.

Knowledge was survival, and Marble decided to throw away the *key*. "And you would be?" Marble shot out pointedly, eliciting another flash of beguilement. Marble supposed it was rare for this woman to not be treated with the utmost respect, admiration, and awe. Her very presence and aura commanded it. *Yes, caution is key, but risk is also reward.*

"No need to be coy now, Marble, and downplay your intelligence." Every word she spoke was measured. "I'm sure you already know." A smirk of her own twisted her lips. So that was how they were going to play, was it? *Very well.*

"She who rules the Bonebridge Outpost. No, not the ruler. The... *Mistress*. What is your name?"

"Mistress will do."

"That's not what I asked."

"I know." *Oh, she's good.* "Interesting garb." The Mistress remarked, her eyes roving Marble's body freely.

"You like it? I made it myself!" She twirled on the ball of one foot to show off her pretty dress, even though the garment could barely be classed as such a thing.

"It must have been quite a feat to fight in it and not lose it completely."

"Oh, t'was a tricky thing indeed. As you can see, it survived, along with me."

"Hmm."

Marble flopped back onto the armchair, doing nought

to preserve any modesty. An indolent grin plastered on her lips, the emissary refused to break the probing silence first. She made a production of scanning the room with a critical eye and cataloguing its occupants and inventory before turning her eagle gaze back to the Mistress.

The Mistress strolled around the breadth of the magnificent bureau she'd been perched against and settled into the commanding chair readily behind it. She pulled open one of the heavy drawers, rifling around inside for only a short moment before retrieving a substantial sheaf of papers and placing them carefully on the desk. *Clever.*

The thundering of running footsteps that could only be made by a heavy-footed, carefree child, preceded said child bursting into the room with barely contained energy. Marble dozily opened her tired yet still vigilant eyes halfway to take in the details. The boy was tall, gangrel, with milky skin speckled liberally with freckles. His yellow hair was tinged with shades of blue, it looked like, dishevelled atop his head. "Sadu. Good." The Mistress announced almost at large to the room as she rose ever elegantly from her seat, her papers finding their way back into the desk drawer. "Marble, meet Sadu." She introduced him with a delicate but strong flick of the wrist. "He will show you around." And with that, the emissary was promptly dismissed and swiftly ushered out of the room by her apparent new charge.

The boy's energy was boundless. He dragged Marble through the building and out into the strange town. Sadu marched his ward through street after street of Bonebridge, barely allowing her enough time to take in all the details that she needed to. His excitement and the honour and joy of his responsibility to *take care* of Marble was a palpable force that the emissary couldn't help but find endearing. He was eager to do a good job and for Marble to see absolutely everything. As they trundled by, many a person stopped and stared with undisguised loathing, mistrust and judgement at Marble herself, especially clad as she was. She stood out like a drik in the desert. Gren and the Red guard were ever-present, both barely managing to suppress their smirks at her discomfort.

The following days followed in much the same way. Marble would wake, taking time to flow through the ingrained activity of strengthening, conditioning and stretching. The daybreak dance was one that required complete control and focus. Every movement, minute and momentous, had to be completed with perfect precision and accuracy. Not even a hairbreadth could be out of place. There was power in those movements. Feeling recharged and dripping with sweat, Marble would cleanse herself and proceed out of her door to be greeted by whichever two guards had been assigned to watch over her. She had not seen hide nor hair of Gren and the red guard since that first day. But the others all seemed just as capable as those two. They would escort their charge down to the food hall, where Sadu would waiting with a beaming smile. A small table right inside the entryway was kept empty for the small group to avoid the emissary walking further into the room and causing chaos.

Breakfast was often a shared platter of fruit, and a small, deliciously light and fluffy bread roll, washed down with a mug of freshly squeezed lemonbeer. Sadu would babble away nonsensically, spurting out whatever random thought occurred to him.

After breaking their fast, Sadu would once again lead Marble up and down the streets and alleyways of the town, their footsteps ever dogged by the shadows of the emissaries keepers. She could feel sometimes how uncomfortable the guards were at the thoroughness of the tours and the information that Sadu happily divulged to Marble, but they didn't say or do anything in attempt to prevent the child from giving Marble knowledge that she, no doubt, should not possess or be privy to. Marble guessed their silence was an effort to avoid drawing attention to the breach.

No matter their attempts at discretion, however, Marble caught every little detail. She saw the tensing and the effort of consciously relaxing and resuming a nonchalant demeanour, no matter how well or quickly the people around her managed to disguise their discomfort. Marble caught it, and she was much better than them at not giving anything away. If the mistress was present, Marble doubted she would reveal anything, and the game would continue. The Mistress had not shown herself in days. Marble was beginning to grow impatient and ever-conscious of the mission that was looming over her head, she was losing time here. She felt herself becoming more and more drawn into discovering the mysteries of this forbidden place. She allowed herself a few weeks to gather herself, build her knowledge, and plan the route to Castan.

Waking, watching the streets, dancing, washing, eating and wandering. Repeat.. She persuaded certain vendors to exchange goods for some form or another of labour. Some of the vendors just wanted the opportunity to sneer and try to humiliate this outsider. Marble exchanged scrubbing floors for some undergarments. She collected pails and pails of water from the well, and it always seemed to have moved a few feet each time. Her guards and Sadu looked on with muted interest. They watched, and saw, and let her continue as she was. Marble didn't care.

Eventually, she discovered the training yards where the warriors worked to hone their skills. Once Marble was happy with her attire]and most general equipment that should see her through to Castan, she turned her eye to that place as the most likely to yield the desired results. The warriors still greeted her with sneers, unlike the weary glances that she received by most of the townsfolk, none of them wanting to upset her or give away any secrets.

Her stride was purposeful and strong as she ambled through the winding pathways to her destination, clad in sturdy boots that thumped satisfyingly with each step and a lightweight but armoured vest and breeches. Her white hair was pulled back and braided severely, with only the occasional flyaway strand, relatively well-behaved. She had yet to replace her scarf, but first, weapons. A small, narrow, curved blade caught her eye as she walked. Made of Cnar tusk, with a simple handle moulded well and wrapped with supple, sturdy leather making it perfectly balanced. The only problem was that it already belonged to someone. It would certainly be noticeable were it to suddenly go missing. She knew how to get it.

The training yards were nothing fancy, the footing here made up of uneven rubble and sand that moved underfoot. There were no fences, but it seemed to be a common understanding that only those welcome and worthy were allowed to enter. She smirked as she passed the invisible boundary.

All of the warriors training stopped short, their movements halted and eyes turned. Ignoring her audience, she stalked towards the warrior that possessed the blade, stopping directly in front of the woman. "I want that." Marble said without preamble. "What do you want for it?" She asked. She was of a height with the outlander. The woman's gaze took on a gleam Marble took for calculating.

"Beat him to a pulp." The woman demanded, pointing out her desired target.

"Done." Marble shrugged, looking in the direction of the man. The one in question scoffed and rolled his eyes with derision. A loose circle had formed already. The man swaggered forward, full of swollen bravado, and like that, he swung. Marble stood fast, unamused and unconcerned as his fists flew towards her face. Her dodge was almost lazy.

The crowd grew, her opponent increasingly frustrated that he could not land a hit.

Dodge left, duck, right. The crowd began to laugh. The man turned red. She saw the vein bulging on his temple. She crouched low and swept out her leg, catching his ankles and sending him sprawling to the hooted hilarity of the warriors. He yelled, outrage making his words garbled and nonsense sounds. Readying himself to charge recklessly at the small woman, he drew a knife from his boot.

A sword to the throat stopped him short. "Now that's not nice." Sadu tutted, turning his blade so the edge bit into skin.

The gathered people dispersed, their interest now lost. Sadu dismissed the man with a look, who scrambled after the retreating crowd. Her saviour turned to face the emissary. The woman's smirk was a dark thing as she pressed the blade into Marble's palm. Then she was gone with the rest. They seemed already on the edge of sight, ephemeral and hazy.

When the outsider faced Sadu, his eyes glittered, yet they looked pained to her. "Just thought you should know. Time moves differently in the Tundra." The blade in her hand centred her, and for the first time in weeks she saw the Creature clearly. She wanted to catch him by the neck, scream at him, do *something*. But Sadu too turned away from her.

It was getting dark, and Marble saw she was alone in the yard. Words filled her head, ones that choked back her own. Among the squalling thoughts, she saw the sun had sunk beneath the buildings.

Still wondering what had happened, her feet started to move towards the setting sun. After a while, one thought stood out from the rest.

It's time to go.

23

NATOLY

The *Merry Raven* rocked gently on her mooring. It was a calm night, the revelry of the camp up on its height a mass of shadowed voices that swelled and ebbed to the verses of a familiar song. Cloudless and still, the dead air sent creepers of mist to swirl across the slow, sluggish flow of the river. A chill threatened to bring frost.

When had it gotten so cold... so dark?

The sun was long gone, the warmth of that wan day already a fading memory. Now it was the moon that lit the sky with her pale-bright light as she appeared above the looming cliffs of Flattop like a silver royal standard tossed onto a dreadblack silk sheet. No stars dared appear tonight.

Nat put a hand to his heart to pick at the loose threads of the raven embroidered there. A habit he had developed on the long days aboard his ship, if he wasn't entertaining the crew with his feeble attempts to learn their glib tongue, or entertaining Sibyl with his agog attempts in bed. His fingers came away empty, plucking at his loose canvas vest. He had left his surcoat with the raven blazon in the cabin with Sibyl.

How could I forget? She liked to wear it in their play, the way it hung on her body, concealing the exciting curves beneath that always made Nat bite his lip and go hard. He had left her there to read when he was done. At least, he thought she was reading. After their tussle, she had gone back to thumbing through the careworn book she had acquired from Govier, some humdrum memoir of an old seafarer called Shazadh, or Sherzod, or Shaizod, or something like that: it was some dunnie name most like, and he had never had an ear for *that* nonsense. It was his custom to have some fresh air after being with a woman. Cold or hot, wet or dry, the air prickling his skin was intoxicating, and he felt as though her hands were still there. So he had retreated without, to take in the Qellish night. Sibyl had not seemed to mind. *She said she likes to watch my backside as I go. Randy bugger.*

The best redhouses in Castan always had balconies, and he would often look out over the under-city and take in the noise of the night, the sea of lights below and the castle on its rise above. The Rose's Daughter had not enjoyed such, his mind going back to that night in Forlorn, and the caresses of the girl that had looked at him with doting eyes. *She didn't love you, fool. Her eyes shone only for gold.* Maybe that was why he had gotten so abysmally pissed that night. He had needed air, and there had been a taste to the wine he could not quite place.

He caught hold of his knife, tossing it underhand to catch at the edge and hilt in turn, spinning it through his fingers deft from practice... *Shit. I need to sleep. I need to...* Try as he might, he had slept little since the Battle at Bagman's Bluff. It was a day he was not likely to soon forget, if ever. It had been glorious that morning, the songs of war emanating off the ships in the vanguard line like the buzzing of half a dozen huge angry wasps. He had positioned the *Raven* on the left flank, keen to blaze the trail for the fleet around the narrowing channel as the rocky upthrust that was Bagman's Bluff rose to dominate the otherwise featureless landscape around it. *Did they build the fort when it was an island, or did the river come to meet it later on?* He had wondered at the time. It was a quick bit of pondering, for then they received the signal from the emissary on the western riverbank to form a line and commence fire. Just thinking of Audeyrn made him scowl. The man did not, *could not*, understand what had happened. Things had not been good after that. They spied the bridges, still standing defiant even in their ancient apathy, bulwarks to the fleet progressing further up the river. He had wondered out loud if they could destroy the bridges, which led to Sibyl opining that they could not sound the waters around them safely, so it would be foolish to advance and risk running the ships aground, potentially blocking their way irreparably. The crew had laughed at his suggestion, first in the common, and then again in Qellish when it was translated. *Laughed at me. I am the captain, and they laughed at me.*

One of the ships chanced a lucky shot at the foundation of the nearest watchtower, the one guarding the southern entrance to the channel. When it started to lean outward, he prayed, silently. With the resulting collapse, the *Lady Cyrinne* was gone, nothing remaining but stone dust and bubbling waters. Her captain had been Arhax the Mouth, a glutton and gobshite, but a good man who had embraced Nat as a fellow captain and warrior. *Dead now, along with everyone on the Lady. They'll never see Wolfsmouth again, or wed their loves, or drink blackwine. How many widows were made that day on the Greenrun? How many orphans?* He flung the knife at the aftmast, where it stuck with a satisfying *twang.*

He had been wroth, the archers on deck struggling to their feet and the crewmen fighting against the turbulent waves of that mighty crash. He ordered them to bring the ship about, to bring the fight to the Godless bastards that crawled inside the Bluff so much like maggots within a festering corpse. He said those exact words, and those aboard unsheathed their weapons and hailed him. All the Godless needed to die, every one, every acolyte and treacher that dared to follow their dark overseers, and he would be the one that brought their end with the edge of his kje. Voicing a battle cry, the men and women on the aftcastle echoed him, none moreso than Sibyl, wresting a bow over a shoulder as she growled out that Qellish curse the Paydar loved so much- *dhereda,* the worst of bastards, evil-doer, incest-born, fuckers.

The *Raven* had jerked hard when her ram hit the fall-stones that ran like scree from the breach in the southern curtain wall. The sight was a barbed invitation, a portal to some hell. He shook off such asinine thoughts, determined not to show any fear in front of these braided warriors. It was a castle, even if it was manned by *them,* and like any castle it could be besieged, the defenders slain. Someone behind him aired loudly that they had not received the signal to assault, but it was ignored. Besides, those nearest the side-rail were already leaping over even as he said it. *Men are deaf to thought when their noses catch the scent of blood*. Thinking back on it all, Nat could not remember much, even the most striking moments a dim haze tinged by red. The rest was blinkered, and he could only recall some vague faces. But he had commanded, *that* he knew, and more important than that, they had followed him.

Sibyl had remained at the aftcastle to command the archers and keep the *Raven* ready should they need to sound a retreat. Those aboard ran at her every order: she had the sailors offload the siege ladders, artillery crews manning the scorpions, the sailors sent scrabbling below decks for bundles of arrows and shot and the like. Haste was everything. Nat gave her a lingering look, and the look he received in return was full of a dark hunger. He had seen that often enough under the covers, but that was the first time in daylight, in clothes even.

He led his men to the bottom of the rocky bluff from which the fort took its name. Jagged stacks like green-covered fingers standing twice as tall as a man littered the beachhead, making for ample protection from the projectiles the cravens spat at them. He was joined by Paydar on all sides, a few young women with flickering, lupine eyes, as though they aimed to leap at the first Godless they saw, and then proceed to tear them apart with bare hands. It scared him, and made him laugh aloud. *Imagine what the Godless will think...*

The sky was a hailstorm of steel and stone. The barrage fell at drastically varying rates, for a few moments stopping completely, and it even seemed safe to move about unprotected. Many of the Paydar had brought their rectangular curved shields ashore, and they hid behind them, bracing as a quarrel would punch into the wood or glance off its edge.

That was all they were good for. While he was waiting for a halt in the uneven volleys, one particularly large Paydar, all grey hair and black teeth, trotted out from a nearby rock to fearlessly advance with his shield held before him. The rocks rose steeply, and his going was slow. He looked strong, very strong, but it didn't help him. His shield was held straight and steady, and remained so, even as the stone took off the top two feet of it, along with a good part of his head and right shoulder.

Gore filling the air, Nat could taste the man's blood on his tongue. His recollection worsened, some things feeling more like dreams than memory. He stayed there a while, moments or minutes or hours, and the next thing he knew he had a shield of his own. He could not tell if he had taken it from a dead Paydar. Then he was scrambling up the rockface. Shingle and broken masonry crunched under foot, and the shield rattled from repeated impact. *Perhaps they know I'm the commander,* but he could not be sure. His surcoat was bleached and freshly washed, while the Paydar were bedecked in their tricolour, striped and gaudy. Otherwise he was helmeted like the rest, the visor restricting his vision to what came in front. To the defenders, he probably did stick out, but the shield hid most of his body. He could not know, and he climbed the rise with a singular thought. *Kill.*

The *Raven's* scorpions cranked and strummed as bolts were sent to arc, aiming squarely on the trebuchets that lined the curtain walls. Men screamed around him. Others, officers in Paydar finery, growled orders to those moving the siege ladders. With some hustle, the siege-crews managed to throw several grapples over the parapets with purchase. The defenders seemed more intent on shooting those aboard the ships than those trying to get over the walls, so the hooks went unnoticed. Five siege ladders were swiftly brought up and erected, the grapples between the merlons acting as anchors. Sibyl had complained heavily about those on the river, saying that they should have brought up something she had called a *cloud bridge*, some Lar'garan contraption that could extend a ladder all the way from a ship to a castle wall. Nat did not know what that was, so he had kissed her then and thought no more of it, letting the river and her lips ease his worries.

Kisses were far from his mind as the breach neared. He was in a shield wall, manned by Paydar he did not know. Another ship had landed, the *Leviathan*. Captain Arodyr had been loath to leave her when Audeyrn commanded him to remain with him on the riverbank, so now it was commanded by the first mate, Arodyr's blood-adoptive son called Egon Sipcup. The man looked like a younger version of the captain as he led the warriors to join those from the *Raven*. He wore a silvered helm shaped like the gaping-mouthed head of a merform, a Leviathan, like the ship. A row of long tapering steel teeth formed a visor across the front, and a ridge of spines made from shards of shining quartz extended from his brow to crown. "*Roqyi!*" the big man bellowed, for a moment extending his arms and opening himself up dangerously. "Why hide behind a rock when there's hewing to be done?"

Nat made a smile, showing his bloody teeth. "Waiting, not hiding. Thought you lugs would never land. Thought that maybe you'd prefer to watch while we cuckold you of all the glory!"

Egon strode forward, and Nat watched as the other Paydar fell away before him in respect. He envied him that. The first mate never stopped smiling. "We shall see who gains the glory by day's end, red raven. Come! My sword is dirty, so very very dirty. I would see it cleaned with the blood of these faithles–" The arrow took him in the foot, puncturing his leather boot and planting solid. The man looked down at the wound, as slow and deliberate as an aurochs. "*Dhereda*! That was my kicking foot. Onward, men! Revenge my foot! Kill them. Kill them all!" The Paydar went forward at the heels of their feather-footed leader.

Something caught his eye. A defender was coming up through the breach, on the hill of stone left by the partial-collapsed wall, his uniform so dusty and torn he looked like a deadman, newly risen. He was helmetless and shouting, and the men of the *Leviathan* stalked forward slowly, their swords and maces and mauls raised tensely, expecting some ruse. Arrows caught him through the leg and his chest. The realisation came to Nat soon enough. The man wasn't one of the Godless... he was hardly a man at all. Nat must have run, dropping his shield, for then he was ahead of the attacking line, what remained of the castle walls towering either side of him, and there was Greg, and he was screaming.

Nat did not feel confused at the time. Only after, when it was over, when the attackers realised what was happening. The defenders had fallen back to the bailey by then, undisciplined rows of children wearing ill-fitting armour and bearing oversized weapons. All of them had a feral, desperate look, and if they were not weeping, they shook or pissed themselves or backed away from the invaders.

It was over. Even the Paydar were not keen on butchering children. Bagman's Bluff was explored, to see if there were any more surprises within. Egon took a troupe up into the North Tower, and there he found forty-three more Godless, infirm and sick and old all. They corralled them into the bailey, for Nat did not know what else he could do. With a Greg that came in and out of consciousness beside him, he ordered for a mess to be constructed in the courtyard for the defenders to fill their bellies. *They may fear and hate them, but at least they won't be hungry.* Only then did the questions finally come. *Children? Where are the rest of them? Why leave these poor bastards?*

Greg had made it inside before any of them, it seemed. When the healers finally disembarked from the rearguard, they came to tend the Godless waifs. Injuries on their side were much more grievous than the Paydar, so their captives received fair treatment. Nat grabbed one by the scruff of his priestly robes as he came waddling past, and commanded him to help Greg. The healer, a barrel-chested man with a jowly face who reeked of onions, was not a stupid man, quickly coming to the conclusion that the tracker was not just some wonted levy. He advised Nat that it would be wise to bear Greg by litter away from the Godless, lest they be afflicted by some malaise. Nat agreed, but not before he made him swear to the gods that he would heal the kid. The healer swore on all the gods, even ones Nat had never heard of.

The questions came after. Nat had his men raise the portcullises, and had the Paydar colours placed atop the gatehouses. Norther and that bitch Sere Rowett were first, riding through the eastern gate, and the adventurer regarded the Godless survivors in mute horror. Aud arrived last with his squire, Hearty, Captain Arodyr and the rest of his escort. The emissary slid from his horse, his armour making him look fearsome and deadly and everything a knight should be. Without thinking, Nat took a step back.

"Where is he?" Aud asked, his grey eyes scanning the fortress.

"Good day to you too, Aud. Greg's fine. A healer is tending to him on the *Merry Raven*. He's *safe*, I say. Sibyl even posted a guard, bless her. She–"

"Your nocturnal conquests don't interest me. Only your loyalty, which has been tested today. *Twice*." Nat could feel the heat of fury rise within, and despite having an empty stomach could feel the bile rise with it. Those around the courtyard had stopped what they were doing at the Emissary's quibbling noise, a good thousand in all. This outburst was not wholly unexpected to Nat, but to do so in front of the men was overkill. "We have won a victory here today, and here you *scold* me. Had I obeyed you, I would be dead, and at the bottom of the river, and that poor bastard Arhax would be here instead." He had meant to sound forceful yet restrained, but he could hear the petulance in his own voice.

"Victory? You call *this* victory?" His hands swept across the mass of huddled old men and women, the lines of children receiving bread and cawl. "The true enemy escaped us. If these were worthless to *them*, how much use can they be to us?" He had not thought of that. But before he could reason with Aud, the emissary said, "You use insubordination to vex me, and to save your own hide. You proceeded to storm the fort without my given command, and in such, you almost killed Greg."

The accusation was too much. *Me? He thinks I could have killed him? He has the gall to think I– that I would–* He fumed, even his thoughts becoming erratic as he struggled to find his justification. "I didn't... I didn't know–"

"Exactly. You didn't know. You still don't know. You refuse to learn, however many times the lesson is given to you."

He couldn't hold it in any longer. "My men were in the water and up the rocks before I had the chance. I can't be held accountable for what men do in the heat of battle."

"That's where you're wrong. You *are* accountable. For their greatest feats, and their lowest failings, it always comes back to their commander. *You.* I gave you the van, but now I think that was a mistake."

Anger choked him. Wanting to punch something, he grabbed the hilt of his knife instead. The Paydar did not like that, especially the emissary's sycophantic blond squire. "Get that hand off your pommel, Sir. Shan't be wanting to kill you, but I will to defend my Lord Emissary." *What was your name again, you mongrel pup?* His hand slid away from the blade, as the Paydar came on him with dozens of spears levelled at his face.

Is this gratitude? Is this victory?

"I didn't want any of this to happen. Greg is my friend, as he is yours. Why would I want to harm him? *I saved him.*" The squire pulled Nat's kje free of his scabbard and trotted his horse toward Nat. "Keep that worm behind your teeth, lest it return to the dirt." He had never been so close to the stripling before, but now that he was he could see that he was trying to grow his own beard. Where Audeyrn had grown a mass of wiry blond and brown hair, the squire only had a thin line of fuzz on his upper lip, and even that was too light and thin to ever be called a true beard. *Hold your tongue, or lose it...* "I prefer to let my steel talk. Can you use that little prick of yours?"

"You…" The squire took a few moments to grasp the insult, his cheeks blazing red. "I'll geld you, you…"

"Quiet yourself, Nyle. Your yowling is irritant noise." Aud stepped up between them. "You didn't know about Greg's mission. It was played by ear I admit, this whole bloody battle. Govier had the improviso plan to sneak inside with Greg. It worked, in a way. I had thought more would die. I suppose we have Govier to thank for that." *The hooded man.* Govier had never given straight answers to any questions posed to him. He had stayed apart, watching, listening, always conspiring. Always. One day he had even had the audacity to ask to sail aboard the *Raven*, to which Aud granted. Curious as to who this strange wanderer was, Nat had broached him in polite conversation. That was met with a hard glance, his eyes sparkling weirdly in the deep shadows of his cowl. "Keep your kje close, *traveller*," was all he had to say. Indeed he never uttered another word for the entire week he had stayed aboard. Nat had hated every second of it.

"Where is the hood now?" He could not see him in the emissary's entourage, nor anywhere else in the crowded yard. Audeyrn looked about quickly, and was about to say something, before shaking his head. *Interesting. He put Greg in danger. Almost like he knew who was holding the Bluff. But how...*

Nat could see the emissary's shoulders drop, the way he seemed to feel the full weight of the armour on his back. *He's tired. Gods, who isn't? Yet it bears down on him like a gibbet.* "Aud... Can we talk in private?" His hand had only touched his shoulder plate when a gauntlet shrugged him off.

"We can talk on the road. The *long road*. My mission has been postponed for far too long. That's all that matters, in the end. Gregyn will be placed aboard the *Leviathan*, under my supervision. You shall retain your captaincy of the *Merry Raven*, for now. We shall talk on the road, when we have closed company." He gestured to a young Paydar ahorse, a boy with a red mark on his forehead. "Tell Crispin Moss he is to command Gregyn's riders until he is back on his feet."

"Aye, Lord Emissary... but..."

"Yes? Anything the matter?"

"No, it's just I... may I stay with the archer?"

Aud eyed him for a moment. "You're his squire... yes. Tell Crispin what I have said, and then board the *Leviathan*. Go." The young lad turned his firemane and galloped off. Nat tried to guess the lad's age, but the emissary would not leave him be, "As your men saw fit to disobey me openly, they are to undertake a sweep of the fort. Anything of worth, anything that could help us in locating the remaining Godless, anything at all, is to be brought to me. You will personally oversee this task."

The indignation of it all made Nat say, "I have already tasked Egon to do that. I–"

"This time you'll do it yourself."

"And what will you do?" He instantly regretted those words, for then the emissary's eyes caused to a hot cinder. Nat took a step back, and this time he meant it.

"I'll question the prisoners."

The knife had dug deep into the mast, and he had to work it well to pull it free. In the moonlight it shone bright, and Nat spotted a dot of rust near the crossguard. Frowning, he made for the cabin. Then, a thought entered his mind. He could not have said where it came from, but it was there, and it soon made him stop. The moon was bright, near as large as that night in the snowmonts. The roc's blood had been close to black then. The cries were almost like a child. *This is not done yet.*

The chill blew against his shirt, and he cursed. Resigning himself to what he had to do, he entered his cabin. And there she was.

"Back so soon? Thought you would be catching your breath a while longer," she said teasingly. His surcoat she had put on the back of the chair, he saw, folded tidily along with his kje and swordbelt. Sibyl herself was on the bed, the blankets all a tangle as two long legs limned in candlelight stuck out jauntily. Sitting up, she let the book tumble into her lap. The covers covered nothing at all.

He caught himself before he could say it. *Yes, yes, yes. A thousand yesses, and more. Always. I...* What? Love her? His doubt was enough of an answer for him. He felt his gaze drift off, he wasn't looking at her, he wasn't even in the cabin anymore. A noise like the bole of a tree groaning under its own weight filled his ears, a visceral keen that sounded half a moan and half a muffled scream. It was totally unknown yet extremely intimate, and it made him shiver. *It's the ship, that's all. It's wood. Hacked riven-timber, that's...*

"Are you thinking about the battle? What the Godless did... that was cowardly. More than that, it was evil. Using the little 'uns like that. Shame we did not find them. They should have been made to suffer for all of it... You know, Shazad is getting awfully boring... I could help you calm your mind..."

He wanted nothing more than to kiss her then, to taste her lips, to tell her everything and show her how he felt. Then the doubts permeated him again, and it choked him, and he said nothing. His silence was enough for Sibyl to cover herself, a deep flush going to her cheeks, for a moment playing with a rogue lock of hair. Then she held out her hand to him. A small gesture he knew, but enough that he could have fallen into her arms. He wanted to.

"Come here, love. You're not in the wars anymore." *But I am. I will always be there...* when he tried to bring Rhyrn's face to mind, it was nondescript, the skin pulled tight until he could not make out her eyes or ears or nose or mouth, only the hair that shook at the edges, a shaking that turned them into wooden roots, heavy and creaking and growing, growing in and out of her face until there was nothing left. *Why can't I remember her face?* The whispering intensified, and it called to him.

Something hard hit the back of his legs, and he was in the cabin again. His hands went behind him to find the table, just the table, with the half-dozen unfurled maps atop. Sibyl was looking at him, her brow creased in something like pain. *Tell her. Tell her now. No. Never. Run. Stay. Find Audeyrn. Find him. Find him now. Now. Now. Now. Do it. Fool. Do it. Now!* Was that his voice? His head spun, and he felt drunk. Nearly as drunk as when he was with that girl in Forlorn. *What was her name? It was a flower.* Greg was there now, kneeling in the sand, arrows sticking out of him to let the blood pool around his feet. He was putting blood on his blade too. When he looked up at Nat, his face changed, aged, the hair lightening and his limbs contracting, until it was Aud that was there. A figure stood behind him, with a crown upon his head…

"My brother came back from the Glede Uprising with nightmares… the sort you dream when you're awake. It's a cruel thing, for us to fight for our land, only for the gods to let you keep your arms and legs and sight, but take away your happiness, your soul, the smiles and laughs you could share with your love. Death to look upon you whenever you close your eyes. The screaming of those you killed, those dying in pools of blood around you, the screams that never end… " Her voice was softer than he had ever heard it. Sincere, but here was an edge to her words, a bitterness that held back sorrow. "I feel it too, you know. I want to be with you tonight, Natoly. I want us to make each other feel safe. Can… we do that?"

"I… I need…" What did he need? She was looking at him deeply, the eyes he liked so much full and glittering in the candlelight. He loved her then. But not enough. He turned, grabbed his surcoat and sword and belt, and out into the night. The wind buffeted at him, making a red veil of uncut hair across his eyes. *When had the wind picked up?* The door slammed shut, and he made his way mid-ships to the gangway. The rigging was restless, thrumming low from the gusts that pulled at the lengths that wound taut about the pegs. It seemed a different world, the warmth and light of the cabin replaced by the dinginess of night. It had even started to drizzle.

He followed the rutted road to the camp by the light of the moon, itself an implacable beacon unabashed by rain or wind. The chill made him pull his surcoat tight about him, cinching the belt a link closer than he was used to. The mud squelched under his boots, pulling at him, as though the very land was holding him back. To return to Sibyl. To fall into her arms. He trudged on regardless, the riverbank giving way to the rise at the foot of the great fay-hill.

As fay circles go, it is oddly beautiful. Old, yet beautiful. Commanding, even now, with only the moonglow, it raises its imperious head in scorn. Wait, what? His mind fought against itself, and it was all he could to keep on walking, each step seeming to get harder and harder, the land giving way to a harsh slope. Thickets made him turn now and again, forced to either stomp them down or push them aside, large masses of gorse with most of their green gone now. Even they knew that winter was coming. Frustration made him barge through them, resulting in the large thorny arms raking his hands and pulling at the threads of his clothing. *Find Audeyrn. Find him. It's Govier. He caused all this. He has to see. I need to warn him. Bollocks to the mission and the war and the fucking Rowett alliance. Govier is dangerous. They all see it! Why is the path...*

He had not noticed when he left the trail, only that he was climbing, his feet carrying him higher, the lights of the camp now in sight. He breathed a sigh of relief, as his eyes were drawn to them like a moth to a naked flame. He needed to find the tent, and the emissary within. Greg would probably be there too, bandaged and hurt, yet unbeaten. Victorious. *He should not be in a sickbed. The lad should be proclaimed the valiant hero of the Battle of Bagman's Bluff, his feats taken back to fickle old Isembard so that he may be raised to knighthood. The king should get off his bony arse and dub him himself. If I were a knight, I would have done it. If I was a knight...*

The wind picked up, to become a howling of a *gray*, the monster-wolves of Old Qell. Then he reminded himself that such beasts were probably used in this land, during the Blood Wars and the Conquest of the Northmarch Kingdom. Even the gutter-rats of Low Castan heard tales of how the sorcerers of Qell had bred their grays to be bigger than any natural wolf, a far more fearsome mount for the Qellish cavalry. They were said to be as big as a plough horse and capable of biting a man in two, even in plate armour. Their breath was a hurricane, their teeth sharper than steel daggers, their eyes roiling like molten gold. The thought of such a thing, and the biting wind, set him to shiver in equal parts. *I do not fear the tales of old women,* he thought. He held the hilt of his kje tight. Then the trees closed in.

He could not remember the walk to the camp taking so long. He tutted at himself, feeling all the fool. He could hear the songs getting louder, so how could he possibly be lost? It was hardly a round-a-bout way to the hidden valley, and despite the closeness of the tall trees around him, at least he was out of the worst of the rain, and the wind. *And the howling.* Leaves fell in lazy succession in a multitude of hues: most every one as light as amber, or dark and deep as blood and wine. As hard as he looked, he could only count a few dozen leaves still green in the high canopy. Even less littered the forest floor, for that was the domain of a leafy field, piles of sodden leaves crunching and squelching underfoot. There was another autumn like this once, he remembered, but now it was hard to pull to mind. All he could think about was his friends, and the things he needed to tell them.

Hearty will listen. He'll scratch his beard and think on it but he will eventually come round. Greg trusts me, doesn't he? I saved his life. He'll listen. Govier put him in that hellmouth, if anyone is angry with the bastard, it's Greg. Norther? He's a pawn. Thinks he's clever, but he's nothing but an upjumped mercen, probably the son of some poxy slattern and village brute, despite his looks. And Audeyrn... he'll hear me. He has to.

Those singing their song neared as far as he could tell. They could not be far now. The words were foreign to him, the tune unfamiliar. He put that down to it being a Paydar arrangement, those marching ballads full of husky tones. They sang well, like the way they fought. Even their mannish women able to give some of the best singers at a Caldish court competition.

So where are they all? The trees gave way to more climbing. He knew he had to go on. He could not stop now. From someways off came the groaning again, this time sounding even more fervent and impatient, a wailing reduced to a hoarse croak. *Hurry,* it seemed to whisper, its owner having an impossibly old and wearied voice. *Hurry now. Make quick. Make quick.* It called, and he followed.

Somehow he found the path, but it was smaller and steeper than before. It zig-zagged on him, forcing him to turn back on himself countless times. The wind found him again, and it kissed the exposed skin of his face as harshly as if from the jaws of a gray. Rain fell in a sideways tumult, making his hair cling limply to his face and his surcoat sodden and heavy. Even his feet felt wet in his boots. Still he pressed on, the undergrowth here reduced to small tufts of mountain heather and stunted blackthorn. Only stone dominated. Stone and wind and deluge. At least here, the rainwater hid his tears.

The song had long ended by then, replaced by a low chanting, an aria to his ears of an unseen chorus, and a woman's voice ringing high amongst it all. Something told him it was for him. Whatever it was, it spurred him on, anticipation filling his blood until he was striding, keen to crest the hill and finally find some godsdamned people. He was nearly *there*, he could feel it. Loose stone moved underfoot, and for a moment he was back at the Bluff, and instead of rain came a shower of arrows cruelly tipped in iron and killing anything they hit. Up ahead came the breach, a narrow gulley between two high standing stones.

I'm here. I made it. The treeline should have extended to the gulley, he knew, but it didn't seem important. He nearly fell as he scrambled between them, desperate to get some respite from the elements. A few more ragged movements, and then he was there, heaving deep breaths as he slumped heavily on one of the stones. It was covered in lichen and moss, and it must have stained his surcoat green, but he did not care.

It did not seem important. The voices had stilled, even the wind had somewhat quieted itself as he lay in his little shelter in the lee of the blowing gale. Flicking his forelocks out of his eyes, he glanced out at the summit of Flattop.

To call it impressive would have been a lie. It was barren. A bald shelf of exposed rock painted a dark brow by the lashing. *No, there's that one...* Nat could just make out the form of a tree on the plateau. Singular, and alone. *I need to...* He knew he had to do something, but the thought kept slipping from his attention. It was more important to reach the tree. The tree was where he needed to be.

Still breathing heavily, shivering violently, he went back into the downpour. He tripped several times on pebbles, his hair kept going into his eyes as he walked. Looking down, he spotted piles of neatly arranged stones piled up impossibly high, large stones balancing precariously on minuscule things that almost looked like gemstones. They were everywhere, every few feet, the rain apparently having no effect on their balance. *What is...*

The thing came upon him quickly, reaching up into the sky with twisted branches that he could not help but think looked like the wrinkled arms of a clawed harridan. The bole was enlarged and rounded, at its centre a hollow gaping wide, the lips either side pulled back to expose something bright and terrible within.

He wanted to look away, to close his eyes and forget, to run, to hide, to find her, to find her... to find Rhyrn. Where was she? He needed her, needed her, no one else, where was she?

The light in the tree was fire, unlike anything he had seen before. Scarlets and golds there were, but also cobalts and indigos, silver and pearl. The blaze swirled and writhed, never touching the wood of its cage, never burning or scorching the hollow. It did not even make a sound. Instead, the voices came, a dirge filling the sky and the moribund ground and each droplet of rain, until the whole world sang with one long, sad voice, singing for him. An odour suffused the air, something Nat thought smelled like the potions healers used on their tools to clean them.

I have to tell them... But then his hand was reaching out, reaching, reaching for the fire. Strangely, he felt no fear. The voices roused themselves, urging him on, now a lamentation, now a battle cry, always meant for him.

His fingers went to the edge of the hollow, finding it cold to the touch. It was cool and still as he climbed in, and he felt nothing, the inferno surrounding him, the glowing fingers wandered as lightly as a lover, touching him everywhere, until there was nothing else to feel. They moved with a frenetic energy, dancing and leaping, alive. Then he felt it. He felt it all, the heat of a furnace wind, and with all the lust he had ever experienced, the anger and the hate, the pain in Low Castan, the great sadness of losing Rhyrn. But most of all he felt the fire. It consumed him. It lasted forever, an unending ecstasy and torment, euphoria and agony, so intense he could no longer tell one from the other. The light blinded him.

Then he felt no more.

24

MARBLE

It was time to get rid of the pest the Mistress had sent her.

She had prepared for colder climates and temperatures, and had finally acquired a scarf. The material was rich and strong, yet soft and sleek and beautiful. The colour was that of the deep Midnight Lakes of the Perygul. The boldness of its hue was mesmerising, changing colour with every simple and sly movement. Marble felt strong again as she donned the covering, she hadn't realised how lost and adrift she had felt without one. The scarf had become so ingrained in her perception and sense of self that she felt that she could breathe again and as though a pressure squeezing at her torso had finally released. Marble was ready. Packed up as heavily as one would see any beast of burden, scarf secure and armed to the teeth, the emissary emerged once more on to the streets of Bonebridge. Now she just had to leave.

Marble was not receptive to the possibility of any further delays on her journey. As she stalked down the streets in the midday sun, passersby stopped to watch. As the emissary approached the outskirts of the hospitable area, the sight of a small group of gathered people caused her stride to slow and caution to creep in. She was leaving today whether they liked it or not.

There stood Grenn, the red guard, the maid, the Mistress, and a man she had never seen before. "Marble." The Mistress greeted stiffly. "Valmar will be accompanying you on your journey." An elegant, strong hand raised abruptly, forestalling the protests and arguments that Marble mouth was poised to deliver.

"You will not leave the Tundra in good time without him." She informed. Her nod was most regal. "We will see each other again, I am certain of it. It has been… interesting." When the woman turned, her entourage followed at her heels, leaving Marble with the stranger, Valmar, amongst stones baked hot by the sun.

The emissary scoffed as the man eyed her. He had thin, dark hair swept back from his rounded face. His ears were small, his eyes sunken into his head, a muddy, murky colour. He was a man of average height but boasted broad shoulders and a rotund trunklike torso. He seemed clean enough to her, but his clothes were old, worn, and stained.

That first day, she refused to speak to or even acknowledge his existence. She was annoyed, but deep down she knew she needed him. It did not mean she had to share her provisions with him, and she would kill him if he tried to take them from her.

So they walked. And walked. And walked. Marble in stony silence, and Valmar unsuccessfully attempting to draw her into conversation every few hours or so.

"So, you Marble right?" Was the first, his voice chipper and expectant. "Where'd about you hail?" He asked, undeterred. "I been places. I probs know where. Hmm, I can guess if you wants? Or not."

The day progressed. *Slowly.* "You the one fighting in the food hall?" Incredibly slowly. "Hows about some riddles? What's black when you buys it, red when you use it, n' grey when you get rid of its? What you's think? You know it? Hmmm? Go ons! You knows." She let the words wash over her in the desert. "Ofs the kings I is blue, ofs the peasants I is red. Frogs cold, dogs hot. What is I?" Painfully slowly. "Ow's bouts a wee ditty? A song? I gots a voice of wonders. Anything you wants to hear? No? My choice? Aws, you good to me!" Excruciatingly slowly.

What felt like an eternity passed before the sun began to sink in the sky, creating a kaleidoscope of colour that Marble would have enjoyed and admired, any other day. The temperature dropped quickly, and while Marble was more than willing to push on, she followed Valmar's lead and set up camp for the night. He was her guide, and until she knew that she was definitely out of the Desolate Tundra, she needed him.

For as irritating as the man was, Marble couldn't deny that he seemed to know what he was doing. He set peculiar traps and alarums that would warn of dangers. Incoming storms and predators and scavengers eager to take advantage as such easy prey, as well as the land as it shifted. They bedded down, she rested but slept little, watching the stranger sleep across from her.

The second day proceeded much like the first, Marble silent and Valmar talking. The only difference being that he kept a running commentary of what they were doing. And walking. And walking some more. And on and on it went.

Rests were short, food and water rationed. Whenever Valmar needed to relieve himself, he just exposed himself there and then. ensuring Marble got a good look. She would always wait as long as she could, trying to find a small dune she could squat behind. Maybe she just didn't want a commentary of her taking a piss. The night was cold, and sleep was fitful.

The sunrise the next morning was stolen away by the angry black clouds behind them. "A storm is coming." Stated Valmar, his face a blank mask of concern.

The landscapes could and would change at a whim. That day they travelled in fear of the encroaching clouds, but by the afternoon it had edged north. They set up camp, and Marble was convinced she would sleep soundly, when one of the alarums sounded.

From snoring to sharp in the blink of an eye, the man paced agitatedly checking each alarum, seeing which of them was tripped. He knelt beside each, to a string of foul curses. Her mind went to the storm, wondering if it turned west to follow their trail. She looked out beyond their meagre camp, and saw nothing.

Valmar's stream of cussing grew more colourful and inventive, and panicked. As he ran between sensor after sensor, more and more of them began to sound. Each toll accumulating to an almost ululating shrill.

Something deeper roiled beyond, a dull *thrummm* that soon overpowered the sound of alarums as it drew closer. Valmar looked panicked. She needed to get Valmar thinking straight again, and quickly. A warm breeze stirred at her clothing, disturbing her scarf. Small whirls of sand took shape, to float in the air.

Marble's first attempt to shout the man's name was little more than a soundless croak. Her second was a hoarse "Valmar!" Her voice carried over the sound of the bells and the wind, reaching the man before it was blown away into the tumult. "Valmar! Pull yourself together! Do we run, or find shelter?". The slap knocked him out of the stupor.

She couldn't quite say what happened next. Valmar produced what appeared to be a random assortment of gewgaws from his pack, and before Marble could see what he planned to do, the sandstorm reached them, grabbing and stinging and *blinding*. No matter where she turned, she was battered with sand. Her scarf buffeted the worst of it from her face, yet she dare not open her eyes.

Unable to see, she was far from blind. She pricked her ears, trying to track her companion through the storm. The sand was thrown in every direction, but the more she listened, the more the discordant song made sense. Through the chaos, the storm was *patterned*, almost a rhythm.

There. She heard him. He was working away at something, an island of flesh in a dry sea. The wind and sand raged furiously about him. Nipping, biting, burning. The sound of the torrent was near deafening, the whole thing setting her teeth hard as she grounded herself and waited, hoped. The air shimmered, her heart beat, and she maintained her poise and her breathing. Then Valmar vanished, his presence dissipated like he was one with the sand..

The bastard better not have left me. Unseeing and deaf, she focused. The twisting, skirling wind and the scraping of the rough tore at her. She wanted nothing more than for a yappor to breach the ground and swallow her. *What a relief that would be.* Her smile was private, a slyful grin hidden from this Desolate Tundra by some fabric. She waited, for the world to turn upside down, for the earth to disappear, for thunder and squall and terror. Her hands found blades, ready and waiting.

Then it was quiet.

Silence, delicate and small. Within the line in the sand the wind was still. She could hear her laboured breath and pounding heart, but not much more. It was as though all sound inside the bubble was muffled. Marble pulled the scarf free, and looked into the gloom. A softlight separated them from the outside. *What has he done?*

Valmar lay prone, his breathing ragged. For a moment she wanted to terrorise him with a commentary of their predicament. With a rueful grin she asked him what was happening, but her question went unanswered.

The bubble was dark, but Marble could see the whirls and twisting formations of the sand without. Every attempt to rationalise leaving the bubble ended with the same thought-*And go where?* Valmar was unconscious, so she resigned herself to waiting. Delayed and delayed again, she sat in frustration.

She realised he had saved their packs from the chaos, strewn haphazardly about by the storm, intact if only getting sand anywhere and everywhere. The emissary packed up what she could and moved everything, including the cumbersome form of her apparent guide to the far edges of the circle.

The storm raged into the night. Valmar woke eventually, exhaust making his movements laboured. In the little hours it let up, the worst of the torrent drifting southwest. The dome of night was inky dark, the air was cold, and the stars winked tauntingly from above. Valmar slept.

They continued on their way the next day, Valmar was subdued, his spirit seemingly gone. He was quiet, and resentful. Marble didn't care. Her mind was too busy, occupied with planning routes and contingencies, and all manner of plans to help her figure a way of outsmarting time. They all ended the same, with her setting her jaw and cursing under her breath.

And so the journey went, Valmar growing increasingly resentful and Marble barely breaking her silence. She kept her vigilance. Days and nights passed begrudgingly as the pair powered onwards.

They walked. And walked. And walked.

Their rations dwindled.. Four more times they were caught in horrendous storms, and the land changed beneath them twice. Once, the dunes disappeared entirely, cracked, sharp, broken clay replaced them. The second time it seemed to reverse. The hard, treacherous ground transformed into a rolling dune that they both had to roll down, to find themselves surrounded by a towering range of hardscrabble sand mountains. Each storm worsened Valmar's disposition until he looked in her eyes as the husk of the verbose man sent out by the Mistress. A husk, ever angry.

Eventually, to her unabashed delight the Tundra ended, the orange sands giving way steadily to earth and sparse tufts of meagre draggrass and cringing byl trees. It was when she passed a particularly dense brush of the dry desert trees that the realisation came to her. *Valmar must leave.* She worked best alone, and did not need this stranger hindering her progress. No. It was time he departed.

He had only had the chance to drop his pack at the foot of a byl before her knife was held firmly beneath the man's fleshy neck, pressing threateningly against the pulsign artery. It took a moment for the husk's uncensored gaze to tear itself away from the blade to meet her hard gaze. Marble allowed her intentions to show clearly in her expression. He looked cocksure, and proud of himself then. *Idiot.*

"It's time for you to turn around and head back to Bonebridge." Her voice was a razor to cut through his bluster. His smirk only grew as though to call her bluff.

"Nah, little lady." His voice was simpering, grating to her nerves. She clenched her teeth hard against the sickening sensation it sent across her skin. "It ain't time for me t'be leaving ya company. Not jus' yet."

"Oh, it most certainly is." She enforced her words with a warning nick of the knife. "You have overstayed your welcome." The emissary watched coldly as the drop of red welled, and trickled lazily over his pockmarked skin. He loomed over her, and his shadow blotted out the sun to make her skin cold and shiver.

"I decide when I come and go. You should watch that ungrateful tongue of yours. Especially when I gained you a month." He twisted his cruel visage into a menacing grin, the threat clear for anyone to see. "I've got an idea of how you can be grateful, though. Grateful, and accommodating."

He leered, taking a tentative step towards her. Any further, and he would spill his life's blood. A trickling red stram. "You should be thankful. If it weren't for me, ya be dead, or worse. You can't even believe what the Tundra hosts. Fell things, demons, shriekers, nightmare things. They make yappors look like moggies." The sneer rolled over his tongue. He man did not heed the warning contained in her gaze. Or he just ignored it.

"You won't get another chance." The emissary seethed. "Leave. Now."

The man just laughed. Blood spattered across his chin.

"You ain't gonna do *anything* to me. You ain't got nobody to help you. I'm a favourite of the Mistress." He made a show of looking around, looking for salvation or threats she could not tell. "You ain't got the gumption nor the balls. You–" He jeered, the words ending in red sputtering.

"My eloquent guide" She left him in the trees.

25

AUDEYRN

Wolfsmouth was much as they had left it.

The Bloodroyal Fleet glided down the wide rush of the Wolfwater, the mid-channel becoming ever more turbulent as it neared the sea. The Span came into view, a thin ribbon arching over the estuary further down, its ends blotted out by the storehouses that lined the riverfront in rough ranks.

A town that surrounded and embraced the estuary of the Wolfwater River as it spilt into the Ruell Sea. The buildings on either side of the drink were enclosed by the massive city walls of fortified stone, the only openings being to allow the channel of the river to bisect the town. Within, Paydar of the lowlands lived and traded and fished the Ruell Sea, here they were much slimmer than their northerly cousins, favouring fish over meat, ships over horses, and songs and joiety over fights in certain colossal mountain fighting pits. From an outsider's eyes, they were much the same, for they both braided their hair in the morning, all spoke the Qellish tongue, and all held the ways of martial combat sacred. The

Qellish tongue was spoken, but here more mongrel in its mixing of the common and trade tongue argot and the languages brought by the travellers on their ships.

The more time Audeyrn spent with the 'low' Paydar, the more he came to appreciate their differences, and how much authority their lady enjoyed. *I must treat with her again.* He did not know if what he felt was anticipation or dread. Perhaps it was both. Lady Adrianne Torrin ruled here. By law, she owed her fealty to the Rowetts of Stonehall-On-The-Tor, and as such, flew the Paydar tri-colour atop the lighthouse in the bay known as the Lord's Lamp. The banner that marked their allegiance to the Rowetts was outnumbered a hundred to one, though, for Lady Torrin's own banner, a green Sea-Dog upon a snowy white field flew everywhere in all its loping glory. Nowhere were the green merforms more prevalent than along the Span, the vast tapering bridge that crossed the entire wide mouth of the river in a high arch. It was built by the Qell of old, and, as such, crafted to be impossibly sturdy for its age and slim profile, rising in a gradual curve until it towered two hundred feet over the passing ships below, safely allowing any beneath with ample room to spare.

Audeyrn had seen the tall tower ships of the Druke, some fabled to reach about a hundred feet or more (depending on who you asked). Even those colourful traders would pass safely beneath the bridge to find safe anchorage in the Jaw, the spacious natural harbour that, once filled, would enlarge Wolfsmouth until it swelled to become the seasonal Floating District, where all manner of spices and goods and materials were bartered and exchanged in a dozen or more tongues from peoples across the continent.

367

Giving a sigh of relief, he went to stroke his chin. *I return with one friend missing and another perilously hurt.* His shorn cheeks felt queer after wearing a beard for so long. Somehow it had felt a nuisance all of a sudden, and there was nothing for it but to sheer it all off. That only helped to make his face feel the growing cold all the more each passing day.

Natoly, where are you?

He had been hard on him, he knew. Unfair? That he could not be sure of. The Rowetts had entrusted him with the command of their warriors, and with it, he had given Lady Cyrinne the solemn promise that he would not dishonour them. They had been insulted once, and even now, the Castan-Paydar alliance was tentative, if anything. *The old Castanni boasted of heroes that wed the daughters of gods, slew the putrid monsters from the unspeakable dreadblack realms, crowned themselves in gold and splendour.* The words from Lady Cyrinne had been thin and hoarse, but the iron was there, and he heard it. *Do not make us regret this, Emissary. The Rowetts are descended from gods too, you know, and like gods, our memories are long and our wrath fearsome to behold.*

It rankled him to think about that. He had been given a grandson of the Lady as a squire, a ship to sail, an army to command, even a suit of armour. The honours had been endless. *And the pride, the pride most of all.* Even the dreams had stopped. The girl in them a vision of Soran beauty, that unknown yet lovely face. But one he knew would fade in time, like all dreams do in the end.

She had led him to the river, as promised, but the purpose of the auspice still eluded him. It had felt like a prophecy, the kind wandering godmen and augers spout in exchange for a drink of wine and a mouthful of yesterday's catch. *So what was the meaning of it all?* She had told him where to find the enemy, yet when they arrived they were already gone, all that was left being the dregs at the bottom of the scummy barrel, those too young to fight, those too sick to be of use, those seen as worthless.

Nyle had advised him to kill them all. He had reprimanded him sharply for that, half tempted to slap the insipid grin from his face. Taking on the squire seemed like a bad idea, looking back. Nyle Rowett was grasping, eager to please, quick to take offence, and proud of that long-storied heritage he had as a Rowett. Worst of all, he had been dogged in his pursuit of knighthood. *But so was Natoly,* the spiteful voice said. *Yes, but he showed his aspiration through acts of valour, not with slinking and sycophantic words.* He should have let Nat duel the squire at the Bluff, he considered, but he could not risk creating a deeper rift between the Caldish and the Paydar. Even if it was an honourable duel, he could *not* risk the alliance. The mission was everything, after all... *isn't it?*

The look Nat had given him had been full of hurting. The emissary knew that his words bit deep into the fox's arrogance. The more he tried to justify his punishment, the less fair it sounded. The thought had even passed his mind to relieve him of command of the ship, but that was too far. To take his ship away would have reduced him to nothing more than an *unblooded* in the eyes of their Rowett allies, and besides, he had fallen head over arse for the captain of his ship. *Sibyl.* One of only two female captains of the fleet, the youngest, and by far the prettiest, she had been wroth to hear that Nat had gone missing. She was convinced that

Audeyrn had killed him, and aired her views in the pavilion that morning as the captains sat down for breakfast. She was not hard to look at, he had to admit, even feeling his urges rise as she bore her teeth at him.

"This is a farce, *dhereda*, and you know it!" She had seethed, storming off and barging past Nyle as he tried feebly to bar her way. He knew that she and Nat had grown close, and he felt the tightness in his gut as he remembered how he had shamed him by mentioning her in the fort. He had mulled over apologising to the fool that morning before they broke camp, to set off down the river, but then Sibyl had come onto the *Leviathan* uninvited, giving the emissary and his officers a taste of profanity that made even the coarsest of the Paydar blush. Arodyr did not even dare to countermand her, despite being her superior. When Audeyrn asked her what she was talking about, she growled, retreated to her own ship, and refused to disembark. She even cast off, and the *Leviathan* and *Sea Eagle* and *Dog o' War* were forced to give chase and command her to stop.

The day was mostly gone when they eventually brought her to heel and escorted her ship back to camp. Then the second hunt across the Outer Qell was finally allowed to begin. The search for Nat brought even less joy than that for the Godless. The last person to see the man had been Sibyl, who initially would not give up anything until Audeyrn had gone to the *Merry Raven* himself, with only Hearty as a guard, both men cautious not to wear swords as the *Raven's* crew glowered at them from the gang ropes. *Even they think I killed him…* She had claimed that Nat had been distracted and shaken the night before, growing quiet only to suddenly grab his sword and go off-ship.

She was no help in regards to Govier, however. As far as he could tell, the last person to see Govier was Gregyn, and he was still delirious from the fever that burned through him from his wounds, and any questions posed to him only resulted in unseeing eyes and shouts of *crystals* and *shadows*. So he had thanked Sibyl kindly and left, not before she called him a *dhereda* again and spat in his face.

The search parties had been arranged for a double purpose. The first being, of course, to find Nat, with the second being to discern the whereabouts of Govier, for sharp questioning. Aud had no way of knowing that Govier was behind the disappearance, but he could not rule it out either. It was Norther who had been the intermediary between the emissary and the hooded sage, and it was Norther who vouchsafed for the man, so it was that Audeyrn brought him aboard the *Leviathan* after his sojourn with Sibyl.

Norther told him everything he knew or as much as he was willing to give, saying that the sage had found Norther in Halfway a whole year before, appearing to know things he had no right in knowing. The spitfire seemed a different man than the swaggering mercen he had met in the Caldish war camp. His wounds at the hands of the undercover Godless agent at the Tor had healed well, but now his tone was grim and his face tight, and he told him that at Halfway, Govier had claimed they would meet again on the river, only then it would be in war and in strange company, and that he must tell no one about their meeting... *yes*, that was the most important thing of all.

The interrogations yielded little, if nothing, of use for Audeyrn. When the torturer Gentle Gaff presented himself before him, offering to whittle out the truth from Sibyl with what he called *a lover's kiss*, he sent the man away with polite words but hard eyes. The look on that man's face had been a terrible thing, as though he were fantasising about the ways he would abuse the captain. He always felt agitated whenever the man was near; he drew rumours to him as easily as flies are drawn to fresh shit. When he had gone, he tasked Hearty with finding out who he was. Something about him made his stomach clench harder than a fist. There was *something*, and he wanted to find out what.

No horses had been taken, as far as the quartermaster could tell. That ruled out Nat and Govier riding off. Them being afoot kindled some hope for the emissary. He had hoped, not that it helped. Five days they held over at the fay-hill. Five days he knew they could have used to travel downriver and rejoin the long road. Then to Silentis. To ending the war. *Five days.* In the end he commanded them to recall the hunters. That took another day, the time waiting enough to make anyone think that Nat was long gone. Unless...

His eyes fell upon Flattop. The Paydar feared the monstrous large fay-hill, some too terrified to even look at it. *What if the fox had never left?*

Arodyr hated the idea the moment it was proposed to him. Nyle begged him not to climb the hill. Sibyl scoffed and wished him luck in acid tones. *At least they didn't stop me.*

The ascent was a haze. The day was fresh and bright, with a bracing wind. The views must have been astounding, but he did not see them. He trudged up, following what looked like a narrow track made by sheep or goats, or the like. A good hour and he was done, passing through a small defile before a broad plateau spread out before him. He found nothing and no one. In the centre, a blackened and split stone marked what must have been a lightning strike, but it must have been old, for the roots that clung to it withered and crumbled when he touched them.

With nothing else to do, he descended, and from there resigned himself to the aftcastle of the *Leviathan*, going over the tidal charts with the lumbering first mate Egon Sipcup, who hobbled about on a bandaged foot. He had looked at the hulking man pour over the parchments with compass and quill, and he heard himself say, "Why do they call you Sipcup?" It had seemed a paltry thing before, not worth worrying over, but he felt like he needed to distract himself. Luckily, the first mate was willing to indulge his curiosity, and he smiled broadly as he spoke.

"I wasn't always as grand as you see me now, my Lord Emissary. Nor could I best the Lord Captain Arodyr or your friend the Hearty Deri in drinking or eating or swordplay. No. I was a small thing born, skinny and weak-limbed. I was *common* too, so my fate was to be that of the unblooded, clearing horseshit from the roads of Wolfsmouth until the day I found someone to give me a sword. I must have been impatient, for before my tenth birthday I heard of a journeyman, a wandering wyrding-man who was visiting a tavern in Sandygate, and who claimed to hail from Lar'gara in the far north. The village was two day's ride from Wolfsmouth, so it was that I came to... *borrow* a horse and pack a nibble of cheese and bread, and I was off. Not long after, I stood before the very man I sought in a mean pub, and I told him to make me a warrior. He stroked his beard for a time, looking me up and down, now and again pulling an ear or poking my ribs."

"In the end he refused me, saying that I was far too spindly and sickly, and too young besides. The men in the tavern laughed at me. Yet I begged him. I said I would give him anything, be his bondman, cook his meals, rub his feet after a day's trek, *anything*, so that I may one day be a warrior like my da, who my old mother said had been a great man. When a drunk came at me saying I'd make a better girl at the redhouse, and put a hand down my breeches, I smashed a tankard over his head. In the brawl that followed, I was ushered out by the journeyman. He told me I was stupid to do such a thing. But then he hesitated, eyeing me hard. 'Or maybe...' I heard him say, just as he took me away by the scruff of the neck. The caravan he travelled with was full of queer folk, a trio of Warretumi mercen, a pair of boltdancers who stroked my hair and asked me to braid theirs, and even a one-eyed Castanni knight. The journeyman explained to them what I wanted, and each looked at me shrewdly. His word was law to them I came to realise, and each offered themselves up to teach me their ways. And what ways they were! The knight taught me swordplay and trained me in the arts of war. From the Warretumi I learned to divine water and track game and shelter from the elements. From the boltdancers... well, they did not just teach me dancing. They were my lovers as well as tutors, despite them being near ten years my senior. I miss them the most, I think. Their hands were oh so clever... But I forget, you wanted to know about my name!"

"Five years I spent in their company, but never did I learn their true names. That was part of the arrangement, you see. We traversed the Paydar and Vastiland, through the Forks of Castan and the Lake Country, and from there south to the tree-cities of Druke on Sunset Point. Each night I was told to drink a special liquor prepared for me by the journeyman. 'Do not swallow in gulps,' he warned me. 'Always sip.' Every night I took that draught, and every morn after I grew taller and stronger. We ate like kings then, for provender was bountiful, and there was no war."

"When the time came for me to finally take my leave, I was a head taller than the tallest of the Warretumi, and stronger than any of them and the knight. The journeyman was keen to be rid of me by then, but he appeared satisfied that his work with me was done. Not that I am not grateful to the man! Look at me now! Whatever wizarding he did surely worked, so even though he did not embrace me by the end, I do not begrudge him that. The old fart was ever distant and far more concerned with chronicling his travels. So I returned to Wolfsmouth, and those I had known before were thunderstruck to discover that I lived, and even more shocked to see how I had changed. I went to the barracks then, for Lady Torrin is always keen to accept worthy blooded into her guard corps. The only hiccup was the man commanding them at the time, a man called Arodyr Rowett. No, not the Lord Captain. This was his father, Arodyr the Elder. He challenged me, you see, for I may have questioned his courage. I soon dispatched him. So it was that I killed a bloodroyal, and earned a place among the warriors of House Torrin. All this, for a man who was told to only sip his drinks."

Audeyrn waited until he was finished before saying, "You killed the captain's father... yet you are first mate aboard his ship. How–"

"Did the Lord Captain not take revenge?" The Sipcup's smile was wide, and violence played in his eyes. "Har! Let us say that he did not always command the *Leviathan*."

They berthed in the arsenal, the ships hailed by chants of *Chja! Chja! Chja!* To the ranks of arrayed guardsmen along the waterfront. *Victory, they shout. They've won a great victory. Yet I only keep losing.* An honour guard flanked the assembled nobles at the head of the quay. There were no Rowett colours here, only the sea-green of House Torrin. He recognised her instantly, and so did Hearty.

"There she is, Aud. Can't say I've relished this reunion."

The emissary had to smile, "Be glad she isn't our enemy. This she-wolf knows who her friends are, and she has more than ample reason to share blankets with the Tourmaline Throne." Hearty looked like he had barely slept. Dark rings formed around his eyes, and his beard was more of a wiry tangle than usual. Regardless, when he laughed, the laugh lines ruled his face, and his teeth were broad and crooked and friendly. "She can sleep with Isembard as much as she likes, like all she-wolves she's dangerous, and we had best be well away from her claws soon."

He isn't wrong. The woman has claws, and they are long and sharp.

The *Leviathan* groaned when her hull knocked against the quay, as though it was relieved to be back home. Whatever peace it wanted was broken however, for then a troupe of trumpeters sprang into a sprightly fanfare to welcome the navy. Aud thought all of this unnecessary, and try as he might, he found that he could not enjoy any of it. The only comfort he took was the solid feel of the waterfront beneath his feet, after being so long on the river. And then she came to him.

"My lady, we report that we are vict–" The kiss was unexpected. Her lips locked onto his, silencing him. It was chaste if anything, made more surprising by the cheers that erupted from those nearby. She was a tall woman, so when she pulled away she needn't look up at him. Lady Adrianne was breathless, and she let loose a deep laugh as she twined her long fingers through his. That elicited another round of cheer. It was silenced with a wave of her other hand.

The prisoners in the hold would be seeking for any sort of opening in the hull to see what the commotion was about. He considered them for a moment. Those that had not died, that is. The children among the waifs of the Godless were strong though, and awaited his judgement. *Maybe they can be sent to Walt. Maybe they could serve as pages and messengers and servants. Maybe even... in time... all will forget that they once belonged to the enemy.*

"I welcome back our glorious Lord Emissary of Castan, our gallant Lord Captains of the Bloodroyal Fleet, and all who followed them into the beast's maw and returned to us with sweet victory! Now, forgive me good folk, but we must return to Brinewater and begin the feast! Lest anyone be forgotten, tonight we shall deliver blackwine reserve to all the inns in Wolfsmouth!" With the promise of drink in mind, their cheers seemed even more passionate. Lady Adrianne herself wasted no time in dragging Audeyrn across the cobbles to a pair of firemanes, both caparisoned in rich sea-green and white of House Torrin, and both kicking at the ground with impatience. Hearty made to protest, but then the elite Merbeast guard advanced to block his way. Audeyrn turned, uncoiling his fingers from hers as he did. "This is Sir Deramun, my lady. He is my protector and leal friend. He keeps my counsel, and can be trusted with matters relating to statecraft."

Her smile was full and her eyes all a-glitter as she bid the guards to let the ageing knight through. Aud could not help but notice how red-faced Hearty looked. *Have faith, my friend. We'll be away from the Torrins and their lady soon enough.* The Lady found the emissary's hand again, and made a show of mounting the firemanes together. He thought then that the last of his troubles were over. Soon he would be supping on a lord's share of roast swan in Brinewater Keep, with a mug of mulled blackwine in hand. Then, when he was hard at work drinking, Nat would barge through the doors to the great hall with his kje bloodied and dripping, dragging a chained Govier past the trestles to fall despondent at the emissary's feet. *Apologies for my tardiness,* the sly fox would say, *but I caught the bastard stealing off, without the courtesy to give us all a goodbye kiss.*

First, they had to get to Brinewater, and that required them to traverse the streets of the town. News of their victory had been brought to Wolfsmouth by the serjeant Crispin Moss. Now the people lined the thoroughfares, squares, and wynds, all chancing to see the triumphant Emissary of Castan, who defeated the fearsome Godless up in haunted Bagman's Bluff. Cries of *victory* mingled in both Qellish and the common by those held back by a neat rank of city watchmen. Lady Adrianne never let her grip lose his hand, and often she would shoot him sweet smiles that he could not help but return in earnest. The crowds met them all the way from the arsenal on the east-bank, across the length of the Span as it rose and fell across the river, and then up on the west-bank along Shipwright's Way and onto the raised heights where Brinewater rested atop its prominence.

The fortress and ancestral seat of House Torrin was not a relic of Old Qell, but the stones the ancient Torrins had used in its construction had been repurposed from a ruined dam upriver. Much like the Span, the masonry of Brinewater looked unweathered, uncracked and polished, inky black and streaked by milky veins of lightning. If the sun hit the stones just right, they gleamed a brilliant iridescent purple, the emissary knew. There had been stone enough to build a double wall around what would become known as Torrin's Hill, with the plenitude that remained going towards the building of the Dome of Life with its huge glass roof and rumoured remains of Quirsus within, and the five high elegant towers of the Keep that rose two hundred foot like elegant black spears. Closest to them on the south side was the South Tower, of course; flanking it left and right was the Tower of Lamentation and the Tower of Hope; then to the north stood broad and strong Otho's Tower; and to his right, placed to have the greatest view of the rivermouth, was the Seaspike, the current abode of Lady Adrianne and her household.

"Woodes, what's the problem there?" His companion asked the captain of her guard, a man he recognised vaguely from his brief previous stay.

"Nothing, my lady. Just an old man in the road." *Woodes Weyland.* He was a small, spare man to hold such a position, but if Aud did not know him personally he had learned his reputation from Captain Arodyr and the Sipcup. *Loyal, to hear them say. Loyal, and ruthless.*

When the lady snorted, her small nose wrinkled. "Really? From afar he almost looks a godman." The emissary looked ahead, to where a knot of guards were busy trying to disperse a dishevelled group of bearded men in beggar's rags from the square fronting the South Tower Gate. "A shabby one, I must say, and scabby too. But a godman, scabs and all."

"He claims as such, yes, my lady. *Him*, and his followers. They say–" When she spoke, all others fell silent. It was then that she let go of the emissary's hand, and coaxed her mount forward. "Remove him, Woodes, but *gently*."

The man Woodes Wayland was quick to obey. He led a half dozen green-mailed guards to the godman and his acolytes, and began to shove them aside, all but gently as commanded. As the Lady's procession passed by, the godman raised a bony finger to them, and spat. A skinny man with a beard that brushed his skinny knees, naked, but for a carved wooden idol on a leather thong about his neck. *"He comes, faithless dogs! He who conquered death and destroyed the monsters that once called themselves gods, he comes! Hail be to he! Hail to him!"* Then something flew towards Audeyrn, Hearty too slow to react, the emissary's own sword not even clear of his own scabbard.

The thing knocked harmlessly against his chest and clattered to the ground. His horse whinnied briefly, and kicked at the wooden image to make it skitter off into the crowds that had somewhere along the way lost all their cheer. Then the gate was opening, great hardiron doors crunching open slowly to reveal a moat and drawbridge.

Adrianne fell in beside him again, placing a pale hand on his thigh. "You are unhurt?"

"Yes… my lady." She said not a word, but squeezed his leg. Audeyrn tried his best to remember whether she was married. A few last noises from the godman and then he was drowned out by the inner gate grinding open.

When he scanned the cobbles behind him, the idol was gone. Knocked elsewhere, or stolen, perhaps. He could not say. He felt a bead of sweat fall down his neck. It had been made of wood, and shaped like a wyrm. *A white wyrm.*

They made their way to Seaspike, but not before they crossed the Grand Bailey to climb the steps to the Dome of Life, where the Hierophant Tar-Ru-Yah awaited to bless him on behalf of the gods. Then the garrison was marched out, and the lords and ladies hailed the heroes on their victory, and wound bright green sashes around their waists. When Aud thought it was finally done, he was ushered along with the captains to the Thundering Hall, where nobles from the lowlands came with hair freshly braided. He saw Crispin Moss sat among similar-looking, thick-bearded Paydar he took to be House Moss. Otherwise, he could see members of the Houses of Jothy and Thyrqell, Mahel and Bligh and Hillborn, yet the only Rowett in attendance was Arodyr, who towered above the rest, and talked closely to the Lords Ransom Hillborn and Ardal Jothy. The emissary thought that was strange.

A girl who could not have been older than five came onto the dais, and who asked if she could 'blood' Audeyrn. Seeing no other choice, he accepted, kneeling down to let the little girl smear a gobbet of red on his forehead. *So now I am blooded in their eyes. I am as Paydar as they will allow. An honour, to be sure. But Nat and Greg should be getting blood on their faces too. Gods, I'm sorry Greg.* Hearty, anointed next, pulled a face to make the little girl laugh. Words were said, and toasts were made, and only then did the progress make it to Seaspike and hopefully to a featherbed.

The gods are seldom merciful, for he and Hearty were sent high up in the tower. Stairs that ascended and twisted maliciously, his footing still being unsteady from the boat made the going hard. Hearty was worse. He was blowing like a bearded bellows as they reached the lord's hall atop. *Why am I here...* Weyland appeared out of nowhere.

"In there, if you please." He gestured to the opposite end of the hall, where a door stood shut and tight. His hand rested on the hilt of his sword as he spoke. With a glance to Hearty, he made for the door, trying to make his long strides sure and purposeful. He pulled open the latch and entered. Lady Adrianne sat in a high-backed chair, a cream-coloured wyrm coiled indolently in her lap. He had not noticed how striking she looked on his previous sojourn to Wolfsmouth, but then again, he had been preoccupied with collecting her fleet for war. He let his eyes wander over her, her dress was made for the chill of winter, a mix of emerald green silk and snowy-white fur, but which left her shoulders bare to allow a single long braid of black hair to fall tentatively down her chest. Her face was flushed from the wind outside, or perhaps from the hearthfire that blazed near her feet. Her jaw was taut, the tenseness in her neck and face only emphasising the sharpness of her cheekbones. When she stroked the wyrm on its scaled head, it raised a pointed snout and opened eyes like pinpoints of gold. Smoke rose in steady plumes from its flared nostrils.

"Your knight can wait outside," she said, giving Hearty only the most perfunctory of looks. Aud was about to talk when his companion spat out, "With the utmost of respect, my lady, I am duty bound to protect the Royal Emissary." That brought a look of annoyance to her face.

"While you are in Wolfsmouth, you are all under *my* protection. Your chatterings are out of loyalty, so I will forgive your little outburst." Her pet gave a low growl, "Leave, knight. Now. Without flapping your gums at me. I will not tell you again." Hearty looked to Audeyrn, gave one last muttered word of complaint, and then he took his leave. The sound of crackling logs and the hissing of the wyrm made for a dissonant song in the lady's solar. He knew that he was not permitted to speak first, especially here, in her audience chamber, alone. Her pet's eyes studied him for a long time, and he found that they were searching and unblinking, the sort of look the herons of the High Forks had when they had spotted likely prey. He made himself look at Adrianne instead, and found a likewise searching look on her face. *What does she want of me? Surely not to bed me. Otherwise, we would not be in the solar, and she wouldn't have that godsdamn beast with her.*

He found his eyes wandering the room, mostly to evade her gaze, and saw a mahogany table placed by one of the high windows. The wan light fell on the neat pile of parchments stacked atop, and one, larger than the rest, with a mass of text filling it. From his angle, he could not tell what it was, and soon enough he found something more alluring. The wine was on a side table, arranged on a silver platter. He gestured, and Adrianne nodded in assent. *I can drink, at least.* It was a Caldish vintage, full and fruity, a welcome change from the overpowering Paydar blackwines. He finished his first, and was settling into his second glass when Adrianne said, "Sweet, no? It's a Mornswood Reserve. It arrived a fortnight ago. Even in this war trade must go one, especially of good wines."

"I could not agree more, my lady." *Why are we talking of wine, unless it has something to do with our alliance? Your alliance. I think I know what that parchment is for...* As he went to pour into a second glass, she called out to decline, all grace and courtesy.

"Your victory is well earned, Emissary Audeyrn, and I would toast you myself, but I much prefer ale to wine." *Then why didn't you put it on the platter? She thinks to get me loose-tongued, then, or else make me drop my guard.* "I have not had a Castan red in over half a year, my lady. Your consideration of me is toast enough." Her nod was curt and formal. Brushing the wyrm off her as though it were but a cat, it slunk away to bask in the warmth of the hearth. Collecting her skirts and sauntering over, Aud could not help but hear the sharp rap of heels on the wooden floor. His head swam, and then he realised that he had not eaten all day.

You didn't wear those when I came for your ships. What do you–

"Enough foreplay. I never did learn to wait for the real entertainment. Tell me truthfully, did you capture the leader of the Godless?" The question caught him unawares. He did not understand. Putting down his glass, he said, "We found no one of importance, my lady. I would have thought Crispin Moss told you this in his report."

"Yes, yes, he did. Yet I thought maybe... oh, never mind.

To the crux, then." Her nostrils flared. He caught himself before he voiced the jape, about how she looked like her pet when she did that. *No more wine, fool.* Her knuckles were white. "What's wrong? Tell me. Is it the–"

The door slammed open. A long shadow fell across the room. Aud's hand went to his sword, and cursed when he grabbed at the empty air. When had he parted with his sword? *My tolerance has gone to shit.* He heard guards shuffling about outside, and Hearty arguing loudly. The emissary's heart beat like he had swallowed something large and buzzing. Then Adrianne Torrin gave an exasperated sigh, to say, "Alright then, come here." The intruder ran with all the speed and elegance of a five year old. At least, she looked to be five. Lady Torrin picked up her daughter in her arms, the little girl immediately making to play with her mother's braid.

"Mother was not to be disturbed. Yet I see this little monster has ruined my plans yet again" Audeyrn tried to claw his way through the haziness of drink. *Of course, she's the daughter. Her husband was a Rowett, and he's dead.* "Elyan, *you* have more sense than our dear Emissary. What does House Torrin want with the Kingdom of Castan, with that old tyrant Isembard?" The girl was too shy to reply, so the lady kissed her on the forehead. The eyes that looked at Audeyrn were big, blue, and full of wondrous innocence.

"I'll tell him." Her face was flushed by the firelight. The light shone in her eyes too, until they each had fires of their own. "Alliance… against our enemies to the north."

26

GREGYN

He fell through a void of shadow.

Day and night meant nothing here, for only the vaguest periphery of a light seeped its way into that glimmering place. No matter how much he tried, how hard he fought, he could not find the source of the glimmering. When he slept, he dreamed. When he woke, he heard voices, and pain was his constant companion. Something held him down, so he was forced to endure the darkness as it engulfed him, a quagmire that smelled of blood and stale sweat.

Talking was a chore. Everytime he tried to form words his tongue proved fat and dry in his mouth, moving sluggishly as he tried. Then a warm liquid would be poured down his throat, and soon after that he would be too tired to talk, too tired to move, even to think. That was when the dreams came for him. Formless masses of faces, half-remembered and mistborne, and torsos bearing far too many limbs. Spiders were often there, or at least he thought they were spiders, coming silent and fast. Black-shelled scuttlers that moved over his skin, at the end of each spindly mucid leg a six-fingered hand probed and grabbed, and left bloody prints wherever they went.

If he listened intently, which again proved a labour, he could just make out a man's voice, halcyon and modulated, a soothing balm to the thumping of blood in his ears. There was a woman too; harsh and clipped and doused in Qellish tones. And there, a third, younger than the man and far less confident than the woman. This one asked questions, endlessly, ceaselessly, to the audible annoyance of the man. *He never spoke that much in the Qell. He sounds...*

His waking moments were ephemeral. Oftentimes, the sounds of his dark world mingled with the unseen, far-off spectres as he lay weightless and buoyant. When the pain in his chest and leg had ebbed to a bearable throb, he allowed himself to be confused. That was when he became aware enough for the fear to set in. Struggle as he might, his formless bonds did not give in to his feeble attempts to escape. He tried *that* several times, each one resulting in strong arms holding him still and then the feel of cold metal on his lips.

And then the dreadblack. The morass waiting for him at the edge of dream. It swallowed him every time, the clutches as soft as the breath from a kiss, the plane dark with the promise of eternal night. Endless and sublime, endless and empty.

Yet the last one had been different. Like all dreams, he could not remember its beginning, only for the fever dream to appear as though starting a book halfway open. Voices, unknown to him, had talked in a tongue even stranger than Qellish. The ground had given way beneath him, and his bare feet burned as they crunched through something soft. A city in the desert rose high above him, and a girl stroked his neck.

It had been exhilarating, if not marred, like trying to look out through a window made of cheap clouded glass, or listening to music underwater. He came to, crying out for water. A vessel was put to his lips not long after, and the liquid within was crisp and cold on his cracked lips, the drink sweeter than anything he had ever tasted. He sucked at the offering like a man finding an oasis in the desert, licking his lips when no more came forth. He hazarded words, each one a stoney rasp, rougher than sand. "Where... am I? Why... can't I... see?"

It was the man's voice that answered him, "We are in the arsenal of Wolfswater, my lord. Safe... and out of danger." His speech was gentle sounding, yet weary. It did little to quell the fear in the pit of Greg's stomach. *Why can't I see?* The light at the edge of sight shifted, and then centred above him like a shrouded star, a will-o'-the-wisp that Old Mart oft said inhabited the Fairy Glen. Now and again, it flickered and shook. *What...*

"He's awake." A boy said, trying his best to sound brave. "I heard him!" Even in his fevered state, Greg heard the tremulous tone, the way his voice broke at the end. "Don't lie to me, Daval. You lied to me last time. But I heard him now. You talked to him. He's awake. He is, isn't he?" the man sighed, and Greg could hear him moving something that sounded like glass. "A momentary paroxysm, is all. Nothing to worry about, child."

"I'm not a child, *dhereda*. You lie worse than Mayred. I heard him."

"I tell you again. It is nothing. He is already away. I doubt he even heard…"

No. Wrong. All wrong. I heard you! I'm awake! I… It was as though the inexorable pull of the sweetest sleep came over him, and he fell unresisting into that silken darkness. The nothingness was painless, silent, and peaceful. It lasted until his mind's eye focused on the light emanating pallidly from a hollow in the earth. Its stink was enough to make him feel awake, yet somehow he knew he was still in the dream. He could hear Audeyrn calling out, and then he felt his bow in his hand, the drawstring pulled back to his cheek as the feather tickled his skin. Before him stood a pale woman, bloodied yet still beautiful in the twilight. His eyes burned. His fingers itched to release the arrow. It all felt right then. Men were screaming foul curses all around him, and the woman mouthed a wordless cry. The arrow flew.

When he finally did wake, the dark of the room's window told him it was night. *The man said we were in Wolfsmouth… How long have I…* Looking about, he found that he did not recognise the cramped cabin. Trying to rise brought back the familiar tightness around his chest and legs, and he saw them wrapped thickly in linen stinking of ointments and sweat. The man detached himself from the shadows. The cowl about his head was shadowed and the face within hidden. *Govier…*

The voice that came from inside the hood did not belong to the man who had led him into the fortress so many days before. Or weeks. Or months. His head spun in the confusion. "So he decides to return to us. Took his time about it, though." The voice pulled back his cowl to reveal a full-faced man with bushy eyebrows, portly, with hands that ended in fat sausages, and a ruddy scalp. Fresh stubble had sprouted on that large pate. Other than that, he was clean-shaven, the skin on his jaw and chin shiny in the lamplight. His thick-limbed body was made thicker by the loosely fitted robe of dun-coloured wool, that looked in Greg's eyes to swaddle the man instead of merely clothe him.

"You know, lad, if your mouth were to open any wider, you could fit an aurochs in it whole." The joke held no joy for the tracker, but he took the hint, and narrowed his eyes at the podgy man. "I know your name. My squire said it... when I awoke before. Dieve? Dasal?"

"Daval, if it please you." With surprising agility he bolted to his feet, to reveal the poor stool that a moment before had seated his huge arse. When he bowed, his floppy sleeves nearly brushed the planks of the deck. "Daval, of the Learned. Formerly of the Journeyman Fellows of Lar'gara, the fair library city in the far north."

Those words made Greg's ears prick. "You're a wizard... from Lar'gara?"

Daval bore a kind smile as he shook his bald head. "Wizards are a poor breed if they look like me." The tracker looked the Learned up and down, seeing the ink-stained fingers, the way he seemed to put more weight on one leg than the other, the small red mark by his ear where he must have cut himself with a razor. If truth be told, he did not look like the wizards he was told of growing up in the Dun Vale. In those stories, they always had long silky beards, and hard knowing eyes full of fire, and all agreed that wizards were tall and old, whereas this man was short and squat, and could not have been more than forty.

"If I were a wizard, I would be a disappointing one, I am happy to admit. Ills and sickness I can ease, bones I can set, teeth and blood and pain I can treat, and I can even be a passable barber when it is required of me."

Greg wanted to know desperately where his friends were, not natter with this Learned, or journeyman, or whoever he was. It must have played across his face, for Daval said, "The Lord Emissary sits in court with the Lady Torrin. He is wont to stay within the Brinewater until the sunset, our leal Lord Captain Arodyr reports." He jerked a fat thumb towards the cabin window, dark and forbidding, "You are in luck, for the nights draw in earlier each day, and we are now two hours since dusk. No! You must–"

Greg rose groggily from the blankets, desperate to escape from what he was beginning to think was his deathbed. "No, please. Rest. I was tasked to ensure your full recovery by the knight Natoly. This is folly. Guards! Help me, he–" Greg was about to ask when Natoly had been knighted, when the door to the cabin creaked open.

"Leave him, *dhereda*," a woman's voice commanded. He recognised the voice. So often he had heard her sing the *Titan's Lament* in the Outer Qell. He turned to face her. Mayred was standing in the threshold to the cabin, looking more like a warrior in her leather and mail hauberk than a lady had any right to be. But then again, she was no lady. One wiry arm rested on a hip as the other wove a dagger deftly through long fingers. The wan glow from the lamp limned her exposed arms.

"I dreamt of you." He regretted the words as soon as they left his lips. But above the blood that burned his cheeks and the squawking from Daval the realisation came to him as sharp and sweet as harvest lemons. *I spoke in Qellish.* The wizard who was not a wizard was still talking, but to Greg he may as well have been talking in Soran. Mayred let one side of her mouth curl into the slightest smile. With the point of her dagger she flicked a rogue braid that had fallen over an eye. "He seems fine to me."

Twenty-eight days. That was how long Audeyrn had lingered in Wolfsmouth, while Greg had lay half-dead aboard the *Leviathan*. During that time, Daval had removed the arrows from his chest and leg, cleaned the wounds and plied him with compresses and healing balms and potions and gods-know-what else. And he had dreamed as he healed. Dreams of things from Old Mart's stories, and things even worse from his past. A dungeon in Mornswood. The Reeve Arran. Some of the shades faded until they were nothing but vague impressions left on the inside of his skull. The rest... they remained.

His chest was still tightly bound and his leg stiff from the weight of the bow across his back and the dirk at his hip. As he stalked across the aftcastle of the Leviathan, a hand resting on Mayred's shoulder, members of the crew thumped their chests or tugged their forelocks in salute. The words *Zjar-eln-Whn* greeted him whenever he passed them. When he tried to work out what it meant, all it did was hurt his head. "What're they saying," he asked Mayred, in slow and simple Qellish, "What does that mean?" She sucked in air from clenched teeth, which Greg did not fail to notice were clean and very bright. A coy and fiendish look met his eyes. "Oh, it is a... *sobriquet.* A moniker. Poetic, if nothing else. They are calling you *stone-voiced*, Greg. It can

have a few meanings in the tongue of the Qell. One being…
talking like a stone, meaning hard and commanding, having
a strong battle-voice or voice that can subdue foes. Another
is that you are someone who talked *from the stones*. A voice
the besiegers heard coming from the breach during the
Battle at the Bluff. It is respectful, don't you worry. I am
very familiar with how you Castanni are sticklers with your
honour."

Stone-voiced. Gregyn Stone-voiced. He did not think it
fit him. After all, it was the battle-borne name for some
great warrior, not a poacher from the High Forks. But he
didn't say that to Mayred. Why would he? The way she
seemed to keep making sideways looks at him whenever
someone shouted *Zjar-eln-Whn* made him feel all flustered
and wanting to look at Mayred too. He liked looking at
her face, her hair and legs, and the way her breeches clung
tightly to her buttocks in particular. He became sharply
aware of how damp he was under the arms. *Gregyn Stone-
voiced,* he tried the name again, turning it over silently in
his head. Then he realised he was looking at her again.

He looked for a distraction. Something to take his mind
off the woman, or the tightness in his crotch, at least. The
gods must have been listening, from whichever haven they
had exiled themselves to, for the sights of a nocturnal
city of golden light filled his vision. Beyond the boom
that closed off the arsenal from the wider harbour came a
river dazzling with refracted light. The sounds of revelry
arising from those celebrating the victory over the Godless
came from both sides of the river, with more than a few
choosing to course the water on skiffs and pleasure barges.
More than three weeks, and they still feel the mirth and joy of

basking in the glory of war. Do they mourn the dead the same way? He could not see the merriment taking place, but he could picture it- the wharves lined with drunks, redwomen plying their trade from open windows and dark alleyways, the cutthroats sharpening their knives. It all made for a calamitous song as he took in the towering storehouses and shipyards that comprised the arsenal. The ships swayed lazily at their moorings, knocking against the quays like fat men rolling in their slumber. Their masts raked a star-speckled sky the colour of darkest ink, their sails furled, so that they looked all a half-submerged forest in the dead of winter. He shivered at the thought.

Beyond the becrenelled walls of the arsenal peaked a few spires or turrets of other buildings, here a guildhall, there a rakish red-house (with lanterns glowing a pale crimson to boot), but above the rest a hand groping desperately into the night sky, five fingers lit by watchfires that even across the town made the castle glow darkly like obsidian. *Brinewater,* said the voice in his head. *The seat of the Torrins.* He wondered which one of the fingers of tall dark stone towers held his friend.

Friend? It took him all a moment to realise why that word felt so queer. "Where's Nat and Hearty?" He asked Mayred, sharper than he had meant it. The comely Paydar seemed to delight in the forced brusqueness in his voice, which did nothing to quell the shifting in his groin. "The knight Hearty Deri sits in court in Eistir's Tower, with Captain Arodyr and the other officers. There, the fat one, you see? As to the Red Raven…" When she shook her head, the bronze links in her braids clattered lightly in the night.

She told him…eventually, and after some coaxing.

Mayred did not want to tell him, that was clear. She said that they had warned him not to scale the Flattop, that it was cursed, sacred, something wholly in between the two. *Can something be revered and shunned at the same time?* The story among the hunters was that Nat, shamed by the Emissary for his disobedience in the battle, had climbed the sheer cliffs of the fayhill to atone. Greg was not so sure about that. He had not known the man before leaving Castan with the emissary, but the long road was a place where travel companions got to know each other well, and he believed he *did* know the man well now. *He went from woman to woman as easily as a man changes clothes,* he mused, rueing himself for being so bitter. *A hiding from Aud would have been nothing compared to what he's been through before.* Yet he still did not believe it. No. Nat was his friend. And he was missing. *What is missing can be found...*

He decided then that he had to see Audeyrn.

Daval made some more noises when they told him that he intended to go ashore. His threats to summon the guards remained only as that, threats. His face was purple and his arms were crossed over his paunch as Greg hobbled down the gangplank from the *Leviathan*'s maindeck, and he was thankful for the crutch under his arm and the way the usually rough-handed Paydar crew gave him a wide berth and patted him lightly on the shoulder.

What did Moss call them? Lowlanders?

Mayred went before him, should he fall, but he was sure-footed enough to get to shore without a splash. There, the hulking first mate Egon Sipcup was there to receive him, standing all six and a half foot, his bandaged foot seemingly painless and forgotten as he busied himself with a stick of a hard sweet. Greg realised he was of a height with the man, which came as a shock. He usually overtopped men regarded as large. It often ended with threats of violence, for having the gall to be taller than others, and it had made him ever painfully aware of his height. Yet the first mate broke off from his rumination when he clapped eyes on the tracker, to reveal a broad smile of even broader square teeth.

"Stonevoice! I see you are sick of having beauty sleep!" He had a keen grasp of the common, with only the slightest Qellish drawl. His dark eyes shifted for all of a moment to Mayred, letting his smile widen a further fraction. "You'll be wanting the Lord Emissary, I s'pose. Guess you're healed enough. Go ahead." He waved them to where a young boy was saddling three horses in the stables. "Oh, and I have heard from the good Emissary of your prowess with a bow, Stonevoice. You must show me soon." With that, Egon Sipcup replaced the stick of sweet in his mouth and went to work. Greg gave his most convincing smile and made for the nearest horse. Muddy.

"Feeling well, my lord," said Jethro Rowett, his eyes on the cobbles as he offered the reins to Greg. The six-fingered hand stood out like a bloody third eye, unblinking and dead. "Thank you. But I'm no lord. Thank you all the same. Call me Gregyn, or Greg, please." His leg began to throb hard, and the blood in his temples felt like a red torrent. The reins were slick in his hand. "Help me to mount up, please." He caught a brief look of concern furrow across Mayred's brow, but it was gone in an instant, replaced by something he could not easily read.

Muddy seemed to be in good spirits as they kept a brisk

trot through the wide road that led from the arsenal to the keep on its high hill. *Shipwright's Way,* Mayred called it. Here and there the cobbles had come loose, to allow puddles to pool from yesterday's rain. The tracker's leg sent hot needles through him as Muddy made his way through a throng of jubilant pissants, his squire and Mayred either side, shouting to make way with hands resting on the pommels of their swords.

He thought that they must have been halfway to the castle when the weariness set in. Soon, his head began to pound, his leg a burning brand from calf to groin, his chest a raging knot. Despite the pain, he found himself dosing, and twice he caught himself falling asleep. *Maybe the wizard was right. Maybe I'm... I'm...*

A hard hand shook him awake. "Greg, you nearly fell from your saddle." Mayred was holding his reins, he saw. He swallowed, feeling the flush claw up his face. "I'm fine. I jus' need to–"

"You're dead on your feet." The boy said, more a squeak than anything else. *A dead man walking.* He tried to argue with Mayred, for he did not have the heart to face Jethro. The boy had watched over him, he remembered vaguely. He had asked for him, even ordering about the Learned. Why had he feared the lad? Something on a hill... a beast, he recalled, the memory strangely misty and faint. It was dead, he knew that for certain. Had he killed it? He thought of a knife, but did not know who it belonged to. "The Brinewater is not far now, Greg. Will you be okay to ride until then?" Mayred was not looking at him when she talked, glaring instead at a group of men eyeing the trio from beneath the awning of a dingy tavern. A languid pat to her scabbard, and they soon lost interest. "Yes," the tracker said, hearing how bone-tired he sounded. "But if I sway again, tie me to Muddy, would ya?"

The guards at the gatehouse were stoneheaded bastards. Their commander wore a greathelm fashioned into the shape of a sea-dog mid snarl, its flews pulled back to reveal rows of fangs shining balefully in the torchlight, and its pricked ears were webbed like the fins of a fish. The face was obscured, but once or twice he saw the flickering of light from behind the steel jaws. *"No one is to enter,"* he said with annoyance, his voice turned metallic from the helmet. *"The Lady herself has commanded that none may disturb the lords at their play. Who did you say you were again?"*

Greg had to clear his throat. "I am Gregyn of the High Forks. I'm part of the Emissary of Castan's entourage. If you ask–"

"Yes, yes, you said! 'Ask some sergeant from the hills. Ask for the Lord Captain of this ship or that ship. Fact of the matter is, boy, that if you are without, you are not getting in. No matter who the fuck you claim to be." That elicited a snarl from Mayred, who dismounted, appearing taller than the dog helm. "You are speaking to the hero of the Battle of Bagman's Bluff, Merbeast. He saved countless lives in the fray, and near lost his own life in the doing so. You'll watch your poxy tongue going forward." The growl that erupted from the dog helm was fearsome, and it was a whole moment before the tracker realised the man was laughing at them. *"I beg to differ, whore. You're speaking to a Merbeast, which might mean little to an ignorant sheep-fucker like yourself, but here, it means I speak with her ladyship's word and will. You, and your pet, and that fool with the broken leg*

can fuck off now, or I can give you some motivation." He gave a brisk command, and where a moment before had been a half dozen lolling guards, now they brandished halberds, their blades shining cruelly sharp even in the night.

Fear clutched at Greg, but not as sharp as the pain in his leg. "Mayred, leave them, please. We'll try again on the morrow." Every word seemed to send daggers into his broken bones. The man in the sea-dog helm grumbled, as though he were disappointed. *"You do that, Castanni. But the answer will be the same. Fuck off, the lot of you."*

They rode back down Shipwright's, and it was all Greg could do not to fall from his saddle. Mayred muttered something under her breath, but it was too quiet and too thick in her Qellish accent for him to make out the words. He turned to Jephro, and saw that the boy too was doing his best to look awake. Why had he feared the lad? He had too many questions. *Even if I were to ask, who would have the answers?* He sidled over to the squire, who did not even register the tall man looming over him. His hair was washed and his mark newly painted, he saw, and his garb was in good repair. The boy was diligent, he could give him that.

"Jephro, do you love your father?" The boy sat up in his seat immediately, but it was Greg who was shocked at the question. He could not even find his own explanation before Jephro answered, "I have to love my lord father the Lord Rowett, my lord... I mean, Greg." *I don't believe you,* thought the tracker, but he said, "I haven't been honest with you, and I think I've misjudged you, if you get my meaning." The boy only nodded, but Greg got the feeling that he did not understand. After all, this was just a boy in an evil man's world. The least he could give him was the truth. "Lord Elmer is a hard, brutal man, Jeph. An' I thought maybe you would be like him. For tha', I'm sorry."

The boy said not a word, and for a time they rode slowly to the calamitous music of Wolfsmouth. The boy who was given to him as a squire stared at the cobbles, his eyes wide and listless, his thin shoulders slumped. Greg watched him, until it hit him. He rode closer to Mayred, who had calmed a little, but still had that brilliant, angry fire in her eyes. It softened somewhat when she caught Greg's eyes.

"Have you kissed and made up with Jeph yet?"

"How could you know that? I weren't talking too loud. Wait, was I? I thought, maybe, I thought I…" Her laugh was throaty and long, and it made him think of her not here, but back in the High Forks, with a summer dress, eating an apple and listening to a nearby bubbling stream. "I've sharp hearing, Castanni. What? Don't look so shocked, you're like to catch flies in that open mouth of yours. And I don't want it full of flies."

"But you do want it, though," Greg could not believe he said that. It made Mayred laugh again, and look up at him over her nose. She did not reply, but her smirk was answer enough for him. That settled it. He would not go back to the *Leviathan*, for he could not endure another minute of Daval's coddling, no matter how many threats he made. Nor could they enter the Brinewater, unless they tried to grapple the high walls, and he did not fancy himself ready for that yet. They would stay in the town then. Sleep first, yes, he desperately needed to fall onto a bed. He could even pay for a featherbed for himself, Mayred, and the squire… or he could save the silver and only buy two. Then they would celebrate. He did not like the blackwine the Rowetts of the Tor favoured, but he would not shy away from trying the ales and wines and spice-liqeurs the merchants brought into the markets from their fanciful ships. He could hire a palanquin and rest his leg, and travel about the town and cross the Span. It was hidden by the veil of night now, but he had been told by someone that it was one of the thirteen wonders of the world. *I could even go on a pleasure barge... maybe Mayred would like that. What would* she *like?*

Mayred herself was still looking at him, and he could not help but notice how she wound the reins round her fingers. "Do ya know a place to stay?"

She took them down Shipwright's, until they left the main road to join a lesser branch that angled up to the west of the town called the Fishcatcher's Walk. It had started to drizzle, so they were thankful when they finally fronted onto a large, three-storied tavern that Mayred named the Deraydia, the canvas pennants that fluttered on steel hooks swinging damply, and painted a faded blue. After a quick once over by the doorman, they were allowed within, where they met the proprietor of the place: a soft, big-bellied man who smelled of queer spices, his hair flowing long and unbraided to his waist in teased chestnut ringlets. He named himself Cosmo Deraydia.

"Been in the family for nigh on twelve generations, has the old girl." He had recognised Greg's accent, and had proceeded to talk in the common, his thumbs tucked neatly in an ohthorl-skin belt. "Aye, you knows, the Deraydias once hailed from a place near old Castan itself. In the lake country. They were lords, you see, lording about in their vast timber forests... I forget the name of their castle.

401

Anyways, may I take a name, my lord of Castan."

Greg's mind ran blank, his thoughts etched hard by tension and pain. He raced to form something quick, something believable. "I'm no lord... but I am a knight." *Why did I say that?* He prayed to the gods then. He felt dizzy, and the room seemed to spin. *Why the secrecy? These people are Castan's allies... aren't they?*

"This is Sir Gregyn Stonevoice," Mayred saved him, bowing her head to Greg as she did so. To compound his embarrassment, Jephro decided then to pluck up his courage to say, "Yes, he fought at the Bluff. He has come to stay in your best chambers." Without much thought, he shot the squire a look of betrayal. By that point it was already too late. Old Deraydia's eyes become large as duck eggs as he shimmied about in what must have been a curtsy. "Yes, I see, I see. Apologies for wasting your time, Sir. I truly am. I will see that our very best is prepared for your lodging. You will not find the Deraydia without hospitality, that you will not." Greg wanted to ask if he was referring to the tavern, or to himself. "Through here, yes, if you would do me the honour of following. Yes, here, we have our main common room. We have fifteen hearths, thirty booths, each good for sitting half a dozen, and the girls are always on hand to fill your glass." He shouted something out, this time in Qellish. A young woman appeared amongst the servitors and hosts to stand beside Cosmo. Greg thought she must have been his daughter, for they shared the same hair and complexion, though Cosmo's girth remained all his own.

"My lord of Castan, I must be impolite now, for the brewers demand my attention, we breached a fourteen-year last night, and the first taste is *always* reserved to

402

the proprietor. My lovely Eppony will show you to your chambers. And not to worry for payment! All heroes of the Battle may pay in the mornings after." Greg gave his thanks but could not shake the feeling that less reputable establishments would not offer the same, nor would their guests be as courteous to their hosts. *I search for a bed while other men look for a rape.* With that in mind, he felt all the more weary, and sick besides. The climb to the rooms led them to the third-story, where Greg had to be carried up the stairs by a burly henchman of the Deraydia. That made him feel like a child, and he could not look at Mayred.

"Here we have the chamber for my lord's manservant," the willowy Eppony announced, leading Jephro through. "I'm a squire," he muttered, but he went in nonetheless. Greg did not fail to see that the doors bolted from the inside. *Good, I can lock the damned thing an' die in peace.* When Jephro was packed away, Eppony led them down the wood-panelled corridor, to the two remaining rooms on that landing.

For a moment, he was relieved, the stress that had been bubbling inside him gone. But then Mayred just happened to brush close to him, the tiny hairs of her arm making him look at the lithe corded muscle beneath. Her hips swayed all the while.

"And these are your chambers," the hostess said, ignoring the second door entirely. The door at the end opened up to a spacious room that was more a hall to Greg than anything else. A hearth was already burning, and there were windows on the west and east walls to catch both the sunset and sunrise. Between them, a corner-posted bed dominated the furnishings. At its foot, a diminutive table held court to a decanter of blackwine, a demijohn of Drukish firewater, and a bottle of brown beer. Eppony made some more pleasantries and then took her leave. There was a buzzing in the tracker's head, and he suddenly felt flustered.

Mayred was already making herself at home, throwing her cloak on a post while she pulled off her boots to stretch her toes. Then she was pulling the stopper from the bottle of beer, not even pouring it into a glass as she drunk it. "Oh, did you want some?" She asked, offering up the drink. The smell had already diffused the room. He could smell ginger and honey, and lemon above it all.

"Yes."

He walked towards her, and then he was holding her. He held her face as he kissed her. The pain had seeped from him as he did it, and he was still kissing her when she swung her arms around his neck and whispered things in his ear. There wasn't much talking after that.

It felt right. An intruder of a thought tried to push itself to the fore of his mind for a time, but it was replaced by that of Mayred. He could not say how he managed to say how he got himself into bed, but he did. All his dark nagging thoughts were gone. Only her lips remained, the way they changed taste as they moved onto the firewater. Somewhere in there she teased him by nipping at his fingers. That made him laugh. And then she was laughing. The world and its woes did not exist. It had never existed. It was only him, and her.

The sound of the hearthfire, and the taste of summer.

27

MARBLE

The days moved quickly.

The emissary had months to claw back. A pretty much insurmountable feat. With the Desolate Tundra behind her, the Soran desert seemed simple and easy. The sand was more yellow than red, the land still and constant. The dunes still towered, but were not so monstrous and intimidating. Sun and moon patrolled the skies steadily and uniformly.

Marble managed at the first mean little outpost she passed through, she acquired a mount. A runty camel, it would take a while for anyone to notice it was missing, along with some well needed provender and vittles.

The temperature was milder than she was used to, her body accustomed to the strong heat of Silentene summers. There had been no steady and gradual assimilation into autumn, and inexorable winter. She knew the cold would only worsen as she travelled further west, the daylight would wane more quickly, and the weather more difficult. The world watched her progress, and hated her for it.

Runty, as the emissary had aptly dubbed the sallow beast, was a cantankerous creature, prone to temper tantrums. The beast refused to bow to Marble's wishes as they wandered through the pale sands, wanting to make circuitous routes that annoyed the emissary no end. Still, despite the seemingly pointless diversions, both woman and beast made decent time. Runty was most adept, it turned out, at finding small oasis areas and avoiding any of the known routes that Marble was aware of frequented by travellers. Marble would feel no guilt when she no longer required the camel and sent it into the desert. The emissary wouldn't be surprised if the dreadful animal lived to surpass one hundred and became the most fearsome creature this side of Wolfswater.

The desert changed frequently, Marble watching the sands roll past, untamed and never-ending. Days merged, and the monotony of the weeks passing was broken up only by the erratic outbursts of her stinking companion. Occasionally, they would come across remnants of roads and paved pathways peeking out from beneath the layers of sand, winking in and out of sight, reminding, taunting the emissary with imaginings of what this place once was. The grandeur, peace, and prosperity… lost aeons before she was born. Before the Godless killed the god Quirsus, before the Thaumaturge Cataclysm, all lost to cruel time.

Yellow gave way to brown and loose sand became cracked mud. The sun shone bright most days, but each passing day hung lower in the sky. Tufts of dry grass became more frequent, along with the occasional tree. Signs that this dry place hosted abundant life became clear. It was the scrublands, the home of the Warring Stone Towers.

The place invited speculation and storytelling, and drawing those with imaginative, fanciful intentions. Marble and Runty walked onwards, side by side, the sun descending and light fading once more. As the sun eddied over the horizon, Marble could see the faint silhouettes, the first of the warriors only a blip in the distance. They would grow steadily upon their approach, she knew, giant monoliths dominating the landscape and colossal to any who drew close.

After hobbling the stupid beast, Marble lay out her thin sleeping pallet a safe distance away, and did her best to rest her weary mind. At day's departure, the cold crept in. She did not imagine the fog of her shallow breathing.

It was cold. Very cold. She stared into the dome of night, no clouds to cover or protect. Marble wouldn't be surprised to wake up to a blanket of frost. It was difficult to drift off into slumber with her body stiffening with each passing moment, but at least the soft sounds of the unperturbed Runty were oddly comforting. Her foggy breath swirled and danced under the light of the moon. Slowly, ever so slowly, and despite the cold, the emissary dropped into a restless sleep, the shapes of her breath taking on terrifying life.

The wind whispered, the breeze shimmered. Merrily, viciously, violently. Stealing away the white mist that reluctantly puffed out from her lips. Faces emerged, there for a second and gone the next. Pulling, pushing with pained haunting expressions. Flashes passed too quickly to interpret. The restless cold stung. The air was heavy, yet weightlessness took her.

Floating. Drifting with the currents but stiff and unable

to move. Clear. Indistinct. Fast. Slow. Then the new sensations bombarding the emissary. Scents tickling at her nose all the while being overpowering and suffocating. Too many merging together to distinguish. Too much and too little. Her head felt it all, but she was helpless to stop it. Pounding heavily and unrelenting. Then nothing.

Nothing. Only darkness and blindness. Just the zephyr of thought. Everywhere and nowhere. Nothing, until she became something. Light and shape and form, the hands caressed and shaped her, and when the wind came again, she was flying.

She was a creature of majestic beauty, powerful wings beating ferociously in the sky, effortless in their strength. The swirling currents bowed at her will, carrying her where she commanded. She watched her desolate kingdom with no fear or threat, for she *ruled* here. She was the predator. She would choose her prey. But there was nothing. Nothing but sand and shrubland and tall monstrous rocks, reaching, stretching pitifully to the sky, a dominion that they could only aspire to. Her scoff was full in its condescension.

She flew on. Searching and watching. Drifting on the currents. Beating her wings harder and harder. She struggled. Her muscles grew fatigued. She grew thirsty and hungry, but there was nothing to done about it. It ate away at her. Slowly. Alone.

When she gave in, the fall was met by hard unyielding earth. Bones snapped and splintered, tendons ripped and red spilled forth. She could do nothing, the pain covering her and filling her every movement. She screamed. As darkness engulfed her, she welcomed it.

She had fins and a powerful tail now, and she breathed

in the water surrounding her. She swam in darkness; the currents pushing her and she moved at their whim. She was alone.

As she was starting to believe she was blind, she was a light. Just a pinprick far in the distance. And so she fought against the world that was trying to kill her, fought with all her might. It would not break her. It would *not*! She fought and pushed and flicked her tail and swept with her fins to break free from the strangle hold. How long had she been here? Vision dimmed, the light grew faint. *I'm drowning...* Choking, flailing spasmodically in the void, and very alone.

Nothing.

She was burrowing through the ground. The world was dirt. Soothing and scraping against the emissary's body. Her strong limbs had no difficulty expanding her tunnels ever onwards. Searching, searching, searching. Finding nothing. No one. Nothing but more and more solitary and loneliness and an empty world. On and on and on.

The cycle repeated itself, and she could not escape. Blackness and darkness and blindness. Racing, racing, racing mind. Forever alone.

Each body, each world, each painful death fracturing her mind. *My name... It's... I...*

It was a slow, stiff awakening for Marble. A blanket of ice cloaked her. The sun was still shy of the horizon. Tensing and relaxing her frozen muscles one at a time, she tried her best to stimulate the blood flow back through her body, to warm her core so her limbs would be able to function at least. More, more, until she could move with a smidge of coordination. On a deep, grunted breath, Marble rolled onto her side, then pushed onto her hands and knees. Slowly and surely, the emissary twisted her stiff neck from side to side as she pressed back onto her haunches, to observe a quiet world. Runty glared back at her balefully.

Dark spots on the skyline betrayed where the Warring Stones stood sentinel, even this far away they were blots on the newrising sun. A moment of curiosity made her want to visit them, but they were behind her now, and going there would only increase her risk of being seen by to many prying eyes.

Breaking fast on dried jerky, she treated herself to a dribble of water. Conservation was key. There would be three three days at least before she could replenish it safely. Another battle with Runty ensued when she broke camp, a part of their routine by now. all packed up, the unlikely duo were on their way again. More nights and days passed, and the sentinels were lost to sight. The land changed, and more nights were cold and restless. The rations vanished.

The solitude and desert scrub came to an end on the fifth day. She untethered the troublesome beast then, letting Runty roam free. It was a bittersweet farewell, despite their differences. Sentiments aside, she did not linger for long. As the beast gleefully trotted away, she took care to pick her way through the sparse vegetation, across the gently rolling land, towards one of the less travelled roads.

Sora claimed this land as its demesne. It claimed every shrub and byl and scorpion, Silentis wanted it out of the hands of the west. What it really desired, were the oases. Lifeblood for pilgrims, the meagre havens were prized, and many would seek to squabble over the finite waters should the enemies of the throne advance this deep into Soran land.

So onwards, ever onwards, she journeyed. She followed the winding path, keeping her visage disguised behind her familiar, comforting scarf, up and down the rolling hills. The ground and surrounding fields showed more and more life, from weeds to grass to billowing meadows that housed and fed wild longhorns, horses, and sheep.

Halcyons soared above, sweeping down now and then to snatch up their prey. The faint outline of farmsteads rose in the distance, dotting the undulating lands, and signs of other travellers and inhabitants of the world invaded her solitary world. She was grateful for the slow acclamation when, late in the day, she arrived at the village.

A full meal in her belly, a roof over her head, and a soft bed was all she could ever dream of. The inn stood vigil, calm and sturdy, beside the road. Three stories high, with an ancient facade. Itr was a welcome sight. A decent-sized stable accompanied the building, a short, quiet snicker sounded through its doors. Slow steps took Marble to the heavy oak and iron entryway of the inn. The doorknobs formed an interesting pattern, a disk with two identical-looking figures. The place was quiet, the innkeeper welcoming enough but, more importantly, not curious in the slightest about her customers.

The interior was well lit, the windows large and wide, sunbeams that would soon be replaced with moonbeams shone through to dust motes dancing in their illumination. Money exchanged for a key, a bowl of hearty broth, fresh bread, a good brown ale, and a promise of a waiting bath when she was done with her meal.

She collapsed into one of the comfortable blue leather

booths that hugged the edge of the room. It was an unusual layout, but Marble appreciated the comfort all the same, choosing one in a corner so she could still observe the entirety of the room. It was one of the only spots that allowed it, apart from behind the bar. The emissary greedily gulped down the warm, homely meal as the innkeeper called in a couple of stablehands, young men, to cart and carry Marble's bath water up to her room. The sole occupant of the inn, and so many to attend her. Pushing her musings to the back of her mind, the emissary devoured the rest of her flavoursome food and savoured the smooth taste of the good ale, before depositing her used utensils atop the empty bar and making her way up to her chamber.

The stablehands passed her on their way back down, hurrying passed but slowing to look back at her. The room was finely functional, small but perfect for her needs. The lantern by the side of the door was lit, as was one across the room near the bed and another next to her steaming bath. Fresh linens, a bar of soap and a clean nightshirt lay folded on a stool next to the cold hearth. With a quick, practised eye, Marble assessed the security of the room and, upon closing and bolting the door, proceeded to set the hearth ablaze and discard her filthy clothing into the flames. There was no saving them.

Taking the bar of soap, Marble flipped her head upside down and dipped her hair into the warm water, letting it soak and the heat soothe her itchy scalp. Raking her fingers through her long, tangled locks, Marble combed out the debris and unwelcome guests. The water turned dusty and grey. Marble wet the soap and lathered her hair, cleansing and scratching her scalp and the lengths of silver tresses.

Pushing herself up with her hands on the edge of the tub, Marble took a deep breath and willed her heavy breathing to even out and her head to stop swimming. Opening her fluttering lids, forcing her eyes to focus, she eyed the grimy water and sighed heavily. At least her head was clean.

She used the wash basin next to the hearth to clean her face and body best she could and luxuriated, using the scented oil left for her, smoothing it through her tangled knotted mane. She would stay another night before leaving, the emissary decided. *And bathe again.*

The nightgown was soft and fervent against her willowed frame and hardened skin. she climbed into bed, surrendering to the call of sleep. After a couple of days, her mind and body would be ready to carry on, she hoped. Telling herself she would be better, she sunk into the soft, clean sheets and allowed oblivion to take her. Tomorrow she would shave and pleasure herself, eat and acclimate to the company of others and probably pleasure herself a few times more if she could not find a suitable companion to help with that endeavour. The air was warm with the bedcovers, and the fire was roaring merrily.

It was the sound of the fire that sent her to sleep, or what she thought was sleep. Light ebbed from sight, and warmth leeched from her body. What started as a breeze to kiss her skin soon whirled and whipped at her, taking her breath and waking her float in weightlessness. It called to her. Calling her away to the place she had never been.

28

AUDEYRN

The Sorans sat hunched and shivering in their saddles, those that had managed to keep their scrawny mounts alive.

The rest stood leaning on their spears, or sat on stumps or stones or even the damp cold ground itself. Their hands were bound into their armpits for the scant warmth to be found there, and pulled their shawls tight, ill suited for this weather, to keep the cold off their chests. The escort was made of some fifty warriors strong, all bearing the strange weapons that those in far off Sora favoured, barbed things, blades on the end of ropes, and cunningly bound recurve bows that allowed for extended range of fire.

All of them were packed away now, all clattering on the backs or hips of their sodden owners. He could only pity them, to have campaigned so far only to be beaten by the hard autumn rains and gales. Beneath thin hoods, they looked on at the emissary and his entourage of Torrin Merbeasts with eyes brimming with hostility. *They are autumn leaves, falling and failing, shivering from the dreadblack shadow of coming winter.*

Audeyrn had never seen a Soran winter, so he could not have said what these people knew of the cold, but guessing from the unkempt men in the camp, the emaciated horses in their stalls, and the way the place seemed more lichyard than battle-camp, he could comfortably guess that they knew little. The thought made him feel all the more pitiful for these people. They were warriors all, yes, those called upon to invade this land for their queen. Did they know why they were fighting? He spurred his horse on, leaving the furtive lights of Wolfsmouth behind to grow dim in the mists of the morning.

This was not ideal, for any side. The Sorans had been camped in a meadow shouldering the coast a league west of the town for nigh on two days now. Their commander was careful to keep their distance, careful not to send his scouts too close to the town, or give any indication that he intended to attack. Not that the townspeople, or their lady, were blind to the thousands of mounted and armed dunnies that had sprung up like flowers made of steel and canvas. *This is not ideal...* and now they all expected him to resolve it.

Wolfsmouth was under attack by the Sorans, was what they heard from the messenger Pluter Moss on the lathered horse that morning, two hours shy of sunrise. That the *dhereda* Lyonis of Ves was leading his hellspawn soldiers from the west, he said. The town had been in a state of uproar as the first furtive grey light filled the streets, filled by Low Paydar and merchantmen and foreigners all scrambling to ready themselves any way they could. Not that they could leave. The Lady had ordered the harbour be sealed, for the booms to be raised, for any sign of desperate escape to be deterred by lethal force. All this she told Moss, who climbed atop a fresh horse to arrange the readying of the town for a lengthy siege.

Audeyrn understood the fear. Adrianne Torrin had strengthened her walls east of the river in anticipation of potential attack by the Sorans; when the alliance of the Tourmaline Throne and the Tor still bore fruit. Despite claiming neutrality after the Rowett withdrawal from their pact, the Lady Torrin had known better than to be idle, for the town had been sacked three hundred years before, no less than by the Rowetts of the Tor themselves, who would come to conquer them and beat them down into mere vassals. Neutrality or no, plunder and virgins looked much the same in the eyes of a raider. He had been there in the dark of the late autumn morning as the Merbeasts formed up in rank, thirty-three strong, all bearing gleaming silver and emerald filigreed armour, yet each one bearing a unique helm marking themselves as a fellow of the sworn brotherhood. Their duty was simple; protect Brinewater, and the scions of the House of Torrin. The bailey crawled with them as the Lady and her councillors stood shouting orders to seneschals and servants, the atmosphere frenetic in anticipation for blood.

A Merbeast with a squid helm strode past him without a glance, barking commands at archers to man the walls. Another, masked as a drik, rode past and delivered a message to the Lady Adrianne, who summoned the emissary with a look. The news that Sorans were coming had inflamed her, and he had to request a private audience to explain the situation. Chiefly, could Lyonis of Ves be trusted? All he had to do was to get the Lady herself to trust a man infamous for his chicanery in war. *It won't be that hard,* he told himself, the bitterness making his stomach sour. At the least, he had managed to persuade Torrin not to give battle to the Soran forces. She had relented, but he had thought for a moment that smoke would rise from her flared nostrils like her pet wyrm.

"You say that this dunny commander can be trusted?" She stood on the steps leading to Eistir's Tower, to look down on the emissary.

"Yes, as much as I can. He is not without guile, but I believe that he will honour the agreement we made."

"Bah!" a cadaverous stoopbacked man shambled over to Lady Torrin, the hardiron staff he bore as Justiciar clanging sharply on the flags as he rested on it. "As he honoured the Ikteti, I do not doubt?" That was a hard draft to drink. Few had forgotten the Soran annexation of Iktet nearly a decade ago, least of all the lands that bordered the poor bastards. The Justiciar was the chief lawmaker and aide to Lady Adrianne, a man named Peon Thyrqell, and if it was to be believed, was just as efficient at ordering assassinations as he was regulating the trade tariffs of the port. "My good Justiciar makes a fair point, Lord Emissary. How can we believe that this Lyonis will not make Wolfsmouth into another Iktet? You yourself admitted to me that the man is vainglorious."

Aud was forced to concede. "Yes, he is that. But you *must* see, there are others that are far worse. His countrymen still hold Halfway, barding the 'water, cutting off your trade to the eastern Qell. They are commanded by a man called–"

The Justiciar cut in with acid in his voice. "Darge Pirellion.

417

Yes, we are most aware of our… neighbour." He stroked a claw-like hand through his lustrous white beard. "Indeed, the man seems like to name Halfway his home away-from-home, the whole sorry time he is spending there. Lord Myddle must be sorely put out that a Soran has planted his sun-burnt arse in his town." Lady Adrianne made a tight smile, yet Aud saw how uncomfortable being reminded of Halfway made her. *How much does she trust this one, I wonder?* The emissary crossed his arms, aware of the vulture glowering down at him. "How very droll, my lord. So you must also be aware then, that the reason Pirellion occupies Halfway is to prevent Lyonis the Yale from acquiring fresh Soran levies to replenish his army."

Thyrqell's fingers tightened on his staff. "It takes less than a thimble of acuity to come to that conclusion." What looked like mischief shone darkly in his eyes, "I fail to grasp, however, the reasoning of your assumption that this one or that one is worse than t'other. From my position, the position of House Torrin and Wolfsmouth, is that an enemy is an enemy, and as such shall be dealt with accordingly."

Lady Adrianne considered them both before snorting a laugh, "He has you there, Audeyrn. Both are primed to engage my town on both sides of the 'water like the horns of a bull. Why do *you* trust the word of this Lyonis of Ves?"

He found no easy answer for her. *Because he promised me. Because he has my respect from mortal combat.* His pause made the Justiciar scoff, and even Lady Adrianne made to frown. He could not find an answer for them. Not an answer they would readily believe, at any rate. The Merbeasts were forming up, men and women wielding death at their Lady's command. *Greg found his answer, amongst the rubble and*

418

ruin. He was broken... and even then he found the resolve to save those wretched waifs. Audeyrn could not bring himself to tell them the truth, so he made his own.

"I can bring Captain-General Lyonis to you, unarmed and bound if needs be, to prove to you that the reason for his being here is not to attack, but to parlay, and allow his men safe passage across the river."

"He's lying," Thyrqell's vulture eyes did their best to read the emissary, so Audeyrn gave it back to him in kind. "What... You're–" His silence came at the raised hand of Lady Adrianne. What was it Audeyrn saw on her face then? Curiosity, or amusement?

"Let the Lord Emissary go to this Soran commander. Let him show House Torrin what a loyal subject he is. Bring him to us, then, and we shall see."

He left at the head of a column of Merbeasts, the mud slick beneath his horse's hooves. He went to stroke his chin, and remembered he had shaved his beard. *Not ideal at all.* The Soran camp was divided into lines of barrack tents, five thousand at a guess with men milling about amongst them. But then again the meadows where they were placed gave way to mists, so in the distance they turned into wraith soldiers of a foggy kingdom, their meagre shelters cirrus clouds drifting forlornly across the mud. The golden glyph of Sora hung on sodden banners, everywhere the gold turned to dun in the overcast of the day. Hearty seemed to read his thoughts as he *hmmm*ed disapprovingly.

"A sorry lot, aye. Makes me pity them, despite them in writ being our sworn foes. Even what those bastards did to Sir Noyon at Kande's Mire... I doubt these boys ever saw damp like this before crossing the Wolfswater. I doubt they even knew that war was." The camp unfurled before them like a wet, stinking carpet, and Hearty was quiet for some time. Then, when the emissary was certain he had no more to say, Hearty Deri said, "I know you blame yourself for Natoly, and for Greg."

"I did what I had to do with Nat, but even so it was hard. It was the dutiful thing to do." High above, some bird of prey called, yet he could not see it. "I'm beginning to think it wasn't the *right* thing to do."

Hearty spat. "Duty is just, aye. Yet who are we to know if those that are duty-bound are good or ill?" The emissary only nodded. He imagined that it was his father being posed the question. Maybe if he was the Royal Emissary still, he could find an answer. Audeyrn struggled with how that would go, his mind wanting only to return to the woman in his dream. *Why are we even at war?*

The Captain-General's quarters appeared where a moment before it was just another among a score of identical worn and ragged tents in a canvas forest. It was not particularly big. It could only have been half as large as the one Walt Iddles used at his war camp to the north. Apart from that, the only indication that this was the headquarters of Lyonis was the pair of Headhunters that flanked the tent flap. They eyed the approaching mounted Caldishman with suspicion, hands on cruel hip knives. *Who could blame them? Four of their countrymen went north to the Tor, and none returned.*

A blur shot out from the tent, making the flaps snap like the wings of some bird. A man was sent hurtling across the ground, his fine enamelled breastplate chipped and scratched, the silken shawl across one shoulder ripped and muddied. He was busy spitting clods of dirt and broken teeth when Audeyrn pulled up alongside him. "This one was planning on removing your head from your neck, Emissary," came the modulated voice of Lyonis. He stepped out from the tent, clad in a wolf pelt and mail, his sword clattering lightly on a greaved thigh. His hair was pulled back in a knot, all but a rogue coil that plastered damply to his cheek. "Lord Savinien here had the bright idea. Hatched it all on his own, didn't you, Ejim?" Lord Ejim Savinien struggled to respond with mud in his mouth.

Audeyrn was unimpressed. *Incredibly good timing for such a show. What does Lyonis take me for?* Another man may have put that done to good fortune, or happenstance, or the will of the gods, but the Emissary had lived at the court of Isembard too long to think he had good timing. *Besides, Lyonis lives and breathes machinations. How has he survived so long, if not for guile?*

"The gods are good," he replied, giving the conspiratorial lord a dirty look. "May we discuss these matters in privy, Captain-General?" The Soran inclined his head, and bid the Headhunters take Lord Ejim to the barrack gaol. Hearty dismounted and tailed Audeyrn, and they entered the dank tent together. A taper was burning in one corner, doing little to banish the gloom, and sending long cloaks of shadow to dance behind the assembled commanders muttering around a long table. They stood, the only chair knocked backward to lay atop layers of musty furs. The table was covered in empty wine goblets and plates hosting the congealed remains of breakfast. "Leave, now," rang the acerbic tones of Lyonis. It sounded too harsh to Audeyrn's ears, and the officers showed their chagrin on bare windburnt faces. A few gave them looks as they went, looks which seemed to say, *if I had my way, you'd be strappadoed from the nearest tree.*

The last gave his most baleful look and went without. The Soran said, "As you can plainly see, my lords, my countrymen have had a bellyful of this land and its rains and drizzles and downpours and howling winds. Everyday it blesses us with some new form of deluge, and we wake with malaise, dysentery and redcough. They yearn for home. For the shady avenues of the crystal city of Silentis, the Oasis of Sharngune, some fucking sun at the least." He gestured to a demijohn on the table.

Aud shook his head, "I am no lord, as you rightly know."

Lyonis picked up the chair, dusting the day's dust from the cushioned seat. "Yet I have heard from a humble crofter on the long road that the great lords accompany the Lord Emissary of Castan himself, arriving triumphant in Wolfsmouth at the head of a victorious Paydar army. You deny that *you* answer to the title of *Lord Emissary*?" Audeyrn should have foreseen the jibe, yet knew better than to react to it. He chose his words carefully. "I have heard that you upheld your side of the agreement."

The Soran resigned himself to the chair, unbuckling his cloak, baldric, and sword as he did so. The spotted Yales on the hilt winked devilishly as he set the scabbard down reverently on the table. "I have. I even received a polite little parlay from a certain friend of yours, a... Walton Iddles. He was *very* confused by my proposal for a summit, and thoroughly *bewildered* when I mentioned our arrangement. It must be said, the man was the very soul of chivalry. He was very happy I could tell. He is a wise man, to prevent unnecessary bloodshed."

"Walt is an honourable man. He knows my mind in this regard. The idea of ending this madness was his idea, no doubt he was acting the ignorant when you met. He *will* continue to make reports to our king that the war effort is progressing, as long as your Sorans advance no further than the Utterings."

"Until I retreat, is what you truly mean." The way he leaned forward caused Hearty to put a hand on his sword. *Careful, this man remains prideful. Appeal to him... appeal to his pride.* The gesture did not go unnoticed by Lyonis. "Please... I have made a sign of good faith by allowing you your weapons within my quarters. Alone, I may add. Yes, my Headhunters remain without, but what is to stop you from stupidly ordering your knight friend here to make me a head shorter?" Hearty scoffed. The emissary touched his arm to calm him, yet the ageing knight remained on edge, the tendons in his arms as tight as hardiron coils.

"I apologise for the mistrust. Since we last met, we have cosened with rogues and strangers, to our sorrow. Our expedition up the river did not reap the benefits we had hoped. Now, I can assure you, I want to end this war. Not for the king, but for all those that will die if we do not act now." The Soran's face was shadowed as he leant on the backrest. Only the outline of his head was vaguely lit, but the Yales on his sword moved restlessly, a mind of their own. "What an altruist," Lyonis said, venom etched upon every word, "I am to believe that you now want to go to Silentis of your own accord? Tell me, do you still carry that chest? The one you held at the Tor?"

"Yes. I mean, I intend to treat with Queen–"

"All I needed to hear was the *yes*. I had not forgotten about that box. It was oft on my mind as I traversed this miserable land. For weeks, I would ask myself: does he still have it? And, what rests within? Gold? A treaty upon vellum writ in Isembard's own bloody hand? The rotted head of a Soran? I came to realise that what I should have been asking myself was this: Why did your king send a message in a box, *along* with his precious Royal Emissary?"

Audeyrn fought to make his face still, devoid of feeling, empty and serene, forcing himself to match the feline glint from the Soran's eyes. When he was ready, he countered, "I was tasked to deliver the chest, unopened, to your Queen. The contents remain unknown to me, to everyone."

"Why still carry out the wishes of your mad king?" He felt his cheeks burn, resisting the urge to set his causting eyes on the Soran.

"I don't know, and that's the truth. But I wasn't sent to you for that. I was sent to save you, and your people. You can pull apart my motives until the gods return, but know that I want every single Soran here to return home alive, safe, to their wives, their children, and their homes. I am your salvation, Lyonis. A bitter draught, but one that must be drunk."

The Soran's response was only to scoff. "And what did my fair lady of Wolfsmouth think of this?" Audeyrn heard Hearty beside him breath in sharply. *Calm yourself.* Lyonis straightened, running a hand through his hair. "She hates the Rowetts more than us, you know? Yet we are her enemies. Invaders investing her lands. She would be wise to slaughter every man and woman with a Soran accent."

The knight thumped his scarred fist onto the table, the

resounding thud as loud as a thunderclap in that quiet tent. "You talk from your arse, dunny. Some shite talk I can palate, but it stank real bad here before you opened your mouth. Open your eyes, and see who stands before you offers you your homeland."

The Soran looked anything but distressed by the knight's outburst. He answered coolly, "I see only a king's lapdog, and his fat oaf of a knight."

"Again, again, again you spout utter shite from your whoreson mouth. The wines you lot drink must addle your wits."

The emissary chose then as his moment to act. He drew his sword, well aware of the loud voices outside. He let his fear wash over him, his heart thumped hard against his chest, and the fabric of his tunic clung clammy to his armpits. Now the Soran showed his face, leaning forward, a hand reaching for his blade. *He does feel dread then... good. This will go smoother if he is put on the backfoot.* At the sound of drawn steel, Hearty instinctively drew his own blade, wielding that ugly blade of his as though it were nothing. Audeyrn angled himself to block Hearty from advancing. This, after all, demanded a personal touch, and he did not think Hearty one for such delicate matters.

Taking a deft step forward, he flung his naked steel at the feet of the still-seated Lyonis. Then, he fell to his knees, the hard-packed earth beneath the thin furs sending jolts through his legs. He heard the knight come up behind him.

"Aud, what in hells are you–"

"Put up your weapon. Now." The emissary could have kissed the old doddering man then, for he did as he was bid, unquestioning, that cumbersome ogre-blade clanging sharply against his own slim longsword. Then the Soran's hands had clasped Audeyrn's own upraised ones, gesturing in a sign of submission, or…

"How is that for trust?" Aud's eyes were downcast, allowing for his wasting gaze to fall mercilessly on the cold metal pooled at the Yale's feet. He could feel the man looking at him, weighing his options. The ones that remained to him, anyway. "You know how to appeal to my ego, at least," laughed Lyonis of Ves, his voice lacking the terse bitterness of before. *Bend, conciliate, humble yourself, until you are prostrate before the defaming suzerain. As long as you act. As long as you do something.*

"Oh fine," the Soran was on his feet. Like that, he was by the tent door. "I have never been within Wolfsmouth. If my history serves me well, I should be the first Soran battle commander to be invited inside the walls. How I wish to marvel at the Span." He threw open the flaps, letting some wan light to silhouette the man. When he looked back, Aud thought he saw the same guile that had made the Yale so infamous across the continent. But he could not be sure, for the man's face was shadowed, and the sun was coming out. He called at an adjutant. "Muster my captains. We break camp."

The rest of that day was a crawl. Audeyrn waited with the column as they formed up. The camp was dismantled in under two hours, leaving behind the usual scars of thousands of soldiers and horselines and wayns, woods felled, midden heaps piled high, latrines overflowing. The sharpened stakes demarking the perimeter were left behind, which Aud did not doubt would be stolen by the usual crows that followed armies, to be used in the construction of a new inn to replace that which had been burned, or replace the rotten support of a stable, or even whittled down into a toy for a Paydar child.

Hearty had been sent back with the Merbeasts, but only after coming to the compromise that one of the masked guardsmen would remain as the emissary's uneasy shadow. The man, at least he thought it was a man, watched from behind the eyes of a sea-dog as his sworn brothers left with the knight. The man spoke only when spoken to, and even then it was clipped and monosyllabic, letting Aud know that he shared no love for the Caldishmen, nor these invading Sorans.

He is a fish out of water, that one. Or rather, a sea-dog. His life is tailing nobles, not these strangers that cannot even speak Qellish. Despite his lack of conversation, Audeyrn did not mind the guard's presence. After all, he had seen how vigilant they were around Adrianne. He needed his protection, not his words. They mounted, watching as the starveling soldiers began their trudge on the long road, cutting along the coastal ridges like a stone ribbon. Soon after, Lyonis joined the emissary and his guard, the latter's firemane whinnying as he caught the scent of the Soran's mare. The guard watched them from behind, Aud having little doubt that he would report anything he heard to his mistress. When the emissary had told Lyonis that back at the tent, he had only laughed.

More Merbeasts hailed them at the gate. He did not recognise these, looking on at those helmeted in the likenesses of eel and mercow. The sea-dog spat out something in thick Qellish, too quick for Audeyrn to catch, and those on the gate looked at each other briefly. For a moment, dread writhed in the pit of Aud's stomach as he saw the beasts look from the sea-dog to Audeyrn to Lyonis. But then one of them removed his metal eel face, revealing a woman no older than himself, who blew into a horn to signal the opening of the gate.

The hardiron of the doors was banded and reinforced with blocks of granite. He watched as the doors swung inward on oversized hinges, pulled within by the teams of colossal aurochs. He had glimpsed them as shadows outlined in torchlight that morning, but now, as the sun traversed a cold cirrus sky, they came into view as the column passed beneath. On high stepped terraces flanking the gate, long avenues had been built into the walls themselves, where dozens of the huge horned beasts were led along by engineers and grooms. *Gods, even their aurochs are braided.*

"A site to behold. Indeed, a wonder of the world." Lyonis had found an apple somewhere and was talking between loud mouthfuls. Aud found that he was only half-listening. He was alone, yet surrounded by a sea of unfriendly faces. Apart from the Soran and the sea-dog, a Torrin escort of mounted spearmen had fallen in on all sides, escorting them along a road that he was sure was named Fishcatcher's Walk. They followed it until it angled north, to join the main avenue of Shipwright's. The emissary was anxious to return to Brinewater, and the vexing meeting he could not avoid. Being back on the long road had made him feel the need to get going, the urge to follow the uneven cobbles a nagging voice inside, one that would not go away. It was inane, and he knew it. It was not even the right stretch of road. *Soon enough.*

An afternoon of scant warmth turned into melancholic

twilight. There was no parade as he returned to the bailey. No one there to greet him or his unlikely companions. The courtiers were either unaware of their return, or had chosen to remain ignorant of the fact. Lyonis made note of it too. "Either these Paydar are afraid of the dark, or they know better than to dignify me with their presence. Shall we see your lady, doggy?"

The Merbeast grunted, the bright lights refracting hard off the Dome of Life to give his mask a slimy sheen. He led the way now, no hesitation in showing them his back. *Indeed, why should he fear Lyonis, or myself, when his brethren man the walls, stand fast to attention at the entrances to the Towers, their hollow eyes singular in their regard for us.* Seaspike was a dark cliff streaking upward like a black-bladed sword. But the guardsman led them not to the Lady's tower, but to the Thundering Hall.

The question caught in the emissary's throat, with something that told him that he would likely receive an unhelpful response, if any at all. His tongue remained behind clenched teeth. Those masked men holding the doors opened them upon their approach, and he entered a cavern of cold and dark mien. A pair Merbeasts were already inside, and they held out gauntletted hands to take their weapons. Aud and Lyonis did as they were bid, but not before Lyonis warned them that the yale could only be used by himself. *This man is either brilliant, or...* The sound of stone on steel shrieked through the hall, music a far cry from the raucous jovial song and dance a few weeks before, all celebrations of victory seemingly forgotten now, the dancers and drunks and running children and barking dogs replaced by only shadows. The shades of those that had drunk in the energy

429

of the living, hollow shapes that skulked away from the light and ate nothing but dust.

Don't be absurd. You think you need fear ghosts? It's the living that should be feared. He clenched his fist hard, until he felt his nails break skin. The shadows remained, and watched the newcomers approach the dais.

Woodes Wayland sat upon the lowest step, sharpening a sword with a whetstone by the light of a smoke-hole in the high slate roof. The blade was six feet long, thick, as wide as the length of his hand with room to spare. The doors to the hall slammed shut, the sound of bars securing them in place ringing in his ears. *No.* He could feel his heart leap up, a nasty thought coming to the fore. He looked at the woman sat in the high seat upon the dais. "My lady, he has come peacefully. You said if–"

"Don't waste your words, Emissary." It was Lyonis who spoke, scoffing as only a noble could. "Our man here looks keen to do his duty. It will be wanting to deny him that." Wayland's face was unreadable as he looked at the men in the hall. It disquieted Aud no end.

"Quiet," The sea-dog growled in a deep rumbling tumult, as though his was the voice of the sea itself. His hand was on the pommel of his sword, and the darkness made his mask fissured and pitted. The fearsome dog turned into a vision of a fel hound from the Hell Unending. He took a few steps forward, slow and reverent. Then he took a knee. "My lady, I present Audeyrn Langholm, Lord Emissary of King Isembard of Castan. I also present my charge, Lyonis of Ves, the Yale, Butcher of Iktet, and Commander of the Combined Soran Army."

Combined Soran Army? Now, where did he get that from?

This one is too loyal by half, and not half so adroit.

"You do know *why* she hates the Rowetts, I gather?" If Lyonis was afraid, he hid it amongst the shadows. The digression was no doubt to break the emissary's concentration. It worked. The Torrins had always been uneasy vassals to the Rowetts, but there had never been outright rebellion. The feuds had always been sorted the usual way, and peace had prevailed across the rolling plains and rocky bluffs of the Paydar. The Rowetts had even garnered good relations with their neighbours to the east, and as far as Aud could recall, had even sent a bloodroyal to be fostered at Ves.

The Torrins, being Low Paydar, had always harboured dreams of secession. With their incomes from the river and the port and Ruell coast, the emissary guessed that they could raise enough levies to face the Rowetts. Enough even to lay siege to the Tor itself. Those lords of Wolfsmouth that had aired such ambitions had always seen such plans scuppered by internal strife, or having to deal with corsairs raiding their coast, or other demanding affairs that tested their resolve and saw them weakened in power and authority.

"She hates them, Audeyrn, because they killed her husband. Bastian, who was my friend."

"How *dare* you say his name." She was clad in a silverthread gown that hugged her body, a mantle of wolf fur adorning her slim neck and shoulders. Her hair was unbraided, he saw, and tousled wildly as she descended the steps, as though dragged from sleep. "You name him your friend, yet where were you when they found his body in the water."

Lyonis straightened himself, through gritted teeth, spat, "I was occupied. I was needed to quell an insurrection."

"Is that what you Sorans call it? An insurrection?" The voice belonged to Justiciar Peon Thyrqell, the cadaverous figure dressed in a featureless dreadblack robe. *Like Man Death come forth...*

"We were vouchsafed protection if he came willingly." Audeyrn found his gaze returning to the sword, and the long sweeping motions of the whetstone.

Lady Adrianne crossed the floor, coming dangerously close to the Soran as though she intended on throttling him. The Merbeasts lurked in the wings, shuffling, loosening their blades in their scabbards. Then she looked at Audeyrn, her hand going to the Soran's cheek. *Don't...*

The slap drowned out the grating of the sword, but only for an instant. Lady Torrin stood half a foot shorter than Lyonis, yet the force of the blow caused him to take a step back. *It can't end like this.* He thought of his father then, and what he would have done.

A laugh erupted from Lyonis. "Were you educated in Soran-Paydar politics, my good emissary, you would know that Bastian, may the gods lay his fine soul to rest, was a Rowett."

"Damn you, Lyonis. You should have been with him," Adrianne's shoulders fell, her eyes hooded.

Then it was the emissary's turn to step backward. "The Rowetts killed their own kin?" The words tumbled freely and stupidly. He felt as though he had been smacked himself.

Lady Torrin shot him a look of all hate. "The idiot and the butcher. The gods are cruel for making *you* our saviours."

29

GREGYN

The sounds of the column never left them truly, not even in the tall grass.

She hugged him from behind, his hands shaking from fatigue as much as excitement. It had been a hard ride. The time they stole to be with one another never seemed long enough.

Mayred had hobbled Muddy and her own playful stallion at the edge of the glade, their coats slick with sweat. A young brook sprouted from between two erratics of granite the colour of a stormy sky, the world beyond the clearing all but banished and forgotten. She had pulled him to the ground after they had halted, to plant a rush of kisses on his neck and shoulders.

They had been racing through the small game trails that webbed through the unruly wild *chejk* grass for weeks, each time he would gain the lead and leave her behind, only for the Paydar girl to burst from the rushes atop Zorul, charging ahead and letting him choke on the upthrown dust. More than once, she would sneak up on him, only to whack him across the skull with a bulrush. The initial shock of being pummelled by the sausage-like top almost immediately replaced with him choking on the explosion of fibres. It annoyed him, but anger never entered his mind. Not with her. It made him want to speed after her, catch her, and pull her reins tight so that he could meet her waiting lips.

He opened his eyes between kisses, glancing at the powerful steed that pawed at the ground. She had brought him hand-in-hand to her horse at the stables in Brinewater. He was a firemane, like most Paydar mounts, but this one had an ashen coat from withers to rump, except for a patch of maroon that ran down his forehead and muzzle like a sunburst. *Zorul, she calls him. Zorul means 'sunfire'.* He would need to remember that.

Qellish was troublesome. There were some sounds he had yet to master, the most subtle inflections of the tongue that sometimes denoted tense, not just timbre. He found that listening was easier, but when he had tried to mimic what had been said, Mayred would only shake her head and stress the sound slowly. Jethro would just bite his lip to keep from laughing, the tracker finding that the boy had little patience in teaching his mothertongue. He could not blame him. He was the same, after all. Despite being a few years older, the boy was short for his age, which made Greg think that he was younger. So he left the teaching to this dark and mysterious girl, the one that had been with him since the hunt for the Godless. Every time she would begin a lesson, he would lose himself in her eyes, and wonder how he had found someone so perfect. Then came the smack across his face, and her telling him that he had lost concentration.

434

That week they had started to tackle the mutations. The beginning of each word could change depending on the subject, which made learning new words all the more challenging for a boy who had lived his whole life speaking only the common. To compound this, he had discovered early on that his strong Forks brogue was a hindrance in pronouncing some common Qellish sounds. His talking had been clunky and disjointed, but he had improved. Both of the Paydar could agree. Mayred had been a patient tutor. The language was the easiest of the new things he had been learning from her.

Crossing the Span over the Wolfswater, they had rejoined the long road, cutting through the easternmost reaches of the Paydar. Then, without border marking or signpost, they entered the lands of Iktet.

With the shortening days, each sunrise felt darker and colder than the last, but he was learning. With each brisk sunrise, he talked in the tongue with greater confidence, until he had even begun to think in Qellish. Riding the long road with his two Paydar companions, he listened to them in their own tongue, hearing them tell of the legendary Six-Fingered Sorcerer, how he had saved the Tor from the Aeromancer and brought the forces of the Qell to their knees.

His nights were no less educational. When the Emissary decided to make camp, at this ruin or that waypost or the enclosure of some local chieftain, Greg would find himself sitting at a campfire and sharing his supper with Mayred, who ate as much as any man and used her fingers to rip apart the meat, if they happened to chance upon game. This land was ruled by Silentis by right of conquest, Captain-

435

General Lyonis of Ves known throughout Iktet as the trickster who made them a dependency of the Kingdom of Sora. Nevertheless, Greg noticed that Lyonis had decreed that sentries were to patrol the camp. When the darkness closed in, the tracker would spread his blankets and raise his tent among the Soran officers, as was befit his rank as adjutant for the Emissary of Castan. He hardly saw Audeyrn now, but he was still referred to as the Emissary's second. He saw Hearty Deri now and again, but the knight had been commanded by the Emissary to maintain the Soran discipline on the long marches.

She would be there too. It was always more secluded in that area of camp, and he was grateful for it, for his nights were all but quiet. He did not have candles, and the campfires were far away, so each evenfall they met in the dark. The tent rebuffed the moon and stars' silvery gaze, so they only had each other. Kisses soon replaced any awkward words, and soon he saw more clearly in the night, and he could see her too.

When the sun sank below the brown haze of the west, Mayred would ask him to help unbraid her hair. He was clumsy at first, but he managed to get enough practice on the days the column marched east to become surehanded, as deft with his fingers as he was firing his bow. Finally, when her hair fell free about her shoulders, she would slip out of that day's grimy garb. Only then did he see all of her. He liked the slimness of her body as she would creep over to him, and it wasn't long before he came to read the movements of lips and legs as though they had a language of their own, one that he was slowly coming to understand. The world bathed in the heady scent of her body, the smell of her hair, the pepper from the officer's supper, the wetness between her legs.

Mornings were no less exciting. Sure enough he would wake before her most of the time, allowing himself to look at her sleeping, her naked body entwined with his own. In those moments, he could take in the curve of her buttocks, and how it met her long, sinewy legs. His eyes wandered upward, to the face he loved so much. Her lips were parted ever so much to allow the slightest hint of teeth. Greg could not tell why, but that made him so happy. Then a hand had cupped a breast, the nipple hardening beneath his fingers. Mayred murmured something in Qellish. Perhaps she was dreaming of home. He kept brushing a thumb over the nipple, long enough until he heard a sleepy voice say his name.

"Have you been awake long, love?" The way she stretched reminded him of a cat. A lazy smile played on her tight lips, with eyes remaining only half-open. One of her hands went to play with his hair, twirling mousy brown locks between fingers. It had grown down to brush his shoulders now. One evening she had even asked if he wanted her to braid his hair in the Paydar fashion, and, in some fit of madness, he had said yes. When it was done, and he could feel the tightness of the twines on his head... she had snorted back laughter and left him to it. The attempts to undo her mischief left had him with nothing but a burning scalp, and he had spent the next few days on the long road garnering queer looks from the Sorans, who at this point had grown too tired and footsore to make comment or jape at the poor Caldishman's misfortunate hair.

The memory had caused a wide grin to spread across

Greg's face. The girl did not fail to notice. She did not miss much. "What makes you smile, eh? Care to say what makes you so happy?" He hesitated for all of a moment. Yet looking at her, he found the courage he never knew he had. When he told her, she kissed him, and then threw a leg over him.

Muddy trumpeted.

The tracker opened his eyes, scanning the glade as he watched his horse and Zorul pull at their tack. He reposed onto an elbow, and heard the soft scraping of steel as Mayred pulled her dagger free. "What? What did you hear?"

The horses were still secured to the dead tree, its exposed roots clawing desperately at the dry earth to reach the cool clear water of the brook not six feet away. Greg scanned the glade, suddenly anxious that Muddy had seen something, or caught the scent of an *yrt* that were said to prowl amongst the grasses. Whatever it was, it must have been spooked by the great firemane hobbled alongside the more timid Muddy. The only sound was the soft hubbub of the brook as it forced the low waters to traverse a string of upthrust rocks between the shouldering erratics. It was quiet... and it was too similar to that other time.

The time he was found.

Found by him.

Him.

It was too late.

He must have found him again. "He's... I hear *him*. He's... " A cruel laugh echoed inside his skull, and he felt cold clammy hands touch his face. He shivered. The face of the Reeve Arran was angled and pitted, as though the flesh had long ago sloughed and rotted, until nothing remained but his skull... and a pair of bloodshot eyes that stared at him in hunger. Yet the hands that extended out from the skull were still fleshy and flabby, the thin hairs clinging damply to the pallid skin. Fingers came, prodding, and he could not help but yield to them.

"Calm, Gregyn." Her voice was a balm to the burning inside his head. "*He* is not here. There's only us." The tracker forced himself to look at Mayred. The instant he drowned himself in those eyes, so dark and blue they may as well have been violet, the memories of that time scuttled off to that dark place again. There was only Mayred. "No one is going to hurt you now."

One last look around the glade affirmed her words for him. A slight wind blew the rushes that dotted the stream, a branch of the dead tree creaked as it swayed, and Muddy swatted at a fly with his tail. "Greg, give that to me." He could not say when he had freed his dirk, but it was there now. He stared at it, uncomfortably aware how tight he held it. He dropped it into her waiting hand, sitting up and hiding his abashed face in his hands.

The soft thud behind him told him that Mayred had stuck his dirk in the dirt. Then she embraced him. He tried to relax, yet try as he might, the tightness in his shoulders refused to ebb. "I thought maybe by now I wouldn't remember what happened. I thought if I made new memories, the old ones would fade and flake away, like old paint. It... It was like I was still there. In Mornswood. You must think I'm weak."

"*Weak*?" Her voice was filled with scorn, but he felt her hand touch his knee. "Is it a weakness to live carrying the weight of the past 'pon your shoulders? Even shoulders as high and broad as yours surely would buckle 'neath such pain, the weight of the past is heavier than hardiron, all agree." He wanted to agree with her too, but his words would not come.

"You aren't weak, sweet Gregyn. You are a fine eye with ya' bow, are loyal to ya friends. A tall and brown-eyed warrior who makes me laugh... with a nice arse too." He knew then that she was smiling. He loved her smiles. When he looked from his hands, he saw that he was right.

"So you may not fight in a suit of plate, or be able to sing without it sounding like a wyrm with its tail trapped in a door." He hated how she teased him for that. Now it was his turn to smile. Her hand went to his chest and stayed there. "But 'ya like some hero from a story. 'Pon a quest to stop the will of evil, slaying the villains in their dreadblack fortress, and saving those too helpless to save 'mselves. They will make songs about you, in days to come. Greg the Archer. The Bow of Castan. Gregyn of the High Forks, Hero of the Paydar."

Greg felt what worries he had melt away like shadows banished by the golden light of the day. The words were there, ready. "I love you."

Mayred's smile broadened until he could see her teeth. So close, he could see that they weren't as white as he had thought, and there was a hairline crack along one canine. He did not care. He liked the long aquiline nose, the sharp line of jaw and tiny ears ever-hiding behind the braids. It seemed like an eternity, but it couldn't have been more than an instant before she said, "I love you too."

Pulling her face in to kiss him, he felt her breath on his lips, her eyes closing as she made the slightest sigh. His crotch was tight, and he put a hand around her waist. Her tongue was busy, and he returned what she gave him. Somehow she had straddled him in their play. He loosened his breeches.

Her hand was there, as though she had read his thoughts. He could feel long fingers pull his cock free, hard and erect. It brushed the crotch of her own riding leathers, making her shudder. "Fuck. I need you." In his fervour, he all but ripped the laces of her pants. Kissing made freeing her legs difficult, but not impossible. When both feet were liberated, he tossed her leathers behind him. He heard Muddy whinny somewhere. "Muddy and Zorul are voyeurs, it seems." Mayred laughed, breathless and open-mouthed.

Wordless, Greg put himself inside her, finding her soaked. She moaned loudly. With both hands on her buttocks, he pushed himself deeper inside her. With her screaming his name, he was surprised that they didn't attract an *yrt* after all.

They left the brook for higher ground. Taking Muddy in hand, he followed Mayred as she led the firemane along a narrow sheepback that looked out over the Ikteti grasslands. They could have mounted up he knew, but Muddy was lathered, and he kept nipping at Greg's hand expecting an apple. His gaze was only for the woman a few feet ahead, watching the rhythmic sway of hip and the way her pants clung tightly to her legs. Then he nearly tripped up on a stone. He wanted to scold himself, but then Mayred was looking back at him, and what was before a grin full of guile and mischief was now almost shy.

It did not take them long to reach the top. The sun had been shining that morning, but as it reached its zenith a thin veil of cloud painted the sky the colour of ripe wheat.

He brought Muddy abreast to Zorul, and caught his rider's hand. Here the grasses must have feared the drop, for the last fifteen feet between grass and sky was only loose stone. *Not even dust, but hard stone.* The fall led down over a hundred feet of empty air before evening out in a scree slope, the *chejk* hazarding upward until giving up not a quarter of the way.

The grasses were dry. It had not rained for weeks, which he found unsettling. Had they been in the High Forks, the autumn rains would cause them to seek shelter for fear of getting drenched and catching a chill on the chest. *But this ain't the High Forks. This ain't even Castan.* The further they travelled east, the more the air became dusty, what scant warmth they had under the sun lacking any mugginess that was rampant back home at this time of year. Even the earth beneath their feet was dusty. The column itself boasted nearly eleven thousand, which on the long road became a snake four miles long, throwing up vast clouds of the stuff. Greg would often take a bath, when they chanced upon such a luxury, only for it to fall off his skin to muddy the bath waters.

It was easy to find where the column was encamped. Below the ridge, the land receded upon a steadily sinking shelf. The *chejk* lay strewn across the land like a petrified sea, the stalks usually the colour of rust now burnished a deep maroon beneath the midday cloud cover. "It is beautiful, isn't it." Her words made her grip his hand tighter.

He turned to face her, watching how her big eyes chased something across the grasses, the sharp nose, the tease of teeth between her lips. "Not as beautiful as you..." She punched his shoulder hard. "Don't think you can butter me up with words so easily, *hero*."

Greg laughed. Gods it felt good to laugh. "It seemed to work for ya' before. Looked as though it put ya' in the mood." She disentangled her fingers from his, crossing her arms to look him up and down. "What's to say I only like the feeling it gives me to fuck the Emissary's favourite banner-boy?"

"If you say so," They had done this dance before. He loved the way her caring eyes broke through the facade of teasing she wore. Had a girl said anything like that to him before, he would have reddened, his tongue knotted and immovable in his mouth, his lanky frame a string of gauche movements. But he had been months in the company of this vexing woman. Like drawing his bow, the quarry need only be found, the direction of movement anticipated, the arrow sent flying to the place he knew it had to be to strike home. The words were there in an instant. "And there I was thinkin' that I only wanted a trophy."

The look of disgust on her face told him his aim had been sure, her mouth wrinkled as she set her teeth. "I hate that. I'm no man's trophy." To make her statement a threat, she lighted upon her dagger.

"Really?" He made his face take on an exaggerated look of dissension and confusion, stepping forward. Muddy snorted, pulling at the reins hard, but Greg ignored it. "You hadn't made *that* clear to me."

Her reply was to straighten to her full height, which only brought her to his chin. "Must not have been listening to me, to think such rot."

"I've been listen'n all the time. I always listen." All the mischief vanished when he looked at her. He pulled her close. Mayred held onto his arms, narrowing her eyes.

"I jape. You know that. I don't. I mean, I want you to feel happy when ya' with me. And I hope you do. I love ya' teasin', I do. But I really think that I–"

"Greg?" Her voice had softened, inviting. Mayred's reins yanked backward as Zorul shifted his footing.

"Yeah?"

"Stop talking." He did as he was told. When they came together to kiss, her mouth opened. He was glad she had not told him to shut his mouth. That would have made it difficult. Muddy snorted now and again, but otherwise the land was silent. So silent that for once, they failed to hear that an army was camped below.

"Quite the view," said a woman's voice. It was far from loud, but in the quiet of the ridge it boomed like a thunderclap. Mayred broke away, a flash of steel and she had turned in the direction of the noise. Instinct made Greg reach for his bow, but it was slung over Muddy's rump and out of reach. He unsheathed his dirk and put on his bravest face.

Three figures had emerged from the grass, standing at the edge of the *chejk* as though they would vanish in an instant. The woman in the centre was tall, but still not as tall as Greg. The other two stood apart from her, and wore the shadows of smiles on their lips. The one nearest to Mayred was ascetic and runty, his dark features made even darker by a mop of thinning black curls. The other was a boy, no more than thirteen, yet more robust, and a head taller than his emaciated companion. The latter eyed Greg through slitted eyes. They all wore garb that he had seen before. Tightly fitted travel leathers, across shoulder and chest and hip pouch belts holding godsknow what. Their jerkins held no badge or ornament, and the clasps that fastened their thin cloaks were crude and practical. Yet he knew who they were. *Sorans.*

"We travel with Lyonis of Ves." Greg knew that the mere name of the Soran commander struck a queer chord with the captains, something between obeisance and dread. He had hoped that mentioning Lyonis would have disarmed these Sorans. The man was infamous, after all. Conquering heroes in Castan were known far and wide, surely his countrymen would know of the deeds of the commander?

"What did I tell you, Dreymon? That drawl of his reeks of Castan." It was the woman who had spoken. Her skin was darker than the others, her heart-shaped face dominated by a pair of eyes the colour of gold in the sun. Her wine-red hair was pulled back, and bound by a length of gold wire. When she smiled, dimples formed on her freckled cheeks. "So the mooncalf seeks to return home. The war is lost, then?"

"The war?" He had forgotten that these people were meant to be his enemies. He grabbed for some answer, something diplomatic he thought Aud would say. "There's a truce. Well, not a truce. But both sides have agreed to–"

"Not here, Greg. Shush." Mayred stood poised, her stance protective in front of Greg as though he were helpless. *Maybe I am, when put next to her.* "Who the fuck are you? Sorans, that's clear. Now state your business."

The woman with the golden eyes stepped forward, momentarily breaking eye contact to pick up a handful of stones. Strolling to the cliff face, she began to throw them in high arcs. "My manners are atrocious, I can only apologise."

A finger pointed from a fistful of stones. "You are called Greg?" He remained silent, but she nodded as though he had agreed. "We have travelled to find Lyonis of Ves. News of a war column upon the long road travels fast. It reached the graceful ears of our beloved queen the moment you stepped foot in Iktet. We are here to escort His Excellency home."

Mayred gave a derisive snort at that. "So, who are *you*?"

The woman threw the final stone, and then crossed her arms. "These handsome bastards before you are two of the greatest alumni of the Garrison." The ascetic man and the boy both chuckled. "I present Dreymon the Pauper and Little Lyster, both of Silentis. As for me, I am Cliada. Now if you would be so kind, take us to this *Lord Emissary*."

Even with all her smiles and affable demeanour, Greg had his doubts about this. But they had no choice. For all he knew, this Soran and her friends could have been assassins sent by Darge Pirellion from the Soran-held Halfway. Lyonis had stressed the importance in leaving Wolfsmouth as soon as possible, before Pirellion could catch on to the fact that his rival was escaping the Paydar, and out of his grasp.

Greg looked over his shoulder, where Cliada sauntered through the ranks of dishevelled tents while biting into a peach. He kept telling himself that it was ridiculous: how could an assassin possibly harm Aud, when he was surrounded by all his allies?

Allies. The word sat on his tongue in a knot. They had chosen their camp for the night at the seat of the local Ikteti tribe, the Yed, their chieftain's seat no more than a roundhouse surrounded by an earthen dyke. That was far too small to accommodate their vast numbers, so now they sprawled around them like a flood.

More knives. At least they're the ones that're outnumbered. Mayred had put away her dagger now, but she remained tense, her gaze fixated. He could see her set jaw and how she kept clenching her fists. *She feels it too.* The realisation hit him then, and the ache in his arm and the pain in his chest returned from his old wounds. *It's the Caldish who're outnumbered, idiot.*

Lyonis chose to command the sortie from a large pavilion of undyed canvas, a parting gift from the Lady of Brinewater. It was white, or what passed as white after weeks of travail on the long road. Greg knew that the idea was that the colour, or lack thereof, would herald them as nonpartisans, who offered no harm as they went about their way. That was the hope, anyway. The tracker did not know if many would respect the laws of chivalry when there was plunder to be had. Not even the army itself.

The hanged men were evidence to that. At the bottom of the rise, three nooses bearing their grisly fruit. The latest that had tried to take their pleasure with Ikteti women. The Sorans had started to call Aud the *Ropemaker* because of it. The rapes had ended after that.

The ropemaker himself was nowhere to be seen. Outside the large tent flaps, a large barrel-chested man sat before a table with food on a large platter, a young Paydar boy sitting across from him reading a book. A healthy distance from them stood the two Merbeasts that had been assigned to protect Aud. They always wore their helms, and would only free themselves of the ghastly visages in their own company. The one with the Sea-dog shot Greg with a death stare as he approached.

"What do you have there, Greg?" The old knight said it as though he had brought a string of strays back to camp. *Guess I have.* Hearty sat cutting into the leg of a halcyon, looking the Sorans up and down while sawing through the tender meat, the way he did it soon making it crumble onto the plate.

Cliada tossed the peach's stone to the dust. "You're the knight, then?"

"Sir Deramun to you. Sir Deramun of the House Montrose. I fought you and yours at the Battle of Kande's Mire."

"Really? I don't believe we've ever met." Her voice was mocking, and she rubbed her jaw in a mummery of thought, "Besides, the Mire was twelve years ago. Hard battle, from what I was taught. Hard won too, many heroes perished. Merhyr the Singing Lance sang his final song that day."

"Aye, the good souls on our side, mayhaps. Lad, go get some food."

"I…" Jephro looked to the Sorans and then the knight. "Yes, lord." Greg hoped the apology written on his face made the boy feel less ashamed about being told to leave.

Hearty exploded when Jephro was out of earshot. "Can't say the devils on yours are worth mourning over. Merhyr the Butcher we call him. I spit on his memory. What would *you* know of heroes? Lanyer Harte the Silver Sword, Sir Noyon Hardress… that poor bastard."

Cliada traipsed over to the table, to look down on the seated man. "I will not apologise for the happenings of war. It seems to me, however, that devils owe no fealty to king or creed, for you lot had a goodly many on your side. Ever wonder what happened to Sandygate when it was sacked?

Did you see Red Ridge after the ambush? How the Castanni treated the women, the children?"

"Enough!" Hearty stood up so quickly he knocked over his chair, and then, with a backhand, he swatted the table away to fly and crash to splinters. Greg had to take a step back from the mere ferocity, Hearty's face turning a deep red, and like that his huge broadsword was in his hands. With the table gone, there was nothing between him and the woman. She stood motionless, having not moved an inch during the whole thing. Her companions looked on with indolent stances. But Greg saw the intensity of their gazes.

The sound of steel singing from sheathes caused him to turn. "This is the commander's lodging. You can take your quarrel elsewhere. I warn you this once." It was the Merbeast with the hammerhead helm that spoke. The Seadog was beside him, both of their sea-green cloaks billowing behind them as they moved to protect the entrance to the pavilion.

Before Greg could do anything, Cliada was moving. Hearty looked on as the woman advanced, only for her to turn on the ball of one foot, planting it square before the Merbeasts. "And I did not come to bandy words with senescent oafs and fish-faced lackeys. I come as the emissary of the Queen Salphyre of Sora, Guardian of Silentis, master of the sands. This land belongs to the crown, so I command *you* to come. You claim to have Captain-General Lyonis of Ves in your company. Bring him forth then, and prove on your precious Castanni honour that he is safe. I will treat with Audeyrn Langholm, or no one." The sun was busying itself in setting behind her, the shadow it

449

cast was overlarge and menacing, and it spread visibly on the road-worn canvas of the command tent. "Do you fear me, as you fear the purifying light of day? Step forth, I say! Where is Lyonis of Ves?"

And then Aud appeared, coated in shade and fatigue. His jerkin was plain and loose-fitting, and the sword he wore at his hip knocking gently against his thigh. Greg wanted desperately to explain the situation, to help stop anything bad from happening. But the Emissary had his *look*, the one he wore when he was angry. His eyes glinted hot and ashen-bright from sockets ringed red from lack of sleep. Greg swallowed, expecting the worst.

"Lyonis is hunting, fellow emissary." He sounded pained, as though it hurt to talk. "In Castan, we usually announce our arrival with fanfare, so that the host has time to arrange a proper reception. This row is unseemly, especially for one with your training."

Cliada grinned. "You know who I am?"

"No. Rather, I know what you are. A prodigy of the Garrison, I assume by guesswork alone. Aside from that, your get-up and whole demeanour marks you as an emissary of that guild. I know you are well-equipped to murder me where I stand, even with my guards."

"*Guards* is too generous by half. They should wear frog helms like the toadies they are." The Merbeasts exchanged a quick glance at one another. Aud crossed his arms, stifling a smile. "Witty, yet uncalled for. Tell me, how could I hope to hold Lyonis captive within his own army?"

Cliada scoffed. "I don't. I wanted to provoke you into leaving your shell, my lord hermit crab."

The Merbeasts bristled. Greg heard Mayred curse under

her breath. *Dhereda*. Hearty adjusted his footing, grumbling. The air was still on the pavilion's rise, and those nearest in the officer's barracks stopped to watch the farce unfolding. The tracker could hear the thumping of his heart. Then it was Aud's turn to laugh.

"It worked, I have left my shell, so here I am. The arms of House Langholm have been a proud oak crowned by a hawk for about five hundred years... but perhaps a hermit crab works better. I have been oft indisposed in the pavilion overseeing the grand sortie, arranging for your queen's army to return home safe." The ease in which he talked made Hearty drop his sword all of one inch. Then the Emissary was patting the Merbeasts on the shoulder, telling them to stand down. Cliada did not move, with a look that dared anyone to challenge her.

Only when the Merbeasts moved away, eyeing the Sorans with righteous anger, did Aud turn to face the woman. He shielded his raw eyes from the dying light.

"Then your mission is ended. Iktet is a client state to the Kingdom of Sora. You can scurry back to Castan now."

"I was advised not to tarry too long in this country by Lyonis himself. The people here mistrust him, for good reason. Besides, my mission requires me to travel to Silentis itself. Shall we discuss this further inside?"

"Not until the Captain-General returns from his hunt." Her tone laid her thoughts bare. Greg knew what it meant. *She wants to see Lyonis herself, to see if Aud's lying.* If the Emissary was perturbed, he hid it beneath his full smile.

"Very well then, We shall have our talk in the sunset. The rest of you may leave us." He moved forward, his long legs carrying him until he came within a foot of Cliada. Then he started. It was like he caught himself from falling, his head jerking backwards and his eyes flashing in confusion. No, it was shock.

It was then that Greg found his tongue. "Aud? I mean... Lord Emissary? Are you okay?" The stranger that looked back at him said, "I need a drink of water. Come. *Now*."

He had turned, already back at the tent flaps, and was beckoning Hearty to join him. Some strange urge made Greg look at Cliada, who looked enthused by everything she had just seen. She raised an eyebrow, the mere act feeling extremely deadly to him. "Run along. Your master wants you at heel."

He's not my master, he wanted to spit out, but his words deserted him as her golden eyes held him mute.

Ripping himself away, he raced to the pavilion, holding his hand up to Mayred, who was busy shooting venomous looks at the Sorans.

What candles that had not yet guttered out within the tent cast a low and wilting light. A hundred or so maps littered the tables and floor. Audeyrn stood amidst the chaos.

"It's her," The Emissary was erratic, his hair suddenly undone, his hands pressed to his temples.

"Who? The woman?" Hearty had planted his sword in a gorgeously illustrated map of the Upper Paydar. "She comes to provoke us all. Dangerous, and not just with words. Who is she?"

Audeyrn did not speak. For a time, the only sound was Hearty's heavy breathing. Greg had time to think. Time to say what the Emissary was too afraid to even utter. It seemed so obvious to him now. It was uncanny how similar she looked to how he had described her. But it was her.

"It's the girl, from his dreams."

30

MARBLE

The tavern was dank and dingy. More of a waystation for weary travellers with no other options.. More run-down than the last place Marble had taken refuge for a couple of days, but the closer she journeyed to Halfway, the more establishments she was forced to frequent. All its patrons bone-tired, and stinking. This was not a cheerful tavern where people would laugh and dance with plentiful booze and hopeful friends.. This tavern, while clean and decent enough, was quiet. The clatter of cups and low grunts of monosyllabic words replaced the rowdy merriment that one would expect.

Marble's scarf was secure, her face obscured, she occupied a table in a dimlit corner opposing the staircases next to the bar. They led up to the night rooms and down to the cellars.

The place was only half full, but as the evening wore on, more and more people packed into the room. The cold, brisk winter night air that accompanied them through the doorway suffusing into the stifling heat of the increasingly crowded area. The quiet hum that had been a constant gradually rose in volume, like a wave. Rising and falling, and unpredictable.

During one such lull, the door opened again, heralding the arrival of a contingent of dusty-cloaked Headhunters, boisterous and clearly already well into their cups. *Shit.* She made a conscious effort not to slink further down in her seat, lest the movement draw attention. Three men and two women stumbled forwards to the bartop. A variety of expressions crossed the faces of the patrons and danced in their eyes as they watched the group.

The tallest of the men, hair cropped close, with broad shoulders and a cocky swagger on him, slapped his hand down against the countertop, demanding the attention of the young serving wench stationed behind it. "Five strong ales and five shots of something good and proper, if you please!" He ordered loudly. His companions tittered and pushed in close as the young woman jumped to his request.

They had an oblivious air about them, ignoring all the attention they drew. Well, that was how they appeared at any rate, and she was happy for them to draw all the eyes to them instead of her.

She removed the scarf from her face as she slid from the booth. Though the style was less commonly worn closer to the border, she was not the only woman in residence using it that night. Small conversations picked up throughout the room. Marble did not recognise the company of five Sorans, but she was cautious all the same. She had lost much weight on her travels, and it was unlikely that she would be recognised unless she either kept her whole face hidden or revealed her hair. The closer she got, the more confident she became. The smaller man did not quite look Soran, despite his overcloak being of typical Silentene make. The other four were quite authentically drunk. *He* appeared very sober.

Bright green eyes flashed in candlelight, the strong line of jaw somewhat hidden by the mass of breadblack curls. She saw the faded scar over the bridge of his nose. He wore a black gambeson with silver fastenings under the cloak. *You don't belong here. I wonder...*

The serving woman gave them their drinks before pretending to notice someone else. The big Soran handed them to his companions, the rounder of the two women stumbling and snorting as she moved forward to collect her cup. Her cheeks were ruddy, her eyes glassy. Marble saw the restive eyes red eyes, the way the *nhere* made her movements jaunty. The other woman, with dark hair and skin and eyes, gazed adoringly at a large plough hand at a table. Smitten, and very young for a Headhunter. The man with the scar on his nose said something to the tall Soran, and he laughed. *You're their fool, and their leader.* A puzzle. He didn't fit in the picture they were attempting to paint.

Marble danced through the room, weaving and gliding, like a ghost, a shadow. No one took note of her passing. She would observe, and learn. She would do what she did best. With the introduction of this rambunctious quintet into the previously subdued place, the once dowdy mien gracing it transformed. From somewhere, someone counted out a beat.

It was time to dance.

Marble caught the eye of the leader. She let him see her.

Could she do this? She was unsure, but she let it continue.

Her pulse quickened, but she did not look away. She did not break eye contact. A body passed between them, severing the connection. Marble flitted away, ghost once more, outrunning his searching gaze. He looked, she knew. She hovered just on the edge of vision. It was the chase. Her blood thrummed. What had she been sent to do? She could not remember, did not *want* to remember. It was all about the game. He searched, green eyes drifting. He was only paying the slightest bit of attention to his companions. He was smiling, this sphinx masquerading as a Soran. She knew. It was just them.

The charlatan and the ghost.

Music sounded and space cleared, the inn all at once becoming a living thing. A conscience that ebbed and flowed, on the verge of something big. The energy intensified, growing and growing, almost overflowing with sudden exuberance. It was all a part of the game. The chase. A song was sung in Soran, a song these people knew well.

Strike now! You lads wantin' blood for gold
Strike now! Die young 'fore ever growing old
Strike now! We've time 'til the end of days
Strike now! Dance for the moon and sun's rays

Those piercing eyes caught her again, green fire ever-vigilant. When he smirked, his eyes narrowed, and his plush lips twitched. She spun away once more. He was wonderfully, temptingly dangerous. *Oh, this is going to be fun.* People took to dance, the four Sorans to start, and then others. Her sphinx disappeared to the dark corners of the room. The hunter and the prey, both on the move. On the prowl. Marble wondered who was the hunter and who was the prey. The air of desperation and tension flowed, unyielding and unending. She was both hunter and prey, and she had a game to play.

> Like the shifting sands I cannot stay
> You know that I must ride away
> Sooner than later all of this must end
> But until the dawn you'll be my godsend

The music was life, and it seemed as though the world was only this dinghy place at the edge of the world. *Alive!* Thump. *Thump, thump thump.* The drum beat pulsed through the place and invaded her body. Her heart danced and matched the heavy thrum. She searched. She hid. She hunted.

She used the shadows. She used the light. She stole sips of unattended drinks. She sweated and she lived. The music invaded her. Consumed her. She let it. She invited it. She drowned in it. She drifted to toher dancers. No longer caring who was hunter and who was prey. She was consumed by the evening, feeling, and freedom. She could do this forever.

> Strike now! You lads wantin' blood for gold
> Strike now! Die young 'fore ever growing old
> Strike now! We've time 'til the end of days
> Strike now! Dance for the Moon and Sun's rays

"You're mine." A smooth, deep gravel brushed her ear, just

as strong arms and large capable hands encircled her waist. He breathed her in as she did the same to him. They danced together. She reached up to wrap her arms around his nape, her face turned away. His sharp jaw found refuge in her exposed neck. Their hearts beat in time with the music. Their hips moved together, they *knew* each other.

> Drink to my love. I know she hears me
> The memories we shared now lost to sea
> In the darkness, I see her there
> The comin' sunlight only a blindin' glare

Together they danced the night away. The crowd pressed in close. It was heady and all-consuming. Speaking without words, they held each other close. The night wore on, all grew intoxicated and intolerable. But still, they played.

> Strike now! You lads wantin' blood for gold
> Strike now! Die young 'fore growing old
> Strike now! We've time 'til the end of days
> Strike now! Dance for the moon and sun's rays

They drifted together. Through the throngs of the crowded tavern. He led and she followed, until they made it outside. The fresh, cold air was exhilarating. Hard bricks dug into her back as their lips clashed in battle. They breathed in each other. They consumed each other. Broken jagged souls.

> Tell me now, or don' tell at all
> Keep me safe while we brave the dawn

459

> I will show you, show you, show you
> Love enough to see our loves through

The commotion of others stumbling out of the tavern broke them apart. It was the Sorans. The real ones. They fell into each other but sobered quickly when they saw Marble's face. "Well, well, *well*."

It was the youngest one that had found her confidence. "What 'ave we here?" She tittered. The others took a while longer to understand, and they all in turn bore selfsame scowls.

"The traitor, so far from home." She did not move, the heady feeling of the night deserting her until she felt hollow. She felt weak. She wasn't a traitor. She had to make them see! The queen, the general, they told her. They told her! They–

Something made her look at the man before her. She saw a curl hiding an eye. He nodded. That was all it took. The emptiness within her was filled by something else, something angry. He stepped back, and whistles a jaunty tune. Marble turned, swaggering to meet the jejune Headhunter. She was going to enjoy this. Then a door opened.

Drunk villagers poured out like a sea of flesh and beer and firewater. Music came with them, a new song that Marble was familiar with. A song she let fill her.

> Crashing Qellmen came on grayback,
> bearing witching blades on high.
> Foemen from the Sundered Peak,
> with them flowed a bloody tide.

460

> The Dread One led them there,
> the nearing victory tasting sweet.
> A spell he spoke from noisome teeth,
> and the Sorans dead 'pon their feet.

The stripling Headhunter was on the floor, wondering how she got there. The others daren't involve themselves. They bowed their heads in deference, and gathered up their loudmouth friend.

She was of the Garrison. She was a warrior, and she would not allow anything to take this night from her. She dragged the Soran who was not a Soran away. She was his, and he was hers. Predator. Prey. Her blood sang. Up the stairs and down the corridor, through the door. It slammed closed, and Marble slammed the him against it. Hard.

They had each other. They had tonight before they were alone, drifting, surviving, with their coldhearted duties. They kissed and kissed and kissed, the song was muffled by the walls and the boards, but she knew the words.

> Alynor, our Alynor,
> lofty gods saw his plight,
> A thunder cry and a will of steel,
> that was when they joined the fight.
> A thunder cry and a will of steel,
> that was when they joined the fight.

He was strong beneath her questing hands, just as she was pliant under his. Her hands were fisted in his hair. Steering his head and his lips down, down her jaw for them to feast on her exposed neck. He licked and sucked and bit and

461

kissed away the sting.

It was everything, the world collapsing until it contained only the two of them. She could feel his length, trapped between them, hard and waiting. The emissary dragged his mouth back to hers and swallowed his growl as she ground against him. A moan escaped her as he pressed in close. Close but not close enough. His fastening ripped violently as she tore at them.

When that was free, she threw it somewhere behind him, to gaze at his muscles rippling invitingly. He unwound the wrap that bound the breasts, and they fell heavy into his waiting palms. His thumbs played on her buds, and their mouths clashed once more as she used her strength to vault them away from the wall.

They separated briefly to rid themselves of their remaining cumbersome garb. But only briefly. He lifted the emissary, fingers digging deliciously into cheeks. She moaned. He growled. There was no stopping or catching the wordless exclamations that escaped from deep within the emissary's body upon her release. Swallowing them up, their tongues battled as she worked through her release. Marble reached down and squeezed its considerable girth punishingly. She had not been expecting the climax. He grunted at the brutal grip, a mix between pain and pleasure. He bit down on the nipple in retaliation. *Ungh*.

Making their way through the room, he hefted her onto the vanity table, spread her thighs wide, and dove down to feast on her centre. She needed him. Needed him. Needed *him*. There was nothing else that mattered. No thrones or kingdoms, no Garrison and no war and no one else. The heat emanated over her and through her.

Music kept playing, but she ignored it.

31

AUDEYRN

His nights were dreamless. A feeble, tired glimmering that traced its way through the veil of darkness, defining itself slowly. It was a long time before he was able to discern the shape properly. An extended muzzle, with flews drawn back in a cold hard grimace. Two pricked ears and two empty eyes aware of the drowsing emissary in his cot, suspended and lifeless and metal. The head talked to him from across the room.

"My Lord Emissary? It is the fifth hour. You said–"

"I know what I said." His voice was hoarse and strained. Winter was nearly here, and he hated being woken by others. He longed for the once quiet long road, where his only companions had been his friends, and he was not responsible for negotiating safe passage for an army, let alone a mass of war-wearied Sorans.

Soon. Ves is not far.

The sea-dog's polished helm shone wanly in the brazier light of his quarters. It was a tent unto itself, a spacious room where the walls were undied canvas and the floor a

464

menagerie of pelts from a dozen or more creatures, many of which he could not name. In one corner his bath tub sat empty, in another, a looking glass and wash basin, next to the armour rack sporting his Paydar suit of plate. The lion cresting the helm, fashioned in the likeness of the winged lion of Castan, looked more like it was yawning than roaring. The sea-dog's head at the entrance seemed disembodied, as though it was stuffed and mounted. The thought of so many beasts keeping him company caused him to laugh.

"My lord? What is it?" Within the hollow eye slits of the Merbeast's helm, eyes peered out fever bright, the only sign that what lay beneath was living.

"Nothing. Go and rouse your brother. The day begins."

No dreams had plagued him since *she* had arrived. He had thought that meant he would sleep better, to wake up fresh, able to gain some new resolve in dealing with the pestilential Sorans. He slept, and woke, and he was still tired. His body begged him to close his eyes, to return to the blissful nothingness, for the limbless embrace of slumber. Rubbing the crust from his eyes, he braced himself for what came next.

The moment he threw the blankets free, cold air stung his skin, goose flesh rising to cover his naked body. Looking at the brazier, he cursed it for giving off more light than heat. The fog of sleep had begun to recede, allowing for his thoughts to return, albeit too slow for the emissary's liking. Very soon, the usual burdens reacquainted themselves at the forefront of his mind. *The fucking Sorans. Lyonis and his perfidious pride. The pox-ridden Garrison sending these thrice-damned incendiaries to treat with me. That... woman.*

He scowled and spat into the brazier when he found that he was apprehensive to even voice her name in thought. The coals were white, the remaining glow still lighting up his little refuge enough to allow him to make himself presentable. They hissed in response to his rancour. *Say her name, gods be damned. What harm could that do? Her name. Cliada. Cliada. Cliada.* He grabbed his breeches from the neat pile on the cotside table left by Jephro. The lad was diligent, and had a healthy sense of awe for the Royal Emissary.

He dressed and washed his face in the basin, the icy water helping to defeat the last vestiges of sleep. The lad was a mystery. He seemed intelligent, loyal to a fault, shy, and timorous. He could not understand why Gregyn had been so spooked by the kid. Of late, however, the tracker seemed to have grown friendly to the young Rowett. *Ever since his recovery from the Bluff*, he had to remind himself. Ever since Greg had fallen nose over arse for his Paydar girl.

The rigours of coordinating the Soran withdrawel had allowed him no time with the tall tracker from the High Forks. Hearty had embraced his role as Quartermaster well enough, so he saw the doddering Deramun often at council. Audeyrn would chastise himself daily for equating Hearty to Greg. Despite all that he had been through, Greg was still little more than a boy. On the rare occasions he would organise the Commander's counsels in the open, when the weather permitted, or when the whim took him, he would often see Greg and his Paydar girl ride away from the column having adventures and making the most of their time together. He did not begrudge them that. Jephro was always somehow at his elbow with flagon in hand when

466

that happened, his painted brow furrowed in longing. He knew the feeling all too well. When his father would leave the safety of the family castle at Langholm to be the king's Emissary, Audeyrn would watch from the battlements, with only Hearty or the master-at-arms Sir Clay Costigan to pat him on the back and assure him that his father would return.

"I shan't hold you captive long, lad. It will just be like any other day. I will relieve you at midday, have no fear," he assured him. Greg had been uncomfortable having a squire, he had guessed as soon after they took their leave of Lady Adrianne. There had been a promise, and Audeyrn was keen to be done with Torrins and their aspirations.

He had focused on the boy. The least Aud could do was help. The young Rowett would be better used as cupbearer and squire to the Lord Emissary himself. It was a safe position, one that demanded respect from the common soldiery and even from the Soran officers. With him, he could watch and learn diplomacy, and return to his scheming family better off than he had left it. Hearty had even helped in bringing the Rowett out of his shell, overseeing drills at quintain and commending him on his swordsmanship.

He was cupbearer the day before, when they had met with the Chieftain of the Yed, called Iza. That had gone on longer than he had anticipated, and Aud hated the unforeseen. The old man was merely an elder, but his people revered him with the blind obedience nominally owed to a king. He had droned endlessly about border disputes with neighbouring clans, and the tax for the Soran army using their land as a marching camp. The sun was low in the sky by the time the Chieftain and his grandsons said their farewells to the party, all grinning, with handfuls of Torrin silver. Lyonis had suffered throughout it all: enduring hours of insults to his face. When they were free from the blathering clansman, he had loudly declared that he was going to hunt to clear his head. The emissary did not put up any fight. He had come to expect the wild mercurial moods of the Captain-General: going hunting seemed anodyne by comparison. He wondered how Walt Iddles had managed to treat with such a man.

Hearty had declared that the day must be saved by a hard sparring session and a good meal. The poor Jephro had been nodding near the end, no doubt the fleeting idea of having some fun that day withering as his arms burned from the weight of the wine flagon. Aud had done his best to make amends. He had pressed into his hands a book, the words along the spine reading *Conquests: A Century of Castan Crowns.* It was penned by the historian and adventurer Elwood Hardanger, a collection of blood-soaked histories of the seven Red Kings of Castan, which Aud had never seen collated, let alone in its original form. It was rare, perhaps the only one of its kind, given to him from the personal library of Lady Torrin. A study of the brutal kings in the eponymous Century of Conquest, incidentally all of them had failed to gain a foothold across the Pinch and into the Paydar. He saw her message instantly.

The boy had taken to it like a drik to water. The book, along with a further apology in the form of teaching him how to wield a longbow, Jephro had been insistent. "I can show you, but I am a poor teacher compared to Gregyn. He might not seem the sort, but he is something of a legend where I come from."

The boy nodded and blurted out, "Greg is good. More than good. I saw him take down a squirrel in a tree from two hundred yards away. I asked him once. I did. But he must have forgot, because he didn't teach me. Mayred teaches him everything, but he doesn't teach me."

I can only wonder what Mayred teaches him. "Ask him when he returns to camp. I'll order him to do it myself if he says no." Jephro giggled. His face lit up as they went for supper.

It had been a good day. Some six hundred pieces of heavy silver coin poorer, but that was a small price to pay for ensuring peace. The tribe before, a people called the Dlan, had only demanded two hundred pieces. Despite what Lyonis could say about the avarice of the Yed, Audeyrn could only sympathise with the clansmen. Not an hour after he ordered the column to camp for the night at the Yed enclosure, four Soran scouts had shirked their duty and stolen young Ikteti girls from their homes. They had been discovered by none other than Hearty, who happened to pass by their cook-fire and heard the girls begging as the scouts used them. It was Hearty, too, that deposited the beaten and bloody scouts before Aud's feet, who begged for mercy between sets of shattered teeth.

Iza was there with the fathers, who were rightly outraged, demanding the men marry their daughters, pay blood money, or be gelded. When Hearty pointed out to the chieftain that rape under Castan law did not constitute blood money, the old man laughed and spat at the knight's feet to show him what he thought of that.

And Hearty wondered why the Emissary looked tired.

That trouble was as resolved as well as it could ever

be. Hangings for those that did not accept the offers of marriage. Those that accepted marriage could no longer call themselves Soran, or so Iza told Aud. They were husbandmen now, and any trouble was dealt with harshly by the tribal elders. Each day the column grew ever smaller, and he had to accept that this would only cause more desertions, crimes, and hangings. One thing they did not lack for was hempen rope. He was the Ropemaker now, whether he liked it or not.

They are almost home, retreating, and a Caldishman orders their commander to hang their friends. Who can blame them for hating me?

It had to end. He wished he had a magic lamp he could rub, to summon the spirit that resided within and command it to stop the war. The thing from the lamp would have to obey him. The story always said so. As if sensing his unease, the box appeared in the periphery of his vision.

Liaising with the Captain-General and his underlings had helped in forgetting about his message to the queen. The message he had to deliver for Isembard.

Deliver this message to that bitch of Silentis, and when you return, I will grant you a boon of me. The king's words rang through his mind like a death rattle, kneeling before the king that stood before the Tourmaline Throne to receive his blessing for the journey ahead. He had kissed the royal fingers, and then Ismebard had said those words. Each one leaving the slightest brush of air on his ear, the breath that smelled like a fruit gone to rot.

The mission...

It was getting lighter in the pavilion. He could see the chest clearly now. The plain old thing moved for no one but demanded that all and sundry come to it instead. The single keyhole was a dark and empty eye socket, allowing only the tiniest of whisperings to leach out, struggling to squeeze through. He wanted to laugh for allowing himself to imagine such fanciful things.

Then it became louder. Only for an instant, but he heard the voice. It was warped and indecipherable, almost like listening to a conch shell to hear the ocean. The harder he tried to listen, the harder it became to understand the words. *What if I...* It sounded familiar.

If he reached out with his thoughts... he could make out words, distinct and lamenting. He had to remember to breathe. It was talking to him.

"Readying yourself for battle?" Came the voice from behind. The Emissary spun, his hand instinctively going to his hip. His eyes glanced at the rangy figure standing dignified and dark against the threshold, the Yales on his blade glittered in dance. He had not heard him enter his chambers.

How long have I been standing here?

"I, too, prepare myself for the day at hand. Those from the Garrison can be... vexing. They do try their best to be diplomatic, bless them." Lyonis wore his hair unbound today, and it looked coiffed and teased around his head like the mane of a Druke cat. He had to look presentable for his queen's emissary. His career depended on it.

"No. I was stretching. Featherbeds make my back ache." It was on Aud's lips before he even had to think about it. The commander looked bemused, seeing through the lie instantly. "Habit of traversing the long road, then. Hard cots and sodden ground must appeal to you more." Lyonis

471

did not move a muscle, yet his eyes moved indolently over to the box and remained there, his smile hooking higher.

"Can you not toy with me?"

"Me? Toy with *you*?" Lyonis took on an expression of hurt, even placing a hard callused hand over his heart. "We are brothers-in-arms, you and I. What would I ever hope to gain from playing you the fool?" Aud was about to tell the Yale that they were not brothers-in-arms, the Pit their only shared battlefield. Even then, they had been on opposing sides. It had been months now, but Aud was certain the fight burned as avidly in the Soran's memory as it did his own. It was said merely to rile him, so he caught his tongue and weighed his response.

Gods give me strength. "Enough of the shit. What are you doing in my chambers? Tell me, or get the fuck out."

Lyonis straightened, the same glib bemusement replaced the hurt in an instant. "My lady Cliada commands your elan presence for breakfast. I believe she has the cooks hunting high and low for some honeycombs. She seems to be in a sweet mood this morning."

"She *commands* me? For breakfast?"

The Soran pretended to ponder that. "Yes. That's what she said. Truly, I recall her saying, 'Lovely Lyo, go and command the Ropemaker that as representatives of our respective gold-hatted monarchs, we must dunk our toast soldiers in our eggs together.' As ambassador-designate, her authority derives from the queen herself. I suggest you best listen to the summons. Just be thankful I am the messenger and that Cliada refrained from using men with spears to escort you. Your companions, however, are being visited by the Lady Emissary's little friends as we speak. Some would

AUDEYRN

say having me run the message was a sign of respect."

"Don't flatter yourself."

The smirk crept wider, Lyonis visibly struggling to contain himself. "It gets worse. The Lady Emissary has ordered you to make the preparations yourself, and to make the command tent ready. Oh, and to find a new table. It seems some oaf broke the last one."

What the Emissary wants, the Emissary shall have.

His father had said that. Coram had been sardonic at the time, having just returned to the island fastness of Langholm from the disastrous summit to resolve the Steppe Crisis. Now it took on new meaning with Audeyrn. One in the form of a dream come true. *No. A nightmare made real.*

Pondering what his dreams meant, he left Lyonis and his simpering grin to find Hearty. He naturally heard him before he saw him, and told him what he had to do. They would be having breakfast within the central chamber of the pavilion usually reserved for counsel. Then he had Jephro check up on the cooks to ensure all was ready. The Merbeasts he found where he had left them, solemn and dutiful and very resentful at their current lot. He had them find Greg and his paramour, wherever they were. He knew he must tread carefully with this Cliada. She spoke with the Soran Queen's voice, and to balk at such would be tantamount to slapping the royal cheek itself. He weighed his options, and even returned to his chambers to check on the box. It was there. Untouched. Conceited. Ordinary. Begging to be opened.

He undressed and washed his face in the basin. Jephro had refilled it with fresh cold water, and it trickled down his bare chest and onto the fur rug at his feet. The urge to wear his Paydar plate was all too tempting to see Cliada's face as he turned up to break his fast in full battle readiness. *That would only give her cause to complain.* Instead, he chose a pair of undecorated breeches dyed a deep green, along with a black leather jerkin and white undershirt he had brought all the way from Langholm. He was not one for jewellery, and would only wear a signet on court days in Castan. The only adornment he allowed himself was the cloak. Black as night, it was meant to be worn along with the plate, a heavy woollen cape that would keep the chill off him. He had told the Paydar seamstress that it was traditional for the Royal Emissary of Castan to wear a garment of fine black silk, and she had done any Caldish tailor proud. Embroidered in gold thread was a lion rampant, his wings spread wide. He swept it about him, a true cloak, long and covering both shoulders. Glad for the warmth, he made to leave. But as he touched the canvas, his mind went to his other cloak, the one he kept safe and clean at the bottom of his pack. The one he had brought from home. *This* one was a half cape, a samite as blue as the summer sky over the Azure Coast. An elaborate oak dominated the cloth in fine thread, crowned by an eagle in flight. It was too tempting.

The sounds of the camp were muffled to a degree and a troupe of crickets provided the only music from some-where. Hearty had offered to play his lute, but Aud did not know if marching songs would make a good impression, especially marching songs performed by the Quartermaster. The Captain-General sought not to appear until after the preparations were complete. He appeared now, the first to sit at the new table hastily positioned at the room's centre, a round slab of mahogany that measured twenty feet across.

The high-backed officer's chairs were encroached on all sides, each sporting ample cushioning on the seats. *Can't be having her whinge of an achy arse.* Then to his surprise, the next to arrive had been Greg. He marched to his chair to the immediate left of Aud with his usual hangdog shambling walk, accompanied hand-in-hand by the fair Paydar girl. As they took their seats, Aud made a mental note to ask him to tutor Jephro.

It was the Sorans who came next. Not Cliada and her diminutive escort, but the high officers of the army. The hammerhead Merbeast stood holding the tent flap open, for the officers considered it remiss that they should push it aside themselves. *The usual farce. Behold! The grand council.* As benefitting his title as the Lord of Ves and the fact that he was the Captain-General's uncle, Ziander of Ves came first, strutting like a man who had never known defeat. He was a coward and a liar if his nephew could be believed. His tanned skin was leathery and wrinkled, that which showed through his bristly eyebrows anyway. Upon a long brocade was a Yale regardant, not as fanciful as those used by his nephew. He took his spot beside Lyonis, but not before bowing profusely in deference to Aud. At his heels was Lord Torquil Ashand, a large and indomitable man who was always seen in scale armour and held a punctilious attitude to the current chain of command. He, too, bowed to Aud and even tugged at a forelock. It had been Ashand who had given him dark looks when he had met with Lyonis near Wolfsmouth. Lord and Lady Eldhyr followed, a pair who could not have been more different. Both in their fifties, where the husband was shrivelled, officious and petulant, his high collar concealing a wobbling chicken neck, his wife was handsome, her dark hair tied and streaked with grey, examining all those in attendance with restless eyes. She proved to be tactful and ruthless in counsel, often overruling her so-called lord with little more than a sharp look. When it was their turn to pay respect, Lord Eldhyr grasped Aud's hand between his own, then proceeded to plant a sloppy kiss on his fingers before he could pull away. His wife was more graceful, making a curt nod and corralling her lord to their seats. Finally the Lord Ejim came limping, having been allowed to leave the barrack's gaol, the bruises given to him by Lyonis replaced by the shame of having lost favour. He made the smartest bow, not too long and just deep enough, a desperate ploy to enter into Aud's good graces. Not that that would do anything.

When they were all seated, a few chattering pleasantries were exchanged, nothing above the low snapping of the canvas now and again from an errant gust of late autumn wind. And then, as the counsel awaited the arrival of the Lady Emissary, Ziander of Ves cleared his throat. The chair creaked as he stood.

"My lord Audeyrn, might I be the very first of our illustrious company to say how fresh you look this morn, and that handsome cloak!" His whiskers moved with an alacrity contrasting his otherwise ponderous tone, his wine-stained lips moving like two wyrms rutting. He gestured lazily to Lyonis. "I cannot contain my excitement like my nephew, to know that our adventure is almost at its end, to find sanctuary in our beautiful Ves with plunder secured, the majority of our men sound of body, and for this wasteful war to finally come to a close." He paused as though he awaited applause. It did not come. "I wanted to wait until we reached the Enamel Gates to say this, but... oh godsbedamned! I wish to present the Lord Emissary with the most august honour in my power to bestow upon a hero of the Veslands."

From inside his brocade, he produced a medallion hanging upon a fine chain of silver yale's heads, the horns of each wrapping around those of its sister on either side, all clinking softly. The medallion itself was angular and embossed, the glyph of the family of Ves carved from amethyst, bordered by tiny purple sapphires, all within a solid silver frame. "With this medallion, I make our esteemed Lord Audeyrn a Paragon of Ves!" He looked very satisfied with himself and with a smile which looked all too forced.

The air was heavy in hard silence, all eyes descending on the emissary, waiting for his response. "Thank you, Ziander, but I must decline. The war is not yet done, and it would be unseemly for me to accept honours for deeds undone."

The Merbeast opened the tent-flap once more.

"I would hope that you are giving gifts to all of us, Ziander, or I will be cross for being left out." The blowhard spun on the spot, the medallion dropping unceremoniously to the table with a *thump*. The others rose as one as Cliada took her seat. Audeyrn remained seated as long as possible, rising last and longest. The woman was clad in a long flowing dress the colour of honey, the hem and collar and sleeves decorated extensively with Soran glyphs, all of the interweaving symbols indistinguishable to Aud. Over which, she wore a mantle made from the pelt of a Druke lion, its maw open and hungry upon one slender shoulder, its eyes replaced by fire garnets. *Is that meant to be a threat, Cliada of the Garrison?* When he looked from her mantle to her face, he saw the quiet amusement play across eyes made dark by the small light of the pavilion, the gold turning to amber. Her hair was down, the locks on her temples carefully curled until they coiled around her ears. Her companions from the Garrison were elsewhere, so she made her way to the seat next to Aud alone. Only when she was seated and comfortable did she say, "Sit, all of you."

Breakfast arrived a moment later, to Aud's surprise. Stewards brought in porritch and toast soldiers, bowls of fresh berries and sliced red and green apple, three dozen poached eggs, strips of back bacon, black pudding, black sausages, placed a large platter in the centre, itself piled high with honeycombs dripping with thick honey, six roast ducks on smaller plates arranged around it, and a few dozen halcyon to top it off.

The food did not survive very long. Soon, the glorious quiet of those engrossed in eating was broken by incessant gabbing by the officers. Audeyrn had forced himself to eat an egg and some fruit, desperate to distract himself from Cliada. Thankfully, she did not try to start conversation. Then the stewards returned, clearing the table and depositing six decanters of wine on the table. They all drank from crystal goblets as they washed down their breakfast. Aud wondered what the soldiers would think once they discovered how they had dined that morning. What they would do.

It fell to him to open the counsel, so he wasted no time in beginning the discussions. It was formal, but he had expected that. He had not allowed any of the counsellors to cozen him during their meetings, despite Ziander's honeyed words and Lord Eldhyr's incessant arsekissing. So what was discussed took on the usual air he had pressed on them early. Only Lyonis chose to rebel and smirk at each passing remark, but that was only to be expected. Aud soon turned his attention to Cliada, despite his best efforts. The Lady Emissary to the Soran Queen had neglected to say anything about Aud reluctantly standing for her, and he was expecting that she would confront him over it. But she instead greeted the lords and ladies courteously and began with the first item of business. She had come to the chamber wearing some exotic scent, musky yet light on the nose, smelling of a flower he could not name. Once, he had dared to look at her hands, both palms set on the table in a sign of authority. Her hands bore countless scars, criss-crossing fingers and knuckles, and her nails were chipped. He looked up at her face and saw that she was looking at him too. What he saw there was the woman from his dreams, watching him now as though he were about to steal her coin purse. Feeling that he had to challenge her arrogance, he looked at her with his burning gaze, making his eyes caust and shimmer, resisting the urge to blink or look away.

Then, as he was about to turn his gaze, she removed one hand from the table. She yawned and covered her mouth with her hand. But he saw the thumb in her mouth, the way it stayed there, the way her eyes caught his again. He wanted her.

The long road brought the army to Ves two days later. Ziander had never failed to mention the fabled Enamel Gates each time they were in session, and now that they finally approached, the Emissary could only watch in muted awe.

They fronted a town that had grown up around the walls of Ves proper, the townspeople managing to erect three-storied houses and brothels and guilds, yet even so they were few and far between, and dwarfed when looking at the Gates. The dusty road led to a pair of ornate bronze doors thirty feet high. The memory of passing through the Mountain Gate of Rowett's Town came to mind, but where those had been hardiron and brutal in their making, here the Vesmen had opted for displays of gallantry, strangely interspersed by scenes of lovemaking. All were outlined and framed by bronze, but the colours and forms were all huge panes of enamel that shone brightly in the sunlight, a plenitude of colour against the brown sandy ground. They opened, and the images fell out of sight, but not before Aud saw one figure in the display stand out. One who looked eerily similar to Lyonis. *A relative, then. Some celebrated ancestor, conqueror, lord, scion of the Veslands.*

There were tapestries in his family's stronghold that did the same, illustrating the storied bloodline of the Langholms and their long history. He had been taught all of it, of course. He could still remember wielding a wooden sword while he gazed up at the men of his house. Lyal Langholm, the fabled founder of the Langholm line, who had first captured and killed the Fay King, taking his holdout of Langholm island as his own seat. His sons took the title of king thereafter, and soon held dominion over the seven islands that made up what would be called the Western Isles. King Royd Langholm, called Red Royd, had made a habit of luring lesser lords into being his emissaries, knowing full well the missions were thwarted with peril. King Kendall the fourth, called the Kind, was the son of Royd and would relinquish his crown to the Tourmaline Throne of Castan when his father was killed in the Battle for the Sunset Straits. He would be the first to hold the title of Royal Emissary, the first to run at the beck and call of the King of Castan. Asterion the Tall, Kendall the Hawk, Audeyrn the Elder, Audeyrn the Younger, Audeyrn the Coward, Aymer the Swift, Asterion Boatsbane (who had always had a ship sunk under him when aboard), the warrior called Rhos the Ruthless. Those that followed in the next five hundred years were good and bad, versatile and inept, men from the House of Langholm were duty-bound to uphold their ancient tradition of carrying out the King's most valuable communication. A punishment, at first. It was King Lucan the Magnificent who had killed the Red Royd, a forebear of King Isembard. He had impressed upon Kendall that it was to be his children's responsibility to make right the wrongs of his house. Forever more the males of Langholm were to serve, not rule. The women however, they would rule the estates and household even if they were not a Langholm by blood. Had she survived, Aud's mother would be on Langholm now, overseeing the accounts and presiding over cases brought for the lord's judgement. But she was dead, the Langholm line reduced to Auderyrn himself and a second-cousin: a boy called Keir Costigan. The role of castellan had fallen to Sir Clay Costigan, after his wife Trista Langholm perished from a bloody fit. He wondered how they fared.

....when you return, I will grant you a boon of me.

He rode at the head of the column. To his right, Cliada sat

high in her saddle, wearing her travel leathers once more, over which she had a shawl of celeste silk wound across her chest and over a shoulder. On his left rode Lyonis and his uncle, chatting amicably to any passersby that shot them a question. The language had shifted again, for here they spoke the Soran tongue. The Ikteti dialects were seldom spoken here. Even the few Ikteti marketmen that chose to trade in the castleton neglected to mouth a word of their mother tongue. The noblemen were well-known, and well-loved, judging from the way the peasants bowed their heads. Ves lay beyond the gates, and more people afoot recognised the Vesmen and hailed them. *They love Lyonis. His uncle, however...*

Ziander had forgotten about Cliada and her disregard for his gift-giving, it would seem. The medallion had vanished, too. Whether reclaimed by him or taken by someone else, Auderyn did not know. The uncle thought he could hide his feelings better than the nephew, but the emissary saw the malice in the dark eyes beneath the exuberant brows. He wanted to tell Cliada about the man and ask her what the Lord of Ves was like beneath the pomposity. Lyonis had told him enough, but all his words came well-salted. He could not trust him, not fully anyway. The thought of having a more trustworthy response from Cliada made him smile.

"Does Ves make you smile so?" The voice came from his right. When he looked at her, he found it hard to look away.

"I was just… remembering."

"A woman?" Her smile made dimples in her cheeks, and her eyes shone a molten gold. "She must be indeed special to make your mind wander when your mission's end draws so close. Perhaps you can tell me her name?"

"Perhaps not," he said, forcing himself to set his jaw. Hard pounding hooves drew up alongside Aud's blindside, a full laugh bellowing out as Hearty tightened his grip on the reins. The cracking of his knuckles made his mount whinny. Cliada leant back in her saddle then. Her only answer was to wind a rogue lock of burnished hair around one finger, and to say, "How gallant of you, Sir Hearty. There I was thinking your sort protected fair maidens, yet all I've had from our resident knight is scorn and threats to violence."

"I protect the Royal Emissary, *my lady*."

"What a chore that must be. Surely, you would rather be drinking with the men?"

"*Enough!*" Aud's shout was enough to draw all the eyes in the cobbled street, from those making their way through the press, to Lyonis, who turned in his seat to watch with a look of amusement.

"Hearty, quiet. She only seeks to provoke an argument. Lady Emissary, with the utmost respect, I would rather we made our progress on the long road peacefully, without cause for complaint. It is in your best interest."

She cocked an eyebrow, white teeth shining through dark lips. "Is it now?"

"Yes–"

He was about to explain when a sudden row broke out among the loose crowd ahead. Audeyrn's hand went to his sword and was about to call Hearty when two hooded figures detached themselves from the chaos, dragging between them a bloodied man in dun-coloured robes the type a wandering godman or journeyman might wear. As they approached, the hooded men revealed themselves.

One was balding, and the other young. *Dreymon and Lyster, Cliada's escort.* Throwing their hostage before Cliada, the older one, Dreymon, said, "Found him skirting the castleton, Cliada. He had a poisoned knife on him, a trope most like."

The Lady Emissary regarded the failed assassin briefly, then turned to face Audeyrn. Her smile remained.

"Seems that you're more interesting than you look, Langholm." She scowled when the two Vesmen approached, Ziander fumbling for words. She answered for him. "Ves is not the haven you would have us believe, my lord. No. Going forward, we are going to do things *my* way."

Aud did not like that, not at all. His thoughts suddenly turned to Greg, and Jephro, and all those that had been put into his care. "And what is that," he heard himself ask.

Her freckled smile was all for him, sending a dagger of fear into his heart.

"Thank the gods you asked. You're going to see the *true* Sora. We're going into the desert."

32

MARBLE

The emissary lurked along the edges of the encampment. She had to leave, soon. If she had known that Darge Pirellion held it, she would not have tasked herself with the trek to get there. There was no way she could cross the bridge with that nincompoop controlling and barring the way. She would have to travel and journey down the river. She was annoyed, and she shunned the bridge. It was idiocy to cross a random stretch of the Wolfswater. If she could find a less violent channel and attempt the the swim...

Fuck.

She held still, her breathing silent, her blood quiet as the Soran scouts passed close by. She did not draw attention, waiting patiently until their rustling movements were distant memories. She had to leave. The emissary picked her way carefully, beyond the sight and the reaches of the encampment and more determinedly, ever onwards. No time to waste. She hugged the edges and the banks of the Wolfswater.

For days, she travelled and journeyed and grew ever wearier. Making temporary camp each night and continuing on each day, until several days later, she halted and chose. The water was cold and suffocating and vicious. But the emissary had no choice. This was her best option. The *only* option. She could not afford to waste more time scouting the river. She would drift too far off course, and the battle was bound to be more dangerous. It was now or never, or admit defeat. She may be broken, but she was *not* a quitter.

She would cross, here. And she *would* make it to the other side. She did not know in what condition she would emerge. Her body would be battered when she clambered out and emerged on the other side. But she would get there, and it would not be the last thing she would do. This is where she would cross. The banks were steep and fraught with debris as she picked her way down the slopes to the water's edge. It frothed around her and lapped at her feet. Hungry, desperate.

It was a long stretch across, eight hundred feet at least. It would be a... struggle. Huge, sharp rocks littered the route across, heavy logs and downed trees bobbed on the surface, the river propelling them, hurtling them downstream at deadly speed. Racing, ready to skewer unsuspecting victims. Marble breathed deeply. The sharp cold air stung her lungs and fog reminded her that if she made it at all, she would likely be freezing. Tempting fate, and death. Nothing that she hadn't chanced before, however. She rested once more, waiting for the sun to reach its peak. She finished her rations.

Even weighed down by her clothes and weapons, she would persevere. She would survive. She would make it.

The emissary prepared herself as the fiery thing in the sky neared its zenith. She jogged on the spot, breathed deeply, stretched and meditated, choosing the eddies she would aim for on her reckless race and battle against the mighty river. *Inhale, exhale.* In and out. Full body shake. *Ready.* As she would ever be. Marble took one more note of the position of the sun in the sky, the eddies she would fight to reach, and the distant back, mocking her, calling to her from the other side of the ravenous, waiting rapids.

She dove in. The temperature of the biting 'water was icy at best, glacial at worst. Bonechilling. Breathtaking. Marble forced her heart rate to steady, her breathing to even and continue despite the burning pain racking her being. She forced her arms to stroke, her legs to kick, and her body to move forward. She fought against the current, and battled towards the first chosen reprieve.

When she looked back and compared it to the distance she had yet to travel, it was punitive and pitiful. *Inhale, exhale.* In and out. Marble took one more note of the position of the sun in the sky. And so it continued. The light waned, the water and the air grew colder. The Emissary's body drained itself, and still, she had a ways yet to go. Next eddie, and the next, and the next. She fought, and she battled, and she swam. Her clothes dragged her down, her weapons.

On the next pass, something like an old fishing net captured her leg. *Shit.* She was dragged down below. *Fuck.* Impact with a rock forced the air from her lungs, winding her, forcing in a lungful of water. Marble struggled not to breathe in, even as her body fought to inhale.

She had to make it to the surface. She had to escape the

net. She got more and more tangled the harder she fought to free herself. She bumped into more and more rocks. More and more trees hurtled towards her. The cold was invasive and numbing and drained what energy she had left. She was battered and bruised… and lost. Dark spots invaded her vision, her limbs felt heavy and useless and pained. The net dragged her to the riverbed. She hit hard, scraped along the rough floor, banged into another rock. Pinned.

Darkness and pain and cold, and nothing. *NO!* This would not be it. This would not be the end. Her lungs and body screamed in agony. It was a blur, a dream, a nightmare, but she surfaced somehow. She coughed, sputtering, struggling to stay afloat, to breathe despite the pins of ice spreading through her body. She floated atop a wide heavy log. She was shivering. She was cold. She was saved. Vaguely the emissary recalled being lugged out of the cold waters, and she was on solid land once more. Shivering, teeth chattering, ever so cold. Then nothing.

She awoke. Something was wrong.

Marble crept, slowly, surely, into the darkness of the night. Her hair was once again covered, bright hue certain to draw unwanted attention. She was but a shadow. Creeping confidently, movements sure and precise, the emissary left her saviours' camp undetected. Into the woods, silently leaping over fallen logs and avoiding the twisting roots and gnarled undergrowth.

Onwards the emissary continued, gloomy night giving way to shy, misty day. The light hardly improved at all.

Only stopping for short respites to find water and relieve herself, she never dallied for long. As she wandered, day turned to night once more, again, the change barely noticeable. Still, the emissary did not stop. Sometime in the night, after travelling down a wooded trail a fair distance, the emissary finally decided to listen to her fatigued body's demand for at least a short sleep and settled into a rude shelter beneath some elms.

A snap jolted her awake, deafening among the silence of the wood. It was a solitary sound, and it soon fell into silence. Following her instincts, the emissary crept along the tree line, not stepping out onto the wide open road, moving cautiously but hurriedly. Barely daring to breathe lest she miss something. No matter how far she walked, the feeling she was being followed did not abate.

Approaching noon the next day, Marble fought instinct and emerged onto the quiet, empty path picking up her pace considerably. She breathed a sigh of relief, and walked on.

The snare was too fast for her. *Fuck.* She could do nothing to prevent her falling forwards to the ground. She landed hard on her hands, the rough path scraping at her palms, biting into her flesh. Rolling onto her back, she unsheathed two of the small knives from her chest harness. She sent one flying back in the direction of the snare's origin. As she pushed herself to sit, figures began to emerge from the trees, surrounding her at a distance. *They didn't take my knives. Why didn't they...*

Quickly, Marble cut the snare away from around her ankles. In one fluid motion, she sent the other knife slicing through the air as she spun to standing, cutting down a shadow and rearming herself with a vicious dagger in her right and another throwing knife in her left.

They could have been anything from brigands to zealot godmen to mercen to just desperate or cruel folk. At that moment, there was no telling. The only thing she knew was that they wanted her.

She counted. Eight standing. Coming closer. Marble stood in the middle of the road, waiting. Watching. She put the dagger away for the time being, and replaced it with a knife. One more glance, assessing. She released both weapons as she moved forward into the trees once more. Six. They converged. Dagger back in hand as the first figure reached her, the emissary stretched around the truck she took cover behind, slashing. Thump. Distracted with number five, the next one crept up on her, managing to slice the emissary's shoulder. Marble spun again before they could get in another cheap, easy shot. Into the eye, he fell heavily onto her, forcing her back out of the woods. Four left.

Another quick glance. There were *more* of them. She hoped to the gods she could outlast them. She set her jaw.

The group of screaming men in front of her charged, sloppily, from the road. Weapons high in the air, leaving themselves exposed. She charged back at them. Careful steps. Precise movements. A slice here, a slice there. She could feel her pace lagging, her energy waning.

She didn't know how long this battle had been going on. But she wasn't the only one struggling. She could see some of her enemies moving sluggishly. Becoming disoriented. The emissary vaguely registered the collapse of men every now and then, but still, the number of foes she faced did not seem to dwindle. She needed to end this. *Now.* She moved towards the men that had been felled with knives still in them. Make them bleed, and wear them out. Crouching to retrieve her weapons where and when she could, releasing them into other men. Standing men, now fallen like their comrades. Again. Again. Again. Tired.

Too close.

She leapt at the figure that was gaining ground on her. Knees sandwiched between their chests, both knives finding home in his throat, momentum sent them towards the ground, forcing the two figures behind him to split to either side. She sliced at their ankles. They fell. Sliding left, her dagger dispatched the man, and she twisted to face another attacker. He swiped. She swiped. He landed a blow. The dagger flew away. Knife found home under his chin as she lunged upwards, then away.

Fuck. Four more. Heavily armed. They knew what they were about. The emissary started up her charge once more.

Another snare shot from somewhere, capturing one foot, tripping her. A knee slammed against the hard ground. The emissary could feel the crunch as it struck, the bone cracking under the force. She gritted her teeth, refusing to let the cry of pain break free, even as tears sprang from her eyes. She pushed to both feet again, trying to dismiss the agony that infused her body. She needed to vomit.

Her adversaries closed in. Caging her. More tears streamed, more blood poured. Ever closer, they came. No Matter. Closer, closer still. *Now.*

Marble struck out. She attacked one of the four armoured shadows. They blocked and parried but did not retaliate.

The emissary rolled onto all fours, spat out a wad of blood and dizzily tried to rise. Something pushed her, and she was beaten down again. Armoured fists raining down, no longer content with playing and toying with their troublesome prey. Another hit, another punch, another slap of metal. And another and another and another. Then they began to kick.

Her vision grew weak and hazy. Spots dotted her sight. But still. She saw him. And she knew as the deep oblivion called to her, that this was not the end, nor the worst pain she would endure at these men's filthy hands.

His heavily booted feet approached as the beating slowed to a reprieve.

There was a long blade in his hands. When he spun it, it cut through the air to make a sleek keening. He asked her a question, and she had to strain to listen. Blood and sweat obscured her vision, but she could make out the sound of mail and laughter of cruel men. When he heard, she saw the leather apron. It was covered in blood old and new.

A pale face,talking in a foreign tongue. He knelt, all too close, and a hand lightly brushed her chin. She shuddered away, as best she could. "You seem like a very clever girl," He said. "I can tell." He took a moment. Looking deep into her eyes, just enough to make her see the darkness.

"Do you want to know my name?"

33

GREGYN

The desert sorrel's movements were sure and steady as she crested the dune. Her rider wore airy Soran shawls to keep the day's heat at bay, not that it helped in any way. With the back of one hand he wiped a sheet of sweat from his brow. For that brief moment he was able to look high into a cloudless azure sky, a slight reprieve from the merciless and unceasing sunlight. The white glare had now sunk low into the west to throw long shadows across the ripples in the sands, like the rakings of some huge clawed beast basking in the heat.

Greg's mind went to the six-fingered hand. The blood-red sigil that marked the unblooded of the noble house of the Paydar. The boy Jephro had been left in Ves, at the command of Audeyrn. He had not cried, for being abandoned so far into the journey. He only looked Greg in the eye and made him promise that he would teach him archery when they returned from the desert. The tracker had grown fond of the young Paydar, but just then, with Aud off talking low to Lyonis and Cliada watching him close,

Greg felt a cold finger wind its way down his back. Each crimson finger of the hand on that brow looked pointed as though belonging to a harridan. He found that he could not meet the boy's gaze. Nor could he deny his request.

Up ahead, Dreymon was nothing more than a scant pinpoint as he moved through the tumbledown ruins of the ancient roundtower. It had long collapsed, the leaning walls that remained giving some shelter from the perils of the desert. A sudden upthrust of craggy red rock had been used as the base of the fortification, now littered by the shattered stones that baked and cracked from a thousand years of sweltering sun, leaving only one story remaining of the former watchtower. There was no roof, and the ring of uneven blocks that lined the parapets made it a jagged crown.

The Soran stopped and was lost to sight among the stones for a second. Greg only noticed him again after he lifted something, to glitter in their eyes.

"He says it's safe." Cliada wore a face veil, but her eyes could still be seen somewhat through the silk. A pair of golden coins, unknowable and dangerous. "We'll stay here."

Her words were a balm to him, the peeling skin of his neck and ears feeling better already. The day had been hot and still, the breeze having weakened until it died completely. The air was heavy, and breathing had become a chore. Looking to his side, he saw Mayred sitting low in her saddle, her cloak draped about her face, so that all he could see were the few strands of hair that stole out. He could hear her licking her lips. It was a feeling they all had come to know very well. After a day of traversing the empty desert, the mouth was left as rough as sand, and their lips would crack and blister. *Gods, I hope there's a well...*

They must have been listening, for as they climbed the ridge and fell under the dreadblack shadow of the tower proper, Greg saw Dreymon saunter over to them with cups of cool drink. Not the longhorn milk the Sorans usually guzzled as they travelled. The milk was made from a creature native to their lands, which Little Lyster had tried to explain to him as best he could. Greg still wasn't quite sure what the longhorn was. When he had asked if it was something like a goat, Lyster had only rolled his eyes. Whatever the thing was, it was bred purely to produce an oily grey liquid lactate that Sorans drank when they ventured into the desert and the Desolate Tundra, the dreaded sun-scorched lands that encircled the kingdom's western reaches. The milk did not evaporate in the sun, could be kept for years if sealed away, and was the worst thing Greg had ever tasted. All things considered, he was elated to see the liquid Dreymon carried was transparent, and cold besides. It was crisp, clear water. When he finished the cup offered to him, he looked for more. Dreymon gave a smile.

"Thirsty work. The pump is inside Meadwater, if you're wanting more. *Eleyri*, here, drink some." Mayred took the cup offered to her without a word. Only when she was finished, and water ran down her chin and down her neck, did she say, "I told you not to call me that. I am not a *lady*. I am a warrior of the Paydar."

"Without a doubt, I did not mean to cause offence, truly. If you will excuse me, I must see that a fire is made." Dreymon had crow's feet at the corners of his eyes, and his whole face wrinkled when he smiled. He disappeared as he ducked beneath an arched doorway. The door long rotted and turned to dust.

"Dreymon is a good man. He was merely being friendly." Cliada was there, her approach as silent as ever. Peeling the veil from her head, she let her damp hair fall across her face. "He is fond of this place, is all. It might seem a dreadful ruin, but once, it was the seat of the Watch, the stalwart protectors who guarded Sora from the fury of the Qell. It is a true desert flower."

A bitter laugh followed the sound of iron-shod hooves on the crumbling flagstones. Audeyrn led his mount across the yard on foot, stroking her neck as he approached the Soran emissary. "Does the Garrison make history scholars of all its agents? I was told you focused on more martial studies." Under one arm was the chest.

Cliada gave a derisive snort. "History teaches us the most valuable lessons. Warfare is merely a facet of the whole. You would do well to learn."

"Truth be told, I am fascinated by your people's history. Perhaps you can regale us over the campfire with the tale of the Watch?"

Her smile was as playful as a cat and as venomous as a yappor. "There I was thinking you prefer the tales our Halfwit Hearty tells. The more colourful, the better. I'm surprised you don't ask for pictures too."

"You're lucky Hearty didn't hear that."

"Am I now?" Cliada took a long drink and emptied the rest over her face, giving a long sigh. She said something Greg did not understand in the tongue of Sora, then handed her mount's reins over to Little Lyster. "Look after your horse, Langholm." She left to climb the low curtain wall that still stood in parts around the mount.

"*Hmm.* Greg, will you see that Hearty hasn't collapsed? Oh, and bring him water. He's like to dry up and shrivel otherwise. Wouldn't that be a sight?"

He and Mayred found the knight at the bottom of the escarpment leading to what once upon a time had been the gatehouse. Over his gambeson, he wore the desert cloak he had acquired in Ves, and still wore a studded jerkin. His face was red, the sweat running down his face in streams to make his hair stick limply to his forehead, making him look like an armoured tomato. His chest was heaving, making his portly frame even more round. "Ah! Lad! Take the horse and mule, will you? I need to crawl into some shade 'fore I fucking die. Fucking Sorans, leading us to this hellsmouth. Fuck. And to think, I was cursing the gods each time they drowned us in the blackwood. What I'd give for a good ol' thunder storm. Pelting rain. Downpours to make you chill to the bones and leave you shivering. *Cold.* Fuck these Sorans, *and* their desert."

Mayred cleaned her fingernails with the point of her knife. "There aren't any Sorans *here*. They're busying themselves preparing your supper. Take off the armour and maybe you can reach the top still standing." She handed him the tin cup, the contents of which Hearty downed in all but an instant. "This desert is full of peril, girl. You *just don't see it.*"

Greg led the horse up the old road. The mule was tethered to the warhorse, burdened with the knight's armour and weapons and gear. He was sure the poor creature gave him a pleading look as they went. "Scorpions. Red scorpions. Black scorpions. Great Claws. Razor Claws. The Stinging

497

Death. Doubled-ridged Stingers. Crabbed scorpion. Cave scorpions. Not to mention the Yappors. You have never seen them, but I have. They hide in the sands, safe from the worst of the day's heat. They feel vibrations. The tiniest of movements. You can be out in the sands, happy as can be, none the wiser about them scurrying hither and thither. Then, just as you feel safe, and drop your breeches to piss, they jump right out, maddened by the presence of so much water in your blood. Heard some tales that their stingers can be as long as a spear. You just don't *know*." One hand he rested on his pommel, the other on any likely hold of the stones around them he could find to support himself. When the castellation hid the sun, the knight undid his gorget a mite to let some air cool his chest. As though on command, the big man's stomach groaned loudly.

"What'll it be tonight, I wonder? Copperhead steaks? A string of scrawny desert mice? You could always find something worth the eating on the long road, Greg. When you hunted, the game never tasted of sand."

"I don't know these lands." *These Sorans are good trackers.* "We never go without."

"Aye, that's true. I know I whinge, but I hunger for something familiar, that's all. Not food, no, but something that I can relate to these Sorans. I've killed so many of them I've lost count. Could be hundreds at this point. No doubt they are the same, if what they say about the Garrison is true. But they're fighters, like me. They fight for their kingdom, like me. Thousands of leagues apart, and at war with one another no less. It is hard for me to trust them, knowing that my friends have died by their hands."

Mayred tossed her knife in the air. "That was years ago.

Cliada didn't kill your friends." She caught it blade-first, then swung it again.

"How can you be so sure? I can't. I want to be their friend. I *must*, if Aud's to end this fucking war. He'll end it, but it will be us who'll have to live in the peace that follows. I am afraid of knowing, now that I think on it. To ask, and to receive the answer you did not want to hear. It'll be to rip open a wound after it's been sutured, to let it fester elsewhile it may have healed. How can I forgive, knowing how they mutilated my friends? Knowing that the sins of the past will go unpunished, instead now commanded to forget. Rage comes red and ready to those seeking blood, and many will find that forgetfulness is a hard skill to master, for a warrior's memory is long and unforgiving. Many will do anything to avenge those they've lost."

Mayred caught the knife one final time and sheathed it. Greg wet his lips. "What will *you* do, Hearty?"

The knight was looking off towards the sunset, so Greg could not see his face. *Is he longing for Castan? For the Azure Coast and the Western Isles? Or is it for someone?* When he did not answer, Greg told himself he must not have heard the question.

Supper that night was a spotted snake. Dreymon had caught it, and it was he who turned the spit as it roasted over the campfire. Beside it, a stew was boiling in a black iron cauldron. Lyster was busying himself grinding herbs in a stone mortar, which he sprinkled over the glistening meat as it turned. Greg had been busy feeding the horses, and as he neared, he saw all the eyes fall on him. Mayred gave him a broad grin and moved over to allow Greg to sit on the woven mat decorated with Yales at their play, another gift from Lyonis of Ves. Hearty returned his gaze to the food, and Greg saw how he still wore his gambeson and jerkin. He had misplaced his cloak someplace. Cliada herself sat nearest the fire, turning a green glass bottle over in hand to watch the flames play across the vessel's surface. The fire was life out here. As soon as the sun sank below the western sands, a chill would descend on the dune seas, a cold that threatened to kill if you could not make a flame. If not by the cold itself, then by the things that made the night's sands their home.

Aud wore a woollen cloak similar to the ones worn by the Sorans. "How do they fare?" The Emissary asked. The firelight shadowed his already sharp features, yet despite the harsh light, it seemed to Greg he looked different, the tightness around his eyes now gone. He kept freshly shaven these days too.

"Well. Aye. An armoured badger spooked them, so it took a whiles for them to settle. They're good now. The only one who seems exhausted is the mule." Zorul had to stop to rest several times a day, but the powerful firemane had soldiered on, even if he did not enjoy the stifling heat. Muddy had struggled from the start. He had been lathered a half day of slow riding into their first day and by day's end, had collapsed, throwing Greg from his saddle. They had stopped then and there, Greg staying with him all night hoping his presence would calm the loving rouncey. In the morning, he was struggling to even breathe. He did not get back up. The sorrel he rode now had been Aud's, given to him from the private stables of the House of Ves itself. He had been bred a pedigree that could trace his lineage supposedly to the hero horse of the famous Vesman called Alynor the Godschosen, who had brought the wroth of the gods down on the army of the Qellish commander Eldred Deathsmouth. In what would become known as the Field of Fury, the once verdant earth of the battlefield burned so hot it turned to glass. The rest turned to sand, and since that day the Desolate Tundra presented an all but impassable expanse for those seeking to invade Sora from the west. In that battle, Alynor survived, along with his horse, returning to Silentis a triumphant hero. But Greg did not care about that. The sorrel was sweet-tempered and had a silky gait as she trotted the sands, but she was not Muddy. How could he forget about his friend? The others had been sympathetic, and Mayred had tried to help by telling him that Muddy was suffering no longer, but… he just wanted his friend back. It still hurt to think about Nat's desertion. Now with Muddy's death, Greg's heart ached almost all the time.

Cliada told him about his new mount's fabled grandsire after they had left the body behind, unburied atop a dunehead. The tears had dried upon his cheeks as the others told them they would catch up. It did not take them long to butcher the horse. Good meat was hard to come by in the desert.

"All is well, then. Dreymon. Is it ready?" Cliada smiled at each in turn. When she shook the bottle, the other Sorans choked back laughter. The meat was stringy, but there was enough of it so each could taste it. When nothing remained of the snake but bones and skin, Lyster began to break and crush them, producing the mortar and grinding them into a fine dust. As he worked away, Dreymon ladled out a stew in tin cups. It was snake mixed in with cloves and *hrizh*, a root vegetable that flourished on the morning dew in the wastes. Greg cleaned his cup, mopping up the bottom with some hard bread.

When the last of the supper had been cleared, Cliada leant forward, the light of the fire playing freely across the comely face, the eyes burning a terrifying molten gold. Only when she saw that she had everyone's attention did she speak. "Meadwater is a sacred place to us. Once, it was a fortress. Haven of the Sun, my ancestors named it. Here is the place that stood an oasis of hope for generations in this sea of dry death. A beacon that stood despite the pummelling of the long years of sandstorms. Here it was whence Commander Harud Fyfe blew the Horn of Strife to warn the Garrison that Lord Math Fadyen planned to rebel against the queen. For the time after the fall of the menace to the north, new and opportunistic foes struck forth to claim the empty lands left by the Qellishmen. Alynor, for his valiance, was married to a princess of the city, making him king in all but name. He made it his responsibility to ensure the western reaches of the kingdom were secure in perpetuity. So the Haven was built 'pon this outstand of stone. His reasons for choosing this place were two-fold. The first was to make it a place of respite for those daring enough to brave the sands. The second..." Greg could see that she was looking at Aud now and smiling all the while. "Alynor sought to strike fear into the hearts of his countrymen's enemies. He had seen with his own eyes the desolation wrought on Eldred and his armies on the Field of Fury, and he did not wish to see something of its like to ever happen again... especially should an enemy manage to worm their way to the gates of Silentis itself. So here he erected a tower that stood a hundred feet higher than the clouds. However, sparse clouds appear here. With the Garrison, he built the hidden road. For he needed a sure way to deliver his fuel to the Haven. To fuel his beaconfire. Atop the tower, a brazier twice the size of a female yappor was placed within wood doused in oil from leviathans of the eastern sea. 'Forever they shall see my fire,' he was heard to have said as he beheld the completed work of the Haven. 'They shall see how bright and far it burns, to ever be reminded the fate that befalls any and all that seek to cross my lands without due leave.' He also installed a tax office to collect duties from the travellers that arrived here, somewhere hereabouts anyway, to pay for his folly. But I doubt you're interested in ancient Soran taxation. His Haven stood sentinel of the sands for fifty-three years before the first challenger came to test their strength against its walls."

She had broken off her watching Aud to send a sideways look to Mayred. Beside him, Greg felt the Paydar girl's shoulders tense. "It was a Yarryn Rowett who trudged his braided levies across the sands after soundly defeating Lord Elyas of Ves and burning his town and raping his womanfolk. Yarryn, who would later become known to all and sundry as King Yarryn Yes-And-No." Mayred exhaled loudly, but said nothing. *What's the Soran's game? She's like to have a blade through her heart before the night is out.*

"This king had promised his men gold and the like. He himself had been driven greedy by the victories he had attained over the insipid Elyas. But the farther they ventured into the desert, the louder his men grumbled, and he had grown accustomed to only sleep soundly in a suit of steel. So he considered it a godsend when the fire appeared on the dunes, an enticing sight that tasted of plunder and glory and women. He led the siege himself, if what our stories say are true. They attacked day and night, for the beaconfire lit the darkness enough to ensure that attrition would always be made. It would be a fortnight before a flag was raised above the parapets, the silk being waved bearing the sigil for parlay. Intrigued, and desperate to take a measure of the commander of the defenders, King Yarryn waited impatiently to be let into the Haven. He was surprised then, to see that the one who was forestalling his victory had been a girl no older than ten. She was Alynslian, Crown Princess of Sora, and granddaughter of Alynor the Godschosen. They drank a flagon of wine as they spoke. He was indignant, and she was defiant. 'You have leave to break the siege and flee my Haven this very night,' she said, her voice high and true. 'As you have seen, the beaconfire will light your way home.' His anger was uncontrollable, for he was the *king*, and how dare this teatless urchin command *him* to retreat. Especially not as his plan was about to bear fruit."

"He left the comfort of the Haven, and returned to his siege lines under the garish light of the beacon. He laughed, and drank some wine, and laughed some more, boasting to his captains how the Sorans had chosen a *girl* of all things to lead their men. Then he confided his plan, for it was already in motion by then; with the wine flowing, and his hosts distracted by his outbursts, his assassin had disguised himself as a serving man. Before the sun rose in the east, his agent would have slit the girl's throat as she slept, and he would ride his firemane freely into the

Haven. But as his captains toasted their king for their imminent success, the strangest thing happened. Yarryn began to doubt his own stratagem. He pulled at his gorget and scratched at his temple, with no more than an hour's passing, he was toasting his own plan, tears of joy filling his eyes and planting kisses on the brows of all his adjutants. Another hour, and he was beating those he saw as *treasonous* to a bloody heap, calling them dunny spies and for being seduced by promises from the whore of Silentis. With each passing hour, as the candles shrunk and the horizon tinged to a deep purple, the king turned more violently from the heights of transcendent joy, to the pits of rancour and despair. When asked what they should do, Yarryn laughed and told them to attack at first light. Yet he had not finished giving the command as he suddenly screamed in their faces, tears trailing down his cheeks as he fled weeping from the tent."

"In the end, as the sun traced its first rays onto the shadowed dunes, Yarryn no longer had the faculty to give commands. He would only mutter 'yes' and 'no' between sobs. Those among his war counsel still assured themselves that victory was guaranteed. The catspaw was within the Haven, lest they forget. The girl commander would surely not survive."

"Poison," Mayred stood then, the blankets falling from here to allow her knife to flash brilliantly from her hip. "It was unjust what they did! Such an ungallant act should not be celebrated, to be recounted as though it gives us some lesson. She poisoned him. He was a monster, I know. Everyone in the Paydar knows the tales of King Yarryn's terrors. However many he killed on his campaigns, he killed

505

sevenfold of his own. I won't stand to have you say you were the cause of his madness. I won't. He is not celebrated among my people, I assure you."

Audeyrn shifted on his blanket. "She is right, Cliada. Why tell us all this if not to rile Mayred?"

Cliada tossed her hair, playing with one lock. She said, "I do not believe he was poisoned."

Mayred spat into the fire. "They shared wine. That's what you said. What are we meant to take from that, if not that the princess wanted to stop the siege by killing the invader?"

"You take from my story what you will, I care little and less. I am recalling a very intriguing time in my people's history. If I may finish the tale, perhaps I can defend my words?"

Greg took hold of Mayred's hand. "It might be different than all that in the story. It might even have a happy ending."

Her fingers fell from his one by one. It was a long moment before he realised that she was looking at him with disgust. "You believe that we can have such things in life? I thought… " the words caught in her throat, and suddenly she had bolted from the campfire, disappearing into the blackened stonework alcoves of what had once been the Haven of the Sun.

Wordlessly he followed, knowing that no words of his could stop her or catch her. No, for that, he needed to use his legs. At least those wouldn't desert him.

The emissary and the Sorans and the warmth of the fire was gone, replaced by the dreadblack niches that clung to the corners of the tumbledown like cobwebs. There was no fire here, not anymore, so he had to rely on the silvery moonlight to keep from tripping on a stone or half-sunken iron bars red with rust.

He called her name, but received no answer. So he ran all the faster, quick enough to outpace her at least. In the end, he did not catch her. She had stopped by a wall, in something which must have been a hall once, but now was much like the rest of the ruin. A gnarled blackthorn had somehow survived there, its roots nestled deep in a cracked boulder at the centre of the hall, its bole twisted and leaning to one side, its branches stretched high to exalt the rising moon. Behind the tree, her face buried in the brickwork, and her hands grasping hard at the crumbling mortar. His breathing was laboured, and his thigh and arm ached from old hurts. The ones he had earned in the Paydar. *It had been the sun glaring down in the Pit, but here it's the moon.* Then the thought came. Familiar, and etched in memory. It had always been there, he guessed, but until now, it had been formless and opaque, absent for most of his life, yet present as he looked at her now. She had clenched her jaw hard so that none could hear her muffled weeping, the hair blown wild as she fled, the knife lodged deep into the wall beside her head. He knew what she was to him, and it made his heart ache. He only wished that he had known her sooner.

As he walked to her, he went to put a hand on her shoulder. He paused, not knowing how she would react, afraid of the rejection he knew would come. The feeling was fleeting, and he was angry at himself for thinking of himself when Mayred was there.

His hand touched her shoulder to give her the lightest squeeze. "I want you to tell me what's wrong. But if you don't want to, I'll still be here for you. I hope that by sharing

it, I can know how to ease your pain. I love you, Mayred."
But there aren't any happily ever afters. This isn't a child's fancy.
Life's a bitter draught you must drown yourself in, or have the
strength to take the lightest of sips. I should know. Happiness is
only for fools and the fortunate. There aren't any happil...

"I love you too, Greg."

She somehow ended up in his arms, how he could not recall. He told her everything after she had told him. There was nothing left to hide now. Only the moon bore witness as he let her have his heart. The ground was hard, the air had a chill, and he was uncomfortably aware of how badly his leg ached. But he was with her, and that was all that mattered.

34

AUDEYRN

"That was cruel."

The emissary stuck his hands over the fire. The night had drawn in, and the draft whipped up by Greg in pursuit of Mayred sent the hairs on his neck to stand on end. He wanted to go after him, to tell the lad to leave the girl alone. Instead, he looked to the Soran sitting across from him. She wore that smirk far too easily.

"Oh, don't give me that look, Langholm. It wasn't my intent to provoke her. Besides, it's not the worst tale I could have told. If I were really wanting to offend your Castanni sensibilities, I'd have told you lot of the lecherous Lord Emissary Camrose, your... What was he? A great-great-great grandfather, give or take."

"Great-great uncle." The history made his mouth twist. Camrose Langholm had been a skilled negotiator, renowned in his day for resolving the Red Snow Crisis in the Snowmonts, and for securing the allegiance of the Vastimen to Castan for King Ellard. His legacy was overshadowed, however, by his habit of sleeping with the wives of the lord that was entertaining him, the last of whom had been adroit enough to realise he was being made a cuckold and shortened Camrose by a head. It had been a bloody affair, soon resolved by the levelheaded Ellard and his new emissary. Audeyrn's father had removed their ancestor's bust and portrait in favour of a dark cellar deep within the bowels of Langholm castle, hoping that part of their family's past would be forgotten.

"You see my point. It's incidental that a Paydar like herself happened to try their luck in invading my country a thousand odd years ago. The girl needs to learn that history is the domain of killers and conquerors. What else makes kingdoms, but the shockwaves of the vainglorious?"

"I disagree, and I think our storytime is at an end, I'm afraid."

Cliada shook her head, the pout that lined her lips full and very false. "Stay a while longer. I am sure our knight here is eager to learn the end of the story." Hearty cleared his throat at her mentioning him, uncomfortable with the sets of firelit Soran eyes poised on him. In his lap sat the lute, and he plucked gingerly at a chord. "I mean, I *would...* were you to listen too, Aud."

There was nothing for it then but for the spoilt Soran witch to have her way. The emissary lapsed into silence, and she immediately took that for his acquiescence. With a smile all for him, she pretended that she had forgotten her place in the story.

"Let me see... The Paydar overtook Ves, led by Yarryn, the arrant arch-cock of the Rowetts. Where was I? His manhood shrinks at the thought of being bested by a girl. He sweats and swears and then comports and quarrels..."

Ah! Of course! His oh-so loyal captains looked to the dawn, awaiting for blood to spill between the merlons. So there they waited, beneath the tower cloaked in smoke and darkness. The levies shuffled their feet and blew into their hands, to get some respite at least from the night. Their suzerain ran loose among the arrayed ranks, beseeching anyone that would listen to help him in his manic state. Telling them to run, to stay, to find an end to all this."

"They saw the body then, for the briefest of moments, their hearts lifting at the sight of the bloodied corpse. Except it was too big to be the girl commander. It was the wrong sex too. The man's body had been stripped naked, his arms made to be strappado as he swung there from the rope, hanging for all that had eyes to see with his manhood stuffed into his mouth. At the merlons, silhouetted by the everfire was Alynslian, the combined light of the Sun and the beacon painting her polished armour a swirling, ever changing visage of a burning landscape, the flames engulfing all that dared trespass on Soran sand."

Cliada stopped then, unstopped the glass vial in her hand and took a handful of what Audeyrn thought were shells from Lyster. In each, he let a small quantity of an amaranthine-coloured liquid fill each shell. Her movements were practised and sure, and not even Hearty could distract her when he asked, "So that was that? They killed the assassin? What about the siege? The defenders were starved out, surely?"

Cliada handed Lyster and Dreymon a shell filled to the brim with the drink. Then, she stood, walking around the fire to hand Hearty and Aud their own. "There was starvation, but not amongst the defenders. The besiegers soon resorted to eating leather and their own dead. The Haven of the Sun has vast vaults and cisterns beneath the tower, some still accessible to this day. No. The siege was protracted. Some scrivens say that it lasted nigh on a year. By the end, the Paydar commanders turned on one another, the army fractured, factions springing up each in support of their own lordling. With no unified leadership, and the prospect of remaining in the desert all too terrifying, disorder took over the ranks. Whatever discipline remained was quickly supplanted by the need to survive, and the men chose to return home, albeit in dribs and drabs across the sands. At the head of one raving group was Yarryn Yes-and-No, who is said to be heard sometimes, arguing back and forth with himself as he struggles to find his way back.

With the invaders gone, Alynslian left the Haven. Her fights were far from over though, as a civil war was raging in Silentis, and it would be up to her to reclaim her rights and win the battle ahead. But that is a different story, and I am not the person to tell it. Besides, I want to drink." The Sorans laughed, Dreymon grinning as he brought out a waterskin made from a scaled hide. He said something, and Cliada replied. She then turned to the Caldishmen. "With the lovesick pup and his girl off at their play, it looks like there's more for us to enjoy."

Hearty sniffed at the shell in his massive hand. "And what is this, exactly? It has a peculiar aroma. Nothing I've had before, that I can tell."

"You wouldn't have. It's a secret of my people. In my tongue, it translates to *philtre of the dunes*. More commonly, it's called *venom*. It's potent, I warn you. You will have to drink it exactly as I say. Here." She gestured for Dreymon to hand the waterskin over to Aud, and it was flung over the fire. Catching it, the emissary felt the liquid slosh within. Unstopping the cork, he gave it a whiff.

"What is it, Aud?" The old knight was holding the shell daintily, as though he was afraid to spill one drop.

"Smells like lemonwater."

Cliada sucked at her teeth. "That's one ingredient, yes, but not the whole. The skin contains a potion meant to be drunk after the venom. It is a... chaser, if you will."

Audeyrn held the shell to the firelight, watching at the inky dark substance filled with colour, plum and maroon, moving in swirls and whorls. "Let me guess. It's called venom for its bite?"

"Something like that. Pass me the skin." She caught it one-handed. The emissary could have sworn she was hiding a smile.

"Why are we drinking it?"

"To celebrate. The war will end, and the deaths of innumerable lives will be prevented. This is a toast to your success. Were others to find out that we're sharing the venom with outsiders... well, Silentis likes to keep its secrets hidden, as you'll find out. But all that is for the days not yet lived. Tonight we drink and laugh and dance. Tonight we banish the dark. We spit in death's eye. We hold one another tight from the daggers of evil. Now, drink, all of you!"

The Sorans finished off their share in a flash. Immediately they were passing the skin, swigging hard and hooting as the draught went down. When Hearty saw that it was safe, he huffed and drank his own. Then it was Aud's turn.

She was looking at him. He gave his drink one last look of unease, and downed it. He tried not to taste it as he swallowed, but try as he might, the flavour flooded his mouth. He had tasted the fire liquors made by the men of the Forks, how it could burn your throat. But this was as though he had drunk burning pitch. His eyes watered as he sputtered.

Hearty licked his lips. "Not bad, truly."

Cliada tossed the skin from hand to hand. "Wait a moment. Let the heat warm you. Breathe. The venom has a resting period, before the lethality returns."

"What?!" Hearty was on his feet. "Lethality? You mean… poison?! You dare to…"

"Oh, sit down. You can drink the skin now. It's not only the chaser, but also the antidote." Underhanding the waterskin to Hearty, he grabbed it from the air, swigged a healthy gulp, and then pressed it to Aud. The antidote tasted worse than the poison. For a moment his mouth filled with the taste of vomit, but as quick as that, it was replaced by honey and smoke, the smell of an island meadow in spring, the scent of a frost after rainfall. He looked to the girl and saw the amusement play across her pretty face, the way laughter lit up those big eyes. The fire made hair look even ruddier than in the daylight. *She is dangerous, this one. Very dangerous. Why have her as an enemy, when she could be a friend?* "That was cruel."

Cliada of the Garrison tossed her head, "You like to use that word, don't you? No, don't answer. I prefer it when you're silent."

"That's rude." Something about the way they drank their venom irked him. "Why did you drink the antidote quicker than us?" She cocked her head to the side, seeing how intently Aud was looking at her face as it was, framed in fire. She exhaled, clearly annoyed by the question, "*Venom* is unique in that it comes from the poison sac of the yappor. It is also the only poison that has an intermittent potency. We... in the Garrison, we have been trained to endure the effects of poisons. For you, you must drink the antidote at a certain point. For us... to drink the antidote immediately after consuming the venom only heightens the toxicity."

"A risky sport."

"It wouldn't be fun otherwise."

Drink ran freely after that. The *venom* was put away, and its antidote. Instead, Dreymon passed a demijohn to Hearty, and they all enjoyed a Soran wine. Aud looked off toward the tower, and wondered what Greg was up to. He thought of keeping his worries within, but the drink had loosened his tongue, so he asked, "Is it safe for them to be out there? Alone, I mean." He had sat next to her so that they shared a blanket. It was a fine wool and, more importantly, warm.

"Without a doubt. Beasts do not come here, it is known. And men... they know better than to intrude upon members of the Garrison." Her confidence did nought to ease the tightness in his neck, nor did it relieve the anxiety he had for this place. The Sorans knew the shifting sands of their native desert, so he would take her word when she said there was no danger. Yet the memories of the desert held an uncomfortable place inside him. His father had been the same, reassuring him that by nightfall the heat will subside, and that no monsters of the night would dare assail the famous Garrison. *Infamous, more like. That had been in peacetime, and we had journeyed the length of the long road without needing to deviate into the shifting sands of the Tundra. How full of life father seemed then.* His da had only seemed world-weary towards the very end. Or had he always been like that? When had the once golden hair become white as newfallen snow? The bright eyes turned cloudy and tired? He nodded at his own thoughts as well as Cliada's words.

"Do you want to walk?" He rose, and saw how close the Soran came to his shoulder as she stood. She took him up the curtain wall, cresting where the tumbledown would allow. From there, the expanse of an ocean fell away before them, a vast seascape of churning waves frozen and turned to innumerable grains of starlit sand. Above, the stars themselves were in their multitude, the Fortress of the Fay dominating all as its starry ramparts and glittering towers lit up the heavens in all its ethereal beauty. "Do you have stories of the Fay?"

"The Fay? Yes… children's tales for the most part. Crystal cavern cities and island fastnesses in the sky. Meant to have had all sorts of magic. A soothsman once came to court claiming that a Fay prince was destined to be born of a Soran princess, but he was laughed out of Silentis as soon as he voiced such drivel."

"Magic." The word felt strange on his tongue. There had been a time when he wanted to be a wizard. With magic, he could fulfil everyone's wishes, and then he wouldn't have had to become the Royal Emissary. However, fate had dashed his dreams and he had found that those claiming to hold magical powers were charlatans and fools. He couldn't decide which was more dangerous. "What are you thinking?"

The question was pointed, but the way she asked was

soft. It caused him to look down at her, seeing how the starlight was bathing her face in a silver-blue moon glow. She looked even more beautiful then than by the fire. "Of things that may have been. Roads less travelled."

"Some would say dwelling on the road less travelled draws predators, of the four-legged kind." Was she sticking her chin up at him, or was it just because he was taller? "Some would even dare say that it's a stupid thing, to be courting trouble."

"What if I want trouble?" His hands were on her waist.

"It's only that I thought you were dutiful, and *well-behaved*." His head spun, but he was unsure if it was drink or his arousal. "I thought you only… oh."

One hand went to hold her cheek. The lightest of a touch, enough to make sure they would look at each other before he had to close his eyes. He could feel her breath on his lips as he came close, the scent of honey and cloves and venom. Her lips opened as soon as they met his. His hand went to her hair, intoxicated by the feel of it through his fingers, the taste of her mouth. Her tongue was restless, forcing him to kiss her harder and faster. She pushed herself against him, so his other hand went to her buttocks.

The world was reduced to the two of them, alone but for the moon peeking above the sands. There were no sounds but for their breathing. It seemed to last forever, and he didn't want it to end. It was not long before his trance was broken somewhat as he felt a hand reach down to rest on his crotch. Her fingers gave his cock a squeeze as she gave him a golden-eyed grin. *Fuck.* With one hand, she was undoing the laces to his breeches, the other digging nails into the flesh of his back.

Somehow they had gotten themselves on the stone, and Aud's shirt was thrown over a nearby merlon. Cliada was standing, just to remove her jack and shirt with exaggerated movements. He saw her then, for the first time. All of her. It was only her breeches left, and with those gone, he was left to admire the slender shoulders, the curve of her hip and buttock that ended in her long legs. As she crept closer to him, he saw how her breasts moved, and he only got harder as he saw how the moon limned them. "Come here."

The look on her face was cruel indeed as she straddled him. Her mouth was slightly open, eyeing his erection hungrily. "No. Wait." He held her by the arm, pushing her down on the blanket until she was looking at him, her ragged breathing causing her breasts tp rise and fall all the more. He kissed her once more on the lips, then traced a line downward. He was sure that he had kissed every part of her until he got to where he needed to be, to make her legs shake, to hear her panting. Only when he was sure she was ready did he start kissing her other lips. He was surprised at how wet she was, but it only made him want her more. Hearing her gasp, he opened her with his tongue. Soon she was screaming his name.

She grabbed him when he was done, pushing him back down, her nails digging into him enough so that he stay still as she rode him. As she slid down onto his cock, she was even wetter. Very soon, he was scratched and bitten enough that he looked like he had been mauled by a roc. When Aud mentioned that, Cliada was unsure what a roc even was, claiming that the most dangerous creature in Sora was a Soran woman, especially if they had not been fed. He laughed at that as they lay covered in a fine sheen of sweat.

"I've never had a Castanni before." She stated matter-of-factly as they walked back to the fire together. That was the last thing she said before they fell asleep.

The morning brought a cool dryness to the world. They broke their fast on sidewinder eggs and sweet well water, boiling the remnants of the night's wine to ready themselves for the last leg of the journey. Hearty saddled up, japing with Dreymon, who seemed to be enjoying talking to the blustering knight despite knowing only a smattering of the common. It was left to Lyster to ready Cliada's horse, but he seemed to be as dour as before. It was Cliada herself that had Audeyrn's attention. They mounted together, breaking camp before the eighth hour of the day and setting out east by south-east. Meadwater... *No, it's true name is The Haven of the Sun...* was soon swallowed up by the sands as they went. He could not help but feel sad. The place had been host to war and subterfuge and madness, and was *old*, but even that lifeless place, it could hold some semblance of respite and happiness for travellers lost in the world.

Greg was there, too, as he looked back at the ruin. He had come back to camp as the first light returned to the world. But not Mayred. According to Greg, she remained firmly adamant that Cliada had sought to provoke her. They rode behind the rest, furthest away from Cliada. Hearty had tried to make light of it, saying that Gregyn would have the honour of being rearguard. The tracker had smiled at that. Hearty himself was all smiles. Where before he watched the Sorans through narrowed eyes and behind plated steel, now he rode with just a silken robe and desert shawl.

Gods, what have they done to him?!

The emissary had to remind himself that he was changed too. He found himself opting for the cool desert garb of the natives over his usual travel clothes. It was a relief, after all, to be free of the encumbering armour. He knew it left him open to attack, but where was the danger out here? The party could see for miles ahead and behind them, and his escort assured him that they had the means to detect natural predators a safe distance off. It had been Cliada who claimed that, and some part of him believed it. The last night had helped. The last time he had been with a woman was little over a year ago, back on the windswept isle of his birth, the Holm. A cousin to the master-at-arms Clay Costigan, had stolen into his bed the night before he was due to sail for Castan to answer the king's summons. Little did he know then, but he would be sent halfway across the world at his monarch's whim. But that night, it had been golden. As was her hair. Calla Costigan was older than him by ten moons and had always been his playmate. Moreso, when they had shared furs in his chambers. Now, in the middle of this empty land, it had been so long he had thought he would not enjoy it or be able to after being so drunk. Aud had enjoyed his time with her, and he thought that maybe she had enjoyed it too.

The heat returned to batter at the travellers the next few days, but it seemed more bearable to Aud now. After all, he along with his companions, knew how close they were to the city. Beneath the hot glare, the days were wearisome, but the evenings were full of drink and talk, and other nocturnal activities. He rode with Dreymon, who was little use with conversation but always marking out points of interest amongst the dunes, giving the Soran names for dry trees and features and creatures. Lyster was more knowledgeable in the common, but what talk came from him was acerbic and monosyllabic. So more and more of his time was spent with their leader. It was a pity her face was hidden from the sun most of the day, but Aud enjoyed seeing the glint of her eyes through the shawl. Then one day, a thin trail appeared on the edge of sight. It soon meandered its way through the sands as though it were a great snake carving a path to the east. It had been cobbled, once. Now the stones were speckled here and there between the hard-packed earth.

"The long road. We're close. We should make Silentis by tomorrow afternoon."

"Gods be praised. I have had a bellyful of Dreymon's tall tales. Tell him, lad." Hearty nudged Lyster, who huffed before translating for the elder of the two Sorans. He chuckled when he heard what had been said and made a retort.

Lyster groaned before saying, "He says the day your belly is full will be the day his hair will grow back." Hearty let loose a loud bellow, and with his hand showed Dreymon exactly what he thought of *that*.

Even Cliada gave a laugh. "Soon we'll be sipping saffron wines beneath cool terraces. Won't you join us?" She spurred her horse on, making Aud catch up to keep abreast. "I will, if you'll have me." A thought occurred to him, one that had been nagging him for days. "When this is done, would you like to come with me back to Castan?"

"What, as your concubine?" It was hard to guess the look on her face.

"No, I... I thought that because we had..."

"Fucked? Is that it?" He desperately grasped for words and found none. "You want me to up and leave, just because we slept together? Thought you were here on *knightly vows*, or whatever the Castanni have to keep you in check."

"The Royal Emissary is purely a diplomatic role, never knighted. We are trained at arms, aye, but it is by royal decree that the men of House Langholm never attain knighthood."

"I'm grateful for the lesson in your family's history, but you forget why you're here."

The accusation stung. "I have not *forgotten*." His cheeks burned, despite the sun. "I'm here to deliver my king's message."

"And what message is that?"

Aud knew when he had been bested. He wanted to throw her words back in her face, to kiss her hard, to tell her that he was here to help. But even if he voiced them, he knew they would be empty. *I don't even know what message I carry.* The chest made its presence known. There were mosquitoes out there, and would buzz around the head until you were like to go mad. The chest was different but not wholly dissimilar. Every step of his mount seemed to knock the chest into his spine, near goading him. His head reeled, his anger flaring until he felt he could no longer hold it. A voice pleaded inside to restrain himself, but the heat of the day and the frustration he felt was too loud, too much, and the voice was soon drowned out by the red rage.

He halted so abruptly that Hearty's horse almost slammed into his own. "Apologies Aud, I didn't see you stop."

"No, I'm the one that needs to apologise. I am sorry to all of you. I should have seen it from the start. I see now." He

AUDEYRN

slung a leg over his saddle. The sand was hot, even though his boots.

Cliada snorted. "See what? Are you going to walk to Silentis?"

Soran laughter echoed at his back as he unstrapped the chest. It was heavy. It was as common and unassuming as the day Isembard pressed it into his care. The sunlight of spring had streamed through the coloured glass of the windows to fall on the scene like a painting. It had made the Tourmaline Throne afire in its halo of iridescence. But not the chest. It had been as dull then as it was now. He had to know. What harm could it do, to see for himself.

Voices called to him, but they seemed far away. Someone was shouting, but he ceased to hear. Carrying the chest onto a rise, he was determined to crest it before they came to bear. He had to know. *Is a secret still a secret if only one person knows the truth?*

It settled in the sands with an unceremonial *thump*. He fell to his knees. The key he yanked from the leather thong about his neck. Tumblers turned. There was a whisper on the wind. It took him a moment to realise he was holding his breath. From somewhere inside the mechanism came a dull *clunk*. Audeyrn opened the lid.

"Aud, are you well?" It was Greg, he sounded all of his sixteen years. "Aud?"

"I…"

What is this?

Within, was sand.

No. There must be something. There must be...

Clawing through the contents, he desperately sought for something that wasn't there. He tried reasoning that

523

perhaps the sand itself was special: precious stones ground to fine grains, a gift for the queen in fabled Silentis. But no, he could wish it all he liked. The chest still only contained sand. Only sand. Isembard's plan laid bare. A spiteful royal joke.

Aye, but at who's expense?

Upending the chest, the sand within met the sands without, merging and melding together until he could no longer tell which parts he had carried for the hundreds of leagues across the continent. The sun set on him there, and what talk came from his companions was some distance away. If a question came his way, he had no words for them. Still he was sat, his legs long having fallen asleep beneath him, his hands getting colder as the evening drew close. He felt little of it, and what he did feel was nothing compared to the pain in his heart. He uttered wordless prayers to his father.

I've failed, Da... What do I do?... Isembard has doomed us all... Should I collect up the sands, present them to the Soran Queen, and give her my best?

You've dealt with them, Da. You know what to do... Please, help me now, I beg you... What do you say to them? The queen? The Sorans? My friends...

They've come so far... for me. What do I...

"Aud... I've come to give you this." Ripped from reverie, the tall man stood amidst the night, the orange glow of a fire burning behind him to give him a flickering, ephemeral silhouette. "You must be cold. I know you're upset. I only... Please take it." He stood there, awaiting a response. Aud managed the briefest nod, and that was enough for Greg. He went to hand him a thick woollen blanket but stopped, instead coming closer to drape it over the emissary's shoulders. "If you want t' join us, you don' need to say a thing. We're here for ya."

Only when he was gone did Aud allow himself to cry. He let the tears flow. They were warm against his cheeks. *They know, yet they don't rant and rage. They followed me through it all... oh Nat... I'm so sorry.*

Whatever message Ismebard had for his enemy was unknown to him. Was it a taunt? A challenge? An insult? He didn't know, and didn't want to. Whatever it was, it was gone now anyway, lost among the Desolate Tundra like so many poor bastards before. *Sand...* His hands curled into fists, and his jaw set so hard he heard a tooth chip.

"He doesn't want the war to end." He had always hated the king, that much he knew. Yet he had always been more afraid than hateful. Now, he felt the anger roil inside. With it, he found himself rising.

"The emissary graces us with his presence!" Cliada leant back, biting a lip before saying, "So what's the sand thing all about? One would have thought you had gold in that chest of yours."

The sallies needed a response, but he let them fall flat and unanswered. He stood, where otherwise the rest were sitting. He was away from the fire, so felt little to no benefit. But he did not need it. The rage inside warmed him against the night: a firestorm that threatened to overtake the fires of the Hell Unending itself.

Mayred lifted her sullen eyes from the fire. "You know something."

Audeyrn shrugged. "I know what I need to do, if that's what you mean." He looked east, to see only the vaguest impression of a dark road on an even darker plane.

"Saddle up."

Cliada giggled, and her companions joined her. "At this hour. Do you want to lame your horse?"

"I *want* to reach the city, and tomorrow isn't soon enough. Now get fucking saddled."

Hearty cleared his throat. "She has a point, Aud. In the morning, we will be refreshed." Aud cocked an eyebrow, directed his causting glare at the Sorans. "And waste more time sweating under the blasted sun? No. We ride now, and we ride hard. I have a message to deliver."

What mad thought had made him say that dissipated as soon as they set off. The Sorans grumbled, no doubt complaining that a Castanni shouldn't be commanding them about. Cliada told them to quiet. The rest of the journey was a gallop, filled with the clatter of steel-shod horseshoes on cobbles. The moon guided them, but the going was still half-blind as they made their mad dash out of the desert. They stopped for a breather only when the lights of the city appeared ahead, heralding that they were close.

He tried to compare it to the dream he had, of a city surrounded by the Desolate Tundra. Then, like now, it was beneath a dome of stars. The only difference was that as they continued their approach, there seemed to be far fewer lights above the walls. He tried to remember the city, and found that he recalled little. Covered arches and domes scraped against the star-speckled sky, growling larger and larger until they scratched the clouds. At Cliada's signal, they slowed until they came to a canter. Aud's mount was blown, he noticed the flanks shining with sweat. He heard

Greg take a sharp intake of breath. "Gods, it's bigger than Castle Castan!"

"Not as high as the Tor." Mayred beside him spat, sneering, " Not by far."

The Soran leader grabbed Audeyrn's reins hard. For a moment, he thought she wanted to bring him closer to kiss, but as he looked at her in the dark he saw only hard eyes in an expressionless face. "From here, you do as I say. Bandits have made the patrols wary of travellers by night, especially any making their way to the palace-port."

"So we're not getting the grand entrance?"

"Oh, the emissary is chipper again."

"Just happy we all arrived safe and sound."

"If you say so..." She said it under her breath, and Aud liked it not at all. The palace-port was a drear thing, a slab of tarred wood five-foot tall. Bolted iron bands two inches thick reinforced the postern, sandworn and rusted against wood the colour of rotten meat. Between two such bands was an eye-slit, but it was closed and dark and all too forbidding. Cliada dismounted, prompting the rest of the party to follow suit.

She tossed the reins of her half-dead horse to Lyster, and slammed a fist against the palace-port. It seemed like an eternity before somebody came, and only after Cliada slammed her fist twice more against the postern. When the eye-slit opened, piggy eyes stared out blindly at the night.

"What you fuckin' want?" The pig-faced man asked.

"Cliada of the Garrison, returning with an entourage from Iktet."

He gave a wheezy snort, finishing his would-be laughter by hawking rheum. "Garrison, eh? Why the fuck you's comin' here at this stupid hour?"

"That's a need to know. General Zadhiyar is expecting me. Now open the fuck up, or I'll have you on latrines for the next moon."

They left their horses outside, for the stair to the palace proper was far too winding and low-ceilinged to accommodate them. Up and up and up again they went. Cliada was unwilling to say where they were going, but Audeyrn did not need to ask. He kept his tongue firmly behind his teeth. The guard before them led them by torchlight, throwing long shadows against the pale nitred walls. Stairs led to bricked corridors led to more stairs. A few times he was sure the Sorans double-backed themselves just to throw their erstwhile guests off the trail. Others detached themselves to run ahead, to tell of the emissary's arrival. It was late into their escort that Aud realised that Lyster held the rear. His hand came to rest on his hilt. His heart beat swiftly, so loud he thought all could hear.

"Here." It was Cliada who told the guard when to stop. It was at a nondescript backdoor, the drab thing holding itself loosely on its hinges. It took a moment for the guard to find the key, sorting through a ring of dozens of keys until he found the one needed. When that was done, they were ushered inside a room lit by a sole torch on one wall, glaring wanly against the unyielding unmortared walls to his left about twenty foot away. "Good luck, don't fuck it up." Cliada looked almost sad when she said that, but it was hard to tell in the half-light.

Cliada was already going through the door again, "*He* must stay here." Audeyrn knew who she meant by that. "She's right." He knew what he had to say, but it did not make it any easier. "I'll see you all soon."

"No." Hearty puffed out his chest. "I've left you before. I cannot leave you now."

For all the world, Aud did not think it would have been Greg who said, "He has to do this. If anyone can do this, it's him."

Is that what everyone thinks?

They left, but it was Mayred who had to be restrained. Aud tried to reason with her, but the guard closed the door too fast for him to say anything worthwhile. It was quiet, when they finally left him. Alone. Not knowing what else to do, he made the first few gingerly steps across the room. The scant light thrown by the torch gave him little inkling as to the dimensions of the chamber. He approached the light like he feared it would burn him. He guessed there must have been another door on the opposite end of the chamber. Elsewise, he was trapped in an empty dimly lit room. *These fucking Sorans. One would think they can see in the dark.* Stalking towards the light, he was all too aware of how loud his boots scuffed against the flags. He was about to leave the pool of light when he heard the voice.

"So it is you." The voice came from his right, from the darkest section of the chamber. A figure detached itself from the shadows. It became a tall woman, nearly as tall as Greg, wearing an elaborate if not sombre shawl and half cape over a shoulder. Her hair was short and hack-shorn, and martial cut, as though she were a soldier. In a face that may have once been comely, her nose had been broken twice, at the least, and an ear was shorn in half. "You look like Coram. Come. Her Majesty awaits, and she hates being roused at this hour."

"Wait." He may have asked so many questions, and was about to, but the woman said, "You're in no position to command me, emissary. Now follow."

At some unknown gesture, a pair of hidden double doors reeled open, pulled apart by unseen hands. Light bled into the room like lifesblood from a mortal wound. She led the way, and he followed, knowing he had to keep up. He squinted to see what was before him.

"I have him, Your Majesty." Was all he heard as the doors slammed shut behind him. *No, no, no! I need more time!*

"Good. You can stay, of course, Dryw." It was far from the throne room that Audeyrn had expected to find the queen. The torches here glittered where common ones flickered. Strange silver-white light emitted from the dozen or so sconces lining the walls, stretching upwards into vaulted ceilings. Not that there were any windows, no, only bare walls were found in this... whatever this room was. It was wider than the antechamber before it, and longer too.

From the walls, tapestries were hung, the goldthread glittering proudly despite the mildew that clung to the rest of the fabric. From the ceilings, he saw great iron automatons, the like he had only heard of in stories. Wyrms and chimaeras and harpies, yappors and rocs and yrts, great eagles and maned lions and snarling wolves, the menagerie was all hinges and gears, lifeless in their mechanised wonder. They were magnificent. A wonder, truly. So distracting, in fact, that he only realised the little woman after coming close to where she sat.

He knew she was the queen just from her dress. The sovereign sat on a humble seat of cedarwood at the far end, a stool by all accounts, for it had no high-backing, and the raised dais upon which it was placed was a mere half step above the flagstones. He had had grander audiences with poorer lords, but there was something about this place... intangible yet implacable, that told him to be wary.

The queen was short, pudgy, and wrapped in a purple and gold pelt of the largest cat Aud had ever seen, which only made her seem more rotund. She shifted as he approached, her diminutive throne creaking dangerously beneath her ample buttocks. He did not find it amusing. He would not even dare. Around fifteen feet away, the general barred his way with an arm.

"No further." She saluted the queen, then said, "My liege, may I dispense with formal introductions?"

The royal eyes were looking up at Aud. They were small and dark in her round face, shining like polished jet dropped into rolls of dough. She shrugged the pelt off one shoulder, letting the emissary see that in one thick-finger, she had a coin. In a flash she flicked it up into the air, faster than he could see what was inscribed on its faces. It was silver, it was silver. Something faint on either side. *I know that coin.* Then it was falling, spinning, and fell flat into her waiting palm. Was it his imagination, or had she kept her attention on Aud the whole time? "Yes. But he should still bow." Her voice was that of a singer, which surprised him.

The general made a gruff noise, looking down her crooked nose at the foreigner. "Bow." He did as he was bid. Taking a breath to steady himself, he made certain that his actions were sure and calm, bowing low enough to evoke respect, but not too low. He had been taught that. Some consider it a mockery. Sorans, in particular, he recalled.

"The monkey has been taught well." The laugh that

531

accompanied the General's cutting words was as deep as any man's. "Wonder what other tricks they taught him." Her tone agitated him enough that he raised an entreating hand, saying, "Queen Salphyre, I do not wish to be insulting, but I would like to discuss my message. It is of the highest importance." The bellicose Dryw was not done. She turned on Aud then with the ferocity of a mastiff about to bite down on a bone. "You are *bold*. I'll give you that. What, may I ask, do you intend to say that will keep your head attached to that scrawny neck."

The emissary rounded on her. "I came here on a diplomatic mission. Is this how you treat with messengers? I came to speak to the queen, not you."

"That's where you err." It was the queen, Salphyre. She had moved only to lean forward, deepening the shadows of her face. "Dryw shares all my secrets. Your fate depends on your next words, for she has not killed anyone today and her patience runs thin. Choose them carefully, for I hate liars, and timewasters moreso."

He guarded his tongue and considered. His mind ventured back to the desert, and to Isembard's chest that still ripped away at his heart. It must remain a secret. He feared what they would do should he let them know its contents.

"So you're the boy," The voice was Isembard's, but it was fuller, less petulant than when he had left him, sounding more as a king should. He was in Castan, and his father was in deliberation with a representative of the Corsair Court. Audeyrn had been exploring the castle, and must have gotten lost, for the white-stoned bailey was unfamiliar to him. Of course it was. It was the first time he had been to Castan.

Then *he* was there, flanked by the lion-crested guards of his Castanna royal guard. "You *look* like him. Audeyrn, isn't it?" His beard was still well-kept. It was dark, dreadblack and forbidding, a stark contrast to the white-gold crown that rested atop his head. "Are you lost, boy?"

"My king!" It was Da. Then a hand was on his shoulder, and he saw something pass over the king's face. A wrinkled lip, for a fraction of a moment. "Coram, dear Coram. The talks with our friends from the Ruell are well, I hope?"

"Most… productive, sire. We have the chance to secure their allegiance. However, they demand that we secede the mouth of the Vast to them, in addition to our acknowledging the sovereignty of Dagger Head."

"Let them have it. They will soon turn on one another. Any successions their successor's claim will be void."

"I… That is not a certainty, my king. Should we relinquish any claims we have on the coastlands, the corsairs will soon spread their plundering across the entirety of the Knifedge Coast. The Vastimen will live in fear of them, as all the lands of the Ruell Sea. The Court also said…"

He was silenced with a hand. The king's smile was amicable enough. "I will hear no more of it, Coram. Their allegiance will be secured. The Vasti will protect their own lands, as will those on the Knifedge."

The hand on Aud's shoulder weakened. "Aye, sire. It will be done."

"Good. The sooner this is resolved, the sooner we can rest easy knowing that they will trouble our shores no longer. Now then…" As he walked past the young boy at his father's hip, he ruffled his hair. "You must come to Castan more often, lad. My son is away, but I'm certain he'd love to meet you."

The king left them, just as the one-eyed knight approached Coram. He whispered something in his father's ear. With a promise on his lips, he returned to the conference, hand in hand with his son.

Why was he thinking of *that*? He thought he had forgotten. All his father's work, the years he spent trying to mend the ills wrought by his king. Ever the faithful servant of his majesty. *His faithfulness to a king that had sent his son across the world, bearing a message that he knew would have him killed.* Coram had nursed his misgivings until the day he died.

Am I going to end up like that? Dying from grief that he refused to talk about, beaten like a dog until it had to be put down?

"Coram would have had more sense." The derision oozed from the general's voice.

I am my father's son...

Natoly's laugh filled his ears as they clashed in the great bailey of Castle Castan. Years had passed, and now Aud wore leather and mail and a blunted practice sword. A few feet away, Natoly Maarten of the Guardcorps levelled his own sword, a blunted longsword replacing the curved Warretumi blade he usually bore. He was goading him into an attack. He knew better than to fall for such a ploy, and instead raised his shield so that it covered his body. Those around them shouted encouragement. His friend grinned his fox's grin. He steadied himself, and leapt forward.

...father's son....

"ANOTHER SONG!?" The great hall boomed to the sound of Sir Hearty Deri, standing on the table after the feast. A roar of approval made the stones of Langholm shake, and soon Deri was trying to quieten enough to bound into his next ballad of drinking and whoring. To the surprise of all, he started the first refrain of *Alder Days*. It was an aria, more solemn than the popular songs marching songs the men-at-arms of House Langholm revelled in. The knight sang alone, his voice carrying true and high so that all in the smoky hall heard the tale of lament and hope. The song ended, like all songs must.

...father's son...

They brought forth the boy, newly freed from captivity at Mornswood. He was near-skeletal, timid as can be, and incredibly tall for his age. "I've been told you can track." The words we heard had been spoken by himself, but the person who addressed the boy was clad in a black cape, and his voice was daunting. "Aye. But... but... but... ya should see me with m' bow." The pride in his voice was strange coming from a lad adorned in rags that smelled like the gaol. The reeve had been loath to release him, he found out, yet the Royal Emissary carried much authority. He had asked Gregyn if he would be part of his household. He had answered, with the first of his many smiles.

...son...

The woman stood over him, but he could not remember her face. There had been a girl, too, clutching at her skirts as though that would protect her from the horrors of the world. What was her name?

...son...

The deserts knew the end. It was night, and it was empty, but for the one from his dreams. She stood there dappled by moonlight, the silvering playing across the curve of her hips and the dark rises of her breasts. When he was inside her, her cries of ecstasy made him even harder. Golden eyes and ruddy hair were all he could see, and that was all that seemed to matter for a little while.

...son...

A man with wings stood tossing a coin amidst a sea of blood and bone. Ankle deep, his richly decorated doublet and cloak shone wetly beneath a black sun. As he looked at Aud, tears drew rivers down his blood-spattered face.

....son...

"Son…" His father's chambers were airy, in a futile effort to ward off the damp. The dying man lurched forward in his bed. All around them, spectral figures leant in too. Men all, similar in ghostly appearance to Coram, similar to Audeyrn. "I know. I know. But this is… not a responsibility. It's an honour. You will blaze your path. I know you will…"

"I am not my father." He was staring up at one of the automatons. The one with splayed wings made from slivers of metal beyond count. His mind had wandered. Stretched back into the recesses of memory, and those other things too, the dreams that would not cease. The other two in the chamber had not moved.

"You knew him, didn't you? *Coram would have had more sense.* No… you knew my father. Not just as the king's emissary. There's something else. Tell me."

The pelt rustled noisily as the queen roused herself, trotting across the dais and onto the flags, towards Aud. The hand that touched his face was tender. "I see it, yes." The creases around her eyes deepened. "Make your argument, then."

Aud felt himself sag with relief but kept his head high. "I

offer a choice."

The General sat on the lip of the dais. "Choice? What *choice*?"

"The choice to bring an end, to all of this. The enemy is not in Castan. The real enemy is in Godswrath." The word alone was enough to cause them to bristle. The fabled stronghold of the Godless emanated fear, no matter who heard it. He could not stop now. He knew he could not. "They are real, and they are growing. With the aid of the Paydar, I was able to destroy a redoubt they had founded in a fortress on the Wolfswater. Also, an assassination attempt by the Godless was scuppered in Ves by Cliada of the Garrison. They are growing bolder, and should they possess the power they had in the stories, we must organise. The perils are coming. We must *end* this war, before they can penetrate each disunited kingdom. Before they bring total annihilation."

There was silence in the cold stone room. Someone was breathing, and he realised it as his own laboured breath.

"Isembard sent you to say this?" The General's eyes bored into him.

Tell them. The voice was treasonous, but that threat held little consequence now. He was free. "No. This is *my* message." *But to someone who will listen?*

Queen Salphyre readjusted the pelt. The look she bore was all sadness, all pity. "I agree… but that ship has sailed. We sent our message to the Tourmaline Throne months ago. By now, it will have already reached Castan."

"No." He felt giddy. Shaking his head, incredulous. His thoughts raced faster than a firemane. "Then why did you want to hear my terms?"

"Oh, Audeyrn," The queen took his hand in hers. He wanted to rage and scream. Inside the pudgy royal hands, his fist was clenched tight. "We had to be certain it was you. As you said, the perils are coming. Do not worry. Some still remember the Godless, and we will inform them of all you've said here. There is still time yet. But as of this moment, this audience is at an end."

And like that, the General was ushering Aud through the same doors he had entered through. She was his only guard as they went about climbing the stairs. All sense of direction left him, he felt stunned and helpless, as though hit across the head with something blunt and heavy. Soon, they were twisted and turned about, the General knew the way of course. To what, he could only guess.

"Here." She stopped him as they were halfway down a gallery. To one side, the walls giving way to fluted columns that led to a garden. All kinds of trees and shrubs and flowers grew. Some, as common as mud weeds, were interspersed by plants he had only seen in illustrations in some of Hector's books. "An oasis?"

"A lichyard. Come."

The confusion was broken almost instantly, when he nearly walked into a half-sunken statue of a woman. Others were newer, and in better repair, but nearly all were covered in lichen and moss, and most home to creeping vines. Men and women, children, crones, even a few hounds and cats peaked out amongst the green catacombs. Some errant light caught his eye, and he looked up, seeing that the sun was painting the tips of the domed towers that surrounded him. *Nothing stops the day.*

Dryw led him to the deepest part of the burial grounds.

There, amongst a grove of silver birch in full bloom, a single tall statue of a young woman stood looking to the sunset. "I have not seen birch since I left home."

"She always loved the birch trees."

"Who was she?"

The light glistened in her eyes. "You know who she is."

Stone was hard to capture the essence of a person. Kings and queens had the most skilled craftsman and stonemasons to capture their image. They had known her during her life, that was for certain. He recognised her, for he had known her all his life. She had always been a part of him, even after she had left. He longed for her embrace once more. To feel her reassuring words and laugh, and to let her kiss his forehead again.

But the only kisses from stone were cold, and his mother was long dead.

35

GREGYN

She told him the truth at sunset.

They stood where the battle had been hardest, but the cityguard had bested the bandits, throwing them back until they broke and ran. That was what Cliada told them had happened anyway. The walls were blackened from the fireballs the invading forces had thrown over the battlements, but they were still intact, if not darker than before. Those who had had their homes within were not so fortunate. Piles of rubble now stood where once had been streets. Pathways had been made by the cityfolk, who went about their day as though nothing was amiss.

I would too, if I were attacked each day.

Today was a quieter day. The gates remained open for the nonce. Trade resumed, with the merchantmen desperate enough to carry out their trade. Children ran naked amongst ruined streets. A fiddler could be heard playing somewhere. And the city was healing. Teams of builders had erected cranes and weighted pulleys to reconstruct new buildings where the old had been destroyed. Tilers and tanners busied themselves in roofing the new structures.

Hammers rang, carts clattered past, and peace reigned. Across the plaza that fronted the gate, teams of oxen were being driven by a scriven at his desk to the sites of work, the man clearly bored by his task. It seemed peaceful to Greg, despite the clangour. After all, noise had been an ever-present part of his life in the Dun Vale. The mill's water wheel had made a deep rumbling as it was spun by the churning waters of the river. If not that, it had been the knock-knock-knock of the gears or the millstone grinding. There was a wholesomeness to the constant noise, making him feel content.

It was over. They had made it. *Most of us made it.* Thinking of Nat always made him sad. He tried not to dwell on it, knowing it would only make him feel more melancholy that their friend had not reached their journey's end. *But he would be happy we made it. He would be proud of us. He would be.*

He told as much to Aud, when he returned from his sojourn with the Soran Queen to the apartments prepared for the outsiders. Greg remembered how drawn his face had been, the paleness of his bright grey eyes only helping to make the dark circles beneath look like old bruises. As he said the words to the emissary, he was certain it was a mistake, that he would not take it well... but the smile on that tired face was everything Greg needed at that moment. He could not contain himself, not even as he pulled his friend into an embrace. "It's over, Greg," he told him then and there, "It's time to leave this all behind. From here, we decide who we want to be."

That had been a fortnight past. With each passing day,

they explored the city. Hearty made his excuses to stay within the Palace, saying that he fancied trying his arm against the warriors of the royal guard. Cliada dismissed Lyster and Dreymon back to the Garrison, the latter of whom was sad to see them go. The first sunrise in the city, as they broke their fast on seeded toast smothered in honey, cuts of stuffed turkey, trays of roasted chestnuts, bakestone cakes with raisins inside, and a crisp lemonwine, she had barged in. Greg had almost dropped his toast (with a generous helping of honey on top) into his lap. He caught it, and felt elated at how quick he had become.

"General Dryw has made me your liaison of the city due to my preexisting familiarity with you lot." *Who's General Dryw?*

Aud had laughed in her face. "Aren't you happy that you still get to be in our company?" Cliada smirked at him, then faster than sight, she had a flagon of the wine in hand, and proceeded to pour it over the emissary's head. She dusted her hands off at that, then stepped back to admire her handiwork. "Oh, I'm giddy."

They had all the time until the Hell Unending. The days were bright and hot, with each sunset bringing cool nights. It was winter, and Greg had to remind himself that the High Forks were probably under five feet of snow and ice.

The thought made him feel out of place, but not as much as Mayred. She had spoken to him less and less the past weeks. He had not pushed it. She was just like him, far from home, surrounded by foreign faces speaking a tongue he could not understand. Sullen more oft than not, never starting a conversation, and even when talking, would give only closed answers.

542

It was so near to being perfect now that the burden of the mission was finally done. Near perfect, for he could not appreciate their mission being complete knowing Mayred was unhappy. When they walked under the shadow of a monument to a dead king, queen, or prince, he would ask her. Never finding the right words in his head, he would end up just blurting out, "I love you," or "You look so beautiful." It always caused her to smile, and she would say she loved him too. He had never been good at mouthing his thoughts. He knew he was not stupid, but neither was he able to puzzle out what needed to be said. In the place of words, he would have painted her something, if he knew how to paint anyway. He wished he had a way of conjuring a way to say the right thing to her. Telling her something that would ease her disquiet.

Cliada guided them across the city on horseback, so they were above the crowds and not at risk of stepping in camel shit. Almost every one of those afoot would move aside as they recognised her. It also allowed them to access the city's great sights. Hierophants of the Dome of the Gods invited them to see relics of the blind god. The Bazaar of Reyzid was a labyrinth, and it was all too easy to become lost inside, and prey for hawking stallowners. The Royal Palace loomed above all, spilling blessed shade over the afternoon.

They surrounded him with things he would never have imagined. Coins of all sorts exchanged hands as the locals bartered, some depicting the proud bearded visages of kings, others with women clad in nothing but beauty, and others still, monsters with multiple heads and grinning demons and queer symbols and flames. As they turned a corner onto the Plaza of Peace they came upon a merchant with cages full of brilliantly coloured birds with crests like crowns. Unable to help himself, Greg went for a gander. A pair of burly men flanked the cages like stone pillars.

The merchantman bestirred himself, quick to sniff out a prospective customer. He launched into a string of the languishly liquid tongue of Sora. Greg blinked his confusion. "I don't understand."

"*Ahhh*, Castanni! You like the birds, lord?"

"Umm, I was jus' looking. I never seen a bird like those before."

The man's smile vanished, "My goods are for paying patrons. See that you do not breathe on them. In fact, do not set your insipid gaze upon them. Be gone, or I'll have my boys beat my words into your skull."

"I thought you had better manners with guests, Partol." Cliada was at Greg's shoulder, and the henchmen were already backing away, their eyes as wide as eggs. She walked over to the closest bird, its plumage a cherry red, while its crest and wingtips and tail shone a dazzling gold and pearl. "Partol is an clod," Cliada cooed.

"*Partol is a clod! Partol is a clod! Partol is a clod! Partol is a clod!*" Shrieked the creature, bobbing its hook-beaked head and extending its wings as far as its confines allowed. Soon it had the others crying out the words too, getting louder and more mocking, until all that came from the cages was, "*CLOD! CLOD! CLOD! CLOD! CLOD!*"

"*Quiet!* Cliada, *eleyri*, I did not know. I didn't. I am wary, as all. With the attacks so frequent, I am taking precautions. There are some that would gladly steal my merchandise just to cook them up over a fire."

544

"I understand. But you *are* a clod, Partol. Even your merchandise agrees with me." Greg could see that the man did not like being insulted so intimately, so publicly. He hung his head and wrung his hands hard.

"It's fine... I mean, I..." Greg found the words. "I want to see the rest of the Plaza, and the sun is almost set."

Audeyrn echoed Greg, "Indeed. Cliada, leave the man be. You promised to show me the Bridge of Kisses at dusk."

She spun on her heel, "So I did. The rest of the Plaza is pretty much the same, dear Greg. They come here to sell their wares from the eastern reaches. Follow me, then."

He was still amazed, despite Cliada's apathy. A comic troupe had set up at the fountain in the Plaza's centre. A dwarf announced the acts, and each came forth tumbling and twirling, and one giant man with the black skin of Warretum predicted a person's morrows. Greg was about to ask Mayred if she wanted to have both of theirs foreseen by the soothsman, but then Aud shot over to Cliada, "It draws late."

Their guide looked at him through a range of fringe that had fallen across her eyes. "One is eager to visit our most famous bridge." The way she looked at him made Greg want to look at Mayred. He furrowed his brow. *Wait, are they...*

"I was told it was important, as all."

"Oh, it's very important. Lest be said I was a bad guide, so I'll educate you ignorant foreigners."

The people of Silentis spilled forth onto the streets as the heat of the day eased. The party had to push through the press that filled the wide Avenue of Alynor, also known as the Road of Heroes and Hero's Way, for the great procession of bronze sculptures lining the straight road through the city. It was the widest road Greg had ever seen, cutting like an arrow from the Gate of the Dawn to the Royal Palace. Alynor himself was at the Palace end, standing with his back to the fortress, his sword raised high in warning to those that approached. His was the greatest statue standing sixty feet tall, not counting the twenty foot plinth beneath him. They had glimpsed him while inside the Palace, but now he seemed tiny and unimportant, being so far and on the edge of sight.

Along the Avenue, they passed dozens of *lorets*, where patrons came to sit on piles of soft cushions to sip venom from ornate crystal glasses. Others reclined to smoke *copezh* from elongated ivory pipes. Only a handful bearing the raiment of officials or nobles noted Cliada enough to warrant a nod of their head, but she did not return the gesture.

"Here, at the memorial to Liya the Lioness. We turn right, yes, now." They near had to barge their way through the press to break from the flow of traffic. They headed for a road half as wide as the Avenue but still able to hold hundreds of Sorans, any accompanying horses, teams of oxen carrying stock, and covered litters carrying notables. This was the Bridge Road, and there it was.

Their guide waited until they came close to explain. "Spanning the two hundred and twenty foot gap between the Manse of Elyan and the Dawnstar Court, I give you the Bridge of Kisses." It arched high as it neared the centre, the span was adorned with a plenitude of whorling Soran glyphs, the columns that stood like petrified limbless trees sheltering those wishing to cross with a peaked stucco roof built in the myriad shapes of sea shells. Beneath the balustrade, an intricate relief mosaic of lapis lazuli, carnelian, tiger's eye, mother of pearl, jasper and fire opals depicted desert flowers growing amongst each other, as though it was a garden suspended above the street. *Gods, tha' white wyrm wasn't even that big. Twice as big? More?*

"It was constructed to help ferry members of the Elyan who had to attend Court, without mingling with the foot traffic or having their robes soiled by nightsoil. In years past, it was a symbol of the forbidden love between those of different Circles. Should a child of one Circle…" Greg reached out for Mayred's hand. It was there, and the feeling of her fingers entwined with his own made his heart leap. The bridge was beautiful, and he was so happy to share it with the one he loved.

"Trysts were made here, on cool nights where they could be alone together, away from the prying eyes of their families. It began with the guardsman whose name history gives us as Liaferro. He was guarding the roadside door to the Court, as he had been unlucky enough to draw the overnight watch. It was midwinter, as the story goes. So he was hunched over his watchfire, cursing his luck, and thinking ahead to his breakfast. It was a quiet night, by all accounts. Until he met them."

"Some have us believe it was an Elyan and her peasant lover. Others say both were merely the children of rival guildsmen, or that both belonged to prominent smithing houses. One apocryphal account claims they were cousins of the Royal House, doomed to live in forbidden love. All that's immaterial. What matters was that Liaferro was there that night when they came, guardsmen hot on their footsteps to send them home."

"With a gruff word and the turn of a key, he told them to get inside the Court. They were desperate, so they did nothing but obey. Good Liaferro was careful to close the door as careful as can be. When the pursuers halted in the light of the fire, they asked the guardsman if he had seen a boy and a girl this way. He shrugged his shoulders and said he would keep an eye out for anyone. The others soon set off, keen to continue the chase for their masters. Liaferro stayed, as was his duty. He stayed, and grumbled at his choices."

"It was further into the night when he heard them first. They were whispering, so he was surprised that he could hear them over the crackling of his fire. But hear them he did. The kisses and the words, the professing of their love, he heard them all. The night passed, and he kept watch for their pursuers. The darkness was their cloak, the guardsman their sentinel."

"When the night was done, he looked for his unlikely charges. He found nothing, but for a ribbon tied to a column on the bridge. Good Liaferro never found the truth of who he had been guarding that night. He burned the ribbon, however, so that their secret would be known only to him and the Gods. To this day, lovers come here hoping to emulate the mysterious tryst of those on the bridge. They also burn tied ribbons in braziers, but only at night."

Mayred laid a hand on Greg's chest. "I… I need to tell you something." The tracker was breathless, and he had the words form in his mind before saying, "Anythin'. What is it? Mayred, what…what is it?"

The Bridge Road was getting busier and busier by the

moment. Mayred swallowed, looking back at the way they came. Cliada cursed. "You lot had your fill of the city? It'll only get busier."

Aud was still looking at the Bridge of Kisses. His smile was wan, and his brow creased. His eyes glistened, too. "Yes. I'd say so. I feel a meal calling me, and a drink."

Cliada made her face again, "Venom, my lord?"

Greg felt himself nodding, but the motion was all too numb. His attention was for his love. She looked pale, too pale for the afternoon heat that still permeated the streets. "It can wait. I'll tell you, but it needs to be a quiet place."

I'd do anything for you. "Aye. I mean, yeah. Jus' tell me when. Whenever you're ready." *You can tell me anything.*

Even with Cliada of the Garrison leading the way, they made for a snail's pace. They rode close by, but Mayred seemed distant as they drifted past the legions of Sorans going to and from *lorets* and winehouses and brothels, wealthy guildsmen returning home atop gilded palanquins after the end of that day's business. It was a frustrating churn, so it was a relief when Audeyrn spotted a group of Headhunters relaxing in one elaborately furnished *loret*. Cliada blew him a mocking kiss and reined in hard at those reclining on feather-filled pillows. They recognised her instantly, dropping their glasses to stand to attention.

They had an honour guard to escort them. The travel was vastly improved, but Greg's mind still grasped at the meaning of Mayred's words. He sent sideways glances her way, but could not bring himself to catch her eye.

What does she mean? Quiet place? What could she wanna say? What makes her so uneasy? Is she unwell...is she... Have I said something? Have I done something? Tell me, tell me, tell me! Please... I love you. I love you so much. You're so beautiful. You're perfect. I wanna be with you forever. I wish it would never end.

They came upon the Great Palace Gate too soon. He had not found the right words for her. He needed to be ready. If he could not be the person she needed him to be, then what was he?

With a word, the sentries at the Gate opened the tall hardiron and bronze doors for the emissaries. It was dark now. The Gate was positioned on the south-eastern side of the Palace walls, so the vestiges of the sun were hidden behind its high walls. When they were inside, he heard himself say, "Aud, I need a moment with Mayred."

He stood tall on his horse as though the weight was no longer on his shoulders. "Of course. Cliada, can you tell the sentries to let them up for supper later this evening?"

The Soran shrugged, saying, "If they want to catch a chill out here, so be it."

With them gone, he was finally alone with the only one that mattered. At her notion, they dismounted, hobbling the horses at the stables used by the common sentrymen. She led him across the empty training yard, with only chickens pecking the flagstones for feed. They found a tower, more secluded than the others, with a sole guard at the threshold to the door leading up the stair. He grunted and led them through. Greg had had just about enough of stairs, but he kept his annoyance hidden behind a wall of anxiety.

"Mayred, where're we going?"

"Someplace quiet," was all she said. He couldn't see her face. She was ahead of him, and it tied his guts into knots.

Without warning the barestone steps gave way to a covered walkway. The way was lit by torchlight, and it made their shadows change into all sorts of shapes as they passed. A turn, and a turn again, and they came to a wallwalk. *Does she know where we're going? What does she plan to do?* He felt a tightening in his groin, his eyes going to the arse before him. Someplace quiet, someplace apart. They arrived, and she was just as surprised as he was. The door before them was unlocked, so they pushed it open for the stars to shine down.

It was half a royal court, and half a bailey. He did not know how else to describe it. To one side a sheltered canvas and stone canopy overhung the openair chamber. The other end was sheltered only by the roof of the world. No torches had been lit here, yet no guards were posted. There was no one. To the left, a crenellated half-circle of a tower top separated them from the emptiness of the fall. Beyond, only domes and spires loomed. Everything was blue, and silver, and night.

He thought about what Cliada had said, about the lovers finding a place for themselves.

She turned to him, her head hung. *Oh please, Gods, no.*

"I think we need to be apart."

The words ripped him inside out. When he tried to breathe, he breathed, but it did not feel as good as before. The stars were dim. The moon was an unwelcome eye, swollen and unwanted. But most of all, he felt relieved. It sickened him.

She looked at him with eyes filled with tears, and try as he might, he tried to get the words out. They deserted him. Keeping her distance, she said, "It is only that I have been given so much to think about. My people…they invaded this land. I came for you, to be with you as you completed your mission to end this strife. But it hasn't solved all the problems. Lord Elmer…my liege…he is *dangerous*. He will bring another war, or worse. I can't be here as it happens. I need to be home. I need to help. If I can help, I should."

Above all that he felt, he was a captive to his confusion. He thought that if he said something, she would change her mind. If there was a chance that she would stay with him, then he should take it…shouldn't he? He needed to be with her forever. He could not be without her. He wanted her. He needed to see her smile, hear her laugh, feel her breath on his cheek, hear the moans as he was inside her.

He could not live without her. But the words that came hid his feelings well. "Okay. I understand. I always tell you that I love you…but it's because it's true. I love you. Everyday, in darkness, and in the daylight, I wanna make you the happiest there is. If that's not being together, then it's okay. I'll wait for you. I mean it. There's only you, Mayred."

The tears ran freely down the face that broke his heart. "I love you too."

As he broke his fast, he found that he had no appetite. Audeyrn was just as confused as he was when he told him. Hearty tried to be sympathetic, but his clunky words and pats on the back did nothing to help. Only the three of them sat at the table that morning when Cliada came to give them her daily scowl of disapproval. Her eyes went to the empty chair next to Greg, and she must have weaselled out what had happened, for she did not ask where the Paydar was.

"Where does the lofty Royal Emissary want to go today?"

She plucked the last rasher of bacon from Hearty's plate as he was about to spear it. *Where would she want to go, after all this? Is she thinking of me now?*

"The hospitality of Silentis knows no bounds, but we have to decline." Aud pushed his chair back from the table, gulping down the last of his wine.

Cliada crossed her arms. "Decline? How formal. Where will you go then?"

"Home."

It took them the day to gather their things. Only the following morn were they ready, their horses and mules assembled in the bailey readying to leave. It was strange to feel so heavy laden after the long leagues with only a few supplies. Greg sat atop his sorrel, the one that had replaced Muddy. He had tried to be angry at him, but that was stupid. His beast was not to blame for his friend's death. He was just a horse, after all. He whinnied loudly when he spotted Greg, which lifted the tracker's sad heart. He chomped down on the bit as he was harnessed and stamped as he sensed their imminent departure. He decided then that he needed a name. *Chomp, that'll do.* It was Cliada who saw them off, showing not a tinge of sadness in their leaving. It was not her way, he had come to realise.

Aud had words with her as they sorted the pack mules for the journey ahead. Greg could not hear what they were saying, but something was whispered in the Soran's ear that made her smile. They left as the sun lit the tips of the highest towers of the Royal Palace. Hearty had his lute in his lap as the party of three joined the first rough hewn cobbles of the long road. That morning, as the warmth was yet to greet them, they fell into the slow dribble of traffic heading southward into the desert. It started slow, but his playing soon fell into the rhythm of the steady hoofbeats of the horses. With a flourish, he launched into *A Song for Winter*.

"I've a story...
To buy my place near the fire, if you'd have me.
A happ'nin' you won't believe, but a tale 'fore we retire.
I always, always I wanted her love,

Knowing...
It would feel so cold, it's chilled my bones.
My woman she's ice and snow, I'd love 'til I was old.
I always, always I needed her love,
Owing...
Everything that was mine, would be all for her.
A cold kingdom all in white, it made me cry.
I always, always I desired her love,
Sowing...
Empty without end, but nothing can grow.
A world empty for us, nothing to mend.
I always, always I dreamed of her..."

"Hearty... please, can we have somethin' a bit lighter." The *twang* that erupted from the knight's lute from Greg's interruption made for a sour note. The knight himself nodded, making his sunburnt chins wobble despite the beard that tried to hide the tomato-red skin. "Aye. You are right, laddie. The *Song* is a dour for such a lovely day."

Aud laughed. "Lovely day? That's an understatement! You've fallen in love with the country, Hearty, and maybe something else too."

The knight scoffed at the sally, and said, "I can get *used to* these Soran winters, is all I'm saying. Anything beats a day on Langholm when it pisses down, clouds shielding the summer sun, then pissing it down some more."

Greg brought Chomp closer to the others. "Ya know it's ill luck to complain about rain when the sun is out. It attracts clouds, and vapours, too."

"You believe that shite?" Hearty slapped his chest. "We shan't see a *drop* until we catch a glimpse of the Wolfswater. Mark my words."

Six days of rain saw them through to Ves, and then four more to see them to the Ikteti hinterlands, to bear down on them in frigid emptiness. They had been given canvas tents by the Sorans for when they made camp. But they were also equipped with broad sheets of oilcloth with a compactible centre pole to shun the winter rains. It surprised Greg to no end. He marvelled at the Sorans' thinking. He would never have thought to pack for such an event. Not that he was ungrateful. Far from it. He gladly crawled under the cover that night, safely sheltered from the cold and wet, and set to stringing his bow. He had chosen to take first watch.

In Ves, they had learned that news had come from on high that hostilities between Sora and Castan were to cease. With a stroke, the war had reached an uneasy end. However, it did not mean those still hungry for blood would suddenly lose their appetite because of the royal word. Dangers persisted, so the party set watches every night and kept their vigilance. He was ready for the monsters, those on four legs and two legs. Lyonis the Yale was not present at the town, his uncle telling them that he was off visiting a friend to the north. Audeyrn laughed hysterically at that.

Sitting cross-legged, he stirred the embers of the fire. The rain had dropped to a drizzle as the night wore on in the Iktet, enough to see the crescent moon ascending. A regular plip-plopping of droplets falling from the edge of the oilcloth made for dismal company. Hearty was snoring, again, and now and then, his tent would stir as the big man turned in his sleep. Audeyrn's tent was silent, peaceful even.

It had been hard, accepting that she was gone. He often woke expecting to see her there, her unbraided hair made unruly by the night. It still hurt, but not as much as it once had. The pain remained, a dull ache in his heart to accompany his other hurts. The cold made it hurt more, so he stirred the fire again, placing some dry brush atop.

Then he heard it. It sounded like a branch snapping. He was standing and had his bow drawn in a heartbeat, an arrow with a grey fletching touching his cheek.

It was dark, and the thick sheets of drizzle lashing down diminished the little light coming from the waxing moon. He thought about calling out *who's there?*, but held off. *Better to be quiet, not give away where I am.*

For a while, he stood, his gaze fixated down the length of the arrow, waiting for another sound amongst the night, a form to move within the shadows, for something, anything, to come nearer to the camp. He was ready for anything. But time crept by, and he heard nothing. The cramp set into his arms, and he lowered his bow, cursing whatever had made him so jumpy.

A fox searching for his dinner, or a rabbit. He did not know if there were any foxes in Iktet, but he had tracked down a rabbit here once. It had been with Mayred. Maybe Aud would know. He would ask him on the morrow. Tending to the fire, he sat back down as close as he dared without getting burned. It was lonely, but at least he was dry. When the moon was at its zenith, and it was finally time to change the watch, he roused Hearty. The big knight emerged from his tent like a bear awoken mid-hibernation but greeted Greg all the same. Then he fell into his own tent and went to sleep thinking of rabbit.

The next day it drizzled, again. They continued, the conversation muted and brief, their cloaks pulled tight about them and hoods concealed their faces. With each passing day, the skies cleared, until their mornings became fresh, and their days were filled with a crisp winter breath. *But it isn't raining though.* The words were kept to himself lest they cause another downpour. They did talk to the passers-by on the long road. Ikteti, for the most part, so talking to them was mainly done in hand gestures and loud repeated phrases. Others were Lowlander from the Paydar, there to trade their goods, and wary of the locals. *A few months ago, they would've been firm enemies,* Greg had to remind himself, *they're afraid their smiles conceal knives 'hind their backs.* Both types were wary of the Caldishmen as they travelled westward. Tanned somewhat by their time in the Tundra, their hair and eyes were still too fair to reasonably pass for Sorans, and they did not know the Ikteti dialects, so they told anyone brazen enough to ask that they were Lar'garans. Those mysterious peoples from the Windscape Peninsula north of Castan were far too remote and far away for them to claim that the party were not who they said they were, so most just accepted, and they kept any further questions to themselves.

A few more weeks having passed, Wolfsmouth drew closer, until they crested a hill to spot the Span and Brinewater Keep and the Dome of Life rise up from the river's estuary as though hands hailing their return. Audeyrn was visibly uneasy. He had been loath to come back, but they had no choice in the matter. The Wolfswater during winter was infamous for its speed and ferocity, and any attempts to cross required sturdy ferries. Swimming was a fool's act, Aud claimed. There was a crossing in Halfway using the Arch, but that would mean them turning north, and into the arms of Darge Pirellion. Lyonis of Ves had been adamant that Pirellion would strappado them. When asked by Hearty why, Lyonis had replied that Pirellion hated anything associated with his rival.

That left only Wolfsmouth, or travelling the length of the 'water to find a tributary calm enough to accommodate them, their luggage, mules, and safety. *No,* Aud had been iron in his decision, *we go through Wolfsmouth, and we do it quietly.* Greg did not think he was the most intelligent, but he knew what Aud was hiding from. He had promised important people to do certain things, and now that the fighting had ended... they would seek him out.

The gate to the city was crammed with people. A customs officer was screaming at those wanting to enter the city in his Qellish tongue. "Get back! Back, I said! You can enter, but it must be orderly. Yes, there is a toll, but it is reasonable. Ask my assistant for the particulars. No, you cannot admit your cow as a child, that'll be for a different concession. Yes, you, come through. Yes, you. No, not *you.* You!"

"Thank the gods the Merbeasts aren't here." Aud had his

hood up and had let his beard grow out the past weeks. Even if the Merbeasts were at the gate, he doubted they would recognise the bearded man in desert garb. As though in an effort to outdo his friend, Hearty had also let his beard grow, until it had reached his chest. "How's this to be done quietly, Aud? Lots of eyes and ears about."

"Aye, but there's more than one way to ensure discretion." He caught the attention of a bored assistant, and then came close to say something that was lost to the crowd. He also planted something hard in the man's waiting palm. Aud turned, and pointed at Greg and Hearty arrayed by their belongings. The assistant walked over to them, with the arrogance only the educated could possess. "Three farmers, newly out of the Iktet, by way of Seaton. Brothers all, you make your trade by trading Ikteti garments. Tired of the Soran occupation, you have decided to set up a company here. Come." The rest was following him as they were escorted through a previously locked side door. Shouted complaints erupted from those awaiting entry, which the official with the strained look about his face tried to quell.

Walls newly made for the war bore down on them as they passed beneath. It did not take long, as another door opened, revealing the bustling streets of the eastern city bank. And like that, they disappeared into the masses.

They crossed the Span, negotiated the winding streets of the western bank, and found their beleaguered way onto Fishcatcher's Walk. The gates were open, the long road thick with those wishing to enter from the Paydar and the Ruell coastlands. Greg saw the teams of gigantic aurochs had been corralled into their pens, and were busy being tended to by groomsmen. There were no officials here. The only guards were civic sentries whose role it was to keep the peace. And still, no godsforsaken Merbeasts. Audeyrn caught Greg's reins.

"Wait a moment, would you?" He caught Hearty's attention, and sat in his saddle, a smile creeping across his blonde beard.

"I know I have asked everything of you. I am sorry for that. Would I have had a second chance, I would have done things differently. I may have been better. I might have not let–"

Nat die? Audeyrn looked away, before meeting their eyes again. "I don't know where I need to be now. But I do know that it's not Castan. I will not be his Royal Emissary any longer. Hearty, you can return to Langholm, if you'd like. I know Clay will have you there."

Hearty puffed up his chest so he didn't look sad. "I will always stay with you, my lord."

"And Greg," There were tears in his eyes, those ashen grey eyes that could be stony and kind, wrathful and despairing. They were happy now, Greg could see.

"Will you go back to the Dun Vale? Or my family's fortress at Langholm? You will not know Sir Clay Costigan, but he is a friend and kin through marriage, and I trust him to keep you safe."

Greg did not know what to say. Langholm was an island, and the castle that Audeyrn held as lord in all but name. It was said to be fearsome to behold. Or home… he could see the mill, walk on the frozen streams again, be at peace… "Where will you go?" He asked Aud. The world around him had turned hazy, so he blinked it away.

"North. I need to find something, something I'm not even

sure exists. Lar'gara!"

Greg spoke before he got even more confused. "I'll come with you. You can't be alone. You may not be the Emissary no longer, but you're still my friend. If you'll have me along, that is."

"*Ha!*" Audeyrn clapped him on the shoulder. "Of course you–"

"What about me?" Asked the boy atop his scrawny firemane. Hearty laughed, and upon seeing Audeyrn's open mouth only laughed harder.

The boy furrowed his brow, so that the six-fingered hand moved. He frowned at Greg. "*You* promised to teach me archery."

Three became four as they journeyed across the coastlands. Much was changed. The land where once hosted armies had healed, newsprung grass fought frost where before had been encampments. Those they met along the long road seemed cheerful, and talked to them happily as they crossed paths. Along the way, they had the story out of Jephro. Escorted back to Wolfsmouth by the remaining Merbeasts, he had tried to find the *Red Raven* in the arsenal, but had discovered that the ship along with its captain and crew had departed. He met his kinsman Captain Arodyr Rowett, who had attempted to marry him to Lady Torrin's daughter. Disgusted at the thought of marrying someone, he had escaped, resolving to wait for the Caldishmen, each day making his way to the gates in the vain hopes that he would see them. And one day, he did just that.

Greg was happy to fulfil his promise to Jephro, and he found that the hand did not disturb him anymore. The boy was not a natural archer, but he was determined. Greg spent his days tracking game, having the young Rowett boy along to listen to what he had to say, and to learn. *One day, he'll be a good tracker. I feel it.* It was one clear winter's day when, finally, after a week on the road, Jephro had asked what had happened to Mayred.

The weather turned, but it was Greg's mood that was darker. Unable to speak for the pelting of the rain upon oilcloth, he shimmied from his tent, and told Jephro that he would relieve him of watch. He sat there, alone with his thoughts. It was almost relaxing, listening to the rain. Soothing, even. His eyes were dropping when he heard the figure approach.

"You, stop! I said stop!" He struggled with his bow, but had it readied as the man was ten foot from the rain cover. At least, he thought it was a man. The large shoulders, and suggestion of a beard beneath his deep cowl gave it away.

"Put it down. You know me."

"Murder! Fie! Wake, wake! Get up, *quick!*" His heart thumped hard in his chest, and his ears burned.

"They can't hear you. Let me speak. Listen to me. You recognise my voice. Remember me now?" He did remember that voice. It gave him pause. *Why can't the rest of them hear?* The thought seemed unimportant, though. Something told him he needed to listen. His bow arm lowered, and the arrow dropped to the ground. With hands raised, and open to show that he was unarmed, the man ducked beneath the cover, and then lowered his cowl. The face beneath was more lined, and the beard greyer than before. His eyes still danced though, with an inner light filled with mischief. *I see it, it's you.*

"Hello, Greg," Govier said with a tired smile.

"Why are you here?" It sounded pitiful, but he needed to know.

"To show you the way."

"The way home? You follow the long road" His mind filled with the sound of the water wheel and the old millstone, the laughter of children playing in the pond at the edge of the village, the smell of flowers in spring, the kiss from his mother as she said goodnight.

"No," The man looked pained.

"Then what?" *Please don't. Please.* He desperately wanted to run away, he wanted nothing but to know. Govier made sure he looked him in the eye when he said, "To the next fight."

Greg shook his head, not wanting to believe what he had heard. "But it's over."

"The fight is never over when there's still good people in this world. You need to tell Audeyrn, and the rest. I will show you where... *they* are."

He fought for his next words. "Who? Tell me."

"The monsters."

36

THE MONSTER

He told them to shut their mouths. The silence was instant, for out here, his word was law, and they knew it was foolish to evoke his fury. Not that it would stop them from talking before too long. They were never loud, not loud enough to draw attention anyway, but he just hated their fucking talking. Talking, talking, talking. It was all they ever did. If he didn't need them so, he would gladly have killed them all.

Loyal. Brave and stupid, but loyal above all else.

They averted their gaze as he unlaced himself and drew out his cock, letting the piss arch high. He sighed in relief. The fountain he made was yellow, and it stank, and he knew he had drunk too little water. Not that that could be helped. They had found no fresh water since leaving the Wolfswater behind them, save for the few villages that boasted a well. This one did not enjoy such luxuries. The water that was left to the company was rationed, and stale. It was a shoddy situation, but nothing he hadn't endured before. The men about him complained, he knew. But not to his face, and

never loud enough for him to hear. They had enough sense
to know *that* would only result in red bloody ruin. Skinner
prided himself on his hearing.

Shaking off the last drops, he tucked himself back in, and
eyed the watchmen in turn. They were two, of the twelve
that now sat huddled in their huts. *Nineteen.* That was all
that remained of those that fled their outpost at Bagman's
Bluff. Commander Garance had ordered him to harry the
locals, while they evacuated the garrison in the fort. He had
forty-four back then. All chosen to be under his command.
All chosen to be left behind. *Nineteen*. Them that had been
deemed worthy had gone back through the rift, the brace
of the gate set to self-sabotage when the last were safely on
the other side. Back home, back to Godswrath. *Fuckers, the
lot of them.*

The village they had chosen as their camp was old, but
those that had been living there had maintained it well,
despite being piss-poor peasants. The meagre defences
helped them not, as Skinner came through the trees at the
head of his blackcloaks. Five families, not including the
village chief's household. Only an old man had decided to
put up a fight as they surrounded them. The screams of the
women and children had caused this certain greybeard to
emerge from his hovel, bearing a dirk crusty with bright
rust and a loud mouth full of curses. The sight had been
hilarious to Skinner. He challenged the man to a duel. The
fool accepted, as he had hoped.

Meat hung from the fires the blackcloaks made in the
hovels and in the open, smoke drifting up in thin grey waves
into a darker sky. He could imagine it turning on the spits,
flesh charred black, grease running off to fall into the flames

with a hiss. His mouth watered. The night was cold, so he had allowed most of his men to claim the stone roundhuts for themselves. Were they to die of a chill, his command would diminish even further. He would not allow that to happen.

His footsteps took him on a round of the village. He needed to be refreshed before he returned to the work. Trees sprung up everywhere, so his walk was crabbed as he inspected his meagre command. The wood that had kept their attack concealed from the village folk had long encroached and breached the perimeter of the village, overtaking it until it was reclaimed fully by the unruly ranks of fir and birch and ash. The ringwall encircling the village was low, reaching to his waist at its highest. That had made him smile when they attacked, whereas now he only grimaced. To the north-side was the keep itself, more a stone longhouse than anything else. A thatch roof and a smoke hole to one end, a pile of firewood arranged flush against the south wall, his lordly seat was covered in lichen and moss, and drying blood. It offered shelter from the rain at the least, and his prize deserved only the best he had to offer.

Silence fell upon the village in the woods. It was cold, and a cloud billowed out before him every time he exhaled. It was thirsty work, was love. He licked his chapped lips, wishing he had a jug of brown beer to warm him. *Wish all I want, it does fuck all.* He wished for many things, and all it came to was to leave a bitter taste in his mouth. *Great One, child of man and child of destiny, where is the rift? Fucking tell me. Tell me. Tell me, damn you.*

The others might follow that twisted mooncalf with the

blind obedience espoused by their betters in Godswrath, but Skinner knew better. It had been the Child and his idiotic followers that had abandoned him here. This… strange world. In preparation, the proctors had drilled into him everything there was to know about the continent. The Paydar, the people, and their alliances, chiefly. House Rowett in its lofty fortress atop the Tor. The Wolfswater and its countless branches. The history of the Qellish conquerors and the ingenious constructions they left behind. The Qellish tongue itself. The war between Castan and Sora, and the pliable idiot who sat the western throne. Everything the Child had gleaned from his travels, or so they had been told. Everything, but for the location of the rifts.

What door can be opened, but has no hinges? Can be locked, but has no key? You may pass through, yet no longer be found?

So the riddle went, spoken by children and grown men alike at Godswrath. He cared not for such glib speech. He knew only flesh. The feeling of an enemy falling onto his blade, coming so close to him he could smell the sweat across his brow, practically taste the blood in his mouth, the semen on his cock. *All that matters in life, not… whatever this is. Ruling here is a bore, but why stop here?* He would have been lying to himself if he said the idea of ruling did not have a certain allure. *Get back home, firstly. Such a return would not be seen as weakness. No, they'll see us as valuable fonts of information on this fucking place. Me, in particular. Me. Who says the rest of these fuckers will even make it back? The Child only needs me. A new commission, a new command… for when the strike begins. I need only do what I do best. Make these ponytailed peasants piss their breeches of the very mention of*

Skinner, the Paragon of Butchery, Lord of Pain, Justiciar of the Damned. A few short years is all that's needed for this world. It will fall, like the others. How can it not? Then a pension, large enough to build myself a strong keep in the Paydar. Why not take the Tor itself? There will be feasts in my honour, all those assembled will drink to my name... my true name. Women will beg to fuck me. Pretty high-born maidens clad in silk and lace, or nothing at all. Left naked, so that I can pour milk down their supple young bodies, and lick it where it pools.

A few wives. Why should their fathers have cause to complain of the marriage? I will be a great lord. No, a king. King. Yes... Wives, to fill my bed and warm me of a night. To suck my cock and to be used. They'll fuck each other too, but they'll think of me while they eat each other's cunts. Who could deny a king that? The order will sniff about now and again, no doubt, to make certain I am a loyal vassal to them, and to the Child himself. No matter. I'll make pleasant noises when they come a-calling, feed them well, and have them bothering someone else in no time. In time they'll even forget about me. In time, I can be a true king. My sons will be the most famous men in the world, after myself. They should fight for my affection, as all sons will when fathers are concerned, and if they forget themselves, the others will simply kill them for me. I will have wives to fuck, and they can always make more.

The thoughts of fucking were making him hard, so he turned about. The smoke from the hovels was hanging low in the air, giving the whole village an eerie, wraithlike aspect. It looked to him as though the place could vanish at any given moment. It hung like a fog, enveloping the village in the wood. Like lich-men disturbed from slumber, returned to this plane as restless wights. The blackcloaks had despoiled the lichyard after all, the tombstones toppled and broken, graves pissed and spat upon. As was custom. *It was only right. Gods are evil, and those that follow them even worse.* It still made him uneasy, seeing the place so… still. Despite his hatred of chatter, he would have loved nothing better than for a thousand loud voices to gabber then, for the place to seem a little less… *Haunted.*

At the very thought of the word, he felt his mouth go dry and his erection subside.

The trees around him shuddered as a gust of wind wound its way between their limbs. Ancient hoary birches and spindly ash, they all creaked and groaned, as though the trees themselves had heard his thoughts. *How absurd.*

Sneering disgust at the whole damned thing, he turned on his heels. He was tired, but not so tired that he could not continue the task at hand. He had only left to take a piss. Dead leaves crunched under his boots as he strode between the sad, low ceilinged hovels. He heard the faint muffled muddling of talk coming from one. He let it go undisturbed.

What the fuck is wrong with me? His stride quickened, grinding his teeth as the voice of his dogs receded behind him. The truth would be revealed soon enough, he did not doubt. The truth behind everything. There was only one distraction he needed to concern himself with, and her name, he had discovered, was Marble.

"I'm not to be disturbed, ya hear? Anyone that comes inside will be gutted." The guard that stood beside the longhouse's door bobbed his head vigorously, saluting as he did. *I'll share my princess with no one. Her secrets are mine.*

The firepit still smouldered angrily, he could see: red-hot spots in the burnt wood were little scarlet eyes shining up from the ashes. To his left, the chief of that irksome little village had his bed. It was ample-sized enough, he had found. The furs were dishevelled now, the sheets stained. To the right, a low table made of splintery old planks was host to the remains of last night's supper, the grease that covered the bones congealed. On the far wall had been a tapestry depicting two figures. *That* had been burned the moment he saw it. The figures had been surrounded by men and women with heads bowed, hands raised, all begging succour from the twin god and goddess. *Blasphemy. Ocrian would have been wroth.* It had been covered in all sorts of black mold, and it had stank when the flames licked up the images of the dead gods. He much preferred what hung in its place.

The fetters that bound her hands to the top corners of the wall by a big heavy chain were made of dark iron. They were long enough for her to rest on the ground, albeit without her being able to move her arms. The feet were also bound in similar fetters that connected foot to foot to hands, the extra links arching behind her back to meet her wrists. The combined weight of all those heavy, heavy chains had eaten into the pale flesh of her wrists, until long streamers of bright red blood flowed down her slim arms. He had to bite his tongue to resist the urge to lick her clean. Other cuts and bruises dappled her exposed thigh, her neck, the slashes across her chest beneath her soiled clothes. The sight would have been horrible for someone who lacked his vision, he knew, but the ignorant would always fail to understand. That was only the start… It was her face that had received most of his attention. One eye was closed shut, the swelling from his latest kiss a ripe plum covering the left side of her face. *It has the same colour of a plum, or close enough.*

"You are so beautiful." His words were met with silence, falling on deaf ears. She remained quiet, until he was convinced that her pain had caused her to pass out. She did not even seem to be breathing. Skinner felt his heart leap into his throat. It could not end like this, he had tried so very hard… he reached down, his hand going to her cheek, only for a pair of bloodied teeth to strike at his hand. She was fast, despite her hurts. He was faster.

"Beautiful, and so very deadly," he said, crying laughter. *She is perfect.* His hand was at her throat then, throttling her. The wheezing noise that escaped her was as dry as dust, almost a death rattle. *How close to death will she be by sunrise?* he mused. The lessons had to be taught. It was necessary, and besides, he was enjoying his time with her.

Releasing his grip, he relished in seeing the marks his fingers had made to the skin at her neck. Her sharp intake of breath made him hard. "So beautiful. You know, I thought I'd never meet you."

A venomous eye peered through the veil of filthy white hair. "Fuck… you… You're going to… die… I'm going… to kill you."

"That's going to be difficult." Skinner pulled up a stool, and straightened out his apron before him as he sat. A lot of the blood decorating the front was hers. "I feel changed by you, you know. I feel so happy." The girl laughed, and it sounded grim. Making a face, she hawked a gobbet of phlegm into his face.

Had any other woman done that to him, he would have

raped them while he ripped the skin from their bodies. It was tempting, but this was no ordinary woman. The splat the rheum made on his cheek was as soft as a kiss. He eagerly spooned it with his hands, licking them clean as he tasted her on his lips. "Do you want to know why I've kept you alive?" *She must have wondered. She must have.* "Why do I want you?"

"You like to... hurt people." Her voice was as unyielding as hardiron, as implacable as granite. He shushed her with a finger to her dry lips.

Skinner shook his head. "No. I want to find truth... meaning, in all of this. Humans... why are we the way we are? Why do we fight, if not to gain something the enemy possesses? I took this village from the people that lived here, because we required a place to shelter. We confronted the villagers, fought them for it, and won. Now I possess the village. It is mine. It belongs to me. Much like you, though you refuse to accept it. But deep down, I feel it. The urge. The desire. You want truth as much as I do, but you tell yourself otherwise. Yet I see it. I see *you*. I know what you are." That made her look up, the dim light of the longhouse making her eye sockets look like hollows in the snow. "You know nothing. But I know something about you." A response from her, at last.

"What is that?"

"You're a cunt, who's going to die screaming."

The frustration bubbled up inside him. He promised himself he would be restrained. The punch that hit her in the ribs made the chains jump and clatter. Marble only grunted, her mouth opening to leave a string of bloody slaver dribble to the packed earth of the floor. Her aversion to his usual methods irked him, and he considered hitting her again, or maybe cutting some things off. He relented. All that required effort, and he did not want to damage his queen too much. "This farce you present to me *will* break soon. You can insult me and spit at me, but sooner rather than later, you will know what you are. I am certain of it. Then, if you behave, you'll have my permission to go about unfettered. You'll even be allowed to touch me." *And so much more. That mouth will be used. And your cunt. I'll use your blood to guide my cock inside you. To feel my love as I hurt you. You'll beg for me to hurt you, my queen.*

The sound of gritted teeth came from Marble as she pulled herself upright. The effort caused new streamers of blood to wash down her arms. She shuddered, but still managed to raise her head to look Skinner in the eye. Her own eye was unblinking, and the more he seemed to regard it, the more the colour seemed to change. He loved that about her. He silently cursed himself for striking her three days past, without regard for that pretty face. He could not wait until the swelling went down. Then he could see both of her fiery eyes dance in the light of his cabin. When she finally changed. When she would become his. Forever.

She smiled. Not her usual sardonic grin, that he had grown fond of despite her aversion to his advances. No. It was full, and she showed him her teeth. His cock strained against his breeches. *Good girl. She should smile more. Those lips, those teeth.* "Why do you smile?" The smile she wore only got wider. He wanted nothing more than to fuck her then and there. Instead, he clenched his fists until it hurt, and leaned in as close to her as he dared. The thrum of the blood in his ears was near deafening. "Tell me."

573

He saw the tongue as it played across her teeth. "I'm thinking, about what hell I'm going to send you to." He had promised himself he would be restrained.

The night drew in. His meal arrived in the form of three knocks at the door. Scorched meat, swimming in fat. The same as the night before, and the night before that. It was seared black on the outside, and the snowflakes that had fallen upon it melted instantly as he collected it.

The blade was wedged in the wood of the table. The tug to retrieve it made a loud splintering sound, one he knew his fickle prize would hear. He felt whole with his *lady* in his hand. It was more than a weapon. It was a tool, able to shape and redefine objects at his will. And it had. The pommel was a piece of moonstone shaped cunningly into a skull, the mandibles open wide to allow for a spinel cut into a red heart to be bitten by the white teeth. The leather of the hilt was dyed a deep crimson, the skin of the first woman he ever bedded. The blade itself was long and serrated, from an iron crossguard two fullers ran down its length. He had debated for a long time whether or not to name his tool. In the end, he had settled on Pet. *And what a good little pet it is.*

Only when the fire had been fed, and the flames were roaring high and loud, did he return to the table. She would also have heard the sound it made as he used Pet to carve his meat. It was sharp. The blackcloaks were trained to care for their blades. It had always been the same, even for Skinner.

Holding a chunk of steaming red flesh in his hand, he made a salute. It was clumsy and effete, the kind that will have earned him a day and a night of lashes back at the sanctuary. Thank fuck he wasn't back there. Not yet. He had every freedom here, in this world, and they had to be relished. Before he discovered the way back. Before Marble was able to see. So until that time, he would make mock of his people, and live a little along the way. "All hail the Child! Son of man, son of destiny! May he reign forever! And the rest, blah, blah, blah." When he had had his fill, he replaced Pet in the table. He found that he was in the mood to talk. He could have done with the bed, to give the girl some *copezh* and tumble her for a while, and then some shut eye. He even reached for his satchel containing the powder.

Not much was left. He cursed, angry that it was near empty. A handful and a half remained, if that. A fortnight's worth? He tossed the satchel aside, and headed for his bed. It was lumpy, the mattress overfilled with feathers and old rags. The furs smelled rank. *Wouldn't smell so bad if I had some beer.* Wishing he had something to swill down the meat, his mind wandered to Marble again. Truth be told, she had never left his mind.

Her hanging on the wall was arousing. With his inner eye, he imagined her walking towards him. She was breathless, and she all but threw off her clothes. His hand went down to his cock. Soon he was undressed, and all he saw was her.

"Look at me." The girl failed to move. *I'm not falling for that again, bitch.* Her hands were all over him, biting, sucking, wanting... He needed her to look at him, to see how much he loved her. "Fucking look at me!"

The door pounded by a mailed fist. Skinner dashed to the table, wrenching Pet out and brandishing it with a snarl. Now he heard it, the sound of alarm, coming from outside. Skinner knocked the stool over in his haste striding to the doors. The pain made him wince. As he reached the doors they burst open, nearly slamming him in the face. "WHAT IS IT?!" His shock was hidden by the fury in his voice.

"Commander! I'm sorry to intrude." The sentry was out of breath, and the blood had drained from his face. Skinner said nothing, and the sentry did not seem to notice that he was naked, and erect besides. "I'm so sorry. But, but, hostiles 'av breached the wall. Sorans, by the looks of 'em. Armoured, on warhorses."

"Sorans? Are you drunk?" That was ludicrous. The nearest client state of the Kingdom of Sora was hundreds and hundreds of leagues due east. The fighting had ceased too, if their last hosts were telling it true. The Sorans were a spent force, long retreated east of the Wolfswater. None remained west of the Wolfswater. None... *So why the fuck are they here?*

Hoarse laughter erupted from the girl chained to the wall. "I'll be cross if they kill you... lover."

"Shut your fucking mouth!" He turned to the sentry. "Rouse anyone not already alerted. The time for subtlety is done. Now we show these peasants who we are. Who we *truly* are. We need to educate them. That the Children of the One do not cower, we do not hide. We lust for blood. Tell the rest! Tell them! No one is to be spared. All must die."

37

THE HERO

The first man fell with a scream, an arrow catching him in his visor. He had not seen where the archer was hiding, nor did his companion. That one went down with a gurgle, the arrow punching through his throat. He fell onto his back, so that a tiny tree with grey fletching sprouted from between helm and gorget. Both fell as one, the clatter of their black plate armour enough to wake a sleeping giant.

No giants came, but another man, wearing the same black armour and cloak rushed over to investigate the din. This one had the sense at least to duck for cover behind the wall as soon as he saw his fallen comrades. He lowered his spear too, so that the archer would be none the wiser as to his position as he scuttled about on the far side.

The attacker kept his bow drawn, but dropped it a fraction to survey the perimeter. Between the boughs of trees, long tendrils of mist clung with a clammy mien, all too tranquil for the hell that was about to be let loose. More mist mingled freely with low-hanging smoke closer to the village proper. It was dark, the new moon a hidden spectre in the night sky. Dark, but the archer had keen eyes, and he saw the glint of mail and spearhead as those within shuffled about, unaware and all too lax that someone might be out in the trees. The ghost in the wood was careful to muffle the noise his actions made, and to regulate his breathing until his heart slowed its pace. His prey was not his usual kind. It was easier to hunt though, all things considered. They were noisier than animals, and clumsier too. Their armour making so much noise as they moved about that he was sure he could have found his mark with his eyes closed.

No one was fool enough to look over the wall. He was a hundred yards away, so any noise the Godless made was too faint for him to guess any hiding places. With a long exhale, he shifted his own location amongst the wood. This far away from the perimeter, he could easily find a shot where the trees just happened to give a clear view of the village. A few steps to his left, a few yards forward, there, he found another view of the wall. Still no one.

Greg let his anxiety flare for all a moment, until he remembered the words that Aud had said back at their makeshift camp. He had been half-armoured at the time, Greg busying himself with the ringmail shirt and coif. The gambeson over that had belonged to someone else, but it fit easily enough.

Take them out, quietly if you can. When the alarum is raised, do not worry. The Paydar suit of plate had been discarded in favour of mail and leather, Greg had not failed to note. *Chaos is the element of all this. Keep moving. Have them guessing. Let them run themselves ragged as we attack from three fronts. Like a hawk we have to strike from a distance.*

Lightning attacks. Let confusion reign within their ranks.

Three fronts. Lightning attacks. Confusion. He had left his friends two hours past midnight, Aud and Jeph mounted on their firemanes, Hearty armoured from head to toe in heavy plate, praying to the gods for a sure victory. Snow came, but it was light, too little to stick. That was for the good. Greg did not want his enemies tracking his movements in white as he picked them off. They separated, opting for their assigned positions outside the village. Aud and Jeph were to attack from the north, delivering weaving raids on any sentries posted there. Hearty was to position himself south-west, and was to simply walk into the village as an unyielding steel golem brandishing his broadsword. *The gods help anyone that stands in his way...* Greg himself was to go south-east, where his skills with the bow would let him dispatch the black-clad foes without risk of being seen.

The signal for them to begin their assault demanded them to remain unseen and quiet. No war horns here, only the sound of the alarum being raised. It demanded that death will come before the Godless are even alerted. *Two dead already, and the one that should be crying bloody murder is cowering behind the wall. How're we to begin?* He shifted his position again, the inability to know where the third man was, gnawing away at his resolve. The arrow was at his cheek, the bow groaning ever so slightly as he moved. The wind was a low murmur at his ear. The snow began to fall. It covered the forest floor, and there it stayed.

Fuck.

He wanted to run to the border wall, but he could not risk stepping on an errant branch, for the sound to echo loud and large in the dead quiet. Greg gritted his teeth and moved as quick as he dared. The trees were silent watchers, their thoughts unknowable as he passed between them, ducked beneath a one of their cousins pulled from its roots by some wind, loped over a young stream with water filled with rotted bracken. The ghost in the wood was a part of the wood itself. Ever so often, he stopped, shimmying up beside the nearest bole, his body all but becoming one with the old sentinel. *Patience. The man can't move. He knows he has t'stay. If he moves, he'll make noise. Then the hunter will know. Patience.*

The ground leading to the wall was littered with bracken. Brown stalks turning whiter with every moment that passed. *Fuck.* He edged up to a hardy old blackthorn. He swallowed hard as he saw how thick the bracken grew from here to his quarry's hideyhole.

The bracken will be cold, and snap. Snaps make noise. Them on the ground'll make even more noise. Snow fallin' from the stalks may worsen it. Then there's the ground itself. Ice crunches under foot...

His bow loosened in his arms. The arrow with the grey feathers was replaced in his quiver at his hip. The one that he now fastened to the bow had black feathers. The bodkin point shone darkly as he pulled the drawstring. He stepped out from the cover of the trees. Greg took a step forward, and onto the frozen earth.

The sharp crunch of snow and ice under foot caused the man to bolt. The black-clad figure sprinted in the direction of the small huts further in the village. Then he was falling, his face planting into the ground as his feet were thrown high into the air. It was grotesque, the joints all moving at unnatural angles. But he was dead. The arrow pointing skyward as the bodkin's shaft stuck out from the black helmet of the sentry.

He's dead. Now what?

The arrows he retrieved from the dead. Searching them, he looked for what he had hoped sentries on duty to carry. Expecting a war horn, he was surprised when the instrument he found was not horn at all, but made of brass. *A trumpet, huh.* Then he looked down at the two leaning against the wall, and the one halfway to the huts. One was grey-bearded, he saw, the other younger even than Greg.

"I'm sorry. I didn't wanna kill you. But you followed the one who kills for pleasure. You might have done some too, I dunno. Whoever you were, I hope you can find peace in wherever comes next. I do hope so." He held the trumpet in one hand, listening to the quiet of the night. He was sad. It had to come to an end. He did not want it to. He wanted to rage and scream, to enjoy the solitude, to imagine the better times. Times with his friends, with the one he loved, of rainy days in the blackwood, of being so high in the snowmonts he could touch the Palace of the Fay, of nights in the grasslands of Iktet, the winters in the High Forks.

I jus' wish I could've shown her. Maybe she'd've liked that. He blew the trumpet.

Battle came to his ears in the form of the song of steel and gut-wrenching screams. Others in black cloaks and black mail and nothing at all hurtled out of their huts. Some bore axes, others short swords and daggers. Most held spears, long shafts of dreadblack wood with large iron broadheads topping them, looking all too much like a forest brought to life. Greg tried to count them, but as more appeared, as they moved among the other huts, he could not be certain of their number. None looked in his direction. None saw their fallen brethren. The bloodlust was up, and they looked instead for direction. They shouted in a language he did not understand. It sounded like the captured Godless in the Outer Qell. He could not recall what his name had been.

Seeing his chance, he vaulted the wall. Knees bent as he landed, dropping to one knee to pull back his bowstring. A dull pain throbbed in his thigh. He was spoilt for choice of target. They could not have been thirty yards from him. It was a sure hit.

Someone else sounded a trumpet. The clamour distorting the sounds around him, so he could not tell which directiocame from. The Godless only became more agitated, pulling on whatever bits of armour they could find in the discord. They did not seem to know where it had come from either.

It must have been chance. Greg was crouched, yet still out in the open. That's how the one sentry saw him. Even from a distance, Greg saw the man's eyes go wide, his mouth agape. He detached himself from the others, running towards the big long building with the thatch roof.

Now or never. Now! His breath came ragged. The air tasted sweeter somehow. Time slowed, and he was the fastest thing in that molasses world. An arrow struck a spearman in the heart, another taking a large brute in his mouth. His scream was horrible to hear. The others fled, seeing now that a hidden enemy was picking them off, one by one. He did not envy the fear they must have felt then. Nor what they were running into. Somewhere out there, a Caldland knight in full armour was waiting, some devil from the Hell Unending clad in steel.

A rivulet of sweat ran down his face. The Soran scarf stuck to his cheeks when he turned his head, wound in the way they had it to shield from the sun, but it also kept his coif from reflecting in firelight. That had been his idea. They all wore their dun and sand-coloured robes, the fabric lightweight yet flexible, and much more versatile than their old Caldish dark travel cloaks. All but Hearty. His role in the attack demanded that he remained highly, and dangerously, visible at all times. The material was well-made, breathable yet insulating, woven for the scions of the Circles. Not for attacking at night. Nevertheless, they wore the coverings. He wondered if this was what it was like being part of the Garrison.

Sudden movement ahead of him made him tighten his grip on the bow. No sooner had one of the Godless emerged from the hut running, than an arrow was flying at his throat. Then he was dropping like a sack. Several voices came from within, Greg thought they were arguing. A few times he glimpsed spearheads slip in and out of view. Slowing his breathing even more, he heard the sounds of boots scuffing on packed earth, struggle as strong men tried to push their smaller and weaker companions out the door, fists meeting faces as teeth were flung loose. The more he listened, the more the world unseen was painted in his mind. It was like he was watching a world only he could see. Not with eyes, no, but with something only he knew. He counted the steps, the breathing, the spears that rattled inside the hut. Then he knew that there were three men inside. One was limping. Another was flatfooted. The third was, in fact, female.

Three. He kept himself low as he approached the nearest hut, the one next to the haven of his enemies. Edging around the side, he pulled the bowstring back until it scraped his cheek. *Now or never. Now!*

A door slammed open, so loud he thought it must have wrenched it off its hinges. It was strange then, that the hut's door remained pulled tight and shut. The sound had come from his right…

"Come out! Come out! Come and see what I have!" Greg hid behind the crumbling wattle wall of the hut. Then he looked at the man cloaked in night. He held a bruised and beaten girl in his arms. Wrapped in a length of thick chain, he had her bound. The way she hung limp told Greg that she was out cold, her face a red ruin beneath a rat's nest of pale hair and filth. He pulled her close, a long face with eyes feverish bright framed by long lank hair the same colour as his dreadblack cloak. Beneath, all he wore were stained breeches, and a baldrick sheathing a skull pommel blade. His chest was exposed to the night's chill, and his feet were bare and caked with mud.

"Here for the girl? Show yourselves, and I might consider not opening her throat. Do it! Do it now, or she dies!"

Only you can show them the way, the fickle Govier had said. He had answered no questions posed to him. He had only shook his head. *I say too little, I know. But even that is extreme. Show them the way, Gregyn of the High Forks. What happens then…*

He desperately searched around him for a sign that the others were close. That they had heard what the captor had said. It couldn't be left up to him. He was only a tracker. He wasn't from a known family or belonging to a renowned guild. He was an archer, a hunter, a poacher (and a bad one at that), he could not be left to deal with such a man. He looked about again, maybe this time he would see the steel apparition of a titan rise from the mists, or a grey-eyed emissary on horseback wielding his long sword. The sound of battle could be heard some ways off. It was indistinct, but it told him all he needed to know. It was him. Only him.

Greg emerged, and faced the enemy. "Here. I'm here."

The man at the threshold slitted his eyes in deep suspicion. "Drop the bow, and that knife o' yours. Quick about it." Greg unfastened his quiver, unsheathed his knife, pulled his bow in hand. He let them drop noisily to the mud. "Good boy. Now kick 'em away." He did as the man bid. He had no other choice. The girl muttered something.

"Shut the fuck up! Now... *you*. You don't have the look of a Soran 'bout you, yet you wear their desert garb." Greg could see the man's mind working away. His hand briefly touched the skull pommel of the long piece of steel at his hip. Then he pulled back, saying, "How did you find us?"

A wizard told me. Greg almost laughed. He grappled for a believable lie. Something told him that this man could sniff out such untruths. He decided to lie, with the truth. "We are on a mission."

"Mission? You trying to fucking stall while your fuck-buddies raid my men? Tell me who you are... now. The Soran whore obviously means something to you..."

Save the girl, if you can.... Govier had left him with those words. He was tired. Of *ifs* and *maybes*, of the world being so confusing. The chaos that breeds chaos. But he knew

585

what was certain in his life. That he was here to help. *I'm meant to be here. This moment. That girl...*

The girl's one good eye opened slightly then. The movement was tiny, but it was there. It was strange, but he thought that she was responding to *him*. There was a voice, too. Telling him to be brave. It was good. It was comforting. The man could not see her eye, and it was dark even for Greg. It was night, but he had very keen eyes.

"The Emissary of Castan. I came with him. Our party has returned from Silentis, and we were told of her." He thought he sounded confident. The words came naturally. He thought he sounded like Aud.

The Godless did not seem intimidated by that. His laugh was nothing but a growl. "The Castanni Emissary is dead. You expect me to believe that you have travelled all the way from the sand-fuckers, to find this little thing?" His hand reached up to hold the girl hard by the face. A ragged wince escaped her.

Think, godsbedamned! Look at her! Do something!

"Your time has run out, my Castanni friend. Tell me how many you are. *Now.*"

Greg could think of nothing to say, so he said nothing. He looked at the Godless straight, and scoffed at his question. He was taller than him, so looking down his nose was an easy task. The Godless bore his teeth. "Fine. We'll all die tonight. I'll enjoy fucking your corpse's mouth in the mud, Castanni." He screamed something in a strange tongue. Greg dived for the bow, he heard a door slam open.

Pain was all there was. Something cold touched his back, cold unrelenting metal driven by strong hands, biting through the mail and leather, through flesh and bone. He

586

felt it go through him. His vision went white to black to white again, and when he looked down, he saw the spearhead glinting in firelight. A sea of torches seemed to come to life around him. He had fallen into the sea, somehow. Confusion crept over him like a chill, he was lost, adrift in pain and fires that fled passed him as though they were angry will-o'-the-wisps, called to war by their dark leader, called to battle against the outsiders. He screamed.

There was no escape from any of it, as hard as he tried. He thought of home, of watermills and rivers, of his friends, of his beautiful Mayred, as hard as he tried, the currents of that river agony brought him back to that place he lay in the mud. There was no escape.

The one billowed above him, the one he thought he had forgotten. He was back at the Mornswood Estate, in the dungeon that the Reeve Arran affectionately named the Cave. There was the table, the wall with the hooks, the cage and the chair, all burned as clear here as they had in life. Greg knew that it wasn't real, but that did not make it any less scary. He had left Mornswood, gone far far away, but he had never escaped the Cave. When he turned his head, *he* was there. It was him, the Reeve. He was taller here, skinnier, and his hair was darker. His face was all wrong too, and when he talked it was in some tongue he had never heard.

It's not real. It's...

It was quiet for a time. The fires had gone, but the gleam remained, to paint the night a lurid orange horizon. He could smell smoke, and he could hear burning on the edge of hearing. Opening his eyes was not so hard. The effort helped him to distract from the bleeding, the all-consuming pall of pain that had enveloped his body. It hurt so much. It was all he could do not to pass out. Maybe that wasn't so bad. Maybe then he could be free of it all, for a time. He would be at peace. It was a calming thought, one that he could find no argument against. Why would he? He had done all he could. It was time for someone else. They could do it for a time. Until the pain was not so bad.

The more he mulled it over, the more time seemed to slow. Sound distorted, light shifted and bent. *Is this it? Is this what everything means?* There was no point fighting the weight of his eyelids. They seemed to get heavier with each wheezing breath he took.

Just for a moment, until I can...

Just until I... I can...

Rest. I need to rest. I can't...

I have to... I need...

So quiet...

He heard it. It was not a sound, not truly. It was clearer, and it was unlike anything he had heard before. Hearing it was the only way he could describe it. It was there. Not spoken, but it was ever-present, a call for those who had ears to hear it. All he had to do was answer.

His eyes shot open. He could see the girl sitting slumped up against the doorframe to the longhouse. Her head was lowered, her breathing not noticeable. A steady stream of bloody spittle extended from her jaw to pool on the ground.

The bow was mercifully in distance, only requiring him to pull it close. The quiver had been trampled, but luckily none of the arrows had been broken. *Mercies. Are the gods looking down on me now? Will they give me strength if I pray hard enough?* The knife was gone. Where, he could not say. Accepting that one of his attackers must have taken it, he pulled the quiver belt around his waist, cinching it two holes too tight. With any luck, it would help close the wound. He had no way to tell. His hands were slick with red when that was done. Now came the hard part. He tried to get up.

Crawling was enough to send lances of pain through him again and again and again, made ungainly by his bow, and the quiver tapping away at his thigh. Rising to his feet was worse. It was not far to the girl, yet every step was enough to make him feel like he was back at Bagman's Bluff, his shattered leg buckling beneath him every time he tried to put weight on it. He wanted to weep. How could he go on, his mind so clouded he could not bring to mind a single sensical thought?

What was there left for him? Everyone he had known was gone now. He was alone. Here, in some backwater he doubted even had a name. He was the ghost in the wood, and now that wood was aflame, smothering him in clouds of smoke and snow. There was nothing, so why did he keep walking?

Something worth fighting for.

He nearly collapsed right on top of the girl. He managed to grab the doorframe, and got a handful of splinters as reward. Catching his breath was a conscious effort. An eye stared up at him from a broken face.

"I'm sorry, Marble." Saying her name gave him courage. The waif did not need to say a single word. She had told him her name regardless. She told him everything in the way she looked at him then. "I can't save them. It's too late."

The Hell Unending came all too quick.

589

A horse screamed a guttural cry. Something fell from its back, thrown to the ground so hard it made him bounce.

"Leave him be!" The titan's voice called in wrath, to the orchestra of metallic clanking. There was another, younger, and Greg saw in the edge of sight another horse with a red mane. It was all wrong.

Skinner sauntered through the smoke as though a demon. He breathed the smoke, basked in the snowfall, and he was spattered by other's blood. Only when Greg focused on the scene around him closely did he realise he had to come to bear over a man who looked like Audeyrn. There was a blade in the hand of the Godless, something glinting red and dark in the pommel. It glowed all the brighter when the man laughed. "How about you die for real this time, eh? They were sure you would die in the fucking wastes. I will gladly correct their mistakes."

"You're outnumbered..." Audeyrn's sword was gone. Pushing himself onto an elbow, he did not seem to see Greg or the girl. There was only Skinner. "Jeph, no!" The boy angled near a round hut, reining in hard a safe few yards from the enemy. As safe as that could be, anyway.

Aud's glare burned savagely at the Godless. "Best watch out for Hearty... he's very pissed off."

Skinner turned to regard the approaching knight. He dropped his blade low enough to clean his fingernails. "Ah, the protector. Let's see what you can do." Hearty's response was to slam his sword and shield together, he advanced like a bull. His opponent wore only a cloak and moved like a shadow. Hearty's sword rose and fell, and in a flash Skinner was ducking and rolling, coming up behind the steel with ease. A confused bluster escaped the breathing holes in the

590

tall helm. It took only a foot to the small of the knight's back to send him sprawling to the ground. Aud had to roll to not be crushed between the falling Hearty and the earth.

"Is this all Castan has to offer me? Weak and old and feeble! I feel insulted."

Aud spat out a tooth. "Give me a sword, and maybe I'll show you."

"Finally, some sense in this inane world."

Greg was afraid he was going to pass out again, and he must have, for the next thing he knew, Aud was standing with a longsword in hand. Jeph had dismounted, and was helping Hearty to his feet. He said something, but Aud was having none of it. "Only one more person needs to die today."

Skinner chortled. "I could not agree more." At the jape Audeyrn set his jaw, his feet apart as he positioned himself, lifting the sword in front of him and testing the unfamiliar weight. "Make your move, bastard."

There were no more words. Only grunts as the Godless broke into a sprint, covering the distance between them with a speed too quick to register. His blade was brought high, but fell to his side for a sideswiping lunge. Aud caught it with a parry, glancing off the edge of his blade with an unforgiving hiss. He pulled back to deliver a blow to the back of the Godless, but the man was already turned and facing him, meeting the blow with a serrated-edged blade, and there it stuck.

Bearing a grin too large for his face, Skinner janked the lodged swords upward with the ferocity of a roc, opening up Aud to a knee to the chest. He buckled beneath the force, bringing his face down hard to meet a waiting fist.

591

The enemy collected himself, pulling back and swinging his blade about in feigned practice strokes. Aud retreated a few steps with his sword before him, chest heaving. Skinner watched, head cocked to one side. *He's playing with him. Oh, Gods, he's not even out of breath.*

The air smouldered. Snowflakes or ash or both nestled in their hair, giving the combatants crowns as they stood in the night. Skinner touched the edge of his blade to his temple. "Make your move."

It was Audeyrn who leapt forward this time. He turned an upward strike into a forward lunge, a nasty movement that would have impaled the Godless had he not spun clear of the sword. In retaliation came a wild slash to the face, the enemy's face lighting up as he anticipated the steel crashing into Audeyrn's skull. Instead, a sword rose up to meet the blade of the Godless. Greg saw how far he extended the move, high enough so that the serrated edge met a crossguard, forcing it to follow its path with a harsh clang. Then a shoulder dug into Skinner's face, and he was recoiling, dealing with an onslaught of blow after blow from Audeyrn.

The men of House Langholm were forbidden to claim the title of knight, by royal decree. Greg thought that stupid. To him, his friend was as much a knight as Hearty. All he lacked was the *sir* before his name. He was a knight to Greg. He was like something from a story. From a song. Unrelenting, he forced Skinner give more and more ground, each blow drawing him closer to the wattle of a round-hut. His sword blazed yellow and red and white, an upward strike, a hit, a hit, a hit, a sideward slash, uppercut, never stopping, he could not stop… He slammed his sword down, causing the swords sing their song of death, and then again and again.

Skinner fell to a knee, holding his blade two handed against the sword coming to cut his head in two. Audeyrn let loose a terrible cry as the sword crashed down. It slid a hair's breadth before it caught on a barb. There it stuck. For a moment, Greg felt the pain leave him. *He's doing it, Marble. He's got him.*

"Yield! I'll only say it once." Greg could see a vein bulging angrily on his friend's temple. His sandy hair was dark and ashen in the gloom, but his eyes burned brighter than the trees. His foe had hair plastered to his face. A cornered animal, he let loose a growl. Lightning quick, one hand went from the pommel to the blade itself, his grip catching the serrated edge. Blood streamed from his fingers like a newsprung river yet he barely grimaced. His mouth opened, closed, and opened again, before any words emerged. "YOU'LL NEVER TAKE HER FROM ME!" It was a shriek more than anything else, a desperate call from a doomed man.

Audeyrn's eyes lost some of their fury, and they drifted towards her. His dry lips moved, murmuring words too quiet for anyone to hear amongst the breathing of his enemy and howling of the wildfires beyond. It was too quiet, for anyone, but her. Beside Greg, she stirred in her dreams.

That was all *he* needed. There came the sound of grinding of metal on metal. Skinner dropped the point-end of his blade. Audeyrn's sword dislodged and crashed into the ground, but not before severing the enemy's fingers as they held the edge. *No...* A pommel was slammed into a temple, and he was falling. The impact of Aud falling again was too much for Greg to watch, but he heard it regardless. He heard the air being sucked from lungs and the resulting sharp struggle for breath.

It took him everything he had to force himself to see. The fires had crept up on the village, he saw. Several of the round-huts were ablaze, the old straw and timber roofs burning despite the damp. They looked like funeral pyres, sending up great black smoke.

"*That* was brave." Skinner got to his feet. Looking at his hand, he saw the stumps where his fingers had been a moment before. Laughter erupted, amidst the blood and snow and smoke. Revelling in victory, he raised his blade high and spoke something lost on Greg.

Hearty wept. Jeph clutched his shortsword close to his chest. The knight's face was dark despite the tears, he made to take a step forward.

The last of the Godless missed little. "Get back, or this one dies!"

No. He won't. Greg's hand slipped down to his hip. Skinner had not looked his way/ He made a slow but sure effort to notch the arrow with the black feather to his bow.

"This world..." Skinner began before seeing Audeyrn attempt to rise again. For that, he kicked him in the face with a steel-shod boot. "You will learn to fear us. As you did before." A loud snapping of trees falling let a flurry of sparks fly, and his attention turned towards it. "The whole world will burn. I wished I could have seen that." The way he said it, he sounded sad, lamentful. Fingers found a bowstring.

"Nothing is certain, but death. Here's to you!" The blade he raised in salute. "A world, reborn in fire."

The broken man at his feet had the insolence to look up

at him. "They'll stop you. You will fail."

Light gleamed like black fire in Skinner's eyes. "Then we're all failures."

His fingers struggled to grip with the blood on his hands. *Now, or never.*

"I may die a failure, but one bathed in the blood of those I've vanquished. A glorious, blooded failure. Fuck, I am tired. Tired, but happy with all I've done. Can you say that, at least?" Audeyrn said nothing, but spat on his breeches.

"I thought not. Now... I weary myself with *this*. Time to die."

Greg heard a voice much like his own fill the burning air. It sounded like him, but older, stronger, loud enough to do what it was supposed to. The bowstring was drawn back to his cheek. He let his breathing steady him. This was what he knew. A language he knew better than any other. The soft caress of the feather on his skin was comforting. The fires in the distance leapt up and high, the flames moving slow, too slow to be real. So too did Skinner, snapping his head towards the source of the noise, until his black eyes fell on the archer. There was confusion in those eyes, and his brow creased, as the realisation dawned on him. Greg let go.

A whistle broke through the air. There was a sound like a dozen eggs cracking all at once, and then, the man holding the blade stood with his mouth agape. His steel fell from limp fingers, settling in a puddle of blood and mud. He only had one eye now. The other was home to a long shaft of ash. The bodkin had broken through the back of his skull. It was a long moment before the body remembered that it was dead. It fell, to crumple in a heap next to Audeyrn.

The relief Greg felt was hampered by the urge to vomit. *Is this what it means to be a hero?* He didn't feel like one. He felt faint and tired, and something inside told him he had lost a lot of blood. It came to him in dribs and drabs. He must have passed out, for then familiar voices were all talking above him. When he came to, they were all around him. He wrestled to keep his eyes open.

"We cannot stay here. Inside, maybe?" It sounded like Hearty.

"No. They need attention. Preferably away from prying eyes." Audeyrn was leaning against a beam. There was a welt on the side of his head. A boy stood behind Greg's head. He thought he recognised him, but there was no mark on his forehead. "I know where we can go."

"Where, lad?"

"It's a safe place. They may accept us, if I–"

A fit of coughing came from the body a few feet away. She still bore the chains. The hair was out of her eyes, to reveal hollowed cheeks and one sunken eye. Her rags barely clung to her chest. "I know... you." It was the revenant of a voice. Greg made himself lean forward. He saw that they all had heard it.

She was barely conscious, and she was looking at Audeyrn.

"Brother."

That singular word caused the former emissary to slump even more onto the beam. He pushed the hair off his face. "Sister?"

Greg could not keep the laughter to himself. It overtook the pain, until all there was in that world on fire was happiness. They had gone so far, hurt too much, and now he had found her. A little thing, but something good in the world so full of wrong. He let himself be content in the knowledge that he had been a part of something greater than himself.

In the end, before the darkness took him once more, he smiled as he thought of her.

38

EPILOGUE

Dreams engulfed him, the pain he felt etched upon his every nerve. He thought it would never end. When he felt *it* call to him, he woke with a start. A skirling wind cut through to his skin and ruffled his hair. Flicking red locks from his eyes, he saw a world lost to the green. It was long grass that crunched beneath his fingers, as verdant as the meadows of Castan in high summer. Amongst the blades, flowers with wide fat petals bloomed peridot and ultramarine and copper, more colours than he could name and all wondrous to sight, nothing he had seen at home, nor along the long road. They were strange, with a beauty about them he could not help but admire. When Natoly plucked one, a flower crowned by the colour of a starlit night, he knew that he was lost. Well and truly.

It sounded again, closer this time. Nothing in nature could make that sound, he was certain. It made him reach for his kje, his certainty shaken and his heart racing. What only caused further confusion was finding his scabbard empty, his hands desperate for something sharp and heavy to grasp. His knife was also gone.

"What in the…" He saw them then, as though conjured up through thought alone. They were not far, and not as he expected. Some twenty feet away, where the grass gave way to a large morass of bramble and gorse, the queerest flower of them all bloomed. Its stalk was curved and sharp, rising to a crown like the hilt of his sword… and the blossom atop was shaped like a knife he had once owned. The one Maarten had given him the day he was made a man of the Guardcorps.

His body was frozen; from fear or confusion or fatigue he could not say, but the knife was *balanced* atop the kje hilt. The point, which he had honed every day until he could shave with it, was placed adroit on the iron pommel, and neither shook nor shivered as the wind barrelled through the glade. It just… stayed there.

Something made his hand go out, to reach for the blade that had been his own for so long. It was nothing to be afraid of, he knew…

Plucking the wayward weapon from its perch, he wanted to voice every fitful question, every inane thought. They remained unspoken: the fact his weapons could offer up no answers annoyed him no end. He sent a dark stare their way regardless.

Wait…

His mind reached back to that night, when he had gotten it in his head to climb Flattop, clawing away at his memory to the last thing he could remember. *It was a fayhill.* There had been a storm, hadn't there? It had been raining, he was certain of it. He was dry as dust now, but he was sure he had felt the cold and the rain on his cheeks, the way it had soaked him through. And the voices off in the night. And there had been a tree, wreathed in terrible flame. He had not resisted when it took him.

It all felt like a dream, a twilit vision shrouded in the malaise of a night spent wasting away on bad wine. However hard he tried, he could not recall how he had gotten to this place. Then he cursed himself for being so dense. *Where exactly* is *here!?*

For the first time then, he took in his surroundings, to find nothing. Only the void met his gaze. The skirling was almost a beckon call as he padded to the edge, watching as the ground suddenly gave way to hard windswept stone, and beyond that only empty air. It seemed to go on forever. He was convinced the emptiness must be endless. He wondered what it would feel like to fall forever.

The thought came to him unbidden and unwelcome, and he felt the bile rise in his throat as he watched the void revel in its unfathomable depths. If he looked hard enough, he could see shadows drift past, dark rocky things floating upon some vast air current.

"What the..." His words were stolen as soon as he mouthed them. A harsh gust took his breath away, jealous zephyrs angry at the man peering down at them from high. They knew that he did not belong here. The skirling only heightened, and somewhere aways it came again, a scream harder than iron, lower than the Hell Unending itself.

Maybe it was the sound of the devil screech, or maybe the vertigo, regardless of what it was, it soon had Nat scurrying back to the relative safety of the gorse brush. His blade was in hand, the feel of smooth hard worn leather giving him a mite of relief.

He stood there for a time. When the call refused to make itself known again, he cursed himself and slammed the kje into its scabbard, and took stock.

His surcoat was dirtier than he remembered it being, and the laces and trim looked as though they had been singed. Apart from that, he seemed sound. The embroidery on the raven looked fine, so no worries there. His captain had loved that surcoat.

What would Hector make of this? Isembard's pet gifted at Castan always seemed to have an answer for everything... maybe the explanation would prove to be as boring as the rest that the so-called court alchemist could conjure. Nat would pay good money to see the man try and wizard his way out of this.

Islands, Hector! Floating fucking lands in the sky! You would shake your head at the notion of it all, I know it. But here it is. Seeing is believing, and I see it. Nat dug his nails into the skin of his palm to make certain he was not dreaming. It hurt. The conclusion failed to make him any less confused.

The same questions barrelled through his mind, until he was exhausted and he could no longer remain inert. He needed to do something. Anything, to stop himself unsheathing the kje to make the gorse a victim of his frustration. Walking along the threshold to the oblivion, he watched as lumbering masses of stone ponderously made their mysterious way through the haze. All dissimilar to the other, some mere barren rock made jagged by some old collision, while others were engulfed in greenery, bearing veritable forests atop while hanging creepers dangled below, making it look like some giant wooded jellyfish. *I must know something. If I can find the where, maybe I can work out the how...*

His erstwhile refuge was larger than those he spied adrift, boasting a forested interior of hoary old hardwoods with limbs as thick about as his waist, and boles as black as ink. The topside of his rock was strangely flat, yet small enough that he was able to make his way around the less wooded periphery in under an hour. At least, he thought it was under an hour. The sun above was veiled in a silver haze, so there was no telling. When that was done, and as boredom set in, he eyed the shadowy wood, and resolved to walk among the dark trees.

It may as well have been night within. The canopy was thick, so only the smallest of shy coruscating pinpricks of light were permitted to enter. The sky pillared by wooded columns, the dome of heaven an interweaving of leaves in the shape of daggers. Nothing grew underfoot. How could it? Only dry, dead leaves crunched under his iron-shod boots. The trees nearest shook, or so it seemed to Nat. Creaking a wooden groan as he passed. *Disturbing their slumber? How long has it been since they've seen someone? They sound as though I've pissed them off.*

Another time came to the surface in his addled mind. One when he had not been so alone in the world. Laughs had accompanied his days, and music his nights. When he was still a Guardsman, not... whatever he was now. He had lived for making the Emissary frown, mocking fat Deri, and the delights to be had beneath the roof of a Castan redhouse. That lanky string of piss Greg had been asked by the Emissary to join them as he set out on an errand for the king. The band of four: braving the long road and the wilds, spitting in the eyes of Sorans, making love to Paydar girls and making the rest hungry with jealousy. *Who wouldn't want to fuck a hero?*

He was Natoly of the Guard, the Red Raven. Wherever *here* was, he would riddle it out. There were worse places in the wide world, more mean, darker, dangerous, where cruel eyes haunted his nights. And like that, it opened up before him. A glade. Fairly lit, but still darksome along its edges, at the centre point a tree grew unlike the rest. Its trunk was the colour of honey, along with the splayed roots running through the earth at its feet, and the high fanning branches that arched overhead. A frozen fountain of gold, or so Nat thought. Indeed, the leaves that crowned it and covered its branches were equal parts transparent and whitest ivory, to make it look as though the golden fountain sent a rain of spray to cascade through the air. The light that shot through the thinning foliage only made the splendour of the tree greater. For a moment there, as he watched the light play across the leaves, and as the resulting multitude of refracted colour was sent to shine in his eyes, his confusion ebbed until it was no more. For a moment, at least, he had no questions.

I don't belong in such a place. A haven such as this. I have to find the way back.

Yet he sat against the tree, where a root had bent and curled until it made for a somewhat comfortable seat. The wind rustled the leaves above, and despite the glare of a thousand colours, his eyes grew heavy. It went quiet after that. A name stuck in his head, of someone he had once known. He couldn't recall her face.

The next thing he knew, he was dosing. He rubbed his

eyes, and saw that it was still bright without. He was hungry, he realised, so cursed and set off through the trees again. His last view of the golden tree was fleeting and obscured by its ugly cousins, yet he could not help but admire the brilliance that bled through the treeline. A small voice inside told him to stay, but he knew he couldn't. Could he?

The fruit hung heavy from the grasping root, shaking every time a gust whipped across the cliff face, shaking like an old man caught in the cold. He could just about reach the nearest, but it took him halfway off the ground, and he needed to hook his boot on a stone. It was a wasted effort. His bounty was a handful of sour berries the colour of rust. They made him gag, but he swallowed them, and licked the juice from his hand.

When that was done, his stomach growled for more. He tried to find more of the sourberries, but they grew too low for him to grasp, and only when his foot slipped and his heart leapt into his throat, did he finally give up.

There must be a way off this rock! I was clever enough to get here! Now how the fuck do I get... down?

He looked over the edge again, hoping to the Gods-in-exile that another island would come close. A half dozen floating specks of land, with no flat ground to stand on, came within two hundred feet of his own. All were smaller, all mean and barren. He noticed something else, too. Far below, the haze was burning away, where a blue-silver screen rippled away from horizon to horizon. He shook his head when he realised. The wind upon the waters was minuscule from that height, but he could still make them out, the way the light sparkled from the far-off sea. It seemed to pull forward. There was a ringing in his ears, and he felt as though his rock was spinning, and no matter how hard he tried to calm his breathing, or tell himself it was okay, he could not stop any of it. The vomit came then, the berries tasting even worse.

Wiping the ejecta from his face with the back of one hand, he watched as the solitary islands came and went. He wanted to talk, but what came next was the scream. Primal, wordless, and all rage, Nat only stopped when his throat was raw and his voice hoarse. Dropping to his knees hurt: the earth here was thin, and stones lay beneath the surface to dig into his legs. The pain was there, but it felt dull and far-off.

"So many things left undone. Things left unsaid. I wish I had the answers. I wish…" What did he want? To go home? Home was Isembard and his caprice, the frowns of Audeyrn and scoffs of Walt Iddles. Did he want Sibyl? His Paydar captain had been there when he needed her. He thought it strange that he was only now thinking of her. He had loved her touch, her scent, the authority she commanded over her crew. Yet when he saw her in his mind's eye, he felt nothing. That should have made him feel terrible, he knew. He should have hated himself. But he didn't.

What did he want?

Nat walked around the cliff face, until he came to the edge that fronted the western horizon. The sun was receding, a golden coin doused in blood, the islands between him and the sunset projecting great ruddy shadows that fell on Nat in beams of shadow. The wind had died down enough that he could sit in comfort in the open. It was calm, to a point. Here it was that he would die. At least he would be warmer than most. He stretched himself out on the grass, surprised how comfortable a bed it made. The sky above was darkening, so he closed his eyes to remember a better place. Where he had been with Rhyrn.

"Someone to laugh with, and all would be perfect." *Let the Red Raven laugh one last time.*

The trees behind him rustled, creaking horribly as he heard their limbs bend and scream. What followed, he could only describe as a furnace wind that buffeted him across the head. A basking heat that enveloped his body, washing the chill from his skin with all the tenderness of a scalding bath. His hand was at his kje, and he spun, seeing whatever foe was waiting for him at the trees.

A red shadow watched on high. It regarded him with a baleful look, a pair of purple slitted eyes limned scarlet by the light of a dying sun. The beast was all neck and tail and wing, and rested on the top branches of the nearest half-dozen trees with the weightlessness and grace of a newfallen feather. Except, Nat doubted that there had ever been a more fearsome feather. A pair of leathern membranes draped the trees, both supported by an elongated set of spindly digits, embracing the canopy with a sure grip. From behind, a sinewy tail came into view and lashed back and forth, at its end a great horned blade the colour of beaten silver. The same silver was found on the great talons and bone-spurs and spines. The protrusions only became greater the closer they got to the head. The neck was lithe, armoured in thick scales to protect the long throat. It was the head, and the eyes pitted deep under a heavy brow, where Nat could not help but look, finding himself helpless beneath the unflinching heliotrope gaze. A pair of tapering silvered horns erupted from the skull crust, and the snout was an extended maw, lipless and agape. A tongue lolled forth from between rows of needle-like fangs. The eyes... they saw him... and they hungered.

"Move, and he'll devour you." Straddling the monster's back, a young woman sat in a high-horned saddle. Even from atop the trees, and with the evening light, her features were sharply etched against the dreadblack hair that framed her comely face. Even there, amidst the creature emanating heat and fury and death, it was her face now that he saw to be the true threat. One word from her, and the creature would pounce. He knew just from sight how agile such a beast could be, despite its apparent ungainliness while perched. He saw the way the neck seemed to coil, tendons beneath the ranks of hardiron scales moving with impatience. The eyes. When he looked deep into the slitted malevolence, his mind seemed to fill with thoughts of food. Where had he seen such a creature before? It was like some kind of freakish overgrown wyrm. The Lady of Wolfsmouth had had such a lapbeast, he remembered, but it would have been swallowed by its crimson cousin and still have room to guzzle a dozen more. He couldn't remember where he had seen it before...

"Who are you?" Asked the rider, suddenly producing a long leather whip to gently tap at the beast's flank. In a blink the red reptilian was aflight, and not a moment later it had landed between the cliff and Nat, with a grace that belied its size and a heat that caused the grass beneath it to singe and hiss. Without removing the locked gaze on Nat, the beast swung its head low, allowing for the woman to swing a leg over the saddle and dismount.

Nat looked her up and down, and for once did not

find himself doing so out of lust. She wore leathers not too dissimilar to riding kit, but she also wore a pair of dark-lensed goggles around her slim neck. At one hip a shortsword was clipped to her thigh, tightly cinched and deadly. In her gloved hands, she held the whip, twisting it hard until it creaked.

"I'm not one for repeating myself. Answer, and if you lie, *he'll* know." As if to reply, the serpentile neck lifted to full height, dwarfing them both, the tongue dripping a long string of slaver.

He had been called many things in his life. A fool, for one. Yet he knew not to question her claim. Something about the monster wyrm disquieted him, and not merely the fact that it could eviscerate him with a word. No… there was something *inward* about it. When it looked at you, it seemed to look inside you. He could feel it slithering inside his mind. He wanted to laugh. He wanted to scream. He considered turning and running into the trees, but if this thing was anything like a wyrm, the place would be ablaze in no time.

"Natoly Maarten." He all but spat out his name, as though doing so would quell the nausea within. "But I am also called the Red Raven. I am a…"

"I highly doubt anyone calls you that. You're more like to have stolen that jack, or removed it from a corpse. Your name, however… *Natolymarten…* It is unusual, I'll give you that, but at least it's real."

"Natoly Maarten," he said, clearly emphasising the two words. He silently made certain his annoyance did not show.

The red shadow gave a low snarl. "That's what I said."

Her face was a mirror to her mount's. "Now, I want you to answer my every question. Lie, and there will be consequences. Tell the truth... and I will consider your fate."

All his instincts told him to kill this bitch right here and now, run for the trees, and hide from the hellbeast. He was quick, but was she quicker? Had he been training in Castan, he would have relished the chance to test new opponents in the yard. But he was here, wherever his little floating rock was. Did it even have a name? He stood still, and his hand did not move.

"How did you get here, *Natolymarten?*"

That caught him in the gut. He considered telling a lie, but the beast's head twitched at that, so he banished the thought deep inside. Then he formed the truth in his mind, knowing that this woman would not even like the taste. *Think! What would the emissary do? He would talk, and talk, and talk some more. Appeal to her, maybe? Reason with this one. If she was not curious she would have set that thing on you outright.*

"The sun sets, and I don't have all day. Tell me, *now*." With one last wary glance at her pet, he braced himself, and told her.

The laugh that broke through the face of disbelief was brimming with mockery. It must have sounded a jape, he knew. She never let go of the whip, nor allow herself to be cosened. The laugh she tried to hold back, he guessed, and it was only for how fantastical it was that she lost her composure. Her face darkened, or it may have been the dying sun. The sun was in his face, the day darkening with each word. The laugh that had filled the island with mirth was replaced by a snigger, and finally reduced to a tittering.

"How marvellous. If I didn't know better, I'd say you've bewitched *him*." Nat did not know what bewitching was, let alone how to bewitch something. He noticed how her words affected the beast.

"That's *all* I know, I swear it." *Reason with them. Disarm the situation. Don't flinch, don't balk, don't fear.*

She shook her head, and the smile she wore held no happiness. Her hair was tied back, dreadblack locks made into an elaborate profusion of knots, a pair of wings here, a tail and head there, shaped to look like a miniature of her mount. "No, it isn't. How the hell did you come here, if not by dragon?"

"You don't understand. There was something. A way to… *walk* into other places. I was in the *Paydar*, for godssake! Not… *here*! I am the guard of the Royal Emissary of Castan. We were on a mission to… to…" The malaise was thicker than soup in his memory. Where were they going? Aud had been sent to do something… "Wait, what's a dragon?"

The question made the woman raise an eyebrow a whole half-inch. She looked at him as one looked at a two-headed goat.

"You're looking at one."

"It beats riding a horse."

"Enough with the japes. Now tell me, how did you get here?"

"I told you what happened."

"Enough!" *I couldn't agree more, lovely girl.* He had had just about enough of monstrous wyrms and floating islands and vexing women. His legs carried him forwards a step. The dragon saw his movements instantly, widening its jaws, a column of black smoke billowing from its nostrils.

"Stay where you are!" He wanted to laugh against the insanity of it all. *I found my way here. I can find my way back.*

With a brusque word, the dragon was howling, a screech to wake even the dead. "I said stay!" Orders, orders, orders. He had taken orders his whole life. Had he really risen from the gutters to do only that? *I made a name for myself. I can carve out my own destiny.* His fingers brushed his knife. It felt right. It felt good. Giving this woman one of his famous smiles for her to remember, he pulled the knife free. *Sun of the day, light the way.* The blade flashed as soon as he raised it. The dragon screamed as the light danced on its long head, dazzling it enough to make it turn away. It was his only chance. A fool's chance, but that was all he needed.

The air emanating near the beast was an overpowering roil as he broke into a sprint. Putting it between him and the woman, he made for the blue beyond. The grass gave way to stone gave way to emptiness.

"No! Don't..."

The feeling of weightlessness was intoxicating. He felt drunk. He felt mad. He felt elated. Natoly let the sudden gust take his breath away. Or was that the sights he saw? The leagues of sky and sea and mountains in the air, the sound of those above fading away until all he heard was the wind singing to him in its strange tongue. He became faster than any horse or cat or hawk. He laughed in the face of the unknowing.

So... This is what it feels like to fly.

Acknowledgments

We would like to thank all our friends and family who have had to put up with us talking nonsense for the past two years, with a special mention to Evan who bore the brunt of our nonsensical natterings. Thank you, for your patience and your ability to tune us out and nod at the right intervals. We apologise for the games of D&D and Warhammer that took three times as long as they would have without our constant interruptions.

This has been a huge project that we have put our hearts and souls into, and we want to thank all of the people who indulged us when we drifted off into daydreams mid sentence and mid conversation when our characters finally told us what was going to happen next.

Huge thanks are due to the amazing Rena Violent for our fantastic cover design. The process and progress was incredible to be apart of and it was really encouraging to have her capture the essence of our story and bring it to life.

Last, but certainly not least, we want to thank you, our readers, for taking a chance on us and our story. We really hope you enjoy and will continue on this journey with us!

About the Author

Morgan Rickards and Rhys Jones are a Welsh writing duo hailing from the Rhondda, UK. Friends since school, they have both been fascinated by Celtic mythology and classical fantasy. When they are not climbing mountains or kayaking the rivers of their beautiful and rugged country, they are writing about alien worlds and bloody medieval sagas. Always wanting to write a series featuring the complex and morally ambiguous characters of Celtic mythology, they embarked on putting pen to paper.

You can connect with me on:

🌐 https://www.rickardsandjones.com

Subscribe to my newsletter:

✉ http://eepurl.com/iq84iU

Printed in Great Britain
by Amazon

29845450R00361